5/6

BOOKS BY

JANICE WARNKE

*

The Narrow Lyre

A Pursuit of Furies

A
Pursuit
of
Furies

Janice Warnke

Random House   New York

A
Pursuit
of
Furies

A
Pursuit
of
Furies

Chapter One

On the other side of the garden four people were sitting on the grass. All were wearing hats. Mrs. Dartley, her violet teagown somewhat disarrayed, frowned and talked beneath a regimental pith helmet of impressive design. The young girl in shorts stretched her slender legs, causing the wide-brimmed Leghorn, the sort that was once worn in fashionable resorts before the First War, to flutter about her upturned face. Both of the gentlemen were in sports clothes, the youth balancing a gray topper, and his companion, red-faced and puffy, supporting a German student cap several sizes too small for him on great bumps of wiry hair.

Campion strode toward them across the lawn. He was annoyed. "What is the meaning of this display?"

"Meaning? What meaning? Must there be one?" Mrs. Dartley replied. The others were silent.

"You are all ridiculous," Campion said.

"You are my guest. Behave like one."

He shrugged and sat down beside them. "I have some reports for you."

"Ah!" She rocked toward him. "Budapest!"

"No. Nothing from Budapest," he said impatiently.

"Tomorrow then." It was one of those days when she felt the lines of control slack in her hands and her exile oppressing her. "Well? Well? What then?"

"For one thing, the American journalist. He's coming here at half past six."

She feigned indifference, said, seemingly out of context, "I have never cared what people thought of me."

At this the American girl turned admiring eyes toward her.

"I think you should take off the headgear—now. Don't you?" Campion asked. Anton Hrubick started, raised his plump, short hands and removed the cap, thus releasing an enormous aura of stiff hair. Posy snickered, then, remembering her manners, quickly turned the snicker to a cough. But both she and Marshall Sears remained as before, in uncertain but relaxed parody of Milady and Milord, which was exactly what Mrs. Dartley had intended them to be.

"Ah Campion, you have always lacked imagination, the spirit of fun, of play-acting . . ."

"Of games," he finished for her.

She smiled appreciatively. "Exactly. Of games. Which is why you're so useful, of course. You are like your name, dear Ernest. As for this," she condescended to explain, "it began as a measure against the sun. The *Helvetian* sun," she added resentfully before going on. "I saw the helmet. Other people's houses disgorge such remarkable objects. That is one of the advantages of renting. And one can change ancestors so easily, not of course that they aren't interchangeable anyway. The helmet seemed to fit my head. Then I saw it to be part of a collection, though why it should be housed in the gardener's cottage I do not know. Children? Do you suppose there were once children here? Before us? *En tout cas,* from a measure against sunstroke, these hats soon became a measure against boredom, which is an infinitely more dangerous malady, don't you agree?" She turned toward the young man in the topper. "My dear Marshall, it is difficult to believe that your father was, as you insist he was, a baker."

"His grandfather," Campion growled.

"Oh?"

Marshall roused himself from a delicious reverie that involved in some interlinked way both Posy and the wines that he would be consuming that evening at dinner. For some reason that was never clear to him Mrs. Dartley always pretended not to remember the details of his lineage. Dutifully he began, "Yes, my grandfather was a baker, but he became a capitalist and by the time he was fifty he owned one of the largest bakery chains in the whole West. My family introduced, on a large scale, the first really terrible bread into that part of the country. You could say that we were pace setters . . . of a sort. My *father* couldn't bake a thing. His eyes are flat, brownish glints, like rubbed, worn-out copper pennies."

"Ah," Mrs. Dartley said.

Marshall hesitated. Did she want him to go through the whole story of his rebellion again? He cleared his throat, but Campion intervened. "Gwendolyn. I have the reports. Are you coming in or not?"

He was the only one of them who dared be impatient with her. It was alarming how these two sometimes fought. Many considered that despite her age, which was variously put at between sixty and seventy and which at the least made her nearly a quarter of a century his senior, they were lovers. Others believed that she knew some dark secret about him and held him in this way, but since this theory did not explain the liberties he took with her only the dullest subscribed to it. Still others of the same mentality put down their relationship to a shared devotion to causes, of which there were, or seemed to be, many. A few believed that he was her illegitimate son. There were specialized interpretations too. A famous psychoanalyst who was once their guest went around afterwards saying that it was an example of the grotesque results of a woman suppressing her natural maternal instinct until past the age of childbearing. Mrs. Dartley, who of course soon learned of this, found ways of taking a powerful revenge upon this practitioner, and for once Campion applauded her. As is so often the case, none of these theories was really true and all were a little true, though in a sense in which the theorists were not likely to comprehend. Those who stayed longest and most happily at the villa were those who did not speculate but who accepted. But even they feared the not infrequent scenes between their hostess and Ernest Campion, and just now the little group on the lawn had stiffened in anticipation of one, particularly since, as they all now knew, there had been no news from Budapest.

This time, however, Gwendolyn Dartley merely commented on how much they all suddenly resembled bird dogs, then sighed and raised an imperious hand toward Campion, a corner of whose mouth was twitching ever so slightly. He helped her to her feet, an act of courtesy, not necessity, and without a word they retreated along the path. She walked lightly, like a woman several decades younger; even her torso had not yet begun to settle in towards the

pelvis. From a distance it was impossible to imagine that tall striding figure as that of anyone but a woman in her prime. She was
talking animatedly now to Campion, and she reached up from time
to time and tapped for emphasis on the helmet, which she evidently had no intention of removing.

"Vitchcraft," Mr. Hrubick murmured slyly, gratefully, and
pulled from his pocket a long Monarchist Virginia cigar. He was
perfectly capable of pronouncing his *w*'s, but on occasion he
found it effective not to.

Two

Sylvia clenched her hands in despair, moved her head back and
forth to the grinding of painfully stiff neck muscles, then bowed
desolately over the littered work table. Her forehead rested for a
moment on the cool surface. "Oh God," she groaned. It was all so
terrible. A sick loathing began slowly to possess her; like a sinister
fungus it began at the back of her skull and also in the region of
her crotch and spread over the rest of her body. How terrible a
disease was despair, she thought helplessly. And the seedbed of this
foulness lay somewhere within her. Where? Mind, heart, soul,
spirit? What word did one use in these clever times? Suddenly she
felt the most violent rage. She leapt to her feet and with wild and
heavy gestures struck papers and pencils and notebooks onto the
floor, trampled on them fiercely like an animal—thump, thump, an
ecstatic trampling on those fragile scrawls; stomp, stomp, a primitive beating of the feet upon those flimsy nothings; rage, annihilation, *nothing*. Ahhhhhh.

When it was over she felt very frightened and weak, and yet in
the most humiliating and abashed way relieved. She stared down at
her feet as though they did not belong to her. She looked at the
red marks on her hands and knew they would darken into bruises,
and she imagined how viciously distorted and beastlike her face
must have been only a few seconds before, and shuddered.

Everything was so pointless. But of course that was it. Everything quite simply *was* meaningless, the flimsy structures of a

seemingly too solid world, herself, her ruined work, which were one and the same thing. Why did she find it so difficult to accept this fact? Meaningless! Nevertheless she stooped ruefully down and began to retrieve the fallen papers. They rustled like dead leaves in her hands.

From out the window a familiar voice announced that Mrs. Dartley was coming along the path. Sylvia listened, but she could make out none of the words, only the familiar intonation. It really was very odd about Mrs. Dartley's speech habits. At times she sounded American, Hyde Park American, Campion had once said, and at other times unregenerate Oxford; and then again she might slip into an English that was faintly foreign in accent, perhaps German, perhaps Slavic, at any rate something vaguely continental. She had lived in so many places, but did that quite explain it?

Sylvia went to the window. If Mrs. Dartley happened to see her she would simply wave at her; that way it wouldn't look as though she had been spying. She leaned out—why, what was she up to now? She had on her head something that looked very much like, and indeed was, a pith helmet. Only, the phrase seemed inadequate, for it also looked curiously magnificent, almost ceremonial. India? The Crimea? The Sudan? It shaded her face as she came toward the house, making it impossible to distinguish her features. Only that firm, somewhat outthrust chin, and farther back in the shadows the refractive glimmerings of the watchful eyes. And that long, confident, vigorous stride of hers. Sylvia sighed; how often this woman made her feel old. It was absurd of course, foolish, the wearing of that helmet, another example of Mrs. Dartley's inveterate exhibitionism. It needed but a plume. And yet there was something admirable and splendid about her too, and almost touching. It was as though the nineteenth century were marching across the disorderly, indifferent stage of the twentieth. Vague and remarkable associations trembled toward consciousness in Sylvia, then subsided.

Campion, she saw, was beside Mrs. Dartley, matching his steps silently to hers, as though a little against his will, looking nervous as usual, and taut. Now they had entered the house beneath her, and Sylvia felt suddenly grateful that Mrs. Dartley had not been there when she had thrown her fit a few minutes before. She missed so little. If anyone else had heard that racket it would not matter.

She dropped listlessly into her chair, succumbing to a familiar sense of disengagement which meant that she would not even try to write more that day. It simply did not matter. And besides, it was so much easier to think about real people who already existed than to try to give form to one's own conflicting selves and to something beyond even that.

Mrs. Dartley, for example; one could spend a considerable portion of one's life thinking about her. How could the woman go on believing in so many things? Causes, people, ideas; all penetrated by some elaborate code or faith, something that Sylvia could not grasp but that had to do, no doubt, with *humanity*. Not that humanity was a word Mrs. Dartley ever used; she was far too absorbed in the concrete, and also too inclined to suspect the chronic wielders of such words of being hypocrites to be caught using them herself. Yet despite all her own posturings, her tyrannical dispensations, her truly outrageous and self-indulged personality, she had retained a capacity for convictions, and it was this, untainted by either ideology or fraud, which gave her her power.

Or Campion. It was curious how a man who had seemingly abandoned any attempt to make something out of his life could nevertheless create the impression that his life mattered.

Sylvia stretched, langorously, stood up, and discovered to her surprise that there was nothing in the world she wanted so much as to go for a swim, a simple enough wish and one which could easily be fulfilled. She had not succeeded in writing anything and she had gone entirely to pieces for half a minute, but at least she had avoided the memory of George Bingham. She glanced in the mirror and thought again of what she must have looked like during her recent outburst. How odd that not a trace of that violence remained on her features. A quick comb run through the shaken hair was all that was needed.

She was naked now and reaching out for her bathing suit. Suddenly she began to shiver, and a powerful wave of feeling surged through her, whether of desire or dread she could no longer say. She stood perfectly still, in arrested struggle, her body half turned as though for flight, one arm thrown up before the head that now drooped forward from the long and slender neck. "*Mon semblable, mon frère*," she muttered at last and dropped her arm. Then, frighteningly, "My partner in crime." But in just what way? One day she would understand. And I shall be free of you yet, St. George, somehow; free of you and love and hate, or whatever it is, this burden of guilt, if it takes me a lifetime, if it kills me.

Then just as all the ambiguities of the past year threatened her once more with confusion a great Wagnerian burst filled the house, set it vibrating and shuddering before a terribly arthritic hand could control the knob and reduce the volume. Lily Halász was at her music again; she had evidently tuned in to Bayreuth. She would be full of joyful excited speech that evening. Sylvia was glad. Mrs Halász had lost so much. If only, for once, Anton Hrubick could contain himself.

Three

It was a pity that for complicated, middle-European reasons, inaccessible to most outsiders, Anton Hrubick and Lily Halász got on so poorly. The dead Austro-Hungarian Empire with its powerfully hierarchical internal relationships seemed to live on in them, and old resentments occasionally flared out across Mrs. Dartley's dinner table. The difference was not wholly that Mrs. Halász had been rich all her life and Mr. Hrubick poor, or even that his background was petty middle-class while hers was decidedly gentry. "Don't prattle to me about democracy," she had once said in reply to a goading remark. "Mr. Halász was the son of peasants. He was a famous lawyer by the time I met him. Everyone knew him, admired him. He was a catch, I advise you. And he was a democrat all his life. If you think that was easy for a man in his generation in Hungary you are very stupid about politics. Even stupider than I am. And I am *stupid* about politics." It was also the old matter of Czech insecurity and Hungarian confidence that made for the conflicts between them. Anton Hrubick, witty and smart of tongue, strenuously intellectual, nevertheless looked at the world out of quick-moving, defensive eyes that seemed never to have recovered from the Thirty Years' War—at least when he was in the presence of Mrs. Halász. She, on the other hand, with her worldly tolerance and no doubt prejudiced belief that no culture had ever been more exciting than that of the Budapest she had known, seemed always, even when she was silent, to be saying: *I belong to a people that fought more nobly against the Turks than all the rest of Europe did, and as for the Hapsburgs, Marie Thérèse came to us, cleverly with a babe at her breast, to plead for the swords of our chivalric lords!* History might thus be said to have conspired centuries before to provide some awkward moments at the dinner table, as well as to have imposed itself upon personality, not to mention more serious matters.

Vaguely national, vaguely class animosities moved them both; the commonest form in which these animosities were expressed, however, was a running argument about music, to which, in different ways, both had devoted their lives, Anton Hrubick as a teacher and pianist whose shortness of fingers (and tendency to be distracted by a number of other interests) had kept him from a concert career, and Mrs. Halász as a passionate listener and amateur. All her life she had sung for pleasure, and until her fingers were crippled by the arthritis had played for herself too. She loved all great music. Anton Hrubick had to some extent narrowed his tastes along polemical lines that gave him the greatest scope for self-assertion, and he had also evolved an elaborate theory about the relative worth of the forms of music which enraged her. He attacked above all opera, vocal music, and singers in general. This was particularly unfortunate, since as a young girl Mrs. Halász had dreamed of becoming an opera singer but had not quite had the voice for it, and the art of singing had remained for her the inviolable higher world, contact with which lifted her above that everyday world of heavy furniture and costly if not always beautiful objects with which her father and later her husband had always surrounded her. She felt Anton Hrubick's contemptuous remarks as a profanation of that higher world and would seldom stoop to direct battle. She also suspected but could not quite manage to prove that in his heart of hearts Mozart did not mean as much to him as those twelve-tone composers whose virtues he so indiscriminately and obsessively preached, and to Lily not to love Mozart above all was the unforgivable sin.

Yet it was Wagner about whom they had their most frequent, open, and violent arguments, to the despair and amazement of the rest of the household, Anton attacking him, Lily seldom failing to rally to his defense. Perhaps only Mrs. Dartley knew what lay behind the mask of this argument, and she remained silent, while the others were forced to suffer what sometimes were days of discord without a hope of understanding its meaning. Then, once in a great while, without warning, the angel of peace would suddenly descend upon Anton and Lily, for reasons which were equally hard to perceive; the battle would suddenly stop, and he would play Schumann or Schubert or Richard Strauss for her, skillfully, carefully, considerate of the limitations of the frail and quavering sounds that issued from her throat. That had not happened now for some time.

Mrs. Dartley had considered that Anton and Lily might provide companionship for each other, but for once her judgment had been in error. It had turned out to be Faustine who responded to Mrs. Halász's musical ardors. In any case, Mrs. Dartley could have done nothing about it even had she known that Anton and Lily would not get on, since neither of them had any other place to go.

It was not because of Mrs. Halász that Gwendolyn Dartley awaited news from Budapest. On the contrary, she had made it understood among the members of her household that the subject of word from Budapest was strictly to be avoided in her presence. Even Anton Hrubick, though tempted, dared not go against so firm an edict.

But he too had heard that burst of Wagner, and he looked forward to a delightful evening of squabbling.

For once, however, Lily Halász was not really listening to the music that came from the excellent small radio which Mrs. Dartley had had installed in her room and which had given her so much pleasure. Instead, she had been rereading a number of letters. She folded them up now and put them all back in their envelopes. She had made a decision.

Four

"There goes Faustine across the lawn. Swiftly. Looking rather like a huntress. What would the right adjective be? Artemine? Do you suppose that's it? Dianic sounds somehow too technical, as though it had to do with electronics, or even perhaps physics, which wouldn't do at all. In any case, it would be misleading . . . as applied to Faustine. Or would it? Clothes can create the most outrageous illusions. She's evidently on her way to swim."

Campion let Mrs. Dartley talk and did not turn his head, though he was curious and it cost him something not to.

Sylvia, presumably as an act of modesty, had pulled a loose, sleeveless garment on over her bathing suit. It came just down to the top of her thighs, hiding the bathing suit completely, and as a result it gave a much greater impression of nudity than if she had left it off.

"What a curious effect. And not the least bit deliberate I'm sure," Mrs. Dartley said, but Campion remained unmoved. He was aware of the fact that she hoped to discompose him and also that for some reason she wanted to delay dealing with the reports.

It was no concern of his what Sylvia was up to or what sort of an outfit she had on. His relations with her had been exactly the same ever since her arrival at Kilchberg some four months before, cordial but distant, and would probably go on being so since this was quite obviously the way she preferred things. It did obscurely annoy him that Gwendolyn always called her by that invented name of Faustine. Sylvia responded to it now as readily as to her real name; nearly everyone else, he had noticed, now called her Faustine too, and even he sometimes did. Of late he had sensed a definite attempt on Gwendolyn's part to make them more conscious of each other. She was not given to matchmaking, he knew, yet she was certainly not above manipulating, juxtaposing human beings to one another in order to be able to gain an insight into them. That was Gwendolyn's real vice, he thought, looking at her now: probing character, exploring its mysteries, trying to pluck out the very center. Perhaps this accounted for the look of unutterable bleakness she was sometimes unguarded enough in this room to let come over her face. Perhaps she had succeeded too many times with too many individuals in touching that center. In any event, one inner landscape was quite enough for him. Besides, no one had the right to see too deeply into another human being. He braced himself. That damned helmet still on her head. Had she any idea of how absurd it was? Evidently not.

"Well let's get on with it," she said abruptly, her voice shifting into those deeper tones that meant she was nervous about something, her hands rearranging several bundles of clippings, flipping through them, abandoning them, turning to some typewritten sheaves. "Algiers? No. That little village with the funny name, not that they all aren't, the one on the Syrian desert. You know, where the Arabs have been murdering Jews, or was it the other way around this time? Why can't I find it? Never mind, I remember what I was looking for. It was a town in Alabama, or Mississippi, what was *it* called? Also a funny name. Nothing seems to be in order here!" Her hands were flying over the desk. It was now perfectly clear to him that her mind today was not on her work. She was not even wearing her glasses, and without them she could hardly read. He was not surprised when she subsided and said, "It doesn't matter. Why should *I* care?"

She was sitting at a large carved wooden table on a sort of dais at one end of the room. From this position she commanded not only the room but in a sense the entire establishment. Even the little garden and park on the eastern side of the villa—on the other sides the forest was close in—could be seen from the casement window to her right. Most visitors who were admitted to this room concluded that Mrs. Dartley had carefully planned the imposing arrangement, but in fact it was wholly fortuitous. The dais had simply been there—no one knew why—and the table, originally built several centuries earlier for a Swiss guild hall, she had chosen for its sturdiness and simple beauty and because the carvings, which depicted a cheerful citizenry going about a number of community tasks appropriate to the four seasons, most especially pleased her. It was nevertheless a comment on her character that while other women would surely, at least at first, have felt somewhat self-conscious in ascending that platform, Gwendolyn Dartley had never given it a thought.

Campion picked up a letter from the desk at which he sometimes worked on the lower level of the room and climbed up to sit at the other end of her table. He waved the letter at her. "You'd better look at this at least. We'll have to get an answer off right away."

"Oh but Ernest . . ."

He slapped it down in front of her and waited. From a chain attached to the front of her dress was suspended a pair of half-lensed spectacles. Wearily she unfolded them and slipped them on her nose. "But Ernest," she said sadly when she had finished, "it is an impossible question to answer. How can I tell them why poor Dragan was a Yugoslav? *Why?* A dog chasing its tail. Why are you an American? Or why is dear Lily a Magyar? That little, fatal, irreversible act of chance. Like one's sex. Oh let's give it up."

Campion doubted that she meant this. He picked up a pencil and began to make some notes on the back of an envelope that was near to hand. She did not stop him.

In the course of a full life Mrs. Dartley had changed citizenship several times, partly because of principles and partly because of husbands, and there was at that moment an act in her behalf pending before the Congress of the United States. She had been born an American but had chosen at the time of Prohibition, for reasons in part connected to that law, to become a British subject. Later, at the time of her marriage to the Chevalier Levin, she also became French and enjoyed the privileges of dual citizenship. Then, shortly before the Second War when she married Dragan, her fourth and last husband, her status became somewhat difficult to determine. Several lawyers and governments were working on the problem when she fell seriously ill, and Dragan, reluctant to have her disturbed in any way during the weeks of her convalescence, failed to get her signature on certain crucial papers, with the result that when she at last recovered she had inadvertently become, like him, a Yugoslav. She did not mind this in the least, but she did feel badly used when after the war she found herself classified as a Stateless Person. Eventually, her bank accounts in Geneva and Zürich being in moderately good order, she got around to acquiring permanent resident papers from the Swiss, and in 1953 settled in the rented Villa Kilchberg. Campion could not help feeling a little sympathy for anyone, even those legislators, who might be so foolish as to become involved with the question of her citizenship.

Mrs. Dartley's retirement into the Alpine reaches of Europe, or her exile as she sometimes thought of it, was not quite voluntary.

She had been quick to sense on her once frequent forays to Washington and London an atmosphere that seemed to declare she was *persona non grata*. This was entirely unofficial of course, but it led to little obstacles being put constantly in her way and it enraged her. "No one," she declared to a former chief protocol officer of the State Department when he paid her an entirely personal visit in Kilchberg, "has the power to force these inconveniences on me. Not yet, at any rate. I have absented myself because I have chosen to do so." To herself she admitted the truth: she had indeed met with a kind of defeat. Hence the furious onslaught of tracts that had soon poured from Kilchberg and that rapid construction of the elaborate network of correspondence, her own private spy system, that extended veritably around the world.

It was not that Gwendolyn Dartley could actually influence the course of history or the decisions of governments but that she had the power to make those who did so feel uneasy. For one thing, she had ways of learning about—or as some thought, of divining— policy changes before those who were responsible for them had quite made up their own minds to go ahead. She also had a way of harassing people about aspects of established policy which they themselves had secret doubts about but could not openly or officially admit to. What was worse, it so often developed later on that she had been right. It was this that made her presence in the centers of power so unnerving, as much to those few friends who still remained in government service and who had known her well in the old days as to those new people to whom she was an entirely puzzling phenomenon. And yet all who had thought themselves well rid of her, even if they were fond of her, freed at last from the full and direct onslaught of her personality when she went to Kilchberg, had hardly had time to enjoy their victory before they were forced to wonder if it had been a victory at all, if her nagging eloquence had not been less troublesome when it had been less public.

She herself, despite the obvious effectiveness of the methods which she had adopted out of necessity, chafed at her isolation, and the previous year had begun to think of giving up the villa and taking an apartment in Paris. But before she could resolve the question of what would happen to her dependents at Kilchberg, the matter was settled for her: certain articles she had been writing

on the Algerian situation began appearing, and on a visit to Paris
she found her welcome decidedly thorny. Since she knew that the
French, if they chose, could be far more difficult than the English
or Americans had ever imagined being, she wisely decided to return to Switzerland. She had determined, however, to regain her
American citizenship, for reasons she had never divulged, not even
to Campion.

Campion had finished making his notes, and both he and Mrs.
Dartley sat slumped forward now in similar postures, each head
resting on a doubled-up right fist. She had taken off the helmet at
last and wisps of grayish-brown hair were matted across her forehead. The spectacles fell from her nose and swung softly to and
fro. She did not move. Campion looked at her, thinking that she
looked tired but neither young nor old. The same tiredness
gripped him. In such moments the comradeship that mysteriously
bound them asserted itself, and he felt only the most intense sympathy for her. Her vices and vanities seemed trivial, what he felt to
be the greatness of her spirit was all. He stood up, gathered the
letter and certain other papers. "I'll take care of this. I'll show you
the draft I've written tomorrow. You'll look at it then." He put a
hand on her shoulder. "Perhaps there won't be any word. That's
possible, you know. It's probable, in fact."

She shook her head, then turned so that her cheek pressed
against his hand in a tender gesture. "No. No. There will be
word." Her voice was melancholy.

"Sometimes I don't understand you, Gwendolyn. Do you want,
do you want . . . a drastic upheaval of some sort . . . or do you not
want it?"

She jumped up and turned frightened eyes upon him.

"I mean," he said, "if it were up to you to decide. If it lay in the
power of one person to decide and that one person were you . . ."

"Shhhh!" she said, refusing to go further in that direction. "Such
things are never decided by one person. Disasters. Triumphs. *You*
should know that." He nodded his head ambiguously. It was
true, what she said, but it had little to do with the question he had
put to her. She raised her arms in a wide, helpless gesture. Then
her tone suddenly changed. "I shan't do the reading tonight."

"No?" He was mildly surprised. "Because of the journalist?"

"Certainly. And he is not a journalist. I have told you that. He is
a television person. Did you think I would with him here? It

would be too much what he wants. It would also be a mere showing-off."

"Are you so averse to that?"

"Sometimes, sometimes."

"Why do you want to fool around with him anyway?"

"I don't know. An instinct. A curiosity. A . . . why should I explain to you?" They had fallen back into their usual manner. "Never mind. We'll work through the reports tomorrow. No, we can't. Tomorrow's one of your days at the academy, isn't it? I'll finish the list of questions that goes off to Rome myself. I'll want your advice about something else. But later. It can wait. Oh get out of here Ernest with your solemn face."

He smiled, put the envelope into a pocket and stuffed the rest of the papers in the drawer of the desk.

"Go out and take some air," she said. "This weather won't hold. It's an illusion as it is; so misleading always these September bursts of summer. Get some exercise. You never do. Soon you'll be flabby. Perhaps you already are. Play ping-pong with Marshall, run around the lawn, climb a tree."

"Do pushups? Swim?"

She tapped him on the shoulder. "Exactly. That's it. Swim. By all means. Swim. Now get out of here."

Five

Anton patted Marshall's beautiful hairy calf. This he could do without fear or self-consciousness since he had never lived for long in the great Anglo-American centers of culture and repression where, particularly among the more worried segments of the population, the least gesture of affection among those of the same sex is taken as a sign of inversion. "Sit down," he said, "sit down. Our enthralled Faustine has obviously no intention of noticing you." He hummed a few bars from the *Erl-König*.

Marshall was still waving his topper after the retreating figure of Sylvia. She sped out of sight into the woods. "But how am I going to find out about the chairs for tonight?"

Everyone in the household had a little task—everyone except Posy, for whom the right one had not yet come along. Marshall's was to set out chairs for the readings which in a sense took the place of what in an earlier and more pious household might have been evening prayer. The number needed depended on whether or not any outsiders had been invited for the occasion and also on whether or not any members of the regular household had been excused. Usually Marshall got his instructions from Sylvia, and it unsettled him if she forgot and he had to ask Mrs. Dartley herself.

"Never mind. You take your responsibility far too seriously, my young friend. Go on with your story, Rosanna," Anton said to Posy.

"Oh but it's finished. That's all there was to it. And please Mr. Hrubick, please don't call me that again."

"Finished? Really? Extraordinary." Posy's stories were usually totally incomprehensible to him, which was why they were so absorbing. He always listened with great attention, hoping he might one day grasp a brass ring or two for his troubles. Mostly he felt he was listening to a charming teller of fairy tales for which there simply were no analogues among all of the other legends of the world. The folk tales of Bechuanaland would have made more sense to him than Posy's. He sighed. Later he would ask Marshall to explain. This one had had to do with a drink called a martini, the mixing of which was evidently a ritual of great significance on the eastern seaboard of America and in scattered coves throughout the rest of that strange land.

"Why did you call Faustine enthralled?" Marshall asked.

Anton did not care to go into all the linguistic implications of the word. He changed course. "Because she is. She's always chasing, or being chased." This too involved word play, he realized, and was no doubt conveying his meaning imperfectly. "As though the furies were after her. Or perhaps it is the other way around—it would be difficult to tell which." Then he added quietly, as an afterthought, "She's very willful, you know."

Posy said, "Well, I know one thing. She's got a demon lover."

"Don't be silly," Marshall said. To him a woman in her early thirties simply did not exist as a woman; she was in limbo, too old to be an object of sexual or social interest, too young to be identified with women of his mother's generation. And what other classifications of women were there? But to Posy, Sylvia was another

matter; she admired her greatly, and as is so often the case when
young girls admire an older woman who is yet young enough to
appear as an ideal image of the self, she was filled with a great
curiosity about her. Imagining Sylvia to inhabit some region of
high and poetic intensities, she had longed, thus far in vain, to "get
to know her."

"She does have, doesn't she?" Posy insisted.

Anton Hrubick endeavored not to smile, the less so at Posy's
eager interest in the question than at Marshall's look of slightly
disgusted incredulity. He would never understand Americans, least
of all the young men. When he was eighteen, younger than Marshall, he had had his first great love, and it had been with a woman
just about Sylvia's age. In Prague or Vienna such alliances were
regarded as great good fortune for a young man, and he remembered that affair as the one uncomplicated yet meaningful love of
his whole life. For him a woman in her early thirties would always
be at the perfect age. Anton had constantly to fight off the desire
to give Marshall a good European education. Perhaps he would
just take him to *Der Rosenkavalier* the next time. But the boy was
still such a puritan, the opera might confuse him more. And the
business about Octavian being sung by a woman, Marshall would
definitely be puzzled at that. He would have to explain that convention to him. And then he would have to explain what lay
behind that. No, no, it wouldn't do at all; you could not educate a
boy just a little, you would have to go all the way, and that would
be much too time-consuming. Anton abandoned the notion. Life
would have to be the teacher.

"At my advanced age," he said to Posy, who was frowning at
him for being so slow to answer, "I have learned to be very uncertain about the exact nature of people's private relationships. I have
even learned not to think about it when I can avoid it. I studied
anatomy once. Everyone should do this. The brain. Oh, the brain.
Even now we know so little about that mysteriously involuted and
complicated organ, and that obscure system, very powerful but all
too sensitive, of electrical energy. Memory we know is there. But
exactly where? Think of that. And what a phenomenon it is.
Think of all the old tribesmen and warriors hidden in us, along
with a great many yoke-bearers and perhaps a priest or two. Do
you ever feel them thumping to get out? And when all this current
of energy begins flowing also, connecting, in whatever way, be-

tween two people, when they have what we call a relationship? Ah
no, thank you no, I am too old to make such guesses. I let others
guess, my little circle of friends in Zürich. I go in once a week
precisely and only for this reason, to listen to them guess. But tell
me, why, why with all this and environment too, the horrors of
infancy and childhood, why then should we be surprised at the
almost infinite capacity for complexity which we show, or rather
which we do not show, which we try not to show, which we hide
in our private lives? Particularly the highly endowed? Consider
the curse that is laid upon them."

Posy and Marshall had learned to wait patiently through such
speeches. They liked Anton Hrubick despite the strange and very
often boring things he said. This time, however, Posy was annoyed. She had understood more of his comments about Sylvia
than he thought, and she had been rather proud of her phrase
"demon lover." "He's called St. George," she said bluntly.

"Is he? By whom? I thought he was called Bingham. George
Bingham. Except perhaps under special circumstances. Whatever
the name, that ubiquitous gentleman has not appeared here for
some time."

"I know. Not since just before I came here. Is it true that he used
to send cables and say he was flying over from New York to go to
a play in London or an opera in Milan and would she join him for
the evening, and that other times he would just suddenly pop up
unannounced and claim her?"

"Claim her?" Marshall said.

"Posy's speech is a little heightened," Anton said. "I believe
there must be some confusion here. Mr. George Bingham has been
with us at Kilchberg once. It is true that his arrival seemed rather
unexpected. Where Faustine was in the habit of going on her
holidays or with whom . . . ah, that is a tantalizing subject let us
admit. What are your sources of information?"

"One learns things," she said mysteriously, and colored considerably. "What does he do, Mr. Hrubick? Is he just rich? I suppose
he's much older than she is."

"I don't think he could be more than a few years older, my dear.
I'm hardly an authority on him, though. I should tell you that.
As to what he does; he is, I believe, what is called an international
businessman."

"Oh," Posy said flatly.

Anton had not the least notion of what picture his phrase had conjured up for Posy, but he knew it had disappointed her. He hastened to make amends. "Not that he looks or acts like one," he added.

"Really?"

"Yes, really. He looks more like a . . . a concert virtuoso, yes, that's good, a man of temperament and remarkable moods. Yes, one could see him striding across the stage with violin bow raised like a lance, a knightly artistic figure." He saw the look of pleasure spreading over Posy's face. "Or like a nineteenth-century poet, one who could dash off love lyrics in between foolhardy turns on the barricades." He definitely had his audience, he saw; Posy was rapt and Marshall annoyed but interested. It would be a pity to let the occasion go now, not to continue with these fanciful pictures. Until then Anton had never thought very much at all about this Bingham person. He had found him rather cold and aloof, but intelligent, well-informed, and somehow of compelling character. A man of unusually moderate habits too, he recalled now, who did not smoke and who drank only sparingly, perhaps therefore interested in being always alert and clear-headed and in retaining that certainly superior physique—he had played tennis and swum with almost joyless perfection. "Or," he went on, "like a Greek hero, a warrior, the sort they made statues of. A *wandering* hero . . ."

As he paused, Marshall said, "Very romantic."

"Oh very," Anton agreed. "But tragic, you understand. Something dark, brooding hangs over him, some curse or edict. A doomed wanderer." For an instant Anton's mind almost came to grips seriously with the man whose person, as even the nickname suggested, lent itself so easily to mythos—some scene or interchange that involved him hovered beclouded but almost visible in Anton's memory. But then he laughed and got to his feet. "Perhaps after all only something out of Wagner," he said. "Some nineteenth-century inflated melodrama, calculated to wring pity from the romantic hearts of young girls. An enviable fate." He touched Posy on the cheek.

She roused herself from her dreamy state. "That's funny. Do you know, that reminds me of a dream I had at The Mothergone. I used to dream a lot when I was there. Come to think of it I haven't dreamed much since."

Anton lifted a hand. If there was one thing he definitely did not

understand about it was the place called The Mothergone. There
had been enough failure of communication for one day. "I'll leave
you two now. A letter, I must write it, very pressing. I hope you
will tell me about your dreams another time, my dear. And Marshall, be at ease about the chairs. I shall find out for you."

He set off across the grass. He heard Posy say, "These hats are
great, aren't they?" and Marshall reply with a vigorous, "Oh Lord
yes," relieved evidently that the conversation was taking a turn
more to his liking. Ernest Campion, in bathing trunks, walking in
the opposite direction, passed at a distance. He and Anton nodded
at each other. Anton began singing a little song. It was a bouncy
folk tune. "*Schwäbische, bayrische Dirndel, juchhe!*" Then he
stopped, turned to look after Campion, and sang the phrase again,
but this time with words of his own choosing—"*Ewig-e,
weibliche, zieht uns hinan . . .*" But Campion was too far away to
hear, and with a disappointed, amused shrug Anton plodded on
toward the house.

Six

Sylvia plunged about in the water with the graceful slow abandon
of a dolphin. Only Mrs. Dartley's pet fish was there for company;
occasionally it brushed its finny way near her. She had been foolish
not to come to this pool every day; it was a part of that ridiculous
plan of self-denial to which she had been clinging ever since she
had accepted Mrs. Dartley's invitation and left Munich behind her.
It suddenly seeemed obvious to her that there must have been
other and better ways, having little to do with her own will. Now
another season was gone, and she had had none of the fruits of it.
Oh but it was delicious, this watery world. Might it not wash away
one's sins, both real and assumed?

It is always difficult to know later on how two people have
reached some crucial moment after which it seems that neither
character nor fate but an implacable third force composed of both
is determining their destiny. Such history can no more be recorded
with exactness than remembered, no doubt because it lies in the

u like to do that, slay dragons? Somehow or other I
 seem the type."
saw that all that incredible alertness which had been
ression of him had now come back. He shrugged, said
 just a salesman."
ere were any dragons, worth slaying I mean? Any
ose? Yes, you can't fool me. I think you'd make a
ier-saint. For God, for England, Harry and St.
 however it went."
 months later, at the end of one of those struggles
 which by then had become so bitter and constant a
r lives, she had said to him—again she was a little
eep forgetting to tell you. I've been doing some re-
 now I will, my St. George, my perfectly named one.
w what he really was, that fellow? I'm sure you must.
filthy rascal, a sainted swine, a marauder, a tricker of
t within the hour she had been holding him in her
 rocking him gently to her, back and forth, and then
ver him while he sank into that light and somehow
 eep that always puzzled her so.
t was the source of this passion that still in some ter-
 bound her to him, even when she knew all and even
ad run off to Kilchberg? It had never become, as she
een so certain it would, a great ecstasy of the senses—if
 could understand and know that with time it would
 omething still more profound and mysterious, some-
 r too. And if what there was between them could never
 inal consummation through the senses, through what
 it?
 talked in the early days she often felt that she had
 wn him. She put this down to liking him so much. But
 times when she could not explain it so easily, times
 med she was experiencing, living in, a perpetual *déjà vu*.
 once she finished a story for him, as though it were
 t of her, detail for detail, whether she wanted it to or
 s exciting, exhilarating when this happened, but in a
 way, and he stared at her with eyes that had expected
 ss. She had developed, too, extraordinary intuitions
 n he would come back or leave. Sometimes she would
 at the Vier Jahreszeiten a few minutes before he was

lost rhythm of so many little things: in fragments of conversation, significances that vanish at the instant they are grasped, sinking into the larger perceptions that could never have existed without them, in quick, suddenly undefended glances, in intonation, even in so trivial a matter as whether or not a bottle of wine is opened, or if opened left half finished and growing warm, losing its bloom by a cracked tile stove.

Sylvia was certain of only one thing, the moment itself and when it had come. She turned and turned again in watery freedom; oh what a bliss of freedom. A pity that even with that ingenious system of pipes which Mrs. Dartley had had the engineer invent in order to warm the mountain stream that flowed into this natural pool it would soon be too cold to come here. The cold winds from the Alps would rush down here as they had rushed interminably down upon the Bavarian capital the winter before when she and Bingham had, it seemed, been safe and warm inside and when she had said, much as one might say, "I've always thought a holiday in Greece would be fun," when she had said instead, "Königsberg's a city I've always wanted to see." That was the moment there was no going back from, not ever it seemed, and this was not because later the same night they had become for the first time what is called lovers.

Once in a great while since that night and all that it implied and that she did not understand she had, wearily, abandoned the attempt to use her rational powers, and just as she now moved with no effort of her own in the flow of this water so had she slipped along the currents of intuition toward the enigma of George Bingham. Whenever this occurred she always got the same startling series of images. First, a scene that showed some Cretan youngsters vaulting once more over the magic horns of death. Then a man, half naked yet far from a savage, garlanded yet heavily armed, moving through a forest toward a tree, followed by dark shapes. The first of these, no doubt a frieze she had seen a picture of, seemed obvious enough. The second—a fragment of pottery, a tomb carving, or perhaps remembered from some deeper and more timeless source?—was mystery within mystery and would simply yield no meaning at all, try though she did to give words to what she felt to be its overwhelming significance. But it was the third image that was frightening, precisely because this one she felt she did understand but was willfully choosing to hide from its meaning: it was a coin showing two helmeted heads, almost identical and almost indistinguishable as to sex except for a slightly more delicate and therefore feminine cast to the features of one. Both heads were on each side of the coin, but on one side the markings of blows or wounds about the face had been reversed to the more delicate of the two. So great a feeling of terror and helplessness would go through her then that weeks would pass before she would again relax a vigilant control over the imaginative, perceptive powers in her which had called up the last of these images. Such powers she kept firmly enleashed, to her sorrow in other ways, since in art as in life there must be a willingness to surrender to the unknown. It was a surrender she could not make, shadowed as she was by the spirit of George Bingham.

Bingham the man was always much on the go, as though he were hoping to outdistance something. The large international corporation, now American controlled, for which he worked, with its vast holdings throughout what is designated as the free world, was organized and run very much like the government. Indeed, there were those within its ranks who sometimes felt it *was* the government. George Bingham himself was far too intelligent to be of this persuasion, but he saw the correspondence, and his own position within AMPERE (Amalgamated Metalurgical Petroleum Electrical Research Endeavors) could be described quite accurately as that of an Under Secretary of State. Much of his work involved negotiations with foreign governments, a task for which his rich gift of languages had well prepared him, and his life was composed of sudden and often unannounced arrivals and departures. From the beginning, however, Sylvia did not attach a great importance to his occupation, sensing that he himself did not.

Yet if his occupation did not matter to him, what did? This thought occurred often to her, especially in the first months of their friendship. Nature, she believed, had meant him for a life of action, and his restless wanderings in a world in which no very splendid form of action came easily to hand struck her somehow close to the heart. The evening they first met, at the home of a wealthy owner of breweries who was also a great patron of music, he had, when most of the guests left, played Mozart on the piano, naming to her amazement the famous woman who had been his teacher. Why had he not gone on? There was no answer, except that after the war he had not felt like it. Did he play much now?

Hardly at all. Couldn't she
she told him, but still . . . H
occupation really required,
because of the music life of
host for the evening. And
because she liked beer? She
her too—someone in the St
duction—but no, she wasn't
Dichterin?" She covered her
pean sense? Yes, in a way I'm
was interesting; he envied her
meeting, some ten days later
nothing had been said of me
that they would—she felt a ne
had in the meantime somehow
her hand had appeared in print

On the first night he took h
that she had given him the nick
looking methodically around
plaster-cracked walls and the w
said was the pattern she had in
last that she had given the plac
tempt she was soon to grow
modes of the newly rich, who,
themselves, purchased the mere
objects, admired the Dutch lith
of the reproduction of the Düre
and there purchased a large n
prints, ikons which she had arra
piece of wall. These he liked mo
Byzantium. Once I was going to
imagine me leading such a calm
though, oddly enough."

Why "oddly enough" she tho
little drunk and her eyes focused
the winged and golden figure
George would be an excellent nick

He laughed. "Why?"

"Oh I don't know. Your name
And he was a noble fellow was

Wouldn't yo
think so. You

Dimly she
her first imp
lightly, "I'm

"But if th
worthy purr
perfect sole
George! Or

But some
between the
part of the
drunk—"I k
search. But
Do you kno
A horrible,
history." Y
arms again,
watching
controlled

And wha
rible way
when she
had once b
it had she
pass—but
thing dark
know its
then could

As they
always kn
there wer
when it se
More tha
pouring o
not. It w
frightenin
nothing
about wh
phone hir

making a quick and unexpected dash for the airport. His voice
then was always hard and closed. "How did you know?" he would
ask. When next they met he would question her closely about it,
with that odd, ambiguous, almost faunlike smile curving his
mouth. When he looked so she always felt she did not know him at
all, felt she had never seen that face anywhere before. In the end
they both got used to the "intuitions"; he attributed them to the
Welsh blood which through her father's line flowed in her veins.

The many things he had been and done amazed and pleased her.
He had even been a sort of farmer. When he was fourteen his
father, an international lawyer who had preferred living abroad,
had died a near-bankrupt. A house in Vermont had been saved, and
from then until the war Bingham, living there with his mother, had
run it as a small dairy and traveled once a week into New York for
the day of piano lessons. Sylvia imagined him easily as this youth,
saw him as a quite pastoral figure, moving among the gentle herds
and the melodies of Mozart. Then war, after which he had gone to
one of the smaller of the old New England colleges, in the summers hiring himself out to the rich on the Cape as steersman for
their pleasure craft. Then had come the Rhodes, the M.A. in history at Oxford. And here for the first time the very variety
seemed to Sylvia to become something else, not plenitude but
confusion, uncertainty. It troubled her. He had felt a growing
revulsion for the life of the academy, he told her, for its inactivity,
for his colleagues. It was not this which she found difficult to
understand but the sequence which followed, for he had then gone
to law school, at Yale, but at the end of the first year, having taken
all honors, had made another sudden change: he had joined
AMPERE. It seemed to Sylvia that he had been meant for some
high and resounding achievement. But what? Not AMPERE, not if
she were any judge. She considered too in those early days the
effect of the war, and there were times when she thought that if
she loved him it was really for the dangers he had passed, the bitter
trials of war so heroically undergone, as she had guessed, and at so
early an age, spoken of once with terrible, oblique eloquence and
never again. Or else that she loved him for some atmosphere of
danger that seemed still to cling to him. And he, he loved her, he
said, for her mind, the only woman's mind he had ever respected,
and for what he called, but did not yet possess, her sexy body. And
she asked, expected nothing of him. He marveled at that. And yet

he was asking something of her, she was certain. Something. They moved toward the wintry moment.

And had not what he told her that night only confirmed those wild, preposterous notions that had sometimes flitted through her head on occasion, as for example the time he lay, as he often liked to do, head in her lap, and the Kuppers' cat had jumped to the top of the couch where he could not see what it was but only feel its intruding impact, and he had leapt up all at once, positioned in the air like a Samurai, a fearful symmetry of readiness in every nerve and muscle and most of all in the mind? These notions she rejected as the product of the all too easily aroused imagination of one who by nature sought always for patterns, believing them to be there.

A furious welter of snow was being driven over the ruins of Munich that night. He had been gone for several weeks, but that afternoon, on instinct, she had made efforts to straighten the two rooms of her apartment and had asked Frau Kupper's son to bring up more wood for the stove. Frequently now he spent the night with her, talking until late, stretching out on the couch and waking himself before six, slipping out before she was up. When he was in a rare gay mood they would dine in his suite at the Vier Jahreszeiten and he would play a little Bach or Mozart for her before they returned to her place. But this happened less and less often. He seemed only to want to be within the walls of her room, almost it seemed to imprison them both there, and certainly to close out the rest of the world.

He arrived in his usual way, unannounced at about nine, two bottles of Moët et Chandon under his arm and a large pot of pressed caviar in his overcoat pocket. He was limping slightly and had what looked like the faint remains of bruises above the left eye and under the cheekbone. He had lost weight and his face was very drawn. He was pleased that she noticed, but waved away explanations with a transparent and awkward joke. She did not ask questions. On the contrary, she felt the strongest desire not to know what had happened. Little by little, as they drank the wine, the tension and fatigue slipped from him. There was one brief instant when she thought there was something supplicating in his eyes, but with a blink it was gone. By the time they had drunk the first bottle he was very much himself again. Should they open the second one? Neither really cared to, but at last he did. Then they were talking of Copenhagen; he had just got back from there—it was a city he liked and he spoke of it with enthusiasm. She too knew Copenhagen, but she envied him his travels, all those other places he went to all the time that she would probably never get to, in Latin America and the Near East and Far East, and every single bit of accessible Europe. It would be fun some time, he said, to take a summer holiday together on one of the Danish islands; one could be very private there, very alone; they would hire a boat and do a lot of sailing. This prospect filled her mind, an image of sails against a north wind. Then she thought of the Baltic Sea and the places that rimmed it, many lying cut off now, behind the Iron Curtain. She said, "Oh there's so much I don't suppose I could see today even if I had the money. Königsberg, for example. Or whatever they call it now. I've forgotten. Something Polish, I suppose, or Russian. Since the war. Königsberg's a city I've always wanted to see. I don't know why."

And he said, "It's a lovely city. Especially in the winter, in the snow."

She felt the blood leave her head. Her expression, however, did not change. Nor did his. She got up and reached for the wine and poured some of it into their glasses while he watched her. It made an enormous sound in the silence. The bottle was still half full. She sat down again. He had not taken his eyes from her. His face had a sort of dark pallor to it. She began to chatter. He stopped her. "Aren't you going to ask me anything?" he said.

"No."

"You understood what I said just then."

Her hand flew to her lips, an imperative demand that he say no more. She jumped up. "Please. *Don't tell me a thing.*" She knew now that she had always known. "I don't want to be your secret sharer."

"But you are."

She shook her head. Chance or intention? How could she ever take his measure now? Who was he? What? Why could she not send him away, *at once?*

He was saying, "Everyone reaches a point at which he slips, if he allows himself any closeness. It's built in. I've tried to tell myself otherwise since knowing you. But what I just said to you proves I was wrong."

"You didn't slip," she said. "It proves that every man reaches a point where he can't bear things alone. Sometimes."

His face hardened suddenly at this. The cool voice said, "I'm afraid I don't agree." But the eyes said something else. An awful struggle was taking place in her. And then she said, "Oh my poor darling."

In the early hours of that morning, while he slept that strange sleep of his, she lay awake. The room was freezing cold. She knew now that nothing but sorrow and pain awaited her. She leaned over his head, saw for the first time its extreme antique sort of beauty, touched the marks on his face. She remembered the fierce, almost joyless embraces, the final coupling. And then words came to her and she wanted to wake him up, tell him, force him to utter them—as though words themselves were magical and the very act of utterance could free him: Close though my love is, yet is mine enemy closer.

But she did not wake him. She put her lips lightly on his and waited. He did not stir. She had somehow not really expected him to. She moved away then and in time fell asleep herself. When she awoke again she could not quite remember what it was she had wanted to tell him.

Sylvia Grierson released all her unsprung energy into a sudden dive, rising first out of the water, then over and down, heels disappearing, plunging deep, deep into the very farthest reaches of the pool, turning there, shimmering, merging at last with the silver-blue light which at those depths seemed the very source of the water itself, then with bursting lungs flashed her way in triumph to the surface. There she turned slowly onto her back and began to float, the dying sun upon her.

Seven

Campion had been spying on Sylvia for some time. It was quite a new activity for him and he was torn between shame and a very pleasant feeling that seemed compounded in equal parts of power and danger. He really hadn't had the least intention of doing this, but when he first arrived at the pool, sneaking up on sneakers as he later put it to her, much later, she had looked so peaceful floating around with her eyes closed that he had thought it a pity to disturb her. Then, before he was quite aware of what he was doing, he found he had crept around to a position in the pine trees where a thick growth of wild berry bushes made a perfect cover for him. Was that body mysteriously rising and falling on the water really Sylvia's? The remote being, with her clipped way of talking, whom he had known, or thought he had known, for the last several months, seemed quite transformed in this grove. No denying it, she was a lovely woman, he decided, thus managing to hide from himself certain more specifically voluptuous judgments he was unconsciously making. And she seemed, for the first time in his memory, somehow not on her guard.

Just then she rolled gently over onto her stomach and to his disappointment began stroking her way lazily in. He knew this was the moment when he had to act, while the sound of the water past her ears would prevent her from hearing him. He had either to come jauntily forward, as though just arriving, or clear out entirely. But he hesitated too long. She was already out of the water and for some reason was standing very still, almost as though she were listening. Damn Gwendolyn, he thought, and then wondered at his own absurdity. He imagined that the pine needles beneath his feet were creaking and that at any moment Sylvia would detect his presence. He was suddenly very uncomfortable, and resentful of not daring to move around.

But Sylvia was wholly absorbed in matters of her own. She had stretched her right arm over her left shoulder and back and was struggling awkwardly with something. What could account for this frantic contortion? An insect bite perhaps? Then just as he realized what she was doing, something was released, the arm came down, and with it the top of the bathing suit. He closed his eyes for a second, imagining the smell of the damp, cool flesh being touched now by the warm air, and his heart began to beat very rapidly. When he looked again she was already peeling the suit down past her hipbones, writhing her thighs and belly considerably in an effort to free herself of that unwanted garment that clung so stubbornly to her; like a fish, he thought, shimmering its way out of an old skin, to be free at last, revealed at last in a new, silken-soft and perfect form. Then, how absurd, he thought; none of that made any sense. Fish don't even do that. Snakes do. But it was impossible to associate Sylvia with a snake. Or was it? What about butterflies? Campion was confused. But no. Fish was right. If fish didn't change their skins then they ought to. Having struggled through this illogical maze of images his mind went blank. Her nakedness was most appealing.

For her part, Sylvia was being very businesslike, wringing out the bathing suit, hanging it carefully on a tree branch. She hesitated now, sighed deeply, put a hand on each shoulder, as though feeling her muscles, then ran them indifferently down breasts, belly, and the top of her thighs, standing all the time curiously straight. Campion fidgeted. He had the impression that she was going to stretch out on the ground and sunbathe. She scuffed at the muddy shore, padded to where the pine needles began and scuffed at them, and then evidently with reluctance changed her mind, for she sighed again and reached out for the shorts and the long shirt she had worn over the bathing suit on her way to the pool. Then, to Campion's astonishment, she tossed them away and flung herself into a sort of dance, leaping high into the air, waving her arms around, lifting each leg in its turn high from the knee and shaking the foot in a strange fashion, while her smallish breasts bounced up and down and the white flesh of her behind rippled. Good Lord! It was obvious that she had gone completely mad, obvious too that he must emerge and restrain her. He took one step forward, but suddenly she stopped, felt her skin rapidly at several spots, slipped into the shorts and shirt, and lay down in the sun and closed her eyes again. She had only been drying herself, he realized sadly. And still he stared. A deep and peaceful, utterly vulnerable and unguarded expression came over her face.

It was then that the relatively casual erotic feelings Campion had been experiencing changed. An undeniable desire to fling himself on her moved him. It was the sudden revelation of all her softness, her stillness, that assailed him most deeply, the lovely relaxed face, the eyes sunk into sleep, the tender limbs that were meant for embraces. Swiftly he imagined her head flung back amidst pillows, brought by his touch yearningly forward, the usually firm lips fuller, larger; saw her head finally, moving from side to side; heard her delicate moanings and little short gasps, delivering herself to him; could imagine too the great quiver that would arch through her, and her silken-smooth, damp face afterwards. God, he was the one who was mad. And furious too, that he had conjured up such a fantasy, like an adolescent that dreams but does not dare, lost rhythm of so many little things: in fragments of conversation, significances that vanish at the instant they are grasped, sinking into the larger perceptions that could never have existed without them, in quick, suddenly undefended glances, in intonation, even in so trivial a matter as whether or not a bottle of wine is opened, or if opened left half finished and growing warm, losing its bloom by a cracked tile stove.

Sylvia was certain of only one thing, the moment itself and when it had come. She turned and turned again in watery freedom; oh what a bliss of freedom. A pity that even with that ingenious system of pipes which Mrs. Dartley had had the engineer invent in order to warm the mountain stream that flowed into this natural pool it would soon be too cold to come here. The cold winds from the Alps would rush down here as they had rushed interminably down upon the Bavarian capital the winter before when she and Bingham had, it seemed, been safe and warm inside and when she had said, much as one might say, "I've always thought a holiday in Greece would be fun," when she had said instead, "Königsberg's a city I've always wanted to see." That was the moment there was no going back from, not ever it seemed, and this was not because later the same night they had become for the first time what is called lovers.

Once in a great while since that night and all that it implied and that she did not understand she had, wearily, abandoned the attempt to use her rational powers, and just as she now moved with no effort of her own in the flow of this water so had she slipped along the currents of intuition toward the enigma of George Bingham. Whenever this occurred she always got the same startling series of images. First, a scene that showed some Cretan youngsters vaulting once more over the magic horns of death. Then a man, half naked yet far from a savage, garlanded yet heavily armed, moving through a forest toward a tree, followed by dark shapes. The first of these, no doubt a frieze she had seen a picture of, seemed obvious enough. The second—a fragment of pottery, a tomb carving, or perhaps remembered from some deeper and more timeless source?—was mystery within mystery and would simply yield no meaning at all, try though she did to give words to what she felt to be its overwhelming significance. But it was the third image that was frightening, precisely because this one she felt she did understand but was willfully choosing to hide from its meaning: it was a coin showing two helmeted heads, almost identical and almost indistinguishable as to sex except for a slightly more delicate and therefore feminine cast to the features of one. Both heads were on each side of the coin, but on one side the markings of blows or wounds about the face had been reversed to the more delicate of the two. So great a feeling of terror and helplessness would go through her then that weeks would pass before she would again relax a vigilant control over the imaginative, perceptive powers in her which had called up the last of these images. Such powers she kept firmly enleashed, to her sorrow in other ways, since in art as in life there must be a willingness to surrender to the unknown. It was a surrender she could not make, shadowed as she was by the spirit of George Bingham.

Bingham the man was always much on the go, as though he were hoping to outdistance something. The large international corporation, now American controlled, for which he worked, with its vast holdings throughout what is designated as the free world, was organized and run very much like the government. Indeed, there were those within its ranks who sometimes felt it *was* the government. George Bingham himself was far too intelligent to be of this persuasion, but he saw the correspondence, and his own position within AMPERE (Amalgamated Metalurgical Petroleum Electrical Research Endeavors) could be described quite accurately as that of an Under Secretary of State. Much of his work involved negotiations with foreign governments, a task for which his rich gift of languages had well prepared him, and his life was composed of sudden and often unannounced arrivals and departures. From the beginning, however, Sylvia did not attach a great importance to his occupation, sensing that he himself did not.

Yet if his occupation did not matter to him, what did? This thought occurred often to her, especially in the first months of their friendship. Nature, she believed, had meant him for a life of action, and his restless wanderings in a world in which no very splendid form of action came easily to hand struck her somehow close to the heart. The evening they first met, at the home of a wealthy owner of breweries who was also a great patron of music, he had, when most of the guests left, played Mozart on the piano, naming to her amazement the famous woman who had been his teacher. Why had he not gone on? There was no answer, except that after the war he had not felt like it. Did he play much now?

Hardly at all. Couldn't she tell that from the way it sounded? Yes, she told him, but still . . . He came to Munich more often than his occupation really required, as often as he could manage in fact, because of the music life of that city. That was how he knew their host for the evening. And how did she know him—not surely because she liked beer? She laughed. No, music was the link for her too—someone in the States had given her a letter of introduction—but no, she wasn't a musician. She was a writer. "A *Dichterin?*" She covered her surprise. "Oh, you mean in the European sense? Yes, in a way I'm afraid I am," she answered. Ah, that was interesting; he envied her and he did not, he said. At their next meeting, some ten days later—when they parted that first night nothing had been said of meeting again, but it had been obvious that they would—she felt a new intensity being directed at her. He had in the meantime somehow searched out and read what little by her hand had appeared in print.

On the first night he took her home, and it was then, that early, that she had given him the nickname. He had stood for a long time, looking methodically around him but seeing, it appeared, not the plaster-cracked walls and the worn and ugly furniture but what he said was the pattern she had imposed on the room. He told her at last that she had given the place beauty, and spoke with the contempt she was soon to grow accustomed to of the fashionable modes of the newly rich, who, so often lacking taste and judgment themselves, purchased the mere imitations of beauty. He touched objects, admired the Dutch lithographs, commented on the quality of the reproduction of the Dürer. She had been to Recklinghausen and there purchased a large number of postcard-size Byzantine prints, ikons which she had arranged over one particularly moldy piece of wall. These he liked most of all. He said, "The history of Byzantium. Once I was going to write books about that. Can you imagine me leading such a calm life? I was a pretty good scholar though, oddly enough."

Why "oddly enough" she thought but did not say. She was a little drunk and her eyes focused slowly on the top center print, the winged and golden figure with raised sword. "I think St. George would be an excellent nickname for you," she said.

He laughed. "Why?"

"Oh I don't know. Your name doesn't seem to fit you somehow. And he was a noble fellow wasn't he? The slayer of dragons.

Wouldn't you like to do that, slay dragons? Somehow or other I think so. You seem the type."

Dimly she saw that all that incredible alertness which had been her first impression of him had now come back. He shrugged, said lightly, "I'm just a salesman."

"But if there were any dragons, worth slaying I mean? Any worthy purpose? Yes, you can't fool me. I think you'd make a perfect soldier-saint. For God, for England, Harry and St. George! Or however it went."

But some months later, at the end of one of those struggles between them which by then had become so bitter and constant a part of their lives, she had said to him—again she was a little drunk—"I keep forgetting to tell you. I've been doing some research. But now I will, my St. George, my perfectly named one. Do you know what he really was, that fellow? I'm sure you must. A horrible, filthy rascal, a sainted swine, a marauder, a tricker of history." Yet within the hour she had been holding him in her arms again, rocking him gently to her, back and forth, and then watching over him while he sank into that light and somehow controlled sleep that always puzzled her so.

And what was the source of this passion that still in some terrible way bound her to him, even when she knew all and even when she had run off to Kilchberg? It had never become, as she had once been so certain it would, a great ecstasy of the senses—if it had she could understand and know that with time it would pass—but something still more profound and mysterious, something darker too. And if what there was between them could never know its final consummation through the senses, through what then could it?

As they talked in the early days she often felt that she had always known him. She put this down to liking him so much. But there were times when she could not explain it so easily, times when it seemed she was experiencing, living in, a perpetual *déjà vu*. More than once she finished a story for him, as though it were pouring out of her, detail for detail, whether she wanted it to or not. It was exciting, exhilarating when this happened, but in a frightening way, and he stared at her with eyes that had expected nothing less. She had developed, too, extraordinary intuitions about when he would come back or leave. Sometimes she would phone him at the Vier Jahreszeiten a few minutes before he was making a quick and unexpected dash for the airport. His voice then was always hard and closed. "How did you know?" he would ask. When next they met he would question her closely about it, with that odd, ambiguous, almost faunlike smile curving his mouth. When he looked so she always felt she did not know him at all, felt she had never seen that face anywhere before. In the end they both got used to the "intuitions"; he attributed them to the Welsh blood which through her father's line flowed in her veins.

The many things he had been and done amazed and pleased her. He had even been a sort of farmer. When he was fourteen his father, an international lawyer who had preferred living abroad, had died a near-bankrupt. A house in Vermont had been saved, and from then until the war Bingham, living there with his mother, had run it as a small dairy and traveled once a week into New York for the day of piano lessons. Sylvia imagined him easily as this youth, saw him as a quite pastoral figure, moving among the gentle herds and the melodies of Mozart. Then war, after which he had gone to one of the smaller of the old New England colleges, in the summers hiring himself out to the rich on the Cape as steersman for their pleasure craft. Then had come the Rhodes, the M.A. in history at Oxford. And here for the first time the very variety seemed to Sylvia to become something else, not plenitude but confusion, uncertainty. It troubled her. He had felt a growing revulsion for the life of the academy, he told her, for its inactivity, for his colleagues. It was not this which she found difficult to understand but the sequence which followed, for he had then gone to law school, at Yale, but at the end of the first year, having taken all honors, had made another sudden change: he had joined AMPERE. It seemed to Sylvia that he had been meant for some high and resounding achievement. But what? Not AMPERE, not if she were any judge. She considered too in those early days the effect of the war, and there were times when she thought that if she loved him it was really for the dangers he had passed, the bitter trials of war so heroically undergone, as she had guessed, and at so early an age, spoken of once with terrible, oblique eloquence and never again. Or else that she loved him for some atmosphere of danger that seemed still to cling to him. And he, he loved her, he said, for her mind, the only woman's mind he had ever respected, and for what he called, but did not yet possess, her sexy body. And she asked, expected nothing of him. He marveled at that. And yet he was asking something of her, she was certain. Something. They moved toward the wintry moment.

And had not what he told her that night only confirmed those wild, preposterous notions that had sometimes flitted through her head on occasion, as for example the time he lay, as he often liked to do, head in her lap, and the Kuppers' cat had jumped to the top of the couch where he could not see what it was but only feel its intruding impact, and he had leapt up all at once, positioned in the air like a Samurai, a fearful symmetry of readiness in every nerve and muscle and most of all in the mind? These notions she rejected as the product of the all too easily aroused imagination of one who by nature sought always for patterns, believing them to be there.

A furious welter of snow was being driven over the ruins of Munich that night. He had been gone for several weeks, but that afternoon, on instinct, she had made efforts to straighten the two rooms of her apartment and had asked Frau Kupper's son to bring up more wood for the stove. Frequently now he spent the night with her, talking until late, stretching out on the couch and waking himself before six, slipping out before she was up. When he was in a rare gay mood they would dine in his suite at the Vier Jahreszeiten and he would play a little Bach or Mozart for her before they returned to her place. But this happened less and less often. He seemed only to want to be within the walls of her room, almost it seemed to imprison them both there, and certainly to close out the rest of the world.

He arrived in his usual way, unannounced at about nine, two bottles of Moët et Chandon under his arm and a large pot of pressed caviar in his overcoat pocket. He was limping slightly and had what looked like the faint remains of bruises above the left eye and under the cheekbone. He had lost weight and his face was very drawn. He was pleased that she noticed, but waved away explanations with a transparent and awkward joke. She did not ask questions. On the contrary, she felt the strongest desire not to know what had happened. Little by little, as they drank the wine, the tension and fatigue slipped from him. There was one brief instant when she thought there was something supplicating in his eyes, but with a blink it was gone. By the time they had drunk the first bottle he was very much himself again. Should they open the second one? Neither really cared to, but at last he did. Then they were talking of Copenhagen; he had just got back from there—it was a city he liked and he spoke of it with enthusiasm. She too knew Copenhagen, but she envied him his travels, all those other places he went to all the time that she would probably never get to, in Latin America and the Near East and Far East, and every single bit of accessible Europe. It would be fun some time, he said, to take a summer holiday together on one of the Danish islands; one could be very private there, very alone; they would hire a boat and do a lot of sailing. This prospect filled her mind, an image of sails against a north wind. Then she thought of the Baltic Sea and the places that rimmed it, many lying cut off now, behind the Iron Curtain. She said, "Oh there's so much I don't suppose I could see today even if I had the money. Königsberg, for example. Or whatever they call it now. I've forgotten. Something Polish, I suppose, or Russian. Since the war. Königsberg's a city I've always wanted to see. I don't know why."

And he said, "It's a lovely city. Especially in the winter, in the snow."

She felt the blood leave her head. Her expression, however, did not change. Nor did his. She got up and reached for the wine and poured some of it into their glasses while he watched her. It made an enormous sound in the silence. The bottle was still half full. She sat down again. He had not taken his eyes from her. His face had a sort of dark pallor to it. She began to chatter. He stopped her. "Aren't you going to ask me anything?" he said.

"No."

"You understood what I said just then."

Her hand flew to her lips, an imperative demand that he say no more. She jumped up. "Please. *Don't tell me a thing.*" She knew now that she had always known. "I don't want to be your secret sharer."

"But you are."

She shook her head. Chance or intention? How could she ever take his measure now? Who was he? What? Why could she not send him away, *at once?*

He was saying, "Everyone reaches a point at which he slips, if he allows himself any closeness. It's built in. I've tried to tell myself otherwise since knowing you. But what I just said to you proves I was wrong."

"You didn't slip," she said. "It proves that every man reaches a point where he can't bear things alone. Sometimes."

His face hardened suddenly at this. The cool voice said, "I'm afraid I don't agree." But the eyes said something else. An awful struggle was taking place in her. And then she said, "Oh my poor darling."

In the early hours of that morning, while he slept that strange sleep of his, she lay awake. The room was freezing cold. She knew now that nothing but sorrow and pain awaited her. She leaned over his head, saw for the first time its extreme antique sort of beauty, touched the marks on his face. She remembered the fierce, almost joyless embraces, the final coupling. And then words came to her and she wanted to wake him up, tell him, force him to utter them—as though words themselves were magical and the very act of utterance could free him: Close though my love is, yet is mine enemy closer.

But she did not wake him. She put her lips lightly on his and waited. He did not stir. She had somehow not really expected him to. She moved away then and in time fell asleep herself. When she awoke again she could not quite remember what it was she had wanted to tell him.

Sylvia Grierson released all her unsprung energy into a sudden dive, rising first out of the water, then over and down, heels disappearing, plunging deep, deep into the very farthest reaches of the pool, turning there, shimmering, merging at last with the silver-blue light which at those depths seemed the very source of the water itself, then with bursting lungs flashed her way in triumph to the surface. There she turned slowly onto her back and began to float, the dying sun upon her.

Seven

Campion had been spying on Sylvia for some time. It was quite a new activity for him and he was torn between shame and a very pleasant feeling that seemed compounded in equal parts of power and danger. He really hadn't had the least intention of doing this, but when he first arrived at the pool, sneaking up on sneakers as he later put it to her, much later, she had looked so peaceful floating around with her eyes closed that he had thought it a pity to disturb her. Then, before he was quite aware of what he was doing, he found he had crept around to a position in the pine trees where a thick growth of wild berry bushes made a perfect cover for him. Was that body mysteriously rising and falling on the water really Sylvia's? The remote being, with her clipped way of talking, whom he had known, or thought he had known, for the last several months, seemed quite transformed in this grove. No denying it, she was a lovely woman, he decided, thus managing to hide from himself certain more specifically voluptuous judgments he was unconsciously making. And she seemed, for the first time in his memory, somehow not on her guard.

Just then she rolled gently over onto her stomach and to his disappointment began stroking her way lazily in. He knew this was the moment when he had to act, while the sound of the water past her ears would prevent her from hearing him. He had either to come jauntily forward, as though just arriving, or clear out entirely. But he hesitated too long. She was already out of the water and for some reason was standing very still, almost as though she were listening. Damn Gwendolyn, he thought, and then wondered at his own absurdity. He imagined that the pine needles beneath his feet were creaking and that at any moment Sylvia would detect his presence. He was suddenly very uncomfortable, and resentful of not daring to move around.

But Sylvia was wholly absorbed in matters of her own. She had stretched her right arm over her left shoulder and back and was struggling awkwardly with something. What could account for this frantic contortion? An insect bite perhaps? Then just as he realized what she was doing, something was released, the arm came down, and with it the top of the bathing suit. He closed his eyes for a second, imagining the smell of the damp, cool flesh being touched now by the warm air, and his heart began to beat very rapidly. When he looked again she was already peeling the suit down past her hipbones, writhing her thighs and belly considerably in an effort to free herself of that unwanted garment that clung so stubbornly to her; like a fish, he thought, shimmering its way out of an old skin, to be free at last, revealed at last in a new, silken-soft and perfect form. Then, how absurd, he thought; none of that made any sense. Fish don't even do that. Snakes do. But it was impossible to associate Sylvia with a snake. Or was it? What

about butterflies? Campion was confused. But no. Fish was right.
If fish didn't change their skins then they ought to. Having strug-
gled through this illogical maze of images his mind went blank.
Her nakedness was most appealing.

For her part, Sylvia was being very businesslike, wringing out
the bathing suit, hanging it carefully on a tree branch. She hesitated now, sighed deeply, put a hand on each shoulder, as though
feeling her muscles, then ran them indifferently down breasts,
belly, and the top of her thighs, standing all the time curiously
straight. Campion fidgeted. He had the impression that she was
going to stretch out on the ground and sunbathe. She scuffed at
the muddy shore, padded to where the pine needles began and
scuffed at them, and then evidently with reluctance changed her
mind, for she sighed again and reached out for the shorts and the
long shirt she had worn over the bathing suit on her way to the
pool. Then, to Campion's astonishment, she tossed them away and
flung herself into a sort of dance, leaping high into the air, waving
her arms around, lifting each leg in its turn high from the knee and
shaking the foot in a strange fashion, while her smallish breasts
bounced up and down and the white flesh of her behind rippled.
Good Lord! It was obvious that she had gone completely mad,
obvious too that he must emerge and restrain her. He took one
step forward, but suddenly she stopped, felt her skin rapidly at
several spots, slipped into the shorts and shirt, and lay down in the
sun and closed her eyes again. She had only been drying herself, he
realized sadly. And still he stared. A deep and peaceful, utterly
vulnerable and unguarded expression came over her face.

It was then that the relatively casual erotic feelings Campion had
been experiencing changed. An undeniable desire to fling himself
on her moved him. It was the sudden revelation of all her softness,
her stillness, that assailed him most deeply, the lovely relaxed face,
the eyes sunk into sleep, the tender limbs that were meant for
embraces. Swiftly he imagined her head flung back amidst pillows,
brought by his touch yearningly forward, the usually firm lips
fuller, larger; saw her head finally, moving from side to side;
heard her delicate moanings and little short gasps, delivering
herself to him; could imagine too the great quiver that would arch
through her, and her silken-smooth, damp face afterwards. God,
he was the one who was mad. And furious too, that he had conjured
up such a fantasy, like an adolescent that dreams but does not dare,

that he was in so advanced yet purposeless a state of sexual excitement, sweating and heart-thumping and erect there among the pubic fineries of the forest. His desire fell as suddenly as it had risen. He felt an utter fool.

The immediate problem was to get out of there without her knowing. It was immensely important to him. But if he stayed where he was, waiting for her to finish her snooze and go back to the house, he might have a long wait, and he was extremely tired of standing there. Besides, it was obviously all her fault. She had not behaved with what one could call circumspection. Slowly he began creeping back, thinking that even as a boy he had been awfully poor at Red Indian. He turned to look back once more, still creeping, tripped over a root and fell thudding onto the pine needles, where he lay with his eyes tightly closed. He decided it was quite pleasant there, but he got up and began circling around to the path. He had scraped his hand against something jagged and his knee hurt absurdly, though it looked perfectly all right. Gwendolyn was right; he was getting out of condition. He must do something about that. When he reached the path he brushed himself off and then to his surprise headed for the pool, whistling and treading as noisily as possible.

At his approach she sat up, blinking.

"Mind if I join you?" he asked. As soon as he saw her he felt furious again and his tone was surly.

She looked at him suspiciously, then shrugged. "Of course not." She did not lie down again but sat watching him while he took off his sneakers. "What did you do to your hand?"

"Oh that." There was a little trickle of blood. "Caught it on a briar."

"I didn't know there were any briar patches around here."

"I suppose you didn't know that it's dangerous to sit in the sun either. Your father never tell you that?"

"What are you talking about?" But instead of answering her he made a great show of running into the water, where he lurched into a resounding and painful surface dive, managed to recover his breath, and began to swim violently back and forth. "From Peter Rabbit to Hamlet to Tarzan," he heard her taunting cry. He ignored her, and for the next five minutes swam the pool with long and increasingly effective strokes. He felt pleased to discover how quickly and easily he was regaining his old form.

Back on the shore he jumped awkwardly around, hopping first on one foot and then on the other and shaking his hands wildly. He saw her looking at him out of the sides of her eyes.

"What on earth are you doing?"

"Drying off."

She frowned, hesitated, then said, "Well, you're getting me wet."

"Sorry." He squatted beside her, affecting to examine his scraped hand.

"Let's see your wounded paw," she said, smiling suddenly, and reached out her hands, thereby revealing their own somewhat battered condition. Before she could pull them back he had seized her quickly by the wrists.

"What have you been up to?"

She looked into his eyes. "I have been beating them against . . . against a piece of wood."

"A desk, perhaps?"

She nodded. He dropped her wrists and slipped his hands deftly under the shirt, encircling her. She did not move but turned startled eyes upon him. He kissed her, gently, as he had not expected to, and then, just as he felt her beginning to respond, she stiffened and tried to pull away. He held on and they fought for a few seconds until he had her pinned beneath him. Then he saw the cold proud expression on the face that looked up at him and let her go.

She got up with deliberate slowness, brushed some pine needles from the tiny shorts and enormous shirt, retrieved her bathing suit, then spun on him with exceeding fury. "You were spying on me, weren't you? God, if you only *knew* how I hate spies." She seemed almost ready to cry. "I've always liked you, Ernest. But you're a swine too. Wicked, blind, monstrous, primitive, beastly, unloving, wretched, miserable, cruel, plundering, savage, lustful . . ." The adjectives poured forth, and as he moved forward in supplication she ran swiftly up the path, from where she turned again and said, "God, if you only knew how I hate men."

Eight

Sylvia was feeling so curiously, so unexpectedly elated that she was even drinking a whiskey before dinner, a somewhat risky undertaking for her. Senseless really, but very interesting, that once back at the house the anger she had felt had been replaced by a light-heartedness that had her bounding and humming about the room as though she were getting ready for some long-anticipated party. It would certainly take some thinking about, this perplexing aftermath of her encounter with Ernest Campion. She suppressed a giggle at the memory of the final scene, she the false innocent, he the false predator. Oh they were both so ridiculous, she and Ernest, much too grim, much too serious most of the time, a pair of misguided monastics.

"Who's playing the violin?" Benjamin Knox asked. His words recalled her to the needs of the moment. She had led the visitor through the first ten minutes on the terrace with automatic ease and without really having to pay much attention to him. He was a decidedly energetic person, however, or perhaps he was just nervous. He never seemed to be still; up, down, back, forth, railing, chair, legs crossed, legs uncrossed, smile, frown.

"It isn't a violin, it's a cello," she said before she thought, and then went on quickly. "It turned up recently in the gardener's cottage. That would be Anton. Mr. Hrubick. He's better on the piano." She listened for a moment to the sounds coming from inside the house. "Schönberg. He's doing it to annoy Mrs. Halász. If he keeps it up much longer Mrs. Dartley will ask him to stop."

Knox smiled. He was still prepared to take command of the terrace, preferably before his hostess arrived, but this young woman, who had just reminded him of the fact that he did not know a cello when he heard one, was making it difficult. He was used to people answering his questions eagerly, desiring to please. But ever since his arrival she had been conversing with him as though the occasion were purely social, or even a matter of indifference to her.

The music abruptly stopped and she smiled too, but that was all.

"I suppose you're a relative of Mrs. Dartley?" he said.

"No, I'm a guest, a rather permanent one it seems."

"I see. Sort of a social secretary." He fixed her with what was meant to be a penetrating gaze.

Sylvia looked closely at him for the first time, and realized at once that he had no idea he had been rude. He had something to do with television interviewing, she remembered. Perhaps that explained it. "Not really," she said. "People often think Ernest and I are her secretaries. But we're not. We all like to do little things for her when we can. She isn't an easy person to do things for."

"Set in her ways?"

"What? Well, yes, I suppose so." By what right did he come into a woman's house and quiz people about her? "It's more a case of her being so unbelievably capable herself that one can hardly meet her standards. She even knows about . . . oh, about automobile engines, how they work and all that. She can repair them when things go wrong. Evidently it was a good idea to know how if you did much traveling by car in the Balkans before the war. Of course she loathes mechancial things, but she loathes being tyrannized over by them even more. Or so she says. Personally I think she enjoys tinkering with the car." Sylvia paused, realizing that in her attempt to forestall further questions about Mrs. Dartley she had ended by saying more about her to a stranger than she had intended or wished to. Benjamin Knox seemed more pleased with her, and with himself, than at any time since his arrival. She vowed to thwart him with silence, and turning to the bar cart began needlessly rearranging bottles and glasses.

"Well, what do you do?" he asked. He had borne the silence for only half a minute and then had come bursting across the terrace and now stood hovering at her elbow. He rubbed an index finger over cheek and chin in a sort of mock shaving gesture. It was a familiar and endearing gesture to his many followers in America, but Sylvia, who had seen him use it several times in the course of their meeting, found it vaguely distasteful.

"For her, do you mean?"

"No, no." He leaned intently forward, his mouth slightly open, his right hand clasping his jaw and moving it from side to side as though he were experimenting with a fracture. What a curious set of mannerisms he had. Where had he got them? From a distance they might possibly be effective, in a theatrical sort of way, but up close they were really grotesque. But of course, they were studied, imitated from one of the big movie stars of the thirties, a man who still occasionally made a public appearance and who now wore these mannerisms, more exaggerated·than ever, as a mask to hide his age. But why did Benjamin Knox wear them? "What do *you* do?" he asked.

"I'm an unknown novelist."

"Oh you write do you?"

"Yes."

"Published anything?"

She was used to the tone of condescension. "Yes."

"What?"

"I told you, I'm an unknown novelist." He was obviously trying to place her within his own special ranking system—or rather, within the ranking system of the culture that had produced him— in order to be able to know just how to treat her, just how much of his interest she merited. Suddenly he reminded her, this sleek, quick man, of that middle-class, on-the-make businessman's world she had been subjected to as a child, a world of grownups who also desired to place, even a child, who could not suppress this desire for longer than a few minutes and who would ask, thinking a child would not know it for a liberty: What does your father do? Meaning—what are you *worth?* How all-pervasive the question still was; and how odd, though not unprecedented, to be a dis- senter from that very class that had given America its chief values. It was rather like being a mutation, one of nature's sports.

"Confidence work," she said aloud. She had just recalled a memorable occasion from her youth.

"What are you talking about?" Knox asked.

Sylvia was struggling not to laugh. "Oh forgive me. I was think- ing of how once when I was a child I shocked a rather plump and stupid and presumptuous woman whose husband owned a lot of trucks and who ... she asked me about my father ... what he did ... oh dear, I'm afraid I'm not making much sense." She let out a small laugh like a yelp and moved to fix herself another whiskey. Just then Mrs. Dartley swept onto the terrace, both hands ex- tended toward the newcomer.

"Mr. Knox!" she said. "How nice of you to come out on your very first evening." He rose and presented himself with style. "I hope Faustine has been taking good care of you. Your letters, I confess, have interested me very much, though not perhaps for the usual reasons. Ah, you're drinking Campari? A moderate man. But then no doubt you need to be, working as you do under so many different sorts of pressure. You're *much* younger than I had expected."

"Thirty-six," he said with the quick eagerness of those who believe that they are indeed remarkably young for what they have accomplished. She had come near to charming him utterly. "You're a difficult person to reach," he went on.

"Not if you had written directly, candidly, at the start."

"The way Jerome did in *A Sunken Journey?*"

She frowned slightly, seemed to flutter her arms. They were still slender and remarkably firm, and they were well displayed in the gray chiffon Balenciaga she had chosen for this occasion. It was never possible to predict what she might appear in. She might well have decided to come out in that shapeless and ancient green tweed skirt she was so fond of, woolen knee socks, and a filthy pullover in the process of unraveling itself. Notwithstanding the fact that the Balenciaga called for all the graceful elegance with which she had made her entrance, she now began to move about as though she had in fact chosen the terrible skirt and sweater. "Ah, you know *A Sunken Journey* do you? How odd. And to whom does a character named Jerome write what and about what? No doubt you can answer that better than I." She seemed almost to be tramping about the terrace now.

Benjamin Knox laughed gently, apparently assuming that her suddenly changed manner masked the desire for praise. During the 1920's when she was between husbands Mrs. Dartley had written five novels, very rapidly and successfully. She did not like to be reminded of them, nor of the extremely long play that had held the boards in the capitals of all the West save Germany in the 1930's. It was unfortunate that the new guest should persist now in recounting in some detail a scene from one of the novels, his voice enthusiastic but subdued, as though he took her silence and sullen expression to be only a particularly unpleasant form of shyness. Sylvia, seeing how she had hunched her head down in her shoulders, listening to her lumber about the terrace, shuddered for Benjamin Knox and looked nervously away. There in the door she saw Campion. He had been watching her. Their eyes met, and then he backed off. She heard Knox saying, "I'm not likely to forget.

When I was an undergraduate your novels were all the rage. They were . . ."

Mrs. Dartley interrupted him. "At Williwaw? Were they? I doubt it."

Knox paled. His hostess sat down heavily in a chair and indicated that he should sit across from her. She pulled the full skirt down around her ankles and leaned mannishly forward, folded arms resting on spread-apart knees. The transformation was alarming, and was meant to be. "My novels were clever hoaxes," she said. "And to forestall you about the so-called play, let me say that it was a tract, only that, a necessary but a crude tract. No undergraduate was reading my novels by the time you were in college, not even in more liberal halls than those of Williwaw, if I am pronouncing it correctly. No one reads them today, thank God, except, I gather, your research men. No one who is even faintly interested in literature looks at the play. Again, thank God. It is important for us to understand each other at the beginning, Mr. Knox." She looked up. Campion had reappeared at the door. "Ah, Ernest. You arrive just in time. Mr. Knox and I have just been being cruel to each other, though we neither of us have meant to be. We each meant to be kind. Didn't we?" She rose swiftly, all graceful again, and smiled down upon her visitor.

Sylvia saw Mrs. Halász walking in the garden in her characteristically rapid and unsteady way. As Campion approached the two combatants she muttered an excuse and slipped down the terrace steps to join her.

Gwendolyn Dartley put a hand on Ernest's sleeve. "Mr. Knox, I want you to meet my very dear friend and on occasion my co-worker, Ernest Campion."

Knox moved purposefully forward in the beautiful new suit which he had just had made for him in London. He thrust out a hand. "How do you do, Dr. Campion? Or aren't you using your title these days?"

Campion's eyes showed his surprise. He shook hands silently.

"My research boys do a good job for me, you'll have to admit that," Knox said to them both. He was taking his revenge. He stood face to face with Campion. "I know all about you, Doctor."

"Do you?" Campion replied coldly. "That's more than I myself can claim."

Nine

When it was all over, that ultimate brightness, and the tower was gone, when they had taken off the dark glasses, slowly growing less blind there in the heated dust of the New Mexican desert, there was little speech. Dr. Campion did not know what he felt. A few minutes later he stood at the edge of a wavering group and stared at the face of the man who had wrought that culminating moment, and he thought then that whatever it was he was feeling was visible in that face, but he still had no words for it. Some years later he read somewhere that Oppenheimer had said, or thought: Now I am become Death. By then Campion understood that. But a little later still he came to wonder if such an idea were not in itself presumptuous, in spite of the sense of horror it was meant to convey, rather as though a priest with the Eucharist were to take it into his head that he had become what he was only serving. Defrocked as he was, Campion felt free to brood upon such matters.

At first he had not known exactly what he was working on, then he had suspected, then been certain. Just at this point he was of course also told, taken therefore into the most outlying of the inner circles. He was very young; he felt pride in the proving of his abilities, in their being recognized. Any other questions were suppressed. The hours were long too, the work absorbed all his energies, one day led into another, and finally into that morning in the desert.

After that his work faltered, in almost imperceptible ways. Or rather it would have faltered but for a conscious act of the will. He put it down to fatigue. In any case, events, so masterfully set in motion by so many men, moved of their own force through time. Hiroshima came, and Nagasaki. The war ended.

Campion severed his connections with government work and decided to take the first long holiday of his life. But first, out of duty, he returned for a week to that house some forty miles up the Hudson. In the two years that had passed since his last visit both the house and Nathalie had grown more cavernous than ever, as though both were being consumed by an inner darkness. He sometimes felt this darkness rushing out at him when he walked the upstairs corridors, and also when he and Nathalie were alone and attempted to engage in speech. He looked at his aunt and struggled to find a connection between her, himself, and his father, whose senior she had been by twenty years. He felt only his separateness, this time not with regret but with relief. She spoke much of God and wrathful judgments. Having departed the folds of the Episcopal faith of her forebears some years before, she had since sought out ever harsher and more fundamentalist sects and had at last settled on one that met her own curious requirements. What little remained of the money, so badly handled since it had passed into her hands, would go to the leader of this sect to help him in his efforts to drive men back to the paths of righteousness.

He walked the long lawn that overlooked the river. Certain rocks, certain trees, the river itself—these were familiar, and the landscape, the out-of-doors, which when he was a boy, returning there from school, seemed always to hold out promises that were denied by the house itself. And before his day, when the building they used for a garage still housed horses and carriage, there had been a forest; it had come right down to the edge of the property. As a boy he had always imagined that in those days, with the forest so near, things had been different, better somehow. Childhood, he realized for the first time, had been a great test of his will to survive. Small wonder that he had turned so early toward an abstract world, purer and more perfect as he'd thought than the real one, and reached through that private tongue, the power of secret signs and numbers and symbols that were not even comprehensible to the rest of a humanity with whom he had so little contact. Yet what a splendid spot for a boy to grow up in it might have been, even in his day, he reflected, had it only been animated by a spirit other than Nathalie's. He regretted very much the lack of human warmth and beauty in the now lost childhood, and accepted the loss resignedly. He was twenty-five, so ignorant of the world, he felt, and of joy, so curiously burdened and set apart. He was sure that when he left this time he would see neither Nathalie nor the house again, and for this at least he was glad.

He journeyed south then, and for months, shy and unskilled in the ways of pleasure, he sat in the sun on a variety of Caribbean beaches and avoided reading newspapers. Afterwards he remembered in some detail only the last of these places. There he made friends with a man of his own age, a Norwegian intellectual who was forever turning the conversation to points of abstract philoso-

phy. Sometimes in the midst of such conversations a sudden rebel-
liousness would come over Campion, and it would seem to him
that what they were saying had little if anything to do with the
concrete, human world about which he still knew so little. It
never occurred to him to ask his friend Eric what he was doing
there tending bar.

In the mornings and in the midafternoons when the hotel guests
had vanished to their rooms full of food and drink, the two of
them went swimming or trailed along the shore simulating an interest in the remnants of marine life deposited there, and talking.
Natives who saw them thought perhaps they were brothers. They
were both of medium height and slender build, and there was
something similar in their manner as well as in the general cast of
their features.

One afternoon, lying in the sun, Campion looked up and saw a
shark fin. Eric was swimming, and although he shouted and waved
and pointed it was only when he plunged in and began himself to
swim out toward that swift enemy that Eric turned and made
frantically for the shore.

When at last they both lay side by side on the sand, dripping,
chests heaving for air, Campion struggled against a most furious
desire to lay hands on Eric, to shake, to pummel him, to force
from him the meaning of what had happened. At last he said,
"What did you think you were doing? Tell me that. You heard me
shouting. You saw the fin. You understood—I know you did."

"It's true," Eric said, and turned his head away, pressing it
against the hot sand. Pity washed through Campion. He laid a hand
on his friend's shoulder, as though to protect, to pull him back
once more from the blade-torn sea.

That evening Campion sat at the bar for the same reason. The
whole evening they bought each other drinks, and when the bar
closed they went to Campion's cottage, where there was more
rum. Suddenly Eric told him, red in the face, stumbling over the
English, dogged. He had been a student at the University of Oslo
when the Germans invaded. At first all of the male students were
put in detention camps. The rumor was that they were to be sent
to Germany as forced labor. He did not want that to happen to
him. He was also interested in certain economic ideas, derived
from the socialist agrarian environment in which he had grown
up, which were perhaps not at odds with certain radical theories

being at least professed in Germany. It was still possible to think so, he insisted. One day he called over a guard. *"Ich bin deutschfreundlich,"* he said. He spent several hours a day for the next few days discussing intellectual matters with the Commandant, who then released him. He went back to his parents' village, far in the north, and there he spent the long, dark night of the war, reading, brooding, regretting—involved too, it seemed, in a bitter love affair, a sort of sexual struggle in which the girl herself became a victim of his conflict between shame and desire. Back in Oslo, when the war ended, the university tried him and passed sentence: he was forbidden to attend the university for three months, a mild and merciful reproof. But he could not bear the knowledge of what he had done; he shipped out.

At first Campion was speechless. The story had meanings he could not grasp. Then he tried to speak reasonably, thinking what a waste it all was, looking at Eric, in body and mind so supremely fashioned for something other than despair. Time collapsed here. Eric began to laugh. He wanted to sing. He often did late at night. "Sing! Sing!" He had taught Campion a song about Madame Olson's son: Madame Olson's son is sick, then he is dying, then dead, while all the time the party goes on unheedingly below the stairs, ssshhhh, don't sing so loud, Madame Olson's son is dead, and louder louder do they sing. It was very funny. They roared it out now, Campion enjoying on his lips and tongue the strange rolling syllables he had learned to form. And afterwards laughed, by now very drunk both of them, and went out to see the moon. It was sinking, already nearly gone. A great warmth surged through Campion. He felt closer to Eric than he had ever done to anyone in his life. They clasped hands, *Blutbrüderschaft* just as the moon disappeared, night failed and for an instant day hesitated.

When Campion awoke the next morning, pain raging in his head but his mind very clear, the first thing that struck him was that he owed Eric a story, that there was something he might tell him in exchange but had failed to. It was obscure even to himself. It would not quite take shape. It also struck him as strange that Eric, to whom he had once let it slip that he was a trained physicist, had never asked him what *he* was doing passing the days on those beaches. Was it a sort of beachcomber's agreement that they had had and that now was so uncomfortably broken? If so, so much the better. It was time for the beachcombing to be over with. He

had a sudden idea: Eric must go back to the States with him, take
after all that doctorate he had once sought. Campion hurried to the
hotel. Eric listened, considered, agreed. They spent all their time
together that day and the next making plans. And the next day
after that Eric was dead, shot cleanly through the heart by his own
hand.

Campion, dazed, full of sorrow and a new, acute sort of loneliness, took a boat back to New York. In the course of that voyage
back it occurred to him that perhaps it needed more than one
thing to break a man utterly, perhaps some deep, personal loss or
defeat as well as the more public one. He kept remembering Eric's
reference to the love affair.

It was June and New York was already rising in its summer
wrath when he got off the subway at 116th Street and crossed the
campus toward Morningside Heights. It was the end of term and
since exams were under way Professor Ransom was, as he had
expected, in his office. In the first instant Ransom looked more
relieved than pleased to see him—the time of the defections was
beginning. But he recovered quickly, and his greeting was hearty.
"Everyone had more or less lost track of you," he said.

"I doubt that everyone had," Campion said, and Ransom chuckled. Then, "I'm looking for a job. Can you give me one?"

They talked. Ransom spoke of several new research projects, in
a generalized way. "Of course you'll have to get a new security
clearance, but that shouldn't be any problem for you."

"I don't want to do research. I don't want clearance. Have you
some classes for me to teach, beginning courses preferably? If not
here, then perhaps you know about some place else in the area."

Ransom hid his surprise; quickly, smoothly he described what he
could offer, apologetic as to rank and salary. It was clear that he
did not think Campion would accept. Campion interrupted, saying,
"That part doesn't matter to me right now. It's fine. For my part,
it's settled."

He thought how changed Ransom was, how like an executive, a
bureaucrat, how unlike a scientist or a man of the academy. "Con-
tracts always come late around here, after the term's begun in fact.
So don't give that a thought. But after you're settled let us have
your address for the summer. My secretary will send along the
few things you'll need to sign."

At the door Campion said, "When you recommended me for the Manhattan Project did you know what it was all about?"

"Of course. Well, I should say that I had a very good idea."

"I didn't, you know."

Ransom hesitated. "I should say that I find that a little hard to believe about someone who is as gifted a scientist as yourself. You made very rapid headway, you know; in the final phases you were assigned some of the really important work."

"But I didn't know. Not at first." Didn't he? Hadn't he? Or had he not wanted to, not chosen to? And would it have mattered had he known in time? To pursue knowledge was the aim, even more than winning the war, for if the truth were told the war had not had much reality for him. But the pursuit of knowledge, that was the only code he had been given to live by, and he had never doubted that it was a fit code for a man of superior intellectual endowments. And knowledge, as every school child was taught, was power. It was one of the most widely known and respected of popular equations. And power—this was the completion of the equation which had been left so obscure—power, it seemed, was sometimes death.

"Then as a man you must have been very naïve," he heard Ransom saying.

"Evidently I was."

That fall he took up his post at the university. His behavior was retiring but unexceptionable, and whatever anxieties he had aroused in Ransom in June he succeeded, he knew, in putting to rest. As term succeeded term his role in the department became fixed. It was convenient to have so unusually competent a man around who was for some reason eager to restrict himself to the beginning courses. No one except Ransom and one or two of the older men even knew that Campion had had anything to do with the Manhattan Project, or for that matter that he had ever engaged in any important research. His students liked him but felt vaguely sorry for him. They knew, these bright, ambitious boys, most of them no more than seventeen, that if a physicist had reached so advanced an age as Campion's and was still laboring with them there was not much hope for him.

Campion himself thought about this, though from another

point of view. He had decided that the collapse of his will beneath a burden he did not yet dare identify by its right name was no more than a reaction to the fact that though he had worked in the midst of so much opportunity and at the ideal age he had not made any significant or original discoveries and that at the end of the war he had known he was never going to. His sufferings, particularly his inertia, which was so great that to go each day to his classes was often a hard-won victory for him, were not, he told himself, the result of some inordinate but indefinable sense of failure as a man, but rather of the simpler matter of disappointment in his professional abilities.

He lived during these years on Amsterdam Avenue in a cramped apartment that looked out onto the soot-covered brick wall of an air shaft. He read a great deal, not as he had once done in philosophy and the journals of mathematics and physics, but poetry, history, and even such humbler forms of expression as the novel. He went nowhere during these years, winter or summer, not even to Nathalie's funeral.

The neighborhood meanwhile was experiencing several spasms of change, unusually fast ones even for New York. He had arrived just before the long-settled Irish began disappearing before an incoming wave of eastern Europeans, most of them Jews. Some of these newcomers Campion liked, some he did not, but with all of them he felt at ease. They were displaced persons too. Surprisingly, most of them stayed only a short time, often no more than six months, and by the end of Campion's own time there nearly all of them had prospered and moved out, to Queens or the Bronx, and been replaced by Puerto Ricans, who filled to overflowing buildings that were hastily being redivided into ever-smaller living units by the landlords, among whom there now numbered one or two of the very Jews who had been living there a few months before. This disturbed Campion. His experience of the conventionally predatory world of social struggle had been so limited and he was at root so benevolent that he had unconsciously come to believe in one of the oldest of romantic fallacies: the notion that those who have suffered greatly are necessarily rendered morally perfect, higher beings than those who have not. When he said something like this to Iza she only laughed at him, and he took the point. His thoughts often ran on such matters now. The victim—

simply as victim—was always in a sort of state of temporary grace; he was always the superior of his persecutor. Campion grew ever more certain of this, certain too that it was the one thing it was death for a man to forget. But beyond lay complexities which were more difficult to apprehend, a bewildering variety of human behavior which it was vain to categorize. The individual's suffering, he decided in the end, could pervert as often as it could ennoble, and more often than it did either of these things it did nothing—it left, in the long run, character unchanged. Character was a mystery, personality an accretion.

Often at the peak of the Jewish influx there had been bitter internecine quarrels, derived, Campion assumed, from regional misunderstandings brought with them and intensified by the dangers and sorrows they had all known. Little by little he had found himself in the role of mediator, a rabbi or otherwise suitable elder not being on the premises. As the outsider, the minority within the minority, he presided, a strict but merciful judge, admired by all— until the time when Iza came to live with him. Then it seemed he had broken a law and was no longer fit to give the law. From that moment on he and Iza were left entirely alone by what remained of the Jewish community.

For nearly a year Iza had lived down the hall with her parents, and the quarrels that took place in their rooms could often be heard throughout the entire building. Her father, who had spent a year of his life hiding in the woods like an animal, was a barber. He worked illegally sixteen hours a day six days a week in a nonunion shop near Times Square and paid no income tax. He also took, under his own name, a sizable check each month from a Jewish welfare agency that believed on the word of an inexperienced social worker that he had no job at all and was not yet adjusted enough to hold one. With the money accumulated from both sources he was able to get hold of a mortgage on a really rundown building on Columbus Avenue. He then declined further checks from the agency and gave up his trade of barbering in order to devote his full time to real estate, and he rented an apartment in a new building in Queens and prepared to move his family there. On the day of the move Campion returned from the campus to find Iza, her belongings stuffed into three shopping bags, sitting in his apartment waiting for him.

Iza took it for granted that in exchange for giving her a place to stay it was his right to sleep with her. He did not claim this right for several months, which amused her but also won from her acknowledgment of the affection she had always felt for him. He fed and clothed and taught her, and in different ways she did these things for him too. As a child she had wanted to be an actress and had worked hard to perfect her Hungarian, to free it of the overtones of the Yiddish which her parents spoke at home. She still wanted to be an actress, and now she set herelf to forcing Campion to work with her on her English. She admired his speech and made him recite poetry and read plays aloud with her. In time he ceased being awkward about this and even enjoyed it; he worked patiently with her accent, bought books on the subject of English sounds and a tape recorder, and ended by learning a great deal himself about the language he had always taken for granted. After six months her Hungarian accent was remarkably overcome; after eight she was as free of it as she would ever be. She began to get a few small parts in television. He had given her money for a new wardrobe. At last she was offered a job as understudy to the lead in a play that was leaving Broadway for a ten-month road tour. They parted sadly but without, it appeared, a great wrenching. As they looked at each other they knew that they would meet again, that they would always be friends, that they would probably never again be lovers.

Several times while she was living with him Iza had had to shake him awake out of those nightmares which set him moaning and whimpering in his sleep. Once she asked him, the next day, "Why do you keep saying that you weren't *deutschfreundlich?*"

"Well I wasn't."

"Of course not. But why do you keep saying so? '*Ich bin nicht deutschfreundlich,*' you say. You've said it three, maybe four times now."

He said, "I knew someone once who was *deutschfreundlich*. And I wasn't, as you and I both know. Evidently it doesn't make as much difference as I thought. Evidently it's no guarantee of moral purity."

"I don't understand you," she said.

"I don't mean you to," he answered.

After Iza left, Campion tried to return to living his life as he had done before she came, but he was shocked to discover how difficult he now found it to bear the loneliness. He noted small signs of deterioration in himself, of withdrawal, and was not surprised when certain nervous symptoms which when she was living with him had largely disappeared began to come back, and to get rapidly worse. He also developed an odd tic of having to look in the mirror. Dozens of times a day when he was at home he would have to stop what he was doing and get up and look. And he was always surprised to see that his face hadn't changed, it was still the same, though each time he expected to see it reflecting back at him something of the nameless horror he felt within him. Even at the university this compulsion would come over him; he barely managed to control it through a class hour and in between classes he would dash into the men's room to look in the mirror. There was something else: every now and then in class, when he was in the midst of explaining an equation, a terrible electronic sound would start up in his head, deafening him so that he could not hear himself speak though he knew that his lips were moving; at the same time a glass wall would come down between himself and his pupils, separating him from them. He did not quite panic at these times, but learned to hang on, to resist the temptation to put his head down on the desk, and he watched through the wavering glass wall, amazed to see by their expressions that obviously he was speaking lucidly and that they had no idea at all of what was happening inside him.

In time he came to refer to these phenomena as his "attacks"; the odd thing was that afterwards he could never anticipate when another one might happen. For happen they did, repeatedly. He bought medical books and read up on such diseases as epilepsy. Then he turned to the standard works of psychiatry and psychoanalysis and decided that he was suffering from anxiety attacks. Anxiety about what? About the condition of the world? About the condition of his own soul? The term anxiety made sense only superficially. He suffered great agonies of insomnia, feeling sleep sometimes creep up his legs, then just as the whole spirit was about to succumb to its restorative measures, in the very instant of succumbing, waking with a great start. Sleepless, he dragged himself to class with a persistent effort of the will. When he did sleep towers fell in his head, reappeared, fell again, fiery winds blew, sand incinerated itself, the desert turned to glass, and he tried to peer through it to vague distorted forms on the other side.

Through all of this he remained, in a sense, objective, curious almost about what would happen next, unable to believe that he could possibly become the permanent victim of such a disorder. The years of formal discipline that lay behind him, the training his mind had undergone, these things seemed to him of no use now, and yet these were the things that saved him.

During the January intersemester there was suddenly a great remission of symptoms, and he was therefore totally unprepared for the fact that when the first morning of classes of the new semester came he did not get up. He lay in his bed for three days, climbing out of it only to go to the bathroom and a few times to drink a cup of coffee. Nothing mattered, that was it; nothing mattered at all. He felt like a soldier who has survived unspeakable horrors and asks nothing but to be left alone, to lie on his back, to let time pass.

At the end of the third day he grew restless. When it was dark he got up, shaved, showered, put on fresh linen and his best suit and took the subway to Columbia-Presbyterian. There he refused to tell the staff clerks what was wrong with him, and only after some argument was he shown into a cubicle where a young resident finally appeared.

"Well?" the resident asked.

"I have radiation sickness," he said.

"You *what?*" the young man cried, pulling his head sharply back.

"No, no, don't worry," Campion said. He was suddenly having great difficulty suppressing cold spurts of recurrent, rebellious laughter. "It's not in my blood cells. Not in the marrow of my bones. It's . . . well, where *is* it? That's what you're supposed to find out. You tell me where it is. That's why I've come to you."

Ten

Lily Halász threw back her head and laughed at herself, her teeth showing still beautiful and white after nearly seventy-six years of eating chocolates, and her violet eyes happily swimming in tears.

She had just had another of her infrequent but prodigious linguistic short circuits. Talking to Sylvia in English about the afternoon's broadcast from Bayreuth she had grown excited and switched midway through a sentence into German, then, her tone perplexed but her speed undiminished, had dashed into the machine-gun rhythms of Hungarian, and, finally, by now wild-eyed, had turned to French, the first language of her childhood, only after a few sentences more to give herself up to that gay and mocking laughter.

"You see what old age has done to me," she said at last. "Europe is all mixed up inside me." As though to comfort herself she hummed a barely recognizable snatch of Bellini. Unlike Anton Hrubick's musical quotations, which were always meant as ironic comments on the situation at hand. Lily Halász's were distinctly private and unfathomable. In the middle of an account of the days of Béla Kun she might break off to hum a few notes of a Mozart trio and then, without apology or even apparent awareness of how disconcerting this habit was to others, pick up the conversation where she had left it. During those seconds of melody her eyes would grow quite distant and afterwards she always seemed noticeably restored, as though she had just returned from a successful cure at Bad Gastein. Now she put an arm through Sylvia's and turned them hurriedly towards that part of the garden where there were roses growing. She laughed again, saying, "Quick. Before the Kaiserin commands."

The Kaiserin was of course her pet name for Mrs. Dartley, who had been holding forth at a great rate on the terrace but who had just then stopped abruptly and got up to stare after them. Benjamin Knox got up too. Campion had disappeared. Mrs. Dartley seemed about to call out to them, then changed her mind. Her solicitude for Lily Halász, who was after all not so many years her senior, was often overbearing, taking the form of telling her what was good for her to do and what was not. Fortunately, Mrs. Halász was quite adept at circumventing these orders. She was a very small, slight woman, and her head was almost too large for her body. Sylvia glanced sideways at her. She could surely never have been considered beautiful, even when she was young, except of course for those eyes and the smile and her spirit—and what more did one need for beauty really? Old age had brought to her face not only a mass of wrinkles, out of which the remarkable eyes

impishly peered, but also a curious stressing of a racial heritage
which had been buried and transmuted now for a millennium.
Sometimes Sylvia imagined behind Mrs. Halász's head a landscape
she had never in fact seen, the endlessly stretching slopes of Central Asia, echoing with hoofbeats and the cries of Mongol horse-
men. So alien a setting for so extremely European and Western a
woman made her all the more appealing. And Sylvia had found her
enormously appealing from the moment she set eyes on her three
months earlier, when she had known only a little of her story from
Mrs. Dartley and had known nothing at all of her character or of
the enthusiasms they turned out to share.

The truth was that Sylvia had a great weakness for the very old,
even for the dull and malicious among them. Death hovered so
arrogantly over them, perhaps that was it; whatever wrongs were
in their past could never now be righted, perhaps that too was it.
In any case, the sympathy was there, and if the old person turned
out to be one whose self or past was in the least bit out of the
ordinary then the sympathy turned to something like devotion.
With Mrs. Halász it was doubly so. Linking arms with her, Sylvia
linked arms with history, with, for example, a white-haired gentleman (Lily's grandfather) who spent half of every year on a for-
ested estate in Transylvania, where he kept, before his house, a
large, round loaf of bread, a knife, and an engraved sign that read:
"Stop, stranger; eat of this bread and be welcome." Sylvia considered this (while talking with Mrs. Halász about the decline in
Wagnerian singers) and considered too that if she now were to
touch Mrs. Halász's hand with her own she would be but three
hands away from that of Metternich. Or to think of it another
way—Sylvia's mind leapt rapidly back, calculating the numbers—
Lily Halász had been held in the arms of that long-lived grandfather, and he, born when his father was nearly forty, had been held
in his arms, and that father in his turn had as a youth bent his knee
in the stately presence of the old Empress, Marie Thérèse, the year
before her death, twenty-one years before the close of the eighteenth century. That was considerably better than Metternich!

Such reminders of the shortness of mortal time both excited and
frightened Sylvia. But she liked unequivocally that sense of contact with the past which people like Mrs. Halász gave her. The
country of her own birth had little patience with history and with
similar invisible realities, death for instance; if it could not really

quite wipe out such realities it could at least pretend they did not exist. Mrs. Halász, who had lived through wars and revolutions and would talk of them if asked, knew the difference, but it was not for this that Sylvia listened, for these were public events, known to her from books; one could grasp them with the mind, as one could the provisions of treaties, the condition of the peasants on that Transylvanian estate, the ideas of Hegel. No, it was the history that is never written, of now forgotten individuals, of personal, of daily life that Mrs. Halász unknowingly transmitted—that grandfather, the peasant parents of her husband, Méltóságos úr Halász himself, a seamstress named Tili, herself as a young girl, as a matron. And as these shapes flickered from the consciousness of Lily Halász into her own, something else struggled to take shape: a deeper and more universal sense of the conjunction between the events and figures one reads about in history books and the lives of those of whom there is no record at all. As for the woman herself, though she had chosen to ignore the "great issues" of her times, those social and political forces which were to end so much that was good and bad and begin so much that was good and bad, she (having decided that there was nothing she could do either to help or hinder such changes) had nevertheless cut through all that was shoddy, tasteless, and overly affluent in the privileged caste to which she belonged and had concentrated with unmitigated ardor, among the bankers and the landlords and the potted plants, on song, on poetry, on things to which no money value could ever be given.

"So with de Rezske," Lily Halász was saying, "for all that they said of his technique I always had the feeling that it was a very ignorant way of talking about his singing. I was only a girl of course when I heard him. Still, if you could not explain it in better than mechanical terms it was better not to try to explain it at all. Ha. It was very funny how in those days everyone tried to explain everything as though they were machines. A silly business."

So, there it was again, another little time marvel; it now turned out that her companion had heard Jean de Rezske sing, de Rezske and others of whose voices there remained not a trace, not even in the wobbly distorted metallic sounds of early recordings. Sylvia wanted to ask her about de Rezske—where she had heard him, when—but Lily Halász had already returned to a discussion of contemporary singers and she found herself being drawn quickly into it. It charmed and astonished her, the number of the great whom Mrs. Halász had seen, heard, and very often known, but it did not awe her—which was precisely a reflection of Mrs. Halász's own attitude. In Venice, as a two-year-old, she had been lifted to the knee of Richard Wagner; she could not really remember this or him, but it had happened. At Sils Maria when she was seven her mother had pointed out in whispered tones the retreating figure of Friedrich Nietzsche. On a trip to Frankfurt when she was twenty she had heard Clara Schumann play and had dined with her. Later, through Lou Andreas-Salomé, she had become acquainted with the poet Rilke. She had known Nijinsky "before Romola and Diaghilev between them destroyed him," and she preferred to remember him as he was when he had first danced in Budapest, not as he was after the First War, mute, fat, and mad, in Romola's overweening charge. She had gone to tea only once in that dreary house of Romola's mother where he was then kept. "Too sad, too terrible, to see it, that long drawn out execution." She had known Debussy and Gustav Mahler, of course, and . . . Lily Halász, tottering along the paths on her high heels and infirm legs, clinging to Sylvia, belonged to the world that had ended at some nameless point in time between the Battle of the Somme and Lenin's arrival at the Finland Station in St. Petersburg.

But Lily Halász herself had been carried on into the living moments of the fall of 1956. She now stopped short and disengaged herself from Sylvia. "You must be careful," she said. "Before you know it you will be talking about Kirsten Flagstad and Sena Jurinac and Maria Callas and Fisher-Dieskau in the same way I chatter on about singers whose names you have barely heard of."

"Why careful?"

"Oh, it's unhealthy to be as interested in singing as you are." She brushed some pine needles off a garden bench, stiffly seated herself on it. The roses had grown very tall there and a few blossoms were on a level with her eyes. She leaned towards them, sniffing their fragrance.

Sylvia sat down beside her. "Why is that?"

"They deceive you about the passage of time, these evanescent arts."

Sylvia laughed. "Oh is that all? I thought perhaps Anton had begun to have an effect on you. I'm not worried then. Most things make me feel I'm being rushed along anyway. Music less than most in fact."

Lily Halász shook her head. "No, no. Singing is different. I'm quite sure there's something special about loving singing as much as I have. You say to yourself, Elizabeth Schumann, Lehmann—Lotte not Lilli—to take only people you, darling, have at least heard on records . . ."

"Lehmann I heard in New York."

"Yes of course, Lotte in America, where I have never been. You see? I think of her as Lotte in Salzburg, Lotte in London, in Vienna. And surely others—no, probably not now—think of her in Hamburg. But you say to yourself, Elizabeth Schumann, Lotte Lehmann, they sing it in such and such a way—you forget they are old women, almost as old as yourself. You forget in fact that one of them is dead. It's a shock when you do remember. Or you remember a certain performance, very special, very memorable. It was when, yesterday, just before the war? But which war? And then you think back, and you find it was fifty-six years ago! Everyone you remember from it is dead. Well, why not? Why shouldn't they be? That's true of families too. But you expect that. Art? You don't. But who else is alive who remembers? Perhaps only you. Those poor singers are gone, and their art's as dead as they. Oh no, these evanescent arts are more painful than the others. Turn to sculpture, architecture, yes buildings—they last." Here she interrupted herself with the mocking laugh. "No darling, they don't last either, do they? In 1944 I had two houses, one in Buda, one in Pest; in 1945 no house at all. And very much more beautiful, more important buildings, they were gone too. So darling, perhaps *that's* the lesson?"

Sylvia said only, "Perhaps." She was disturbed by Lily's tone, which despite its edge of irony betrayed a depth of loneliness she was usually at pains to hide. Beneath the words the void had opened up. And the subject itself? Sylvia said, "I wonder if one were to take up gardening."

"Ah," Lily said, "now perhaps I might better have done that than run around to concerts all my life and tried my poor husband's patience playing and singing all the time in his own house. Of course in Hungary one didn't garden, unless one did it for a living. My first time in England I was stunned at everyone's interest in gardening. Literature, music, if they talked of these things at

all they seemed very embarrassed. But roses? That was all right to
be enthusiastic about. Or even train schedules. I often felt very
inadequate, but *amused*. Not that I have anything against roses,
especially when they are so kind as to bloom this late in the season.
Nature lasts? I suppose that's the idea. Very reassuring in a simple
way. Every year roses die, the next year they will be there again.
But this rose?" Here she reached out and very gently touched one
of the large blooms; when she did so its petals shattered and fell
upon her lap. She said triumphantly, "You see, one might as well
stick to singing."

"Unless one believes in the idea of garden as garden."

"Ah, but where does that idea come from? Out of someone's
head, not out of nature. You should have seen our garden in Buda,
my darling, one year after the war. It simply wasn't there any
more. Only wildness and disorder and weeds. Nature, all right. But
not very comforting. But why do I explain this to you? Poets are
born knowing such things."

Sylvia no longer felt uncomfortable when Mrs. Halász referred
to her as a poet, and yet the whole conversation had begun to
depress her, as though she were being tested in some way and
feared in advance that she would fail. She said, "At the moment the
only connection I can imagine between myself and what you've
just been saying is as someone who might some day read about it if
someone else writes it."

"So?" Mrs. Halász smiled. "Things are not going well for you at
the moment?"

"Things aren't going well. Not just for the moment, for quite a
while now." This was the first time she had articulated her sorrow
about her work to another person, and she felt a very definite and
pleasant sort of relief. It corresponded in some way to that general
mood of release with which the swim had left her and which the
encounter with Campion had so oddly emphasized.

Lily sniffed at her. "That will change." She was holding one of
the rose petals to her cheek. She turned towards the terrace and so
did Sylvia. It was empty now. Sylvia wondered where Campion
had gone. Mrs. Halász said, "What is the new visitor like?"

"Benjamin Knox? He's, well, he's like a great many other men in
his generation."

"That's not very helpful, darling."

"He's an operator."

"Of what? Machines?"

"Something like that." She laughed. "He'd be conniving his way up in the church if the church still counted for anything. Nothing really *matters* to him, except I suppose his own ego. He's an opportunist. But I don't know why I think I've the right to make these judgments, since I've just met him. I suppose it's really just because he said something that annoyed me. He seems to be rather good at that. He annoyed Mrs. Dartley too." Remembering that, she found herself feeling almost sorry for him.

"You know, sometimes you remind me of a girl who stayed with us during the siege. Did I ever say this to you before?"

"No." Sylvia knew only vaguely, and largely through Mrs. Dartley, of that large mixed gathering, mainly Jews and deserters, which the Halász' had risked sheltering during those weeks when the Russians laid siege to Budapest and the Germans attempted to hold the city, both wholly indifferent to the fate of its inhabitants. Mrs. Halász scarcely referred to these events, but Sylvia had often thought about what it must have been like in that city, the enemy both within and without.

"She was, oh I suppose seventeen, a funny little thing. My son's wife's closest friend was Jewish—an old school chum—and everything was so confused after the bombardment began that we lost contact with her. Then we found out she had been put in one of those columns of Jews they were supposedly marching to Vienna, mostly women and children, it was January. My son got hold of some petrol somewhere and some false papers and got through to the road. Two days I think he was gone looking for her—I was frightfully worried—and then he found her. It was quite easy to bribe those young soldiers who were supposed to be in charge of the march, most of them country boys without a great taste for what they were doing. She was walking with a friend, someone we also knew, and this young girl was beside them. He brought all three of them back. At first she hated us—a class thing you understand, she was poor and from a little village in the east, Galicia I suppose. And then after a time she didn't hate us. I quite liked her from the beginning. She wanted to be an actress, I remember. Sometimes I got tired of the cellar and stayed upstairs during the raids, playing and singing, Brahms, Schubert. Why not, I thought. She liked to stay with me. Oh she was eager to learn things. She hated that village and had always wanted to come to the capital.

But not that way, of course. After the war I thought maybe she would stay on with us. My own daughter was grown by then, naturally, a matron, not very interesting or amusing I'm afraid, quite snobbish—somehow I suppose our fault. But my husband and son thought it important to find her parents, if they were still alive; they took her to one of the refugee groups. Well, then we were all scattered. I was with friends in Buda for some months, cut off from Pest. A long time later I had a note from her through a Jewish organization. She was in a DP camp in Germany. They'd found her parents—I don't think she got on with them very well, though. She said perhaps they were going to America. I never heard again. But perhaps she did write and I never got the letters. Mail from America by then . . . I've always wondered what became of her."

"Have you thought of going to one of the refugee organizations here? It shouldn't be hard to trace her."

Lily Halász looked annoyed. "What would it matter to her now? She wasn't really my child, after all. Why should I bother them?"

There was a pause. Sylvia said, "Why do I remind you of this girl?"

"Oh I don't know exactly." Lily hesitated. "She was a very uncompromising creature. And perhaps the voice a little. I don't know, really. You don't even look like her. And you're not Jewish."

"No, I'm not."

"What are you? Americans . . . that always interests me about them."

"Nothing very interesting in my case, I'm afraid. English mostly, some Scottish, and through one side of my father's line Welsh."

Lily Halász brightened. "How interesting. Welsh. Ha. I know almost nothing about them. A very small nation I think. Like the Hungarians. But that's such a funny word, 'Welsh.'" Do you know what it means in German?"

"Yes. It means a foreigner doesn't it? An *Ausländer?*"

Lily seemed amazed, impressed even, that she should know this. Then she reached out and removed some kind of late-autumn seed which had caught in Sylvia's hair, held it a moment, let it drift away. "Yes, my dear. A stranger." Then, "Well, I suppose it's time for us to go in to dinner. I must get Gwendolyn alone some time during the evening. I have had a great many letters from a relative in London, very distant, a young woman—well, forty—a chemist. She wants me to come and live with her. I have decided to go. Gwendolyn will make a fuss. I want to get it over with."

Sylvia could say nothing. She had not been in the least prepared for what her companion had just told her, though she saw now that it had been in Lily Halász's mind during all their conversation. And it did not really make sense. Was it that her extremely independent nature felt stifled by Gwendolyn's oversolicitude, her pride offended by her generosity? Sylvia doubted it. Was it then the desire at the end to have contact with some remnant of family, someone who spoke her own tongue? But even in Budapest there had been remnants, yet she had chosen to leave when the way was at last cleared for her. Did she regret that leaving now? It was not unlikely. Or did Lily Halász, uprooted and adrift, even herself know why she was moving on? Sylvia felt a clear, deep pang of regret at the thought of her going. She said, "I'm very sorry. I shall miss you greatly."

"Well thank you, darling. That's very sweet of you. I shall miss you too."

She stood up now, the rose petals falling to the ground. But one of them she held on to between her aged and arthritic fingers.

As they moved back towards the house Sylvia saw that Campion had come back onto the terrace, had evidently mixed himself a drink and was standing there with it in his hand. He looked almost as thought he were waiting for them. It was pleasant to think so.

Eleven

"Six million Jews," Benjamin Knox intoned, somewhat more loudly than the discussion he had been having with Anton really required. Other heads turned towards him. More wine had been brought in, and bread and cheese. Everyone was seated at the dining table, their shadows jumbled together on the walls around them. He had been placed at Mrs. Dartley's right, and in spite of the setbacks he had thus far encountered in her house and the curious bargain she had struck with him before dinner, he now felt himself in a position of sufficiently secure and proper privilege to begin to establish his image with her. Besides, the phrase he had just uttered was in itself somehow satisfying. "Six million," he repeated, looking down at his untouched wine glass. *He* had never killed a Jew, his tone said, *he* came from the land of innocence.

Anton gathered in his breath, but before he could speak Mrs. Dartley, who had been discussing the American presidential campaign with Marshall, leaned towards their visitor. "Beware the fallacy of statistics, Mr. Knox." Her voice was so gentle, so careful, that Sylvia at once paid attention.

"Facts are facts," he said. "You can't change them." Sylvia felt a coldness creeping into the room and a heat into her breast. The expression on Knox's face could only be described as one of smug satisfaction. Here it seemed was another man who was capable of turning murder into a profitable commodity. Merchant of false remorse was the phrase that came to her. But she resolved to say nothing.

"Ah, that is true," Anton said, nodding vigorously, his face puckish beneath the wild, wiglike hair. "But what do the facts really mean? Perhaps that is what we should ask. Or at least perhaps we should ask why it is we find these facts so irresistible. Is it really because we are ashamed of what our fellow men have done to other men and feel pity for the dead?" All his *w*'s were coming out strong *v*'s. "Or is there a secret dark reveling in our blood too? Do you Americans not share comfortably in the deed from a distance, much as the Germans and the Poles and the Lithuanians and my own compatriots did even when they did not actually deliver the strokes? Possibly all of us feel safer because in the face of so much slaughter of others we are still alive?" Anton laughed. "Or perhaps we are really so horrified, so fascinated, because we feel in ourselves the old secret lust for a universal dance of death. Ah yes, Deutschland, Deutschland, where the archfiend so recently held sway."

Mrs. Dartley intervened. "Anton, you are ranting." It was not that she disapproved of what he was saying but that she knew her guest would not understand it. She wished therefore to avoid the kind of pointless wrangling which she was sure such a misunderstanding would lead to. "What I meant, Mr. Knox," she said in much the same gentle manner as before, "was, can the mind take in such numbers even if it wishes to? Is the repetition of the terrible statistic a true admonishment for us all, does it bring the events closer, make them real? Or does it have just the opposite effect? I have often wondered. And somehow I am reminded of the two attitudes it is possible to take toward meditation. One, that by assuming the posture of meditation one will inevitably achieve the spiritual condition itself. Two, that the posture may very well remain . . . only a posture."

"Are you suggesting that . . . ?"

"That the phrase six million Jews repeated often enough may become only a sort of placebo."

The others turned away now, as she had expected they would, Anton toward Mrs. Halász with a shrugging motion which suggested that if he were not going to be allowed to have some sport with the new visitor by enlarging on one of his favorite topics then at least there was always Richard Wagner.

"I suppose that is a possibility," Knox brought out with slow intensity, frowning the while as though his head were heavy with thought. He was secretly annoyed that he did not know the meaning of the word placebo but was satisfied that he was not under attack by Mrs. Dartley, who was the person who counted. When they had emerged from that private conference of theirs before dinner and she announced to her household that she had agreed to let him do a program on her he had not failed to notice surprise beneath their polite acceptance of this news, and in the case of Campion, disapproval. Not that it mattered; it had been all too quickly and disappointingly obvious that no one here was of any importance except possibly Campion, whom he would certainly not use for other reasons. The old Hungarian woman might be worth talking to. Hrubick, or whatever his name was, was out of the question, a jester or a madman or both, possibly even a former Nazi. Perhaps that was why he had left Czechoslovakia after the Communists took over. He would have to check carefully on him, and if need be omit all reference to his existence. Now that he thought about it those wild and incomprehensible things he had said about the extermination of the Jews had sounded suspiciously like Making Excuses for the Germans. Knox shuddered to think of what audience reaction to that would be in New York.

"Did you ever know a Kulak?" Mrs. Dartley asked.

"Kulak?" A Kulak was a peasant of some sort. What was she driving at? "Afraid not," he answered.

"Neither have I. Stalin killed eight million, mostly through a deliberate starvation policy. Who cares?"

Knox experienced a flicker of angry confusion. Nothing at the Villa Kilchberg was as he had expected. And the initiative kept slipping from him. On the question of the Jews at least he had expected a more manageable response, which was why he had brought it up. Her own record was clear; in fact he had planned to make much of it in the program. There was that play of hers which he had exhumed, the speeches she had made, the officials in America, France, and England whom she had pursued with what one of them had recently called when he talked to him in London "impassioned nagging." There were even some who claimed that indirectly she'd had a lot to do with Franklin Roosevelt's having called the Evian Conference in 1939. Was she deliberately trying to make things difficult for him or did she simply enjoy going against the tide?

Now, as though she had read his thoughts, she said in a confiding voice that excluded the others, "Not an exact analogy, but a suggestive one. I think it would be such a pity if this retrospective moral outrage about the Jews were to become a sort of *substitute* for conscience. It is so easy to take a firm and self-righteous position when something is over with, a splendid way of ignoring whatever calls for moral perception at this very moment. I find this annoying, in part I confess because I know what the real attitudes were at the time, both official and unofficial. I beat on a fair number of doors. With very few exceptions the only people who cared about what was happening to the Jews—and the first withdrawal of civil liberties in Germany was a fairly certain sign of what worse things might be coming—the only people who really cared, as I say, were the Jews themselves, and quite a large number of them, understandably, didn't care either, or to be more precise, could not allow themselves to care very much so long as they had the hope of being left untouched. Even as you or I might have reacted, Mr. Knox. Or they could not bring themselves to *believe* it, again understandably, until the Haman, the holocaust, was actually upon them. A gigantic rescue operation was called for. It was not carried out, for a variety of reasons, some of them quite valid, alas. Do you, for example, save the Hungarian Jews by

trading them for military equipment which will be used against
your own soldiers? Certainly not, not if you are a good commander. Men in high position often face terrible decisions which
the rest of us are spared. It wasn't the first time for this sort of
failure—the rescue operation, I mean—nor will it be the last. Although I prefer to be a trifle more optimistic about the race of man
than my good friend Anton. Purely on faith you understand, not
on evidence; the evidence is overwhelmingly on Anton's side. I do
confess that I find much that is being written and spoken today
about the murder of the Jews a trifle hypocritical, even sometimes
a trifle orgiastic in tone. I also find it depressing that the remem-
brance of the sufferings of so very many individuals should on
occasion be exploited, for political, or any other, purpose. Don't
you agree?"

Benjamin Knox did not know whether he agreed or not. Her
manner was so reasonable, her attitude seemed so confidently to
place him on the same side with her, that it was difficult to find a
point of attack or even of control. And yet he sensed that the
simplicities, the set phrases and responses, the very rituals of his
trade were somehow being called in doubt. He looked around the
table. He was adept at taking the measure of groups, at mastering
their lingos and special ways and thus winning his place among
them. Otherwise he could hardly have got on so well as he had in
America. What bothered him about the collection of people in this
room was that they failed somehow to be a group. He squinted at
them now, their reality difficult to grasp, to seize. He could not get
them in focus, bring them together in one clear picture; it was as
though the knobs on the monitor board were stuck, resistant to his
manipulations, or had suddenly developed a will of their own. He
blinked hard, half expecting to see only lines and shadows when he
opened his eyes again. Instead, they were all there, animate, sepa-
rate, distinct, yet flowing towards and away from each other in
bewildering ways.

Ernest Campion was at the foot of the table. Both he and Sylvia
were listening attentively to the girl called Posy, who was seated
between them. Now her young voice rang out excitedly, "Then
when you've got the architect's paper absolutely secured with the
tape you take the heel-ball and get to work rubbing."

Knox turned to his hostess. "What is she talking about?"

"Brass-rubbing," Mrs. Dartley replied firmly, although it was one of the few things the details of which her mind retained but shakily. Even now when she said the term she immediately conjured up a picture of someone rubbing a devout hand over a brass effigy in more or less the same way in which pilgrims in Rome kiss the toe of St. Peter.

"Oh. And the heel-ball?"

Marshall broke his long silence. "It's a piece of cobbler's wax."

"Posy's a very skilled brass-rubber. One might almost say it's her vocation. That is how we met, actually. She was working on a crusader. At Margate in London." Mrs. Dartley spoke rapidly, as though she wished to be finished with the troublesome topic. "I had gone to visit Billy, the rector. Billy was on a committee that was trying to get the laws on homosexuality liberalized and he was about to write a very important letter to the *Times*. I've had a great deal of experience writing letters to newspapers in recent years and he wanted my advice. Here was this child doing this splendid brass-rubbing. So patient. So persistent. Later when I learned from Billy that she was having financial difficulties I thought she might join us here. So I called on her at The Mothergone . . ." This last phrase was nearly lost entirely as Mrs. Dartley crammed an enormous bite of bread and Brie into her mouth.

Knox smiled. If he had Posy pegged correctly any financial difficulties she had ever had were of her own choosing. Nevertheless, he was pleased at the turn in the conversation. An atmosphere of the deliberately, amusingly eccentric—this was how he had seen the whole program and this, with the addition of some shrewd name-dropping that would give his viewers a sense of glancing contact with the great, was the context he now definitely wanted for Mrs. Dartley, so that she and some of her more disturbingly unconventional views and activities should seem interesting without really having to be taken seriously. He waited until she had consumed what she had in her mouth, then asked affably, "But what *is* a brass-rubbing?"

"Why it's, oh dear me, it's an image of the dead, a reproduction, very often quite remarkable, quite striking when it's successfully transferred to paper. That is, they are memorial effigies of the dead, in brass instead of stone, they are in churches, to begin with I mean. And then . . ." Her arms fluttered helplessly. "Marshall?"

Marshall began. He knew that Mrs. Dartley disliked having to explain anything of a technical nature. "Suppose you have a book.

And on the cover is an embossed design of some sort. You lay a piece of paper over it. Then you begin to rub a pencil over the surface . . ."

At their end of the table Anton Hrubick and Lily Halász had reached the point of open conflict. "The greatest art," he said, "is never free of the demonic."

Sylvia caught this and wondered if it were true. "What about Rubens and his bride Isabella?" she asked. "The one where they're both wearing the Florentine hats, I mean." An image of the painting rose in her mind, the young, prosperous, handsome, very well-cared-for bridal couple, sitting there so happily if rather smugly in the honeysuckle bower. It was almost enough to make one believe in an ideal of marriage. "Or what about the one he did of his second wife, Helena Fourment, the one where she's holding her first-born son on her lap?"

Anton dismissed both. "We are discussing music," he said.

"*Così fan tutte*," she muttered under her breath, but not loudly enough for him to hear. Anton was such a great one for categories, which she decidedly was not, and such a stickler for terms. Their arguments almost never got anywhere. Besides, she wasn't sure that she didn't more agree with him than not, at least about music. About painting she was less certain. Perhaps those Rubens canvases had to be talked about in another way. They were certainly very beautiful. In any case, Anton, like most middle-European musicians of his generation, could never talk for more than a minute or two about any art but music.

Lily Halász had been shaking her head from side to side, little quick movements of negation that set the flesh of her face shaking. She said at last, after emitting a great sniff, "You surely are not trying to tell me that you complain of a lack of the demonic in *Wagner*."

"I complain of its inflation."

"*You* do?"

"Therefore if it is inflated it is the false demonic, which is worse than none." He struck his fingernail against his wine glass, causing a little chiming sound. "Compared for example to *Don Giovanni* . . ."

"Ah but what can be compared to Mozart? Good, let us talk of Mozart. That pleases me far better."

"No. I will tell you why in Wagner it is the false demonic, mere morbidity and dark posturings. Because otherwise it could not be vanquished so easily! That mechanical and empty victory he ended by contriving for the heavenly forces, that false triumph of good over evil, that is what I criticize him for, what I cannot forgive."

"Contriving? Bah. If you know so little of his music as that one can discuss nothing with you." A faint pinkness was spreading over her high cheekbones. Ernest and Sylvia had both stopped listening to Posy and were being drawn in. Posy looked down at her plate, trying to resign herself to their loss. She knew very well that they had been less interested in brass-rubbing than in each other, yet she had enjoyed the role of go-between. Sylvia and Ernest were different tonight somehow, warmer than usual, both of them; friendlier; they had taken her into their own orbit. And, as always, it was a pleasure for her to talk on the one subject she knew something about. She had got as far as describing how you had to rub the transferred image with silk and had hoped to move on to an historical account of English and Flemish brasses, but now she would have to relinquish, grateful for the moment she had had.

Anton shook his head. "Not bah, gnädige Frau. Da, da-da diiiiiiii, di di da dum," he reproduced the great Wagnerian leitmotif in a long satiric hum, gesturing so dramatically that he almost knocked over a wine bottle. "Bah to that. Redemption through love! The favorite delusion of European romanticism, of a secularized and failed Christianity. Of course with Wagner it was always some wonderful, but extremely neurotic, woman, some Elizabeth or Senta—it was she whose howlings you were listening to today was it not?—or some transformed Kundry. At any rate, some female principle, never mind all her names, the ameliorator of the heroic but brute male force without which that force can never be a holy instrument, an instrument of the divine, the savior therefore of the race, the victor—over what? Death, demons, Lucifer himself. False! No, Wagner was always a pagan—the idea of Christian salvation was foreign to him, as foreign as to us, a *theatrical device!*" He seemed quite serious and yet at the same time amused, as though he were indulging himself not only in argument but also in the subsidiary pleasure of teasing. Now he winked broadly at Sylvia and said, "Of course Wagner is not entirely stupid. He knew that woman is a most imperfect vessel. Along with being divine, a goddess, she is an instrument of Satan, a temptress, a seductress."

"How interesting," Sylvia said flatly. She wondered if he could have known anything of that encounter by the pool between Ernest and herself. Or was there something in their manner now? Anton was always so full of wickedly shrewd guesses. She glanced at Ernest and saw that though he was smiling he too was wondering.

Lily had thrown up her hands in disgust at the end of Anton's tirade and turned to Knox. "How is it possible not to hear that longing for redemption, from *The Dutchman* on, in all of the music?"

Knox replied that he did not know.

Sylvia said to Anton, "I'm surprised that at the least you're not grateful to Wagner for giving expression to all those things you're always reminding us of—imprisoned souls in bondage to the dark of preculture, infernal torment, the primitive longing for violence, for universal death, for the destruction of this world."

He grinned at her. She had parodied him in voice and gesture as well as language. "So you have opinions on Wagner too?"

"Naturally," she replied. Until that evening she had never taken part in the Wagner quarrel, if that was what the quarrel really was.

Giovanni had come into the room and whispered to Mrs. Dartley, who left the table so quietly that the others were hardly aware of it. Sylvia said, "Oh well, at least you ought to give him credit for prophecy."

Anton's cheeks puffed out as though the effort to keep from laughing would cause him to burst. "Ah, the mystery of art? I had forgotten about your druidical ancestors."

"My what?" Sylvia said, then shook him off. "I meant the power state as evil, and all that. Think of the stupidity of the Nazis, failing to understand so completely their favorite composer, think of the *madness* of emulating *Wotan* when at the end of the *Ring* everything's in ruins and flames, just the way Germany was at the end of the war. After *Gotterdämmerung,* and the terrible vision, the miracle's those last chords you've just made fun of, Anton. And after those chords the only other possible music was *Parsifal. Parsifal* isn't charlatan. Nietzsche knew it wasn't, which is exactly why he felt betrayed and turned on Wagner—and of course went mad. And you know all this perfectly well."

Anton turned to the table at large and said, though without

malice, "One of the difficulties with the new new woman is not just that she is so independent. It is that she is so annoyingly well informed." He turned back to Sylvia. "But then, intelligent women have always been my great weakness." Knox's facial muscles underwent some sort of spasm.

Sylvia, full of wine and in complete gallop, ignored the proffered truce. "Christianity did hold out the hope for life in a new and higher way once. I'll give you that, Anton."

"I don't want it," he said.

"You don't? Why? It was such a lovely idea. Sacrifice and atonement, yes. But now instead of lambs or maidens or any father's son . . . well, you know. And then that revolutionary thing about forgiveness."

Anton guffawed. Campion, who had not taken his eyes from Sylvia, had the most sudden desire to hold her in his arms, to protect her. She seemed to him as vulnerable now, though in a different way, as when she had been lying by the pool.

"I'm only saying that this was the idea implied in the Incarnation, that . . ." She hesitated. What did she know about the Incarnation? Almost nothing. And was it not hypocritical of her, despising as she did the debased and meaningless remnants of belief with which the so-called Christian world was so poorly shored up against its ruin, to talk of Christianity at all? Yes. She had been babbling. She had also been holding forth again and had made an utter fool of herself.

Anton took advantage of the hesitation. He put both hands flat on the table and leaned towards her. He was quite red in the face. "And now will you please tell me how it is possible in the middle of the twentieth century even to think of the possibility of forgiveness, let alone redemption?"

She saw at once his meaning and felt too that for the first time since she had known him the real Anton had emerged. So that was it: he could not bear Wagner because he could not bear to be reminded of the visionary hopes of the nineteenth century. The music of an earlier age that had expected and projected less—yes, *that* he could still love. And certain musical proclamations of his own time, above all those that proclaimed the broken-apartness of the world—these too he could honor, would insistently honor, even those he knew to be bad art. Her heart began a frightened thumping. The falling towers of Europe, the toppling of the holy

West, the crown of culture spinning into the pit, the last gleams of its intricate gold fading—wasn't this what he meant, what he saw behind his fool's mask, what he could not bear? How great the fall, and how could it seem that it had not been sought for from somewhere within mankind itself? The death camps. Auschwitz, Buchenwald; the nameless ones to the east of Moscow with their older, slower, but equally certain methods; Dresden, Guernica, Leningrad, Berlin, Warsaw, Budapest, Hiroshima. And yet when she answered Anton, she said, "How is it possible not to?"

Everyone at the table had been listening to them. Now, except for Ernest Campion, who continued to look at her, they all turned in some surprise to see Mrs. Dartley entering the room. She took her place once more at the table but said nothing. An odd sort of excitement was coursing through Sylvia. It was as though some long-delayed engagement of her spirit was taking place. She felt set in motion in a way that neither the whiskey nor the wine could explain. It was not happiness she felt, but some deeper flowing of her energies that was not unlike it. In another instant, if she were not careful, she would jump to her feet and run around the table, or praise God, or kiss Ernest Campion. For the first time she became aware of his looking at her. Their eyes met and then, as though by mutual accord, gently parted.

Anton persisted. "The idea of Christian salvation is imposed upon his music, just as it was upon us."

Ernest Campion leaned forward, poured more wine for himself and Sylvia, and said to Anton, "You deny him then his leap of faith?"

"A false leap—and he had better have made it in philosophy if he had to."

Oh but where better than in music? Sylvia thought but did not say. In the beginning was the word, the lyric word.

Lily once more addressed herself to Knox, who, surveying them all, had just been struck by the strange composure of Posy and Marshall. Were they actually listening to all this talk, or were they off in their own world? He envied them if they were. For himself, he thought he had never heard so much talk about nothing, and yet there was something compelling about it. What an offbeat notion of a dinner table conversation: demons, redemption, good, evil. And how long were they going to go on sitting here? Did dinner always take the whole evening? He had thought of entering

the conversation once when the name Freud was used, but there
had seemed no easy way. Besides, he had never actually read
Freud, and Sylvia Grierson no doubt had. As for her, for all that
she did not look it, she was nothing but a damned bluestocking,
which explained why things had not gone well for him on the
terrace. How he loathed bluestockings; they made him want to
smash things. "Anton is the one who is always turning music into
philosophy," Lily was saying. "He is worse than the Germans. I
am always trying to talk about *music*, but he somehow is always
talking about something else. Very often things that do not even
greatly attract me, philosophy, theology, abstractions, sometimes
even politics." Knox nodded noncommittally, but for the first time
since he had made his name in television the worm of discontent
was unexpectedly stirring in him. He simply did not know what
they were all so excited about, and worse than that he did not
know why it should bother him that he didn't. To his left Mrs.
Dartley smiled but was silent. He was grateful for the fact that she
at least was not involving herself in the discussion. Nevertheless,
he was full of uncomfortable misgivings. The idea of doing a program on her was clearly a mistake, and it would be wise to abandon
it now.

"Tolstoi? Dostoevski?" Campion asked.

"They also lied. And everyone else. The so-called rational
prophets were no better."

"Certainly no better. I agree with that."

"Lies. Not only those half-mad poets, those mystics, with their
painful attempts at Christian belief, but everyone who expected
miracles. Wherever that expectation was transferred, into the secular faiths too, science, social ethics. It made no difference. Those
visions of a better world, a miracle of love and harmony, a para-
dise, no matter whether on this earth or elsewhere. But you will
note, always eternally hereafter," Anton added ironically. Then he
asked, turning toward Mrs. Dartley as though he expected her to
answer, "Now tell me, tell me, how is it possible to think for one
moment that these higher, these ideal worlds can ever exist?"

It was not Mrs. Dartley who spoke in answer, but Sylvia, half
muttering under her breath. "I think that as long as we can imagine them existing, they do."

Ernest Campion immediately said—and when he did, Sylvia,

forgetting the embarrassment that had just overcome her, looked at
him in half-delighted amazement: "It's the nineteenth century
you've got a grudge against, Anton. You're against it because
every one of its great articles of faith has one after another gone
awry. Every miracle contained a hidden serpent in its bosom."

"The failures, the failures," Anton said.

Campion's voice was light now. He was making a clear attempt
to turn the conversation into the more accustomed grooves of
satiric banter. "Wagner's just your whipping boy. We're on to
you now. You're really attacking the whole nineteenth century."

Anton bounced in his chair. "And who has a better right than I
to attack it, I ask you?" He turned to Lily, as to an ally. "You and
I, we know that century, don't we? We were born in it." There
were several smiles at his tactful exclusion of Mrs. Dartley. "It
gave us our ideals, and this century has proven that they were not
fit ideals. They were delusions, at the very best illusions, *nicht
wahr?*"

"I never think about things in this way. Everything is always
changing."

Anton said, "You accept things the way they are too easily!"

She shrugged. "What am I to do but accept? My husband was
arrested because of charges brought against him by Hungarian
Nazis. It was really because he was a known democrat. After a
time the Hungarian authorities finally got him released. During the
war he supported Horthy against Hungarian and German Nazis,
and especially to prevent the Germans from taking over direct
control of the government. When they did take over and Horthy
was out, the Germans came looking for my husband. He had to go
into hiding. Two years after the end of the war the Russians called
him a fascist because he had supported Horthy, and because he was
a rich bourgeois *and a democrat* declared him an enemy of the
people, a class enemy, and sent us both into exile to a house with a
mud floor in a peasant village near Roumania. He was born in a
peasant's cottage and he died in one. In between? What did it
count? I have no idea. My son deserted in order not to have to
carry arms in combat against the Allies. The Russians said he was a
spy and sent him for three years to prison camp in Siberia. Now
what am I to make of all this? And even if I make something of it,

what am I to do about it? I prefer to listen to Mozart. Or Wagner."

Knox thought that his instinct about her had been right. Part of her story might be useful to him. Carefully edited of course. He brightened a little.

"But listen, listen, Mrs. Halász," Anton said, now almost desperately. "I understand what you mean. But now understand me. Do you remember the old Emperor? Franz Josef? Did you ever see him?"

"I saw him very many times," she said.

He plunged on, ignoring for once this reminder of the difference in their social status. "I saw him twice. Once when I was a boy, again when I was a soldier during the First War. Never mind that. But the first time, I was in Prague, standing in the street when he came by, and I cheered and had tears in my eyes and felt that I would gladly die for him. Later I became a nationalist, a social democrat, a pacifist—all my fervent idealism went into such things. Good. But let me tell you, what I felt for the old Emperor, *that* was idealism too, not the kind we give approval to now, but it was there. That, I tell you, was also the nineteenth century."

No one commented on the fact that the approval in his voice could not be misconstrued, that he had made, at least for the moment, an extraordinary shift in point of view. Lily Halász merely said, "But of course. Why not?"

He lifted his shoulders and made a face. He was obviously still dissatisfied with her response. He turned to Campion. "Well, let me ask you, a rational man, what is *your* opinion of that leap of faith? For one way or another, we have agreed, that is what the whole century was trying to do, the poets, the composers, scientists, social thinkers."

Campion said slowly, "I think it was an historical inevitability."

"You mean because of the decline of the church and the advancement of learning?"

Campion nodded.

"But then what happened? What went wrong?"

"Perhaps many things. Perhaps the goals were lost in the machineries of power which were supposed eventually to spew forth the miracles."

"But was the failure of"—Anton hesitated, then used for the first time the term that had lurked unuttered behind all of his exchanges with Campion—"secular humanism—was the failure of secular humanism inevitable?"

"I can't answer that," Campion said.

Anton shook his head again. "But the leap, that historical necessity . . . ?"

"Inevitability, I said."

"Yes, well, inevitability. You said *was*. For the rational man today is such a leap inevitable? Possible even? You, for example? Do you believe in it?"

Campion paused, then said very distinctly, "I believe in enlightened despair." Sylvia's head turned sharply toward him.

"Bravo," Anton said, lifting his wine glass. Gwendolyn Dartley, smiling faintly, still silent, held them all in her eyes. Benjamin Knox, who had made almost nothing of the last few minutes of conversation, had nevertheless felt its intensity. He was only confirmed in the opinion he had formed earlier of Anton Hrubick, although now it appeared that he had been not a Nazi but a Communist. But as he looked at Ernest Campion he felt unreasonably ill at ease, and began to regret that vain boast he had made when first he was introduced to him on the terrace. "Bravo," Anton repeated. "Out the window with redemption. Just like Jan Masaryk."

There was a great stillness in the room. Then Campion said, "I should have added that I also believe in the long view." Then he nodded at Mrs. Halász and smiled. "And oh yes, in Mozart, of course."

Lily's head went back and she laughed. Anton moved his eyes jerkily from one face to another, smiled a smile which they were all meant to see was false, then drank off a huge pull of wine. A general murmuring started around the table. With relief Knox imagined that at last this long dinner had come to an end. Instead, to his horror he saw now that there was a new passing around of wine bottles, and all that had happened was a rearrangement of attentions. Mrs. Dartley made some desultory remark about coffee, but he doubted it would come to anything. Then she said to him, "There was a message for you just now, Mr. Knox. Apparently there was some language difficulty and Giovanni called me to the phone. It was a Mr. Ralph Bledder. He said it was only necessary to tell you that he would be here with the car at eleven-thirty."

"Fine," Knox said. "Bledder's my assistant."

"What a pity I didn't know about him. He would have been most welcome too."

"That isn't necessary," Knox said in some surprise. "Besides, he had a lot to do in Zürich."

She drew him out now about his work, expressing an interest in all the details, especially when he explained that his staff had been busy for weeks preparing material on her. "But what," she asked, "would have happened to all of it if I had not agreed to the program?"

"Nothing," he said. "We just wouldn't have used it, that's all."

"But isn't that rather extravagant? As it were, unpeopling Egypt?"

He smiled and said with satisfaction, "That's just the way we work, the way it has to be."

"Amazing," she said. "And all this effort just to bring me into several million living rooms. That is the phrase, isn't it? Or perhaps not to bring me there. But I still don't quite understand. After all, our arrangement only became definite this evening. What if I had said no? What would have happened to your scheduling?"

"Easy," he said. "We have to stay flexible in this business. Be prepared to add things, drop them, alter dates. Before every season starts we've got two or three programs completely ready on tape. Then if something falls through or nothing better comes up in the meantime for one of the open spots we're all set."

"Ah," she said, "how very interesting."

At his end of the table Anton had returned to his usual manner. He was saying to Campion, "Now why should a woman want to be a writer?"

"Why should she not?" he replied.

"But life permits a woman to live mindlessly amidst sensations. Why should she want to relinquish so enviable a state? Besides, women believe in happiness—they can never quite give up that goal. It makes it so difficult for them to accomplish anything, other than what we might call their historic mission." No one replied to him, and he grinned.

"And where will you go when you have finished with us here, Mr. Knox?" Mrs. Dartley asked.

"I'm scheduled to do a program from New York, live, in late November."

Anton said to Sylvia, "I'm very curious to know which role you fancy, my dear, the Magdalene or the Virgin?"

"I don't fancy either one. And I certainly hope these weren't my only alternatives."

"But nature seems so generously to have cast you for the Wagnerian passion. Temperamentally, that is. You will find it difficult to escape."

"You are a rogue," Lily Halász said.

"Yes, a talking rogue—impossible at my age to be any other kind, I fear. I hope I haven't offended you, Faustine?"

Sylvia smiled and shook her head. She was really hardly listening to him.

"Good. I should hate to arouse the wrath of those bardic ancestors of yours. Imagine if all the gleemen in your blood should start to chase me. You are a heretic, my dear. Do you know that?"

"Me? Why?"

"A double heretic in fact. First, because you are a poet, and all poets are heretics. Second, because you are a woman. And a woman who is a poet has fallen into double heresy."

Just then Benjamin Knox said in a way that drew to himself the attention of the whole table, "As a matter of fact, I may not be going directly back to New York from here. There's a possibility I may be in Germany for a couple of weeks. I can't say I'm looking forward to it." His tone made it perfectly clear that he felt he would be going among those who were the exceptions to the rule that evil was but a temporary absence of good—during the earlier discussion he had searched his mind and struck with relief upon this apt phrase, a quotation perhaps; at any rate it certainly made more sense to him than all the complicated things they had been saying. But he had forgotten this now. In Germany he would move among the forever damned, among a people essentially different in kind from all the others in the world.

"And what is it that takes you to Germany?" Mrs. Dartley asked.

Sylvia blinked at Knox. His tone had annoyed her. What a hypocrite he was, really. Two swift images came to her, two little dramas in which he was the protagonist. Benjamin Knox walking through a German park, recoiling with horror at the mark of Satan which he would find on the brow of every babe in its mother's arms. Benjamin Knox, Christian hero, snatching a Jewish child from out the grip of a be-weaponed and sinister figure in an S.S. uniform. Or flinging himself bravely against the gates of Dachau. She nearly laughed. But she felt a sort of sick depression too. How she hoped they were not now to have the standard conversation about German guilt, the cant phrases and incredible moral and historical simplifications, a conversation which in its sordid assumptions about the innate and unique depravity of all Germans who had ever been or who ever would be always eerily reminded her of the racial theories of the Nazis themselves. Oh if only the question of what had happened in Germany—in Europe one had better say, for there was complicity—could be stripped of the hypocrisy with which both the Germans and those who had at last won victory over them had in their different ways enshrouded it, then one might begin to dare to face some truths.

Sylvia closed her eyes and suddenly realized how much she had drunk. Her mind was reeling with perplexities. When Turgenev was a boy his father had struck down peasants before his eyes. His mother, on her deathbed, had had a chamber orchestra playing polkas in the next room, had caned her servants during her last hours, and ordered her overseer to set fire to the house and village as soon as she was dead in order to deprive her son and the peasants of them. Turgenev was the gentlest of men. Sylvia opened her eyes. It would never do. It was as though some braking mechanism on her powers of association was simply failing to work. She was now thinking about Troy, of all things, about how old Schliemann when he had dug at New Ilium had ended up finding not only Troy itself but—how many was it?—eight other cities as well, culture after culture which over the millenia had risen, endured for a time, and then nine times in one violent way or another been destroyed. Aloud she said before she could stop herself, "Boum. Pouw. *Finito!*"

"What?" Posy said.

"Troy," Sylvia said mysteriously and decided not to try to explain. And yet you could put it another way—how often on the ruins of the dead had men and women raised a new city. And even after that last and longest wait—had it been complete annihilation, or a moving on of a few last survivors?—had not Schliemann in a sense raised on those same ruins a tenth city? On this idea, Sylvia's mind, for a moment, came to rest.

In the meantime Knox had answered Mrs. Dartley. "The possibility of doing a program on the generals' plot. But from the angle of the civilians who were indirectly involved in it, the ones who'd probably have had a role in any new government if the attempt on Hitler's life hadn't failed."

"Ah. The July 20th. The von Stauffenberg plot. But why don't you center it on von Stauffenberg himself?"

"Absolutely out," Knox said. "Officer caste, decorated by Hitler, in the inner military circles at the time. Nope. We can't afford to make a hero out of him."

"But he was a hero, my dear Mr. Knox. Perhaps if you had known Germany before the war you would know just how much of a hero he was. For a German officer to commit an act of treason, however necessary . . . ? Besides, Americans are so fond of military figures."

Knox ignored all of this. He had waited a long time for the floor. He did not intend to lose it now. "The point is that we've got to concentrate on something, someone, less controversial. For a program like this, I mean. We've a line on one man in particular, clean hands, absolutely no doubt of that, no Nazi involvement, that's established. He's a type that's hard to find. Of course people are bound to raise the question of why he didn't get out of Germany when he saw how things were going."

"They are?" Mrs. Dartley asked in a bored way.

"Naturally. That's no particular problem. We can handle that. The other problem, why he didn't do something *sooner*, after all '44 was practically the end, they were losing the war—we intend to go into all of that very frankly, no holds barred, on the program itself. We're not going to do any whitewashing."

Sylvia pondered his habit of shifting to the pronoun "we." Bingham had the same habit.

Campion seemed extremely interested in the conversation. "What did he 'do' in 1944?" he asked.

"He didn't actually do anything towards the plot itself, except indicate his support of it. I suppose you could say he wasn't in a position to do anything very effective about seizing power. Not that I particularly go along with that idea myself. Where there's a will there's a way, you know."

"*Sancta simplicitas,*" Anton said.

"What was that?"

"An old Bohemian exclamation of heartfelt sentiments."

Knox nodded and went on rapidly, "The point is that if they'd
pulled off the coup he'd have been an important person in Germany after the war. We had to turn to whatever civilians there
were who'd been anti-Nazi and were still alive. There's no question about it, this Greifenberg would have been a natural."

"What was the name?" Campion asked.

"Greifenberg. Andreas Greifenberg. Quite a mouthful. He was
a dabbler, a sort of high-powered dilettante, but he seems to have
been fairly well known and respected by the right people. He left
a widow, much younger." A certain boyish enthusiasm was in his
voice now, and his attitude was in part that of one eagerly sharing
information with those less in-the-know than himself. "As a matter
of fact, the whole business depends on her; there are things we
can't use without her permission and I'm against doing the program
at all if she isn't willing to be interviewed. The night they killed
von Stauffenberg—that was the 20th of July—the Gestapo went
straight to his office and turned up these lists of just about everyone who'd been involved in the conspiracy, including the civilians.
Kind of a stupid thing to do, leaving lists like that around. It was
Skorzeny who took them directly to Goebbel's house. The men
they killed that night, like von Stauffenberg—he was dragged
down into a courtyard and shot—they turned out to be the lucky
ones. Later it got pretty nasty. They strung some of them up from
meat hooks; you know, just put a sort of thin cord around their
necks and hoisted them a few inches off the floor, so they'd
strangle—Himmler got it all on film and ran it off later for Hitler.
They rounded up the people on those lists for weeks; the usual
Gestapo techniques, needless to say—beatings, torture . . ."

Everyone at the table was watching Knox. He talked about these
events with so naïve and impartial an excitement that he left little
doubt as to how good a story he considered it to be. Sylvia saw
him then in a new way. It was as though those people of whom he
spoke had never really existed, except as providers of a macabre
entertainment. She'd had the same feeling about his references to
the six million Jews. Knox did not seem able to comprehend what
had really happened. He was, without even knowing it, without
even having to think about it, a henchman of executioners. He
would preside retrospectively over this man he was talking about,
as, she was sure, he would over the crematoria, in order that an
audience might select from among the horrors its special thrills, as

the crowds who in the old days flocked to watch a man drawn and quartered had done, but even more safely than those crowds, because it was already over with and at an even greater distance in space: satisfaction without risk or remorse or guilt or responsibility. And besides all that, the name Andreas Greifenberg was familiar to her; she knew it in quite another context.

"They threw most of their families into prison too—that's when a lot of them broke. One thing we have to be careful about is not to give the impression that even in 1944 there were very many Germans who were willing to take the sort of risks involved in defying the Nazis."

Mrs. Dartley brought him up short. "I should think that would be perfectly clear, perfectly, painfully obvious." To Sylvia her expression looked strained. Campion somehow looked different too, and he seemed about to speak when Mrs. Dartley went on, "Mr. Knox, are you aware of the fact that Andreas Greifenberg was an old friend of mine?"

Knox was genuinely taken aback. "He was? Is that right? I had no idea." His manner became suddenly solemn, respectful, but he also looked pleased; perhaps this information would be useful, an unexpected windfall.

"He was a very close friend too of my second husband, Bob Dartley. They traveled together in Greece and Italy before the First War."

Knox tried to be offhand. "I'm sure we'd have run across the connection eventually, Mrs. Dartley. We're still researching you, you know."

She said with quiet brutality, "People who pry into other people's lives very often miss the most important things."

He ignored this. "Do you know his wife too?"

"His widow? His young widow? No, I do not. He married her during the war. I have only corresponded with her."

Knox said, "I've heard he left a diary of some sort, a sort of record of life in Nazi Germany."

"Have you? How interesting."

"I wonder if he did."

Sylvia said, "I wonder if we're talking about the same man who did all that work on Greek art."

Campion said, "Yes we are."

She turned reproachfully to Knox. "I don't see how you could call him a *dabbler*. He was practically the century's greatest authority on classical antiquities." She was about to go on and say that she herself actually knew someone who had known him but she hesitated, reluctant to give Knox any information of a personal sort. She felt too that complicated things had been touched on which she understood only a little better than Knox did and that Mrs. Dartley did not want any of them to continue with this conversation.

Mrs. Dartley said, "I should be interested to know if you have had a favorable response from Andreas Greifenberg's widow."

Knox frowned. "I can't say we have, so far. She's refused us, in fact. But I'm writing her again, a new tack; I don't think she understood what we're after."

"I see. A language difficulty no doubt." She stood up. "Giovanni will bring the coffee in a moment." She gestured toward a sideboard where there were also brandies set out. Everyone else got up too. Knox felt a great sense of release; things had really gone wrong towards the end of dinner, but once freed from that table he would surely be able to handle everyone in his own way. "Ernest," Mrs. Dartley said, "I wonder if you will be kind enough to act as a sort of proxy for me with Mr. Knox. From time to time. Help him with whatever he needs, give him whatever information he asks for that seems to you suitable."

It would have been difficult to tell which was more surprised at this, Knox or Campion. "If you wish," Campion said. Sylvia felt that he too was under some sort of strain.

There was a moving about now.

"I shall say good night to you," Anton announced. "I am dying for a Monarchist, Mr. Knox."

"What does that mean?" Knox asked Marshall.

"He smokes them. They're a special sort of cigar. Mrs. Dartley can't stand them."

Lily Halász, in a corner, was singing to herself in a sort of struggling undertone. It was evident from the rapid shifting of octave and beat that she was attempting to manage several parts at once as well as to intersperse an orchestral line. Darkly, gravely quavering *"Trotz Teufel und der Höllen Port"* hardly hung on the air at all before it was vanquished by the light and cheery *"Ihr Wüten wird sie wenig nützen."* She was unaware of the fact that Anton had approached her on his way out and was standing with head cocked at her. *"Was kann uns tun der arge Feind? Sein Grimm kann unsern Trost nicht rauben."*

"Can it be that I have at last caught you in a statement?" He startled her, taking her arm suddenly, affectionately. *"Das neugeborne Kindelein!* Or are you simply rushing the season?"

She said sniffily, "I have not been in church since my daughter's wedding. Must there be a special reason or time of year for so very beautiful a piece of music? I sang in the chorus of the Budapest Bach Society for over forty years. I have more than a few cantatas stored away in my head. Marshall, do you know that part just before the trio, the soprano recitative accompanied by three flutes?"

"No," he said.

"What a pity."

Knox found himself next to Posy. "I meant to ask at dinner. What do you do with these brass-rubbings of yours?"

"Put them on walls," she answered. "That was one of the troubles at The Mothergone. There wasn't enough room."

"Now just what is The Mothergone?"

"Oh just a place where I lived in London before I came here. A kind of rooming house for working-class girls. Some rich Englishwoman endowed it, so it doesn't cost very much at all to live there."

"And the name of this place is really The Mothergone?"

"No, not really. I called it that. I made up the name."

Hearing this Sylvia wondered for perhaps the twentieth time about that term. What did Posy mean by it? Was it a lament or a cry of triumph? Or did she even know herself? As usual, her wispy little voice told one nothing. How different Posy was from most of the students she had taught, always pouring out their little domestic histories, unaware of how interchangeable they often were, touching nevertheless. Posy was touching in another way; uncertain of whether or not she had ever had a history, she seemed to be desperately in search of one. Marshall was next to her now, bending over and saying something in her ear. Sylvia had remarked the trio on the lawn that afternoon, Anton waving around one of those cigars, the behatted youngsters, and had deliberately avoided them. The young lovers, as she referred to them, though as far as she knew they were not lovers at all, more like brother and sister really. That sort of thing could change quickly, though. And really one could never be certain. Posy at nineteen was quite formidably beautiful, and Marshall, who had looked like a mangy tomcat when he first came to them, was now gleaming and handsome. A curious, a cryptic pair. What else they had besides the beauty of youth she did not know. Perhaps that was enough for the time being, especially for someone Mrs. Dartley's age. Perhaps, for that matter, it was just enough. Looking at them she felt herself recovering her pre-Knox good spirits.

"Cognac?" She jumped. Ernest was holding out a glass.

"Why not? I might as well finish myself off."

"My idea exactly."

They smiled at each other. "Are you pleased with your new assignment?"

"With Knox? Now what do you think?"

"Do you know," she said, "somehow I didn't want to go on talking about it in front of him." She turned her head toward Knox. "But about that German, Gwendolyn's friend, Andreas Greifenberg. It's such a coincidence. I know someone in Munich who knew him when he was a boy. Stefan—I knew Stefan when he was at Yale for a couple of years, he's an architect—Stefan revered him. He said Andreas Greifenberg corrupted him. He meant that knowing him, talking with him, kept him from ever being taken in by the Nazis, and though he's never said so I suspect it had a lot to do with other things in his life too besides politics. There's one story Stefan told me that I've never forgotten." She knew that the vast amounts of wine she had drunk were having a marked if unpredictable effect on her and that she was no doubt talking far too much, but Campion seemed interested. "When the Nazis came to power Andreas Greifenberg was one of the directors of the Glyptothek in Munich. Well of course you know what they were like, they took over everything and corrupted it, theatre, art collections, history, and you know what they were like with their misunderstanding of the ancient world, how perverted they were. Stefan says it would have been just a matter of time before Greifenberg went because he never had made a secret of what he thought of them, riffraff he thought them, but that what did it was his insisting that their swastika went in the wrong direction. Have you got a pencil?" Suddenly she interrupted herself, laughed wildly, looked Ernest Campion provocatively in the eye and said, evidently to her own surprise, " '*N'oubliez pas de me rendre mon crayon.*' "

"I won't forget," he replied swiftly.

She cocked her head at him, seemed puzzled, and a little uneasy. Then she said, as though to dismiss the whole matter, "It's just a quotation. I hadn't thought of it for years. I used to say it to every man I went out with—well, to a few of them—just to see if someday someone would know what it was from. They never did, so I was safe."

He said, "The Russian hotcat. Clavdia Chauchat, Clavdia of the *Kirghiz Augen*. What do you mean 'safe'?"

She was plainly astonished, and not quite so sure of herself as she had been. It was as though after years of being the trickster she had now been tricked herself. She feigned amusement. "I made a little pledge with myself once that I'd marry the first man who knew what it was from, who knew what I meant." In order to avoid his eyes, which had not once left her face, she now laughed again, hiccuped, begged his pardon, and then said, "That was when I was young and silly and didn't know any better. About Andreas Greifenberg, I've got to show you. Matches will do nicely." She began tearing them out of a matchbook and laying them out on the sideboard until she had two *croix gammé*, one turning to the right, like a Buddhist's prayer wheel, 卐 , and the other to the left, 卍 . "Look,'" she said, pointing to the first one, "that's *swastika*, it's supposed to mean that all is well, everything's good, and that's the one the Nazis used. Andreas Greifenberg couldn't stand that, and according to Stefan he told them that if they had to have a symbol it should be a *croix gammé* turning to the left, which means all is evil. In Sanskrit it was called—let's see . . . a very similar word . . . but I've forgotten it, I guess."

"*Sauvastika*," Campion said. He had such a strange expression on his face.

"Yes. That's it. Stefan wasn't sure the story was true. It would have happened just before Andreas Greifenberg came to live in their village, in 1934, when Stefan was about six, I suppose, but he heard it somewhere later and believed it because he said it sounded like him. I wonder if it was true. One hopes so."

"It was true all right," Ernest said. "In fact, he said it to Goebbels at a party given for Goebbels by the Bavarian Culture Ministry. He said he objected to any modern state reviving and worshiping an archaic symbol, and then went on to make the remarks about *swastika* and *sauvastika*. He took out pen and paper and drew both symbols and labeled them and handed the piece of paper to Goebbels. There were a number of witnesses."

"So that's how it happened? Then it really did. I'm so glad. I must tell Stefan. He'll be glad too. Does Gwendolyn know about all this?"

"Yes." He was smiling patiently and at last it struck her.

"How do *you* know so much about him?" she asked then.

Knox was on the other side of the room. Campion said, "In part because he did leave a manuscript behind, or several related ones which were intended to form a whole. It's more than a diary. He left it all to Gwendolyn. Some of the letters he had been able to get out to her until about '43 were supposed to form a part of it too. It's a fairly complicated piece of work, or she finds it so. You know the trouble she has following through on anything that can't be done in a day or two. She'd been making stabs at putting it together for years."

"And did you . . . ?" She understood now.

"Yes, I took over the job."

"You're a sort of secret archivist," she said.

"Nothing of the sort. That's your métier. It's simply that Gwendolyn doesn't want it talked about until it's in the hands of a publisher. I think her reasons are purely practical—she doesn't want to be hounded about it. At first I thought she had maneuvered me into taking over for her. Maybe she had. But after I'd looked at parts of it I couldn't see letting it just molder away. The idea of someone she didn't know working on it, editing it—that idea was entirely unacceptable to her. It's a work that has very deep, very personal meanings for her. I know about your friend Stefan Zimmermann, incidentally—that is, there are some references to him and his family in Andreas' manuscript."

Sylvia's head had cleared rather rapidly. Looking at Ernest Campion she realized at last that there was something personal for him in all this too, something perhaps that was even painful. She said, "I'd like to see some of it some time if I might."

"I'd like you to," he said. "A few more months and my part in it will be finished. Then Gwendolyn and his widow will have some decisions to make. And I'll be back among the unemployed, or the half-employed." He was trying to be light.

They stood looking at each other, both a little tense. She said, "How strange this is."

He said, "It isn't so strange really."

"I meant my knowing Stefan," she said quickly. And then, "I wonder that Andreas didn't go to Switzerland. That's what Hans Knappertsbusch did when Goebbels started fooling around with the opera house in Munich. But instead he went off to that little village; within an easy walk of Switzerland, Stefan told me. I suppose that was deliberate. He finished the work on the Munich Vase Painter there, didn't he, and he did all the volumes of *Attic Figure Vases?*" Campion nodded. "Stefan," she went on, "was always going to take me there, to see the village I mean, to show me where he'd lived and where Andreas lived too. But we never got around to it. The year I spent in Munich was an awful one for me, a wasted year. I didn't do any of the things I wanted to. What was its name? Alte something or other?"

"Alterbrunnen."

"Yes. Have you ever been there?"

"No."

"That's funny," she said. "I'd be so curious if I were working on him." There was a very long silence now. At last she said, "Well, at any rate now I know why you had such a funny expression on your face when Knox brought the subject up."

Campion looked about quickly. Knox was still on the other side of the room. He said, "You know in part. In part it was also because Andreas Greifenberg was very nearly my step-father."

"Oh Ernest," she said.

"Yes. He and my mother met and . . . and fell in love."

"Oh Ernest," she said again. She reached out and put a hand on his sleeve. Somehow the gesture touched him deeply. "And did you know him?" she asked.

"Not in the sense you mean, dar—" He caught himself in time to keep from saying the whole word. "I was a child. I have only the vaguest memory of someone who I was told later on was he."

"Oh what a shame. He must have been someone worth knowing."

"He must have been. My mother certainly thought so."

"But aside from that."

"Of course. Quiet now." He turned towards Knox, who was coming towards them from one side. Mrs. Dartley was coming from the other. When they converged she said, "Mr. Knox, you will excuse me, won't you? I leave you in good hands. Lily and I have something we must talk about."

Knox looked at his watch. "Certainly." He turned to Campion. "My assistant Ralph Bledder's picking me up at eleven-thirty. Maybe we could use the next half hour or so to get a few things lined up in?"

Campion nodded. "Splendid," Mrs. Dartley said. "And Ernest, why not take Faustine with you? I'm sure her comments and insights would be very valuable to the world at large."

"What's the world at large got to do with it?" Campion asked.

"That's the name of my program," Knox said.

"Oh."

"Why not?" Sylvia said. "Let's go." She suddenly felt tipsy again, but pleasantly so, irresponsibly so. It had been an evening of revelations, but they had left her charged with a sense of purpose, of confidence even. She felt too that there were all sorts of mysterious bonds now between herself and Ernest Campion. She grabbed one of the brandy bottles from the sideboard and clutched it to her.

From the door where she stood with Lily Halász Mrs. Dartley once more addressed them. "Now, remember, you are all to tell Mr. Knox everything he wants to know about me. So nice having you, Mr. Knox. I look forward to seeing you on your return from England. Good night now."

Twelve

"Sylvia, stop it." Campion spoke firmly. "You're only confusing things."

"I am? Sorry." She subsided.

Knox, who was being very brisk, prepared to go ahead.

The World at Large had actually begun in small as a local New York program and at the outset had consisted mainly of interviews with theatrical celebrities. With success, however, and the award of a network hour, Knox had moved determinedly in other directions as well. He now took all knowledge as his province, and the very fact that he was so ill-prepared to do so and so untroubled by any awareness of the complex nature of whatever was under discussion was an asset; it enabled him to communicate the more readily with a mass audience without in the least offending their democratic sensibilities. This was perhaps what his admirers meant when they said he had a "flair." Though much of the program, which made its appearance approximately twice a month during the season, was now constructed on the principles of the pseudo-documentary, the chief interest, for Knox as well as his viewers, remained in that confrontation between himself and the subject. Strive though he did to create the impression that he was dealing with "issues," labor though he and his staff did to provide an authentic context of seriousness, his real gift was his capacity for exploiting personality, favorably or unfavorably as it suited his purpose. There were few in an era of public relations and propaganda who could allow themselves the luxury of refusing his invitations, even among those who had retained a natural taste for privacy. His questions, indiscreet but naïve, had won him more than one newsworthy coup; and always, beneath a surface that was respectful and enthusiastic, he had a way of regarding the Prime Minister of India as though he were no different in kind or achievement from America's ranking crooner. This very blurring of distinctions struck, subliminally, a responsive chord in many of his viewers, who, feeling Knox to be, as indeed he was, no different from themselves, felt too a comforting egalitarian glow. Even among his detractors no one could deny that he had been born with the skills of his trade.

Recognizing that in the autumn of 1956 national interest would be centered on the presidential election—for a time the specialists as well as the experienced staff correspondents would have their day—Knox had planned his own activities accordingly. The first two programs should have as wide an appeal as possible—his choice was led naturally to the topics of sex and war—but the third program, which in spite of his protests was scheduled for two days before the election, and could not therefore be expected to do well in the ratings under any circumstances short of having the two candidates themselves appear, was to be used entirely for enhancing his prestige among the so-called serious critics of the medium. When it was not otherwise inconvenient he liked to do this, to devote a program to some little-known but extraordinary personality, the choice of whom would reflect credit on his taste, judgment, and apparent willingness to sacrifice popularity to merit.

Up to the point at which he had arrived at Kilchberg all was going according to plan. The first program, which had just appeared, had been about a Hollywood sex queen; her childhood miseries and history of nervous disorders had enabled him to use what he thought of as the Freudian approach to the interview. It had been a great success. Now he would be flying back to England to complete work on the second program, for which he also had high hopes. It would focus on a famous British field marshal who was just publishing his memoirs, and great use would be made of films taken of the desert campaigns in Africa during the Second War. And then, for that difficult third program slot, Gwendolyn Dartley—and, judged by entirely different standards, this just might do fairly well too.

Mrs. Dartley had been drawn to his attention by one of the brightest members of a hard-working staff which consisted mostly of youthful Phi Beta Kappas from the colleges that had been beyond his once-humble reach—a year or two working with him was now considered a choice way of getting on in the industry. The more Knox considered Gwendolyn Dartley the more likely she seemed, and the idea of having a Swiss holiday while putting the program together appealed to him too. In the end he had decided in favor of Mrs. Dartley with every confidence. The Algerian tracts had given her name a certain publicity the year before, and it appeared that she had a small but intensely devoted following for those other curious things she had been writing in the last few years. Her novels, though now forgotten, had once been popular and would no doubt "ring a bell or two" with the older generation, as he had put it. Best of all, her personal history was colorful, a version even of the good old rags-to-riches theme. Of humble American parentage—"people of good blood who had known hard times," one of his sources said—she had made her way with notable ease among the great and famous of the world. Knox

saw clearly of course that the chief instrument for her success had
been marriage. Dartley had not only belonged to the leading intellectual circles of the time but came from a family which for several generations had had at least one member in high government
service, so that even after his death she was well connected in
England. Levin had known everyone worth knowing on both sides
of the Atlantic.

It was Knox's oblique references to the cleverness of these alliances and his much less oblique suggestion that the first marriage
had been purely calculating that had elicited a sort of half-serious,
half-mocking tirade from Sylvia. She had been rattling on for
several minutes before Campion stopped her, about why was it
that no one was ever willing to use any imagination, and suppose
Knox had been a very intelligent and very good-looking girl but a
very poor girl too and he had been stuck in a little town and the
only available rich young man in town wanted to marry him, or
her, as the case was, she corrected herself, well why not, if a
woman didn't have any money or any way of earning it that was
pleasant she certainly didn't have much other choice in those days,
and suppose that afterwards it turned out to be just utter despair.
Both men had listened to this patiently enough, but when she had
gone on to complain of the lack of a courtesan tradition in America "because of the bloody puritanism," and did they know how
many brilliant woman in Europe had been courtesans and did
either of them think that Pompadour's hold over Louis for example had been primarily sex and—it was when she had reached
this point of muddle that Campion had felt he had to stop her.

Now she flopped back on the couch and narrowed her eyes at
the two men. They struck her as ridiculous. Each was making a
great effort to stay on a surface where the uneasiness they so
obviously felt with each other could at least be handled. Knox said,
in a way that pointedly excluded her, "The last one seems to have
been something of a hero. What we're interested in knowing is
whether or not he was a Communist."

"Gwendolyn has never said."

"It's something we've really got to find out."

"I'm surprised you haven't already done so."

"Oh we've learned quite a lot. Just no definite evidence so far
that he was."

Campion now said, dully, as though he were delivering a report,

"Dragan was a great patriot, and certainly a socialist, quite likely a
Marxist of sorts. But he was educated in Paris and Zürich—the
medical degree's from Zürich. Of course you'll know that. At any
rate, the term I imagine you're looking for is 'Western-oriented.' I
think you could use it safely. Naturally the royal government-in-
exile thought he was a Communist. Hardly surprising. By 1942
he had decided that the Titoists were the only hope for successful resistance to the Germans. He was able to make these views
felt in other areas in London. But I'm afraid you'll have to ask
Gwendolyn whether or not she thinks Dragan would have supported Tito after the war."

Knox's head and eyebrows moved up and down in assent. "I
wonder if we could talk a little about how you came to throw
your lot in with Mrs. Dartley."

"The term is inaccurate, and I fail to see the relevance."

"It's widely thought that you're her . . . well, let's see, co-
worker was the term she used. That's the relevance. Don't take this
the wrong way. We have to get the complete picture. We end up
using only a fraction of what we get."

"And you want me in the picture?" With an effort Campion
kept himself from saying that he thought Knox already knew
about him. Then he said, "Gwendolyn's comments on the contemporary scene, her polemics one might call them, sometimes involve
a certain amount of technical detail, and a sorting through of a
considerable amount of information that comes to her. I help out
with this side of her work. From time to time. I do it because . . ."
He paused. "I do it because it seems natural for me to. She and I
have never discussed it. Those other little things that she turns out
sometimes—those I have nothing to do with." He considered what
word other than "things" he might have used; perhaps "essays"
would have been better, but that term did not really describe those
curious and often startling pronouncements, always incomplete
somehow, yet always provocative, those fragments which seemed
to have been wildly snatched from out some larger vision which
evidently visited her from time to time but which was destined
never to be given a coherent form.

"Then your coming here was not really in the nature of a com-
mitment?"

"My coming here was by invitation, a perfectly ordinary invitation."

"You've been here close to two years."

"Yes I have. I like it here." He was determined not to show the anger and resentment he felt at being questioned in such a way by Knox. As though to get it over with, he said, "On Gwendolyn's last trip to New York, shortly before she took the house here, she was the chief speaker at a fund-raising meeting of one of the refugee organizations." It had been in fact her last speech in public. He himself remembered it with a kind of amused awe. She had spoken eloquently, it was true, about the need for funds, but she had also terrified that audience of good and comfortable people by invoking a picture of a new *Völkerwanderung*, of endless crowds of refugees in flight across the surface of the earth, and she had ended by saying that although they were quite right to support such organizations—and she herself would not be there if she thought otherwise—they were nevertheless deluding themselves if they believed they were accomplishing very much.

"I went to the meeting, and spoke to her afterwards—I had met her once or twice before. I'd had an unpleasant illness that winter and, having come into a small amount of money, I was about to leave for a year or so in Europe. Mrs. Dartley suggested that I pay a visit to her here. After spending some time in several European cities I took her up on it."

"I understand you also paid a visit to Niels Bohr in Copenhagen."

"That's true."

"I also understand that you've been offered the chairmanship of the New York Nuclear Disarmament Committee," Knox said.

"You're very well informed," Campion said, in the same precise, flat way he had been using throughout the inquisition. He and Knox accented each other's peculiarities to great disadvantage, Campion's disciplined way of talking making him seem stiff, unnatural, and even pompous, and Knox's strenuous attempts to assume authority coming out as a sort of crude bludgeoning. Sylvia glowered at them. "I declined. I've learned to live with my own history. Certainly I think the need for an international ban on nuclear weapons is a pressing one. And eventually disarmament. If there's ever a time when any action of mine could bring this about I shouldn't hesitate to take it. But it's most unlikely. I'm unable to make myself believe that it will be accomplished by a few of us marching around with placards of protest. And I can't think I'd make a very good messiah—prophets of doom we've enough of, most of them telling the truth accurately enough and hardly any-one listening to them anyway. Sorry, but the spectacle of one repentant scientist—I'm sure that phrase, or one like it, would be the rallying point—such a spectacle wouldn't, I think, be quite enough to sway the ultimate decisions of government. If I had it to do over again I wouldn't involve myself personally in the Manhat-tan Project. Will that satisfy you? But that's another matter en-tirely. A personal choice. Now isn't there someone else here among us whom you'd like to discuss?"

Sylvia could stand it no longer. She got to her feet. "Who do you think you are?" she said to Knox.

"Sylvia!" Campion said.

Knox laughed uneasily.

"How about Posy and Marshall?" she asked. "Let's get to work on them. Mow down the lilies of the field. Why not? Well, I've probably drunk too much, I'll admit that. But I don't think . . . oh never mind. I'm going to bed." She lurched out of the room and Campion followed her.

"Are you all right?" he asked.

"Now that I'm out of there I am. What's the *matter* with him?"

"It's not worth being upset about."

"It isn't? It is too!"

"Come to dinner with me tomorrow night in Zürich."

She shook her head. "Can't."

"Why?"

"I think I'm going to be sick tomorrow. With a hangover. And if I'm not then I think, I think I'm going to be working."

"All day? And night too?"

"Well, no."

"Good. It's definite then. We'll go to the Zum Rüden."

They looked at each other. "Never kiss a drunk," she said, and turned and ran unsteadily down the hall. He watched her take a corner, then returned reluctantly to the room where Knox was.

"A really charming wisp of a girl," Knox said nastily. "Even when she's had too much to drink. I'm a little confused about her name, though. You call her Sylvia, and I was sure that's what she told me it was, but the others seem to call her Faustine, don't they?"

"Sometimes."

"Well . . . which is it?"

"Both."

Knox bounced from his chair to a position near the fireplace. "Very clear. As clear as you want it to be. She's a necessary part of the stage props. Well, that's fine with me, useful in fact. Or you could put it another way. She's part of the collection. Our hostess does collect people, doesn't she? I want to go into that. What about those two kids? What are they doing here?"

Benjamin Knox was plainly rattled, and Campion was pleased. Very seriously he began, "Gwendolyn met Marshall at a Hindemith concert in Zürich."

"A what concert?"

"Hindemith."

"And that's a . . . ?" Knox made sounds in his throat.

"That's a concert at which Paul Hindemith's music is played. Gwendolyn, if I remember correctly, introduced Marshall to him afterwards." Campion hurried to change the subject slightly. "Gwendolyn believes that nature sometimes imitates art and that the American obsession with parent-child relationships is an example of this. Freud, you know. She thinks that Marshall and Posy are refugees from the great American Oedipal drama. I've never asked for more details. Posy had been sent to England to live with a woman who was paid to introduce her into British society. She escaped from her and got a job folding letters and putting them into envelopes for something called—I think it was called the Protect Our Birds League. And she rubbed brasses. That's her main accomplishment."

Campion had every intention of elaborating further, but Knox interrupted him. "Oh for God's sake. I get it. And where did she find her?"

"Who?"

"Faustine. Sylvia. Whatever her name is."

"In a brothel," Campion replied. Suddenly, in spite of himself, he felt an extreme revulsion at the prospect of answering more of Knox's questions.

Knox flared out his hands in protest. "Now look here, Campion. I don't mind a few jokes at my own expense. I don't even mind the phony atmosphere of mystery that you all go in for here. But if I can't get a few straight answers then let's wind it up now."

"That would please me well enough. But it wouldn't please Gwendolyn, evidently. My apologies. It was a poor joke. I don't know much about Miss Grierson, or how Gwendolyn came to collect her." Privately he wondered now if Stefan Zimmermann hadn't perhaps been the link. "I remember her talking about her last winter. And then, around the end of May or first of June, she turned up here. From Munich." He was certain that what Sylvia had referred to as the waste of her life in Munich had to do not with Stefan but with Mr. George Bingham. It now seemed to matter to him very much that he knew so little about her past. "She'd been living there, fairly poorly I gather, in a half-bombed-out building in Schwabing. Before that, in America, she was a college instructor, I know almost nothing else about her. I'm sure you're in a better position to uncover her history than I am. I'll tell you what I can about Gwendolyn. Since she wants me to."

Knox shrugged, somewhat mollified, and looked at his watch. "Too late to do much now. Bledder will be here any minute. Some time I'd like you to look through the dossier he's bringing, the stuff we got on her before I decided she'd do for *The World at Large*. Before I make final decisions on what and who, whom to use." He moved about the room, plainly more relaxed now that Sylvia was gone. One of his greatest assets was his capacity for memorizing, for absorbing vast amounts of material and information and for pulling out the right details under the pressure of the cameras. It was this that gave the impression both of spontaneity and authority to his television manner and accounted in large measure for the fact that even relatively sophisticated people could watch him without being too bored. He said now, in an intense but otherwise quite new voice, "A vain, bothersome, but withal prodigiously effective old meddler . . . a corrupting influence upon society . . . a reformer of incorruptible integrity . . . a taker, a mad egoist . . . a generous friend . . . a disappointed publicity-seeker . . . a museum piece . . . a woman who is always ahead of her times . . . a terrible old phony . . ." He paused. He had made it clear they were quotations, and the first Campion knew very well from its ring and from something Gwendolyn had once said was Churchill. Until then Campion had not actually realized how thorough and uninhibited Knox's investigators had been. He had a picture of hundreds of faceless agents oozing into offices and living rooms all over the world, asking questions the answers to which they would then pass on to Knox. It was a little unnerving, especially since his purpose quite plainly was not to illuminate but to anatomize.

Campion said, "Yes, Gwendolyn's all those things, I suppose. But they're all superficial remarks. Her personality is prismatic. Her character, if you're interested in that, let's say . . . elusive."

Knox did not seem to be listening to him. "And then the facts of her life," he intoned. "Sort of impressive, to put it mildly. I admire the old girl, I really do. You know, what really strikes me most of all is that she always seems to have known exactly what she wanted, exactly what her purpose in life was." He paused, as though out of politeness permitting his companion to respond if he wished to, but not expecting him to.

"I wouldn't agree with that at all," Campion said. "I'd say her life has been very fragmented, even if most people would think glamorous, a series of experiments—which is something of a sign of dissatisfaction. No, on the contrary, I'd say that all her passions and interests and gifts coalesced rather late in life. Perhaps in a way this was even forced on her. By circumstances. It's sad in its way that she's accepted only very late in life the burden of her true purpose."

Once more Campion had the impression that Knox wasn't listening, and this time he was immediately glad, for he suddenly realized how difficult he would find it to say exactly what it was he had meant by that phrase "her true purpose." But Knox did not take him up on it. Instead, he said, in the same intense voice, "Just remarkably in control of everything, it seems to me. Always knowing what she wants. Somehow, for example, somehow I can't imagine her ever crying. *Has* Mrs. Dartley ever cried? I can't imagine it."

Campion felt both pity and contempt for Knox. "The first time in my life I can remember seeing her she was weeping," he said. There he was again in that darkness, being huddled into his clothes in the middle of the night, being taken to the strange house, the tall woman with the swollen red face and the tears that kept streaming down it while upstairs lay that huddled inert form.

"Really? When was that?"

Behind Knox, at the door, the servant Celeste had appeared with

a young-old man who was carrying a brief case. Both hesitated in
the doorway. Campion had an impression of almost indecent servil-
ity about the stranger. But his face was one that made hardly any
impression at all; it would not be easy to identify later on, or even
remember; it seemed to have emerged uneasily from amongst the
faceless crowd, to which in an instant it would surely return. It
was evidently Ralph Bledder. With part of himself Campion perceived all this, while with another he struggled in disbelief with
the fact that Benjamin Knox was once more blundering into the
painful inner confines of his life. He knew too that he was about to
take a bait that had somehow been carefully prepared for him. Yet
he could not keep himself from answering. "When I was not quite
six."

"And what may I ask was the occasion?"

"The occasion was the death of my mother. Not that it's any of
your business."

Thirteen

He was lying on his hospital bed, as usual half asleep, when Mrs.
Dartley appeared in his life for the second time.

"Open your eyes, Ernest," she said. The voice itself frightened
him, provoked uncertain memories. Reluctantly he obeyed her and
then sat up. Beyond her was the Hudson, looking just as it had for
nearly six weeks. She put out a hand and he took it. She was
wearing a soft tweed coat and there was a considerable amount of
snow on its collar and shoulders. Afterwards he wondered why she
should have been out walking in that weather, a woman of her
means, and yet she must have been. The freshness of the outdoors
seemed to cling to her, strange against the overheated, dry, unnatural atmosphere of his room, his little province. A forest after
the first snowfall, he thought, and a tremendous impatience at
being where he was welled up in him for the first time. But he did
not really know who she was.

"Of course you don't remember, do you? Not quite."

"The voice," he said. "The eyes. But . . ." He was struggling, he realized then, *not* to identify her.

"Gwendolyn Dartley," she said.

He remembered it all then, and stiffened against it and her.

"It was I to whom she came."

He did not reply.

"Does that mean nothing to you?" she persisted, leaning nearer, engulfing him in that forest smell. He was not deceiving her. She saw that he knew her. For an instant he wanted her cool hands on his forehead, pressed over his hot eyes so that he might know nothing but that abiding forest. But he resisted. Her walk, he reminded himself, could have taken her through nothing but the tenement-lined streets of Washington Heights, where what trees there were were as bare and alien as himself.

"Oh yes, it means quite a few things to me," he said. His voice was firm and natural. "Among other things that she had to turn to someone, somewhere. Abandoned women usually do." His tone left no doubt as to his meaning.

She stepped back a little. "I admit I'm surprised, not pleasantly, to hear you speak of her in this way. Your mother was indeed an abandoned woman, in the sense that she was a forsaken woman, forsaken by fortune, one who deserved much better of life than she got. But then, who doesn't?"

He snorted. "Perhaps we could spare ourselves argument if we agreed to say that at the least she was an abandoning woman?"

"Ah, so that's it?" She held him with eyes filled with contempt. "I see I should have come sooner. I see that now. I had no idea you had been so misinformed. I had no idea that you yourself were not clever enough to have penetrated through that misinformation to the truth. What a pity for you. The wretched Nathalie. She was always in love with your father. Everyone betrayed Louisa in some way, even I did, inadvertently. Only you, I suppose, never failed her. But it was her destiny to be failed, even when she was in her grave. You complete the circle." She whirled away from him, thrust her hands in the pockets of her coat, looking as inexplicably masculine as a few moments before she had looked overpoweringly female, and paced several times rapidly back and forth between his bed and the door. She said grimly, "I'd have spirited you away from them, if I could have. If there had been any way.

Brought you up as my son. Think how lucky it was that there was no way. It's obvious we'd never have got on." She moved purposefully toward the door.

He was afraid she would go. "I've been under the impression," he said, "that what I've been doing all these years, at some cost to myself, I might add, was choosing not to lie to myself about her."

She whirled toward him. "Oh you're not ready for the truth. Let me know when you are. If you ever are," and she began to laugh, a long, low, gentle, taunting laugh. "It is time too for you to rid yourself of this vain notion that you are the guiltiest of men."

"Why have you come here?" he asked.

"There hasn't been a time when I've not known where you were and, to some extent, how you were. Except once. You will know the period in your life I'm referring to." She was standing close to the bed again. The snow was melting on her coat and the smell of the damp wool was very pleasant and very disturbing to him.

"That isn't an answer," he said.

"I see only your father in you at this moment, Ernest Campion. He was monochromatic. He had only one range, the range of himself. I believe, however, that you are your mother's child too. Else I don't think you'd be in this hospital bed now. I see . . ."

" 'I see, I see, I see,' " he interrupted. "You sound like a fortune-teller."

"Oh? Perhaps I am."

He realized that they were smiling at each other.

"To be brief," she said then, "your mother was once very kind to me, when I needed kindness. She gave me some money. It enabled me to run away. No. That is imprecise. I could have run away without a penny. It enabled me to run with a purpose, not just away but towards something. Wasn't I lucky? I have deposited a certain amount of money in a bank in your name. Sometimes even money can be a kindness. I imagine you'll be getting a letter about it in a day or two. The same amount will be deposited next year at this time. After that, nothing. I'm not going to try to persuade you to accept it. I'm not even sure I care whether you do or not. But it's there. I owe it to the memory of your mother."

"It seems hardly worth the effort," he said.

"Worth it? What a lot of rot, if you mean your mother. She was one of the most worth-while persons I've ever known. As to

whether *you're* worth the effort or not I shouldn't hazard a guess.
I'm late. I'm leaving for London in two hours. Perhaps we'll meet
again."

When she was gone he closed his eyes and for a few minutes
imagined only the forest.

Fourteen

Claude-Simon Levin, born in the ghetto of Kiev, Parisian by
choice and temperament, early collector of Picasso, patron of
Bayreuth and Salzburg—until history made him unwelcome in
these places—stockbroker by trade and knighted member of the
French Historical Society for the distinguished monographs he had
written on the decorative arts in the period of Louis Quinze, had
been a small, neat, very handsome and compact man. Gwendolyn
Dartley, his second wife, had ranged nearly half a foot above him,
and his old dressing gown, of once magnificent silks and velvets,
which she was now wearing, fit her very poorly. She had been
pacing her room with agitated steps for some time. "I am an old
woman," she said aloud, "wrapped in the garments of the past."

This was certainly true. In addition to the Chevalier's dressing
gown, she was wearing the terrible and indestructible green tweed
skirt which dated from the bluestocking days of her marriage to
the Oxford don Bob Dartley, whose name she had also kept. And,
bulky and ridiculous beneath the dressing gown, was the black
turtle-neck sweater that had so well set off the manly chest of
Dragan. It was only of her first husband that no trace remained, in
object or spirit; that bewildered, ordinary and well-intentioned
young man, that hard-working heir to a textile mill, from whom at
the age of twenty she had fled to England two years before the
First War. And there, without any doubt, she had cut something
of a swath, and had been doing so ever since.

Mrs. Dartley was much less afraid of death than she had used to
be. This was the gift old age had brought her, as she had always
hoped it would. There had been times in her youth when she
could imagine no other reason for wishing for a long life, though

few had ever guessed this about a woman who had seized experience so ardently, on occasion so ruthlessly. Now, while she did not yet welcome that relinquishing of self, that dissolution of personality which in a secular age is the basis for the fear of death, she accepted it without much anxiety. Given a few years more she might even meet that moment gladly. She remembered Bob sitting in the garden those last months, every day the face narrower, more waxen beneath the unraveling brim of the Panama straw he wore to shade his eyes from the sun. If ever a man had relinquished with grace it was he.

Yet why should she not want to be freed from that massive and torturous personality of hers, when all too often it overwhelmed whatever was best in herself, and in others too? And always when she felt she had contained and shaped it into something acceptable, even useful, even now when she was old, it would assert itself in the old raging way. Benjamin Knox—how inexcusably she had crushed him even if his lies, his manipulating ways, had also been inexcusable. And later, what she had done to him when they were alone during that conference before dinner, was disgusting, was wicked. By what right was she the scourge of God? Yet she had paid her price afterwards, in the pain and shame she felt. All her life there had come these terrible, lonely moments of bitter self-knowledge, as surely no one around her now guessed. Then she saw her every action as small and self-seeking, her very eccentricities, which usually she felt no need to defend, as merely the sign of a disordered spirit. Self-hatred, in short. Yet that, Bob had said, was a form of vanity, of self-indulgence too. And he was right. How had he known so much, so young? Claude and Dragan had merely smiled at her moments of anguished despair at the ambiguous powers of the ego that was rampant within her, having neither of them, different as they were from each other in other ways, ever felt a moment of doubt as to their worth as human beings. If Bob had lived, what? Could they have sustained that curious balance between them once she had caught up, as catch up she did? He had taken her with all her grievous faults, made worse by being young and insecure, made worse by her fearful struggles towards the only world in which, she knew, she could survive—taken and loved and praised her, amused at the many of his friends who shrank politely from what he called her vigor. "Robust, darling," he would say. "Wonderfully robust. Sane too." And her mind, when she first knew him it had leapt wildly about like a young horse—the simile was his. "Have you heard? Poor Bob Dartley's turned himself into a private tutor for that American girl." Oxford had been cool yet unperturbed—in those days the English did not yet feel the self-doubts that later were to complicate their attitudes toward Americans.

Another world, England in 1912. And Germany too, where Bob had taken her that first summer, before their marriage. How different from Bob's English friends Andreas Greifenberg had been, how warm and committed to the variety of experience, how unafraid of expressing his feelings; the golden glow of those weeks at that house he had taken in the Odenwald, the warm scent of a German summer, forests, rivers, sunsets over the pastel towns, the poems they read aloud, the music they listened to, and all three of them in love with each other. And by then her mind had begun to feel at home in the pastures it had always longed for. How he had worked with her, Bob; it was too late for Greek he said, but no matter, pounding in the logic, German, French, Italian, pacing her through art galleries, quick and sensitive, never forcing, but casting always the net of his enthusiasms and taste both wide and truly for her. What beautiful years. Taking them for all in all, they had been the best she had ever known.

Gwendolyn Dartley stomped towards the cabinet and pulled out a Swiss music box that contained Turkish cigarettes, the same brand Dragan had favored. So quickly and roughly did she open and close the lid of this box that only the tiniest chiming sound was released, a cry really, a little protest version of whatever musical composition lay hidden within, unrecognizable, cut off now behind that rift in time. A match spurted. She had smoked but rarely since her marriage to Claude—his own extreme moderation had had at least a few effects upon her. But there were still times. She paced now, trailed and wreathed by smoke. She disliked intensely being drawn back into the past, and it did not happen often. At her age she had most particularly resolved to live in the present, to concern herself with the future, lest she give others the excuse for turning her into a mere monument . . . to what? To realities that now existed only in her own mind? Ah, that very phrase itself, was it not the sort of phrase that came so easily to Bob? He would have seen through those novels at once, seen how utterly they failed to transmit the realities, how sham they were, things to please her ego with, to win a specious kind of name and place with. A female Pope, darling, he had once said, a learned Mother-Monarch, oh yes, definitely but never in a million years an artist. She had laughed, having never intended to be one. She was far too busy living life to want to write about it. And that had never changed really. And had she not in a sense been his mother, rooted earth-strength to his overdeveloped and thus somehow frail sensibility? And Claude, was he not her father, the most perfect father imaginable, who left her free, yet petted and spoiled her? That comfortable life she had hewed out in London after Bob's death, her own house and enough money for travel, had been as nothing compared to the world of subdued luxury into which Claude had taken her and for which she had always had so natural an inclination. Wealth he had had, though not so much wealth as to have turned himself into a principality and not so much as it appeared. Nevertheless, the choicest of all the things that mattered to him, and most of all the minds of those guests who partook of the Chevalier's talk and hospitality. How surprising after all that elegance, those forms that were almost too perfected and con-trolled, had been the coming of Dragan, a man who was driven by the single, overriding purpose of achieving the political and social freedom of his countrymen, whose personal courage had matched so supremely that purpose. And it was he who had aroused in her the physical raptures which made all her experiences of bodily love that had gone before, save one, seem mere shadows. There had been a scandal, her marrying him so soon after Claude-Simon's death, so soon indeed after their first encounter. But by then she had learned not to hesitate where the feelings were deeply touched. Gwendolyn Dartley had difficulty with numbers. She stood quietly in the middle of the room now and figured back. Forty-six she had been when they married, and Dragan forty-one. She smiled, secretively, standing so for a long time. Then her mouth tightened, she spun towards the cigarette box, lifted and slammed its lid in the same harsh way she had done before.

It was of course the visit of this young man Knox that was unleashing the past upon her, that and the prospect of the ordeal by television which lay before her. The few questions he had already put to her, his general attitude, had shown all too clearly that he regarded her as an old woman with an interesting past who was now engaged in the pointless and eccentric writing of a vari-

ety of tracts that were perhaps newsworthy. And why was she so
engaged? His expression had told her he did not need to ask. He
knew, he thought. A response to a few slights here and there, real
or imagined. The discovery that time had passed her by, as it had
so many others, the stubborn refusal to accept this, the need for an
audience, an absurd setting of everyone to rights even if in no
more elevated a form than writing letters to newspapers, which
was how it had all begun. She would not justify herself to him. Let
him think what he chose. She would certainly not enlighten him
with an irony that he could never comprehend: that she herself
did not know what it was that drove her to the penance of writing,
except that this time the driving spirit was an honest one. Nor
could he know what torment it was for her, how awkward and
unnatural a task the act of writing was to a woman for whom talk
was the superb and natural element. And by what right did he
come here to judge her? By what right did he speak of things of
which he knew nothing: of Andreas Greifenberg, his death, of
meat hooks and gas chambers, no more than a spectacle, as it was
to those who had killed him? And why should she care that he saw
her only as a monument, and a not very important one at that? Oh,
but if only he could see, could be made to see, he and others like
him, that the past she had lived through was his past too, connected to and shaping every dire and present moment. She could
not hope of course to do this. He cared only for personality, not
truth. And mere tracts, written or spoken, which was all she was
capable of, could never do this anyway. Which was why she had
consistently refused to write her memoirs. There was no point
unless she could convey the essential things, which had not only to
do with husbands, or one or two lovers, or conversations with the
great, or the abundant romantic friendships with men and women
alike with which she had filled her life, but which had also somehow to do with history. Personal relationships, she understood,
were the root of everything that mattered to the individual; they
made him happy or unhappy and were not just a senseless game to
be parodied as it was now fashionable to do. Bob and his circle had
been right—let those who mocked have their day, it was a fashion
that would pass—but they too had limited themselves, had deliberately chosen to tell only a part of the story; they had lacked the
stamina to try to say more. The hovering over the individual of
events that lay beyond him, beyond either his control or will, in

history, this mattered too. History—ah, did she not know it, was
not her whole life a summation of this?—was constantly colliding
with the individual, with his little world of love and hate and failure
and success, even when he did not know it, even when it seemed so
far removed. Gwendolyn Dartley thought suddenly of Faustine,
and she knew why it was she had invited her to Kilchberg, and
what it was she hoped of her.

She walked to the window, opened it to let some of the smoke
out, looked down to the forest. There was a new chilliness to the
air. She hugged her garments close to her. It was all so sad really,
her life; beneath the glittering and in many ways enviable surface
lay but a series of elegies, for men, for women, for the century itself, and yet it was not for the intoning of elegies that her voice had
been fashioned, but for rebellious hope. How unpleasant an irony!

They were all gone now of course, the husbands, at least the
three she knew about, the three who had mattered, and nearly
everyone else she had loved too. She had survived, she was the
widow of them all. Thrice-widowed and thrice-bereaved. It had
not been so bad with Claude; she had missed him but not mourned
him unduly, too grateful for his peaceful death, a good year for
him to die in, 1938, before the full horror descended—he had
never been able to believe the truth about this century, formed and
shaped as he was by another; only when the suicide lists began
coming in from Vienna had the old ancestral wariness begun to
flicker in his eyes, and sixty-four a decent if not a ripe age, the two
happy grown children, the memory of having been a good husband to their mother, dead long before, and also to herself, the
excitement she had brought him during the years of their marriage. Oh she could never have imagined Claude-Simon leaving
Paris. He would not have done so. Bob she had mourned even
while he still lived—sent back to convalesce after the Somme, to
die—watching the narrow hand that labored still at the austere
resounding prose in which he set forth his theories of art while in
his lungs the violent rotting went forth apace around the wound
that would not heal. And Dragan, after the muddy, risky, confused
months in Belgrade, the return to Paris, the last-minute flight to
London, the government-in-exile that would not accept him,
socialist-radical that he was, the British government that did at last
accept him, so that in 1944 he was dropped behind the lines in the
Carpathians and there died fighting, and she a woman in her fifties

who for one extraordinary day thought of death in the high Roman fashion, but knew herself, for all the grief, too well.

And Andreas . . . Andreas . . . who survived the First War, who came years later to see her and walk with her by Bob's grave, who visited in London often thereafter, and who later, on one of those visits, met in her house Ernest Campion's mother, who loved her, who endured her loss and the nightward plunge of his country, beaten, shot, or hanged—killed at any rate—disappearing in the communal smoke of Dachau, up those chimneys which for so long had been sending out the signals of distress. For what purpose? So that a young man named Benjamin Knox might one day interview his widow?

Gwendolyn Dartley sank into a chair. "I am the widow of them all," she said aloud. "I am the widow of this century."

She sat with her eyes closed, like one who was fashioned out of rock, sat until the cigarette burned her fingers. Then she saw before her on the table the documents, the letters, some of them still unopened. Tomorrow perhaps there would be some with Austrian postmarks, and among these might be a few that had been smuggled out of Hungary. They would tell her in a variety of ways, these letters from a few friends, that something was in the air. And could one not sense that even in the remote fastness of Switzerland? Could not even a careful reader of newspapers in the past months have caught an occasional vibration? The giant scales, hung as it were over Europe, had begun again that fateful tipping, back and forth, between hope and fear. Was it any wonder that old age had not brought tranquility? It was absurd to hope for anything but the long slow spinning-out of the agony of the race. And where place responsiblity in a time of great and general indifference, a time in which, benumbed by violence, men had lost the capacity for imagining otherness? To do what then? Nothing. Except to speak the truth and know that even if one had more eloquence than she no one would be listening. And what, after all, did it matter that an old woman, her sins still all too full within her, cared desperately, confusedly, impotently, that still once more a cataclysm was gathering force, and that if it came no matter what its final result, men and women would be its victims.

Gwendolyn Dartley's head slumped forward onto her chest. She seemed to sleep. Time passed. Then she raised her head. The firmness came back to jaw and spine. There was a knocking at the door.

Fifteen

It was Campion. He made no explanation. He never did when he appeared at her door in the middle of the night, and this night in particular he felt no need to explain; the smoke in Gwendolyn's room told him that she would welcome conversation. For a time they talked about official matters and then, suddenly, they were back to the old subject again. Exactly how they had got to it was, as always, a mystery. Afterwards the precise steps could not be retraced, they blurred in his memory.

It was odd how those few simple events could bear a seemingly infinite scrutiny. This had happened, and that, and then that, one could say; thus it was and so, no changing of it now. There they were, those few events, caught forever in the amber of the past. Yet to say this was not enough. Not at least for him. Nor, it seemed, under the impulse of his desire, for Gwendolyn either. Or did she perhaps only humor him, in the only possibly effective way, through these rare but recurrent seizures? Who knew? Together, the one who remembered all and the one who did not, they held the amber to the light yet again, turning it to a thousand new and different angles, as though both hoped one day to catch it, so, ah, at last, the only and absolutely truthful angle from which all could be apprehended. Sometimes Campion thought that this was what it really was that kept him staying on with Gwendolyn.

"On her face," Gwendolyn said, "was a look of unspeakable, gloating triumph." There, for example; Campion had never seen that before, the look on Nathalie's face. Each time Gwendolyn approached this scene there was always at least one new detail that flickered up in that prodigious memory of hers, that memory which he had learned in other contexts could be trusted to an extraordinary degree, and this flickering in turn seemed then to illuminate the scene itself in a new way. "I remember I wanted to lay hands on her, that creature of no sex. I wanted—yes, it is true, and I don't believe I've felt this more than one other time in my life—I wanted to strike her dead. It was she of course who had devised that net that had her quarry so utterly entrapped. He lacked the subtlety for such devices, but welcomed them. She had mastery over the situation—oh there was no doubt of it. And over him as surely as over your mother. Only it would be some time before he would realize that."

Campion remembered the afternoon his father lay dying. He was ten by then. The long red mark of the blood-poisoning had traveled the length of the stricken arm and he had been in a coma for several hours by the time Campion arrived, rushed down from his school. Only once did he regain consciousness before his death, and only for a few seconds. He had looked at Nathalie and then at his son standing beside the bed and his eyes had widened, and then he spoke one word: *Louisa.* Nathalie had screamed and flung her hands across his open mouth but he was already dead before she touched him. Campion knew it was his mother's name; he could not remember ever having heard his father speak it before. What were the syllables of that name to the dying man? Were they even at the last an accusation, or were they as near to an act of contrition as he could come? Or had he perhaps meant for Nathalie to tell his son the truth at last? This scene too was a fixed event, but there was no hope of holding it to the light. Here was nothing of amber, but another substance entirely, opaque, impenetrable. He had long ago accepted this. It was not even worth telling Gwendolyn about.

Gwendolyn was stalking about the room, Levin's dressing gown flapping open. He said: "And his face?"

She hesitated. But tact had never seemed as important to her as truth, and it was clear that Campion wanted her to pursue the matter of faces just now. "*His* face? It was the purest abstraction of revenge. Vengeance saith the Lord and vengeance is mine. Or however it goes. The God Jehovah I thought. Yahweh. Just such an expression must lie behind the mask of any Lord who could call himself by such terrible names. The male rage for power. Naked, fearful. In a room filled with the furniture of the Enlightenment."

Campion smiled in spite of himself. He remembered once having asked her why his mother had married his father and she had sniffed and replied, "Why does anyone marry anyone?" and had then added that in any case he must not forget that in his way his father had been an impressive man and one who was accustomed to getting what he wanted. Something had been wrong with him. As to what it was, it was not Gwendolyn Dartley's place to say. Perhaps if at the least he had had an occupation of some sort. It

was a strange family, odd ideas about blood; they all hated the
outside world, withdrew from it very early in life. "All the details
that lawyer of theirs was spewing forth. But your father wasn't
even listening to them really. And poor Dick Currier—when I saw
they'd a lawyer with them I got mine over as fast as I could you
may be sure . . ."

Dick Currier was a familiar detail, a part of that formal rhythm
into which he and Gwendolyn so naturally slipped when they
discussed this event, much as when one member of a family tells
another for perhaps the hundredth time a story that is well known
to both, the very repetition itself the sign of a shared and undiminished interest. "Poor Dick. How upset he was. Your father
wouldn't even *answer* him. He had withdrawn into his own world
of righteous terrorizing. He was judge, judge of all he did not
understand. She had broken the law. How? By asserting *her* powers, which were quite unlike his. The face of an executioner. I
thought all this at the time. Or did I? Well, perhaps not. But
Jehovah, I'm sure I did think that. And all of this . . . this fierce
primitive drama, this ritual murder, for that is what it was, was
taking place in my living room."

Campion felt suddenly how deep Gwendolyn's agitation had
become. It was now as though she was searching all this out not
for his sake alone but in some obscure way for hers too. He had
never quite felt that before. "*In my living room,*" she repeated. Ah
that was it, he guessed, her own sense of powerlessness; that scene
had been, at least retrospectively, a defeat for her too as well as for
his mother.

That the final scene but one had taken place in her living room,
he of course knew, though even that had been kept from him all
the long years of his childhood, youth, and early manhood, along
with the more important, central fact which had been so deeply
hidden from him. This fact was that his mother had loved him,
that indeed it was because of him and not the man whom he used
scornfully to think of as *her lover* that she had been driven to that
final deed. And yet what was important was no longer that fact
itself, the narrowly personal assurance of having mattered to her,
but what it was that lay behind this, the character of a woman he
could not remember, and behind that inevitably misty figure the
spirit of love itself, which had been missing from his life because so
terrible a violence had been done it long ago. "She had a talent for

love," Gwendolyn had told him once, "yes, decidedly. That was
the essential thing about her. Not in the sentimental sense of
course—it had nothing to do with being a good wife, a good
mother, a good citizen. I have no idea of whether she was any of
these things or not. No. In the biological sense, for that's everything, isn't it, defined in the proper way? I have an idea that it is.
Capricious she was, yes, and I must admit more than a little
spoiled, though not by him, by others, but her capacity for love
was infinite. Most people have just a very little of this capacity—
and some I think really none at all—it is not love that such people
feel for their children, for example, but something quite different.
And so often they want to narrow everything down to that very
little bit of love they can manage, to protect it, I suppose, and they
want everyone else to do exactly the same. But others, with them
. . . well, it's a quality after all, not a quantity, and therefore it's
simply always there. Very distressing, very frightening, to people
like your poor father, for whom possession was the chief thing."

How, nevertheless, could he have been expected to know? What
can a child perceive of the complicated doings of adults, and what,
for that matter, even remember beyond an isolated happy scene or
two which in time he does not feel certain really happened, particularly when he has been schooled, directly though subtly through
Nathalie and indirectly through the silence of his father, to a remembering of events not as they were? What for years he thought
he remembered had been imposed upon him by them. That she
had taken him from his father in order to be with someone else, in
itself a terrible action, and that she had abandoned him in a foreign
country, having sent a telegram to his father, who then arrived
with Nathalie to rescue him. And certainly he did think he remembered being with his mother in a place by the sea where there
was always sun and where at first he could not understand the
language which those around him spoke, and a stranger who was
often there with them and who sometimes spoke that new tongue
with his mother and sometimes a slightly strange English. And
then playing alone in the garden when Nathalie and his father
arrived, out of the shadows, and then a long journey to a dark and
rainy city where black dust fell in a constant shower upon himself
and the huge stone buildings, in one of which he was kept for what
seemed to him years, until that night when he was taken to see her.
How easy for them to have manipulated all this without even

having to know they were doing so, even to the point where as a youth he had secretly regretted the weakness which had caused him, a boy of not quite six, to weep inconsolably all that night. That was the one thing he had never forgotten—"Your mother is gone, Ernest," Nathalie said—being taken to see the dead mother who presumably, it turned out later, had not even been worth his tears, flinging himself with childish passion upon her lifeless body, being pulled away. After all, was her death not a judgment from on high?

Gwendolyn had set a saucepan of milk on the little burner she kept in one corner of the room. She was completely calm now, and soon, he knew, would be redirecting the conversation. "And my mother's face?" he asked her. What a sad sense of pleasure it still gave him to feel the unfamiliar phrase, my mother, on his lips. How seldom in his whole life had he had a chance to use it, and when he did it was almost always in answer to a question, to say, "My mother's dead."

Gwendolyn was pretending she had not heard him. He recalled the precise and unequivocal language she had used when first he learned from her how things had really been. He had waited for her after that speech he had referred to earlier in the evening when he was talking with Benjamin Knox. He had gone up—she was not suprised to see him—and said simply, "I'm ready for the truth now. I think I already know it." And of course he did by then, but he wanted it confirmed. Yes, his mother had taken him away, that much was true, to the south of France in fact. Andreas joined her there. He should understand that the marriage between his father and mother had been a disaster. Beyond that one could only guess; his mother was not the kind of woman to discuss her private life, not even with a close friend; letters spoke of frequent illnesses, psychogenic disturbances she had assumed, reactions to unhappiness; it was not like Louisa, she had been such a healthy young girl. She was happier for a time after his birth, and then . . . unhappy again. A short visit to London coincided with one of Andreas' visits. "He fell in love with her at once. I saw that. And she with him. I was not surprised when a few months later I learned that she had taken you and was in France with him. To be entirely honest, Ernest Campion, I knew beforehand. From Andreas. They had my blessings. For what they were worth. Not much, I fear." Time passed there in the south, idyllically one hoped, one was certain.

There were great threats and complications, from the Campions, held off, at a distance, but eventually to be reckoned with. "Above all they hoped still to make it impossible for your mother and Andreas to marry. A friend at last persuaded her to make, for her part, one last conciliatory effort, one more personal appeal, before she and Andreas were forced into a long legal struggle. This was a mistake. It gave them the scent. I was that friend. Soon the pursuing figures of Nathalie and your father were in London, setting in motion that vast maneuver. I knew this because they called on me, descended upon me repeatedly, forcing me to become a kind of intermediary. They wished only to make a clean, an amicable settlement of matters, they insisted; there had been enough struggle, they saw that now; and a fair arrangement about the child. You. I myself did not know what to think. Louisa concluded at last that she should meet with them and the lawyers. If they were telling the truth, all might yet be well. Of course she did not bring you to London with her because she mistrusted them—how well she knew them. The date was agreed upon. This was the key part of the ruse because somehow they had learned where you were. When she got as far as Paris she had an instinct and turned back. She also sent a wire to Andreas, who had gone to Germany for a week. The two trains, the one bearing her back as she thought to you and to Andreas, and the one bearing you towards London, must have passed each other at some point. She found you gone and raced back towards London in a frenzy. She refused to let Andreas go with her. She feared a meeting between him and your father. With good reason. Your father was past reason. The owner outraged." All of this Mrs. Dartley had said coldly, directing her contemptuous gaze upon him. Then she said, "It was after they made it perfectly clear to her how helpless she was—your aunt's phrase was 'You will never set eyes on your son again'—that your mother killed herself in one of my guest rooms."

Killed herself? And when Gwendolyn Dartley saw that he really had not known this, when she believed him as he stammered out, half unconscious from the shock, that he had always been told that it was his mother's heart, a weak one, they told him with heavy irony, that had suffered a sudden attack there in London, then she began to soften towards him. "Oh it was ambiguous I grant you, but I have never been in doubt about it. It was one way of opposing tyranny. It wouldn't have been mine of course. I do not think your mother consciously resolved to kill herself. Nor do I think she simply made a mistake in the dosage. I believe that at that moment she wanted to die, that she felt too unhappy to go on living, and that this wish unconsciously expressed itself when she took more of the capsules than was usual. And in her state of acute nervous distress . . . the poor tired body . . . the three sleepless nights beforehand. Call it suicide. Call it an accident. Call it murder. It was all of those things. The half-finished letter to Andreas on the writing desk . . . I did not read this of course . . . later all he would say was that it was the letter of a woman whose light of being was flickering out."

"And my mother's face?" Ernest persisted now.

But again she ignored him. Artfully she returned to what had long been clear. "Yes, a jealous God. Nathalie had certainly taught him the pleasures of being worshiped. But there was more to it than that. All the variety of life that was not the self, all this was, somehow, anathema to him, a profusion of rival images. Today the terms would be clinical I have no doubt. He was even jealous of you, though this he disguised by competing for your exclusive love. What he could not possess or command wholly he wanted to destroy. Nature did not intend your father to be this way, I am sure. He had done something terrible to himself at some point. Made some fatal denial of a part of himself perhaps? Do you know what else it was she was fleeing from when she finally left, not just this atmosphere of tyranny—it was their coldness really, his and Nathalie's, their lowness of spirits, the terrible dwindling away of their energies. It could not have been just anyone she fled to, of course. It had to be Andreas, or a man like him. Someone with some of the old instincts left in him, someone in whom they had not all dried up in the name of money or power."

"Gwendolyn," he said firmly, "I've asked you about my mother's face."

She banged some mugs together. "Oh Ernest, why do you torture yourself in this absurd fashion? And why do I let you?" Yet he saw that she understood that, however painful, it was after all his past, that he had been denied it and had a right to it and could claim it only through her. "Yes. Well then. Her face, that evening in my living room. How did I start on faces? Well. Very very white—she was always pale of course—but this was really whiteness, and the eyes kept getting larger, brownish green, with the green taking over, like a fire, like a fire burning deep in the earth, far underground, not to be put out, ever, at the very center of things."

She moved rapidly then to the saucepan where the milk was about to boil over. "It's time for an Auld Man's Milk," she observed. "Or rather, in this case, an old woman's." It was made from Bob's recipe, and it was he who had made up the name, mockingly, in the last months of his illness. She lifted the cognac and poured two large mugs half full with it, then added the steaming milk and held out one of the mugs to him. He took it and got up to turn off the electric coil, which, as usual, she had forgotten to do. Both made efforts through all this not to look directly at each other. There had been something disturbing in the extreme in what she had just said about his mother's face; *their* faces she had been able to make interpretive judgments about, statements, impassioned perhaps, but clear and rational and comprehensible; but about his mother, only those images. Well, perhaps it was wiser to think no more about it. Facts, even painful ones, were easier to handle than poetic truth. The consequences of that meeting in Gwendolyn's London living room he knew. Later that night the woman Louisa, his mother, had begun a letter to Andreas but had never finished it, had then spent an hour or so with Gwendolyn, listening without hope to the battle plans Gwendolyn was drawing up, had thanked her, kissed her good night, gone then upstairs, and there in the guest room made an end. It was in that room the next night that he had been allowed to see her, coldly laid out, the tidied corpse—was it she?—and at that he had been allowed only because Gwendolyn Dartley had threatened them if they refused with the one thing they now feared, an enormous and public scandal.

Campion drank, deciding to let it all drop. It had been such a long time ago, that brutal wrenching of the order of things. Nothing to be done now. The bright cognac flavor and the soothing milk were beginning to work, easing him into the present. He and Gwendolyn were looking at each other again.

Greedily, she had consumed most of her drink. "I suppose you'll want another one?" he said. She nodded—it was her nightly medicine for sleep—and he moved to put the pan on again. "You still haven't explained to me why you've agreed to this television thing. I don't think Knox can be trusted."

"One can never be sure. Besides, I don't particularly have to trust him, do I?"

"If you think he'll let you say whatever it is you want to say you're fooling yourself."

"But I've no idea of what I want to say."

"Whatever it turns out to be he'll edit it to pieces. You can be sure you won't recognize it afterwards."

"But my dear Ernest, it's to go out direct. The interview part. He has decided to do that part 'live.' That's the term he used. The rest I have no control over anyway."

"Exactly the point. Are you aware of the fact that he can turn the whole thing into a sort of anatomy lesson if he chooses?"

She shrugged indifferently. Then she said, "You think Mr. Knox cleverer than I? Well, we shall see. Besides, I've another reason for doing the program. He's going to pay me a great deal of money."

"He's what?"

"Yes. I thought you'd agree that it was nice of him."

Campion looked disgusted. "Why do you want to take his money?"

"Why, Ernest? Why? You ought to know that. So that I can keep this place going, so that we can live here a while longer."

Campion could never understand why her ever-sinking resources were a cause of guilt in him. Certainly he was costing her nothing; he could live well enough on what he earned. It would be a good thing in many ways in fact if her establishment were to come to an end, and yet he knew that she did not yet want it to, and with a part of himself he did not want it to either. He remembered suddenly that portrait of Levin which was stored in Paris, the one canvas she had hung on to.

"What about the Picasso?" he asked.

"It's already gone," she said.

"What? When?"

"About six months ago."

He said angrily, "Well, my God, why don't we start making some economies? Wines. That's the place to start. Let's drink Swiss wines. What difference would it make? You yourself hardly touch these vintage beauties you're so keen on serving up."

"That's true," she said. "But my abstinence is irrelevant. There was a time when good wine mattered to me. It's nice to know it's there."

"Nice to know it's there," he repeated. "A childish luxury!"

"Now, now; stop it. Marshall likes it so much. And Faustine. And so, for that matter, do you."

"Not to the point of bankruptcy!"

"Ernest, the villa is paid for through the end of the year, which you know. Perhaps I should tell you something you don't know, that as things stand now we may just be able to live for another six months." She waited for his reaction.

He looked at her, then rapidly made her another cognac-milk and poured a large portion of plain cognac into his own mug. "You might have told me sooner," he said then.

"I might have, but what was the point? Besides, this extremity is a new development. Several little projects of mine consumed far more than I expected them to. But you do see that there's no sense in making ridiculous economies, not having nice wines to offer one's guests and that sort of thing, in the meantime, don't you? The most difference it could make would be a matter of a few weeks."

He did not ask her which little projects had cost her so much. There were so many it might have been. Instead he said, "I didn't know these television people paid for an interview. I thought one did it for publicity."

"Oh they don't usually," she said. "Although they will if you are in a position to name a price, if for example you've just been involved in some tawdry scandal or other and are really interesting. Not if you are simply in yourself, as I am, a *personage*. I have my own methods, however. I blackmailed Mr. Knox."

"That's disgusting."

"I suppose so."

"How did you do it?"

She snickered. "All I did was mention something about the nutritive value of chocolate. It was very simple. *My* research methods are quite good too. And I had a bit of luck. I'm not sure I'd have done it if he hadn't said what he did to you. But maybe I would have anyway. It was such a good opportunity. I'm not even going to tell you what it's about. I must keep my part of the bargain; good blackmailers do, I'm told. He'll forgive me. Just as I've already forgiven him for his reference to *A Sunken Journey* and as I hope you've forgiven him. Oh Ernest, it's not going to last long here, I've faced that at last, you see. Even with this money it's just a reprieve. I'll end as I began, poor but honest. But with no country to call my own. A pity in a way that the Chevalier was so clever about everyone's money but his own. A bad Jew, that's what came of him assimilating to so great a degree I fear."

"It's ridiculous of you to try to put the blame on Levin," Campion said. "I know what you've been doing with the money he left you. And you had years to work away at it before I came along."

"Never mind. The point is I'm not being a fool. I've kept enough to have a decent little flat someplace when everything goes. I'll miss all this. I hated it at first. Being off from everything. But now I'm used to it, my own little kingdom, as it were. Why do you think I'm not going to prevent Lily from leaving?"

"Is she leaving?"

"Yes. She told me tonight. I've been very upset about it. Some London kin."

"Has she said why?"

Gwendolyn Dartley shook her head. "Not the real reasons. If indeed they are clear to her. My guess is that she wishes she had not left Budapest at all, that she thought there would soon be a liberation and she could return. Now that she is out and reads the newspapers and sees how little interest there is she has lost this hope. I blame myself for urging her to come here. But when I learned about her family . . . Yes, well, enough of that. I do not urge her to stay now because I know things cannot last here. She'll be miserable among the English, she always was. But there I can take care of her, if need be. One advantage of not being able to get money out of England is that I still have some money somewhere. The one person I don't worry about in the least in all this is Faustine. She can take care of herself."

"Or Mr. George Bingham can take care of her," he said.

She looked at him steadily. "I didn't know you were so interested in Faustine."

"Her name is Sylvia," he said. "I wish you'd use it. And I didn't know it either. I'm sure it's only temporary."

"Are you? Well, we shall see." She walked to the great guild table on the dais, sat down heavily in the chair, raised her mug towards him and took a long drink. Then she startled him by saying, "Your father, your mother, she was, oh somehow completely his opposite, which was what both drew and enraged him. He could break her of course, as it turned out through you—I doubt that otherwise he could have—but he could never change her, which was what he always wanted to do, long before Andreas."

Out of the mellowness of the drink which had been enveloping him Campion was suddenly painfully alert. If she were now to turn that amber to the light, ever so slightly . . . He waited. If, in the hands of Gwendolyn Dartley . . . "Do you know, Ernest, it occurs to me only now that from the very beginning what your poor father was trying to do was *to unsay her*."

Louisa, his father had said, even he, with his last articulate breath. And that was it. She had once been, she had died in despair, but she could never be unsaid. On the contrary. A feeling not unlike happiness rose in Campion's breast.

He said, "But he didn't manage to, did he?"

Gwendolyn Dartley did not answer. She came slowly down towards him, looking suddenly very old and crumpled in and tired in a way he had never seen her look before, like one who had endured much and would endure things yet to come. She laid a hand on his shoulder and leaning heavily on him walked him towards the door. Both knew that the amber had been laid aside forever. "Ah sleep, it is a blessed thing," Gwendolyn uttered, in a sighing voice. Then, as if by some spiritual sleight of hand, she changed. "How does it go from there? Who is it, anyway? Shakespeare, Coleridge, Keats—I always mix them up. About sleep, I mean. They all said so many interesting things about it. Insomniacs, I suppose. Like you. Like me. Like other watchers in the night."

She laughed then. Their lips met lightly in a good-night kiss.

"Oh by the way," he said with his hand on the door, "it seems I'm in love with Sylvia. At least I suppose that's as good a way of describing it as any."

"Of course you are, my dear, and it should prove to be most interesting indeed. For everyone."

Sixteen

Mrs. Dartley had been right about the weather. It did change, abruptly. Higher up in the mountains the heavy snows began, and the Villa Kilchberg itself was enveloped in a perpetual damp swirl of mist. Campion, commuting on certain days to his classes in Zürich—where the busy commercial rhythms of the city were unchanged—and climbing on other days with Sylvia up the piny paths to where they sometimes had a view of the ever-changing and mysterious waters of Lucerne and of the snow fields and peaks beyond, noted the difference that place can make in one's attitude toward the seasons. He preferred the upper reaches. There one knew unquestionably that the solstice of winter was coming. There there were no deceptions. Yet, paradoxically, he wondered at the same time if he were too old to take up skiing again.

Sylvia these days, after the months during which she had alternated between iron clockings of the self and long flights into sleep, was waking early, long before the rest of the household, shivering in the cold, struggling to get the fire going in her room, giving up usually and sitting encased in sweaters before her desk. She was entranced by the strange new book she was writing; reading parts of it over later in the day she often wondered who had written it. Herself of course, but no longer the narrow self of personality, the mere and insubstantial *I*. Once she wrote on the bottom of a page, without being aware of what she was doing, these words: Proteus Unbound.

Three things had altered the general atmosphere at Kilchberg since the night when Benjamin Knox had come to dinner. One was the weather, another was Mrs. Dartley's increasing anxiety about news from Budapest, and the last was Knox himself. Having departed for the better part of a month he had now returned and was frequently on the premises, asking questions and moving furniture about, conferring with technicians about where to install cameras, and with Ralph Bledder, who seemed to have a way of appearing quite suddenly when he was wanted, about more obscure matters. The animus between Campion and himself if it had not actually been conquered had at least gone underground; they were scrupulously polite with each other. The struggle Knox felt himself in with Mrs. Dartley remained, beneath great streams of speech, a silent one, and he had succeeded in not having to have much to do with Sylvia, the one person at the villa who really made him feel uncomfortable and whom he therefore disliked. He would never forgive her for having corrected him about the violin-cello business.

She, however, had been watching, fascinated in spite of herself, the day he had an enormous television set installed in the sitting room in order to accustom Mrs. Dartley to what he referred to as "the medium." There had been some sort of technical difficulties while they were putting it in working order, and for a time the most hideous and frightening shapes had been unleashed on that screen: black and silver flashings of violent, unidentifiable shapes, forms that were surely never human, coursed and chased and careened at incredible speeds across it, accompanied by equally frightening and unidentifiable sounds, accusatory moans and shrieks—all of which Knox had explained as "interference from a wandering electromagnetic field." It would soon be remedied, he assured them; and it was, she discovered later, but at the time she had not waited to see.

If the most amazing thing to Sylvia in what was happening to her was how out of doing nothing, out of finally surrendering the will, the act of creation had at last begun again, the next to the most amazing was the amount of energy with which her still secret early morning hours of work left her for the rest of the day. Gone entirely was the dreadful lassitude that had made the smallest task a loathsome burden. It disgusted her to remember the wasted months, particularly the self-incarceration since coming to Kilchberg. Now she wanted to see, to touch everything around her. Even taking her shoes to a cobbler in Dreilindenegg, the nearby village, was something that gave her pleasure, especially if she could find an excuse for staying in the shop for a time to watch him work. She lingered in bakeries, inhaling their fragrance, watching the shaping of bread doughs, the structuring of beautiful pastries. She visited the workroom behind a shop that sold carved wooden objects to tourists, saw how the carver, a man of her own age, brought forth birds and animals and men and women and children. She was drawn to all who mended or created things, who with their hands gave form, even the simplest, the humblest forms. She also began to look at faces unguardedly again, seeing in them nothing to fear, feeling in her self nothing to hide. It seemed to her that for so long she had been running in a dark and spaceless landscape that had no beginning or end. Now she was returned to the world of dear, familiar forms; illusory and impermanent they might be, like that world itself suspended in a void of emptiness, but she was prepared to honor them. She felt a new and deep connection between herself and nature, even if, as both Lily and Anton in their different ways had suggested, it was not very trustworthy, and even if, perversely, at the very time of year when nature itself seemed to decree the declining of the world. No matter; she would pay her debt to the world by watching over it during the time of darkness. The light of the year would spring forth again.

What exact role Ernest Campion played in the new rhythm of her life she did not feel pressed to consider. They were often together, he an agreeable companion, full of easy speech and revelations modestly made. It astonished her that so serious a man, a man whose name, as Mrs. Dartley liked frequently to point out, suited him so well, should also turn out to have such a capacity for pleasure. Several times a week now they drove into Zürich for the evening, or met there in the late afternoon. They met sometimes in the Lindenhof, from where they could look down over the roofs of the old city onto the Limmat flowing through the center of town, and sometimes by the Fraumünster, watched over not by gargoyles but by the four beautiful leaping fish that guard its clock tower. If the weather was not too bad they walked along the Limmat Quai or along the gardenlike shores of the lake, or bought bread and, standing usually by the Zunfthaus zur Meise, fed the gulls, the Möwen, who, sweeping towards them in a happy frenzy, would, with confident raised wings and thrown-back beautiful heads, catch their offerings in midair. Afterwards they dined, sometimes in a small tavern behind the Grossmünster that hourly was shaken by the male-toned ringing of its bells, the higher pealings of the Fraumünster coming to them from across the river, and sometimes in the Zum Rüden or the Zimmerleute, those *Zunfthäuser* from out whose windows they could look across to the other bank and see the old city rising towards the Lindenhof. And sometimes they would dine greatly, at the Kronenhalle, Sylvia never failing to tip a nod to the drawing of Joyce as they passed it, or once they were seated—upstairs, beneath the water lilies of Monet —to call for fat Molly the cat, who consented to sleep beside her,

opening an experienced eye as each course was served and appearing to sniff to see if all was well with the Margaux which Ernest
favored. Later they often crossed the river again and climbed the
streets in the neighborhood of the Peterskirche until they found a
likely place for a nightcap.

It was in one of those streets in a jewelry shop window—*eigene
Werkstätte* the sign said—that they saw what at first, but only at
first, struck Sylvia as amusing. There, in the one small window of
that old house, a number of tangerines had been placed in pat-
terned intervals on a simple black jeweler's cloth, and scattered
about among them were loose emeralds and diamonds cut to such
uncommon brilliance that the eye was forced to see what was truly
there. But that was not all. Stuck into two of the fruits were two
of the most delicate, jeweled pins, the one a floral burst of diamonds and emeralds, the other of diamonds only, mysterious, abstract, hard to give name to, like a snowflake perhaps, or an expanding crystal, something at any rate that suggested the most
exquisitely strict and formal yet free and mobile patterns of nature.
What, she had thought, must it have been like for the Incas, trying
to explain to the moist-lipped Spaniards before they went down
beneath their swords? There in that window, she knew, was something quite different from either power or the vulgar commercial
customs, the standardized carbon on every bride's finger, with
which until then she had associated such jewels. She was fascinated, and three different times returned alone to stare in that
window, which was never easy to find. If she set out directly for
it, it escaped her, but if she began by the Fraumünster and simply
followed the winding, circling streets up toward the Peterskirche,
eventually, as if by magic, it would appear. At last she understood
what it was that made the difference, why for the first time in her
life she had seen the beauty of precious stones, what it was about
those emeralds and diamonds, those rocks now glittering in the
hard but beautiful substance of their own inner truth. It was that
the human imagination had been at work on them, and without in
the least betraying their nature. On the contrary, here nature and
art had blended. Or rather, here nature was transformed by art
into the beauty that lay hidden within it; here too the complex
truth of its inner structure was faithfully revealed. Nature became
its highest self, art, but remained . . . nature.

At the Villa Kilchberg no day passed now, however inclement

the weather, when at some point Sylvia did not feel impelled toward the out-of-doors. These were the times of the long walks, the
wanderings through the mist-veiled forest, which so amused or
puzzled the other guests at Kilchberg. Except for Ernest, who
liked, when he could, to go along with her. Alone she frequently
lost her way, but was never frightened. Here was a different
world, it was true, ambiguous and mysterious, but not, she felt,
particularly unfriendly. The strange sounds that underlay the apparent silence when she sat very still to listen, the prolific shadows
in among the trees—how easy it was then to understand the old
stories about the spirits and minor deities that inhabit such places.
They were harmless enough so long as one did not deny their
existence—or power. Perhaps that was why she did not feel they
were hostile towards her, but on the contrary seemed often to be
calling and beckoning to her as one of themselves. It was only
when she was again safely down from the high forest that she was
sometimes frightened at having been alone up there. Yet even in
the midst of her first great relief at feeling herself once more
breathing the air of a more prudent altitude she knew that she
would go back up again the next day.

This day she had wandered even higher than usual and had
delayed a long time about turning back. Yet somehow the charms
of the place had refused to reveal themselves to her, and the more
she sought them the more they eluded her. Something had clearly
gone wrong with the magic. When at last she started down it was
with a feeling of extraordinary reluctance. She chose paths at
random and where it was possible followed no path at all, almost as
though she were deliberately trying to lose her way. But no matter
what she did, she was being led steadily, efficiently down. For the
first time the spirits of the place seemed to be rejecting her, driving her out. There was nothing for her to do for the moment but
obey.

Reaching the gardens of the villa she lingered among the last of
the roses, the few that had budded only in time to die stiff and half
formed on the cold stem and the even fewer which, having somehow attained a full blooming, were now wearily spread open to the
blast, their petals in a last trembling. The oldest poets were right,
she decided, looking at them; autumn after all was the saddest
season, full of such painful reminders of a golden time. The absolute sleep of winter was perhaps preferable; it smoothed over loss

and pain and deterioration; it gave rest, the end of struggle. She turned towards the house and was walking slowly towards it through the rainy darkness when she heard the Bach. It was clearly not Anton Hrubick at the piano but someone who had once been quite good but no longer played very often. It was not so much the occasional false note as a hesitancy of rhythm, a brokenness of span. If Bach was architecture then this was Bach with certain arches missing. It sounded like a ruin. Perhaps it would stop. Perhaps he would go away, St. George. Sylvia leaned against a tree, mournfully, her head bent forward from the slender neck, her mouth half opened in a silent cry of pain. *Perhaps he would go away.*

Seventeen

George Bingham did not look particularly American, which was very useful to him in his profession, at least as useful as his remarkable command of the tongues of Europe. On his mother's side there was a curiously mixed lineage, Prussian, Greek, and a bit of unadmitted-to Venetian; on his father's the usual blend that is called, for lack of a more precise term, Anglo-Saxon. Bingham's eyes were a dark golden brown, his complexion smooth and healthily ruddy around the cheekbones, his brow both high and broad, and his hair, though graying a little, inclined to the tight curls with which Praxiteles endowed his youths. Altogether it was a strong face—and one would think memorable. But the essential disguises, he had once told Sylvia when she raised this question, were spiritual ones. And to that there was hardly an answer. One would also think that his looking well-born would be a handicap, considering that at times he needed to pass himself off as a worker; even a change of clothing or speech could hardly be expected to disguise this. It was a tribute to his great gifts of adaptability, of assuming magical forms, that even here he had succeeded. But as for nationality, it would not be easy to place him. With a change of costume, speech, manner, he could easily become a Latin American businessman in Leipzig, an Austrian intellectual in Warsaw, an Italian musicologist in Prague, and all manner of Anglo-Saxons and

Teutons. And in the distance behind all these figures it was possible to discern still another, far older figure—a lapse in history or in the genes?—someone who in the modern sense had no nationality at all, someone set wandering long ago.

A few minutes before, he had come into the music room. He had a light, tennis player's way of walking. The room was large, and nearly empty of furniture: only the piano, a bench, and with its back to these a long, high-backed couch which faced an unlighted fireplace. His fingers had moved with depressing uncertainty over the keys. Yet he had persisted. Now he stopped, looked toward the door, and waited. She was moving slowly toward him along the corridor. When she finally appeared, bedraggled and damp, he stood up.

She did not speak. Still looking at him, she took off the raincoat and threw it on the back of the couch. He too was silent, patiently self-possessed yet not quite hiding his eagerness. She said then, "Go away. Please go away."

He moved a little towards her, stopped. "Not a very friendly welcome," he said.

"I'm sorry."

"So am I. There's a Monteverdi cycle in Lucerne. I thought you might like to go."

"You were mistaken."

"I'm disappointed. But never mind. I've got a few free days anyway. I'll forego Monteverdi for you."

"I don't want you here."

"I've already been invited."

"You haven't been."

"Oh yes I have." He was adopting the offhand manner she knew so well. "Mrs. Dartley. I had a glass of sherry with her. Two or three hours ago. When I first arrived. While you were off on your mysterious jaunt. You've picked up some new habits, I guess. Somehow I'd thought you might be expecting me."

"That's over with." She turned her back to him and walked towards the windows. "I can't imagine why she invited you again. She doesn't like you."

"Doesn't she?" He followed her. "She disguises it awfully well."

"What does that prove? We all disguise things well. Or badly. Does that fact change anything? God, if she only knew what you are."

"What am I?"

"Go away."

His tone changed. "Don't be unkind. Turn around. Look at me."

"If she only knew," she repeated.

He turned her slightly, forcing her to look at him. Both of their faces were reflected in the window. No longer mist but rain was hitting against it. He said slowly, carefully, as though to remind her, "I'm just a salesman."

If this was love, what she felt for him, then she could almost wish to be free of love forever. Yet soon, she knew, there would again be nothing but her self, his self, and that shared and secret burden that marked them off from others. She felt the last phase of a terrible struggle had begun, but that the terms of that struggle had changed utterly since his last visit. "You told me once your life was in my hands," she said now. "In Munich, during the snowstorm. Remember? A terrible thing to say, to do. Haven't you understood that this was what I ran from finally? And every time you come back you try to thrust it upon me again."

"Nonsense," he said, but his face was pale.

"Not nonsense. I can't bear it. Someone else, perhaps. Not me. I've work to do. You chose the wrong woman. I beg you to leave. The only thing you've accomplished with me is to make me your fellow conspirator, to render me deaf, dumb, and blind to everything in the world except *your* destiny, a destiny I've no control over, really—none."

"Walking in the mountains does strange things to you."

"Don't you understand? I can't save you."

"Will you calm down? I never asked you to save me."

"Didn't you? I think so. Didn't you long to give up a little of your aloneness, your precious individuality, your remorseless, murderous code?"

He took one step and covered her mouth with his hand. Then he seized her by the waist, pressed his face painfully against her neck and collarbone, lifted his head and kissed her. But she spun and dodged out of his arms, and he let her go. They were both breathing heavily. Neither moved now. She said slowly, sadly, "And that doesn't work either. Not for you. Leave me alone. I beg you. Let's say I've failed and leave it at that. Say that I did want to save you and that I failed. It was a very unequal struggle from the beginning. I was poorly matched against a rival who was far more powerful than I could ever hope to be, an enemy who already meant everything to you."

"My work," he began, but she interrupted with a bitter laugh. Never had his incredible aliveness struck her with more force than at that moment, and because it did pity ran sharply through her when she had least expected it. The old fatality of their relationship was asserting itself. She struck out against it, recklessly. "Your *work?* That? Oh that's despicable enough, I grant you, but that's not what I meant by enemy. Why even the Russians aren't my enemy. Nor yours. They're just a convenience. The enemy's death, you poor fool."

There was a small sound in the room. Both turned towards the door, which Posy, traversing on tiptoe the distance between it and the couch, had almost reached. How was it possible that neither of them, with their extraordinarily developed senses, had until then been aware of her presence? Clad in purple leotards, she stood there now looking at them with frightened eyes, her mouth moving but no sounds coming from it. Instinctively Sylvia moved closer to George Bingham, so that their two bodies were touching. Then Posy managed, "Oh I'm sorry, sorry, sorry," and she backed away from them into the dark corridor. Just then there was the familiar sound of a heavy car pulling up before the house. Campion had arrived in Mrs. Dartley's old Phantom II.

Eighteen

For the last ten minutes Anton had even given up humming that gross imitation of *The Ride of the Valkyries* and, like Marshall, was concentrating on keeping his seat in the swaying vehicle. "I was looking at those black swans and somehow lost track of the time," Marshall had explained, arriving half an hour late at the Saint Gotthard Café. Black swans, black swans—what went on in that young man's head? Spoiled, drifting . . . a twenty-one-year-old male, old enough to be a father, or to have conquered half the world, daydreaming along the Limmat Quai, standing in the rain

watching those hideous swans while the minutes passed. For
Campion a day of vexation had culminated in a sudden impending
sense of disaster just as he had turned into the café where they
were all to meet; this had been followed rapidly by a feeling of
urgency about getting back to Kilchberg. And then the boy had
been late. Staring at swans! It was offensive, and Campion had
made no effort to disguise his anger. All those crucial minutes lost.
But why did they seem to him so crucial? He did not know;
nevertheless, he had driven the twenty-five kilometers between
Zürich and Kilchberg with incredible recklessness, swinging the
Rolls past every vehicle that got in his way, slowing down only
now as he turned past Dreilindenegg into the rutted private road
that after another few kilometers would end at the door of the
villa. Anton sighed elaborately.

And what was the difference between Marshall and himself?
This was the point, he now recognized, this was why he had
reacted so violently. What was he doing, at his age, heeling around
after Gwendolyn Dartley, a sort of ludicrous first minister of her
domain? What was he doing patiently trying to put together another man's work, a dead man's work, and two times a week going
into Zürich to run errands and to tutor at a girls' finishing school?
He had felt an extreme revulsion that morning as he mounted the
steps of the academy where he would spend the day taking half a
dozen or so American *jeunes filles* (who no doubt had upset their
distant and rich parents by resolving to seek admission into a university—normally one did not expect that to result from a stay at
such a school) through the paces of mathematics and physics. The
Phantom II bounced heavily and Anton groaned. *Ubi sunt* someone had written on the blackboard that morning. Now which of
those girls was either so witty or so despairing? Campion had no
idea. He had felt very odd when he turned his back to erase it.
Later he had considered sadly that the *ubi sunt* of his life was no
crouching tiger ready to spring at his throat and fling him into
eternal damnation—that was over with—but only a slow dwindling away. Between the pursuit of power and the mastery that it
presumably gave one over experience, over one's mortal destiny—
an absolute mastery which Campion could not but regard in the
light of his own history as totally deceptive—and the passive
submission to experience there ought somewhere to be other
choices. In the last few weeks he had come to believe there were.

But in this century? Out the car windows he saws the undulating, damp darkness around them, a few leaves caught meaninglessly in the headlights. He had the most fatal sense of the world dying. It was only the time of year, surely; autumn had been making people feel this way for a number of centuries, possibly since before there was even language for expressing it. Or was that so? Perhaps it was only after the poets began to do their work. No matter; a great sad emptiness filled Campion. He had been silent for the whole drive. Now he began to feel ashamed of this and of his treatment of Marshall. He said, "Miserable time of year, isn't it?"

Marshall, beside him, pulled out of his slumped tense posture, muttered agreement eagerly. A few seconds passed and then Anton's voice from the back seat began, a slow deep rumble, emerging at last into syllables:

> *Wer jetzt kein Haus hat, baut sich keines mehr.*
> *Wer jetzt allein ist, wird es lange bleiben,*
> *wird wachen, lesen, lange Briefe schreiben*
> *und wird in den Alleen hin und her*
> *unruhig wandern, wenn die Blätter treiben.*

Silence fell on them again. Marshall had not understood the German words, and Campion had understood them only too well. He repeated a few phrases to himself. Anton's voice had for once not been mocking. Perhaps through that darkness he was remembering the lost towers of Prague, or perhaps for an instant during that drive he had been turning the corner of a familiar street on an October night that no longer existed, seeing a familiar doorway, almost home. For the first time it struck Campion that Anton was old as well as, like himself, homeless. *Wer jetzt kein Haus hat . . .* But after all there was a house, Gwendolyn's, only temporary of course and not his own, but still, it was there, better than none; perhaps that was true for all of them. Who now is alone will long be so . . . restlessly wandering the barren paths . . . Suddenly Campion admitted to himself how fervently he hoped this might not be so. He thought of Sylvia, and a surge of feeling, compounded both of excitement and content, raced through him. Warmth, contact with another human being, love—how much after all these things mattered. Love was no general cure; that was another fallacy of a century which rocked uneasily between faiths. It was foolish as well as unfair to expect love to bear the weight of the world's woes and failures or even of one's own; it could not change these things, but it might mitigate them a little. It could not take the place of achievement, but its existence could matter. How remarkably his mood had changed. He drove the car lightly, easily now. They came around the last turning and there was the house, massive, solid, real, lights shining forth from it.

Campion pulled the car up by the door, reached for the packet of mail he had put in the front compartment, stuck it in his leather portfolio. He had decided to garage the car after dinner and was about to tell his companions this when another idea occurred to him. "Why don't you put the car away?" he said to Marshall. He had already resolved to apologize for his earlier harshness, and this indirect way was much easier for both of them. Campion knew of Marshall's secret passion for the Phantom II, one he could never indulge because of Gwendolyn's fixed notion that no one but herself and Campion should ever sit at its wheel. The car dated from the days of the Chevalier Levin; it had miraculously borne her and Dragan along the difficult roads of Serbia, Croatia, Macedonia, Dalmatia; they had dashed in it to the relative safety of France when the war first began; later a friend had hidden it in a barn in Normandy when they made their crossing to England, and it had survived the war to be triumphantly reclaimed by her on her return. It meant a very great deal to Gwendolyn Dartley.

Nineteen

Campion entered the house just in time to see Mrs. Dartley descending the staircase with a half-grown and very unruly-looking cat clinging defiantly to her shoulders. She paused for full effect and rested one arm gracefully against the bannister. "Well now what are you up to?" he asked.

"Surely you mean what is this cat up to. How it does purr. Almost as though it's having a sexual frenzy of some sort. Do you think it is?"

He could not keep from smiling. "Where did it come from?" he asked. There were no pets kept at the Villa Kilchberg other than Posy and Marshall and down in the pool that absurd fish which by now he supposed had gone to sleep for the winter—if that was what fish did in the winter.

"I haven't the faintest idea. It was sitting at the top of the stairs like a watch-cat, surveying things in a most calm and deliberate manner. I stooped to pet it and it sprang at me as though it were going to rend me. Instead it settled down and became quite amorous. Ah, sweet kitty." The animal had begun to rub its chin along hers. "I must find a mirror. I imagine the decorative effect is quite striking."

"Oh it is," Campion said. He was losing interest. "Are you coming down or not? I've got some letters for you." Mrs. Dartley kept a postbox in Zürich under a pseudonym, and one of his tasks was to collect the mail from it. She insisted that many of her correspondents use the Zürich box, on the theory that there was much less chance of mail being tampered with if it never left the post office at all. This made no sense to Campion. He could not imagine how deliveries to the villa could possibly be tampered with unless the postman himself—an elderly *Swiss* postman—had been subverted, and this was something he simply found impossible to imagine. Besides, there was nothing that could really be called secret in the information she received from so many parts of the world, however strange or startling the uses she made of it might sometimes be. Still, he had never been able to dissuade her from these elaborate measures, which were perhaps the result of the years with Dragan, when she had either been, or thought she had been, surrounded by spies, informers, agents, and counteragents of provocation.

"Here," he said, taking the packet of letters out of the portfolio. He was getting quite impatient. He wanted a drink and he wanted to find Sylvia, not necessarily in that order. "I'll put them on the table for you." He spun swiftly on his heel to the right and his extended fist made immediate and jarring contact with a resilient object that gasped and went "oooouff." The object was the solar plexus of Posy, who with lowered head had come out of the corridor to the right of Campion and was trying to cross behind him to the opposite wing, and whom he had just sent spinning. "Oh good Lord, I'm terribly sorry. I had no idea—are you all right? You'd better sit down. Now take it easy." Bent over, her hands to her middle, Posy was wobbling. Campion caught at her and half carried, half propelled her to the only chair in the entrance hall.

"Ernest," Mrs. Dartley said, starting to come down the stairs as rapidly as she could with the cat clinging to her, "there was something I meant to tell you, something you must know."

Campion ignored her. "That's it," he said to Posy, who was letting out all sorts of pitiful gasps and choking sounds, "that's it. Lean forward. I've got you. Don't be afraid. Relax. Try to breathe slowly. Relax, I said." He was supporting her forehead against the palm of one hand while gently applying pressure between her shoulder blades. Slowly she was beginning to get control of her breath.

"My dear child, if only you had not been *creeping* it would never have happened," Mrs. Dartley said, having finally negotiated the stairs.

"Gwendolyn! For heaven's sake shut up."

"But it's perfectly true. And if you, Ernest, had not been so impatient with me." She twisted her head around so that she was staring at the cat, who returned her gaze with equal stubbornness. "Will you get down now, you obstinate, beautiful beast? Very well then. Take your chances." The mail was scattered all over the hallway and she was determined to retrieve it, but the instant she bent over, the cat began a high-pitched and ominous growling and by dint of using its claws clung more tenaciously than ever to her. Mrs. Dartley cried out and straightened up at once. She was furious now. "Who let this ugly cat into the house, anyway? Where did it come from?"

"Better now?" Campion said to Posy. She nodded and tried to speak. "No, no; quiet," he said. "That's a good girl." Her deep pallor had worried him, and he was relieved to see a little of her natural color returning. He continued to watch her face, patting her as he would a child, and now he also became aware of the fact that Sylvia had come into the hallway and was struggling either with Mrs. Dartley or the cat or both. A male figure with his back to Campion was there too, squatting on the floor, his head bent over and almost hidden by his shoulders while he gathered up the fallen letters.

The front door opened and Anton and Marshall appeared.

"What form of disaster has struck here?" Anton asked. Then, addressing the squatting figure, "Ah, my dear sir . . ."

Campion looked and saw the figure get to its feet, saw that it was George Bingham and that he was handing a neatly stacked pile of letters to Mrs. Dartley. He shoved Posy back against the chair and started forward, intending to strike him. Instead, he stopped after he had taken a few steps and said, "Will someone please get a glass of cold water? At once."

No one responded, and Sylvia, looking distressed, only moved closer to Bingham. Mrs. Dartley, with flung-out arms, said to him, "Now, if only your efficiency could extend to removing this leopard from around my neck." George Bingham smiled and strode toward the cat, lifted his hands toward it. There was the sound of a minor explosion in the room, and he sprang back. Posy yelped. "What in the name of God was that?" Mrs. Dartley said. Marshall said, "The cat spat." He was looking annoyed at everyone. "Haven't you ever heard a cat spit before, any of you? When they're really afraid it sounds like an electric light bulb being popped." He touched the animal, and at once it became mild; in another few seconds it was curling up affectionately in the crook of his arm, transformed utterly from fierce beast to household god.

"Well, thank you, Marshall," Mrs. Dartley said. She was trying to smooth down her hair. Then she began brushing at her clothes. A huge cloud of cat hair rose around her. Anton coughed. She said, "Now if we're all intact perhaps I may attend to introductions. Ernest, Anton, I believe you both know Mr. Bingham from his other visit. Now let's see. Of course. Oh Posy, how *much* better your color is." Posy's face was indeed crimson. Mrs. Dartley said, touching George Binham's sleeve, "Our young accident victim here is Miss Rosanna . . ." At that Posy began to sob. "Dear me, what is the matter with the child? Faustine, perhaps it would be better . . . would you be so kind?"

Sylvia hurried forward, but Posy only began to sob the more violently when she felt Sylvia's hands on her shoulders and heard her saying, "Everything is quite all right, Posy. I assure you it is. It was just an accident. I assure you we understand."

"Of course it was an accident," Campion said angrily. "She isn't an idiot, which is perhaps a distinction around here. You don't think she thinks that I hit her deliberately, do you?"

"Oh Ernest," Sylvia said.

Lily Halász, followed by Benjamin Knox and Ralph Bledder, came in through the front door. The hallway, though quite spacious, was beginning to look crowded. Campion muttered between clenched teeth, "Why didn't you tell me you were expecting a visitor?"

"I didn't know. Be careful."

"Then what's he doing here and what am I supposed to be careful of?"

"Please. I'll talk to you later. Trust me."

"*Trust you?*"

"Ernest, please . . . Posy is . . ." Posy was moaning quite openly and she now reached up and covered her ears with her hands.

"Posy's quite all right. There's absolutely nothing wrong with her. She's breathing perfectly well." He felt very absurd after he had said this.

Now Sylvia was getting angry. "I didn't mean that. Haven't you any sense? Don't you understand that you don't understand? Oh *please!*" She leaned over the girl. "Posy, let's go upstairs now."

But Lily Halász was walking towards George Bingham, who was standing in the middle of the room perfectly still, surrounded by all the movement. "Ah Lily," Mrs. Dartley said with relief. "You must allow me to present an old friend of Sylvia's. He'll be staying with us for a few days. A pity he didn't arrive sooner. Our Lily leaves us tomorrow. Mr. Bingham, Mrs. Halász."

Lily extended her hand, which George Bingham took with grave courtesy. She was looking at him expectantly. She said, "But surely we have met before."

"To my regret, no," he answered.

"Oh, but I'm sure of it. In Budapest. At a sort of party my son gave."

He shook his head. "I'm sorry. I've never been to Budapest."

There was a silence while Lily Halász continued to look at him, her violet eyes flickering, her mouth turned slightly down. Then slowly she withdrew her hand, which he still held, smiled, laughed. "Very silly of me. Of course we haven't met. I'm mistaken. I beg your pardon. It is so easy to get confused at my age."

"Not at all," he replied. "You must tell me about Budapest. I've always wanted to visit there. But AMPERE executives aren't particularly welcome in Budapest these days, I'm afraid."

Campion observed Anton pursing his lips to whistle, then evidently change his mind.

"Oh well, these days," Lily said, turning from him to look towards Sylvia. "You're not missing so very much. Budapest is a sad city."

Mrs. Dartley said, "Well. Well. I must keep my promise to you, Mr. Knox. My room. Shall we say in ten minutes? Now that we are all here—though why we *should* all be here in this depressing hallway I do not know—I suggest that we . . . disperse."

Posy rose and Sylvia, an arm about her shoulders, started up the stairs with her. George Bingham followed them with his eyes. Mrs. Dartley started up too. Then Campion said in a loud voice, "Oh Gwendolyn, just a minute. Would you mind one guest more? I had a cable in Zürich today, from Elsie. She arrives tomorrow."

Mrs. Dartley turned her head back but continued climbing the stairs. "You need not ask that, Ernest. You know that Miss Crown is always welcome here. Or indeed anyone else who is dear to you. It has been far too long since she has been with us. What is the occasion?"

"I've no idea." He stared hard at Sylvia, who had paused on the staircase and was looking down at him. Until that very moment he had intended to take a room for Elsie in Zürich.

Benjamin Knox bounded up the stairs after Mrs. Dartley and said to her in a voice he was careful that no one else should overhear, "Who did you say was coming?"

"You are irrepressibly curious, Mr. Knox," she said. "A young woman whose name is Crown, Elsie Crown. If that means anything to you."

Benjamin Knox did not reply.

Twenty

Posy was rapidly recovering from that primal scene she had witnessed in the music room. She had made her explanations amidst subsiding sobs, amidst brief but soothing comments from Sylvia, who had at last said, "Now please. Stop sniffling and chattering

your teeth at me. There's really no need for you to explain anything. Please." She had tride to obey, had let herself be wrapped
around with a coverlet from the bed, and, snuggling down, had
given in to a most perplexing sense of well-being, especially when
she saw Sylvia cross the room and drop into a chair, evidently with
the intention of watching over her for a little while.

An older and more experienced person than Posy might have
said that it was a sense of the futility of her own existence that had
settled upon her earlier that afternoon, might also have seen her to
be suffering without knowing it from the still unreconciled needs
of the child and the woman. Posy herself knew only that she had
been terribly bored and restless, and lonely. Marshall was in Zürich
for the whole day, and everyone else had either gone out or was
busy in their rooms—even Mrs. Halász, who had been taken away
somewhere by the television people. The first thing she had done,
therefore, was to go through all the imprints of her brass-rubbings,
the great stacked rolls of them which filled her closet and drawers,
and finally to take down those which had been on her walls and
replace them with another arrangement. This pleasure behind her,
she had lapsed again into her former state and had at last put on the
leotards and gone into the room where the piano was. There,
pretending there was music, she had begun to prance and dance
and flutter about. It was with this curious fact that she began her
somewhat incoherent account to Sylvia, though naturally she had
said nothing of how she had watched her own reflection admir-
ingly in the French windows, bright and airy against the darkness
outside, of how for a long time she had danced just to herself,
thinking she was the most beautiful creature she had ever seen,
until, suddenly, in the midst of a graceful turn toward this image
of herself it had all seemed dull and silly and even, somehow, not
right, and in a panic she had jumped onto the couch, curled up
there, and eventually fallen asleep. Later she awoke to music. It
had surprised and bewildered her; she had thought perhaps she was
dreaming. This much too she told, explaining how she had peeked
over the top of the couch at the stranger at the piano, feeling
confused, embarrassed, not knowing what to do, hiding again, hoping that he would soon go away. How could she also have admitted to the fact that she was certain of his identity and that she
had *wanted* to stay in that room, the more so after Sylvia arrived?

Now, beneath half-closed lids, she continued to stare at Sylvia Grierson, seated among the shadows. Her room, which Mrs. Dartley had let her choose for herelf, had once been a library, but books and bookcases had long since been removed. It was a very large and draughty room, full of echoes, and poorly lighted. Sylvia had not moved for what seemed to Posy the longest time—only with great effort was she able to keep herself from wriggling about under the coverlet. She looked in that dimness almost like a statue, noble and prayerful, but at the same time angry and burdened and helpless. Her elbows were on the chair arms and her hands lay curiously across her breast, her eyes a haunted stare, her head bent slightly forward, all as though she had been fixed in some violent, agitated effort. It saddened Posy, to see her so, and the memory of what had happened such a short time ago in the music room came back to her. She shivered a little. That atmosphere of struggle, the scuffling sound of bodies in some desperate, forced embrace, the contesting shadows which had been thrown on the wall behind where she lay hidden. It was natural that in her fear she had tried to escape. And those words that had been spoken—it now struck Posy that she must under no circumstances repeat them. She felt a sort of pride in understanding this, especially when she recalled that Sylvia had for her part asked nothing of her. Even the public humiliation she had suffered in the hallway—a just turn of events, a fit punishment she had felt even while it was happening to her— began to lose its importance in the light of her now certain awareness of what infinitely more important things were happening to her elders, those into whose lives she had so childishly blundered. Brought up close now, this woman whom she had admired from afar, made unmistakably real by the fact of her vulnerability, Sylvia seemed to Posy no less admirable than before, yet changed somehow. She remembered too the words that had passed between Sylvia and Ernest Campion. Everyone seemed changed now to Posy, involved in some wild, unending struggle, and although it all still remained just a little beyond her comprehension, it would not, she knew, remain so for long. With a part of herself she wished she could stay warm and protected, safely beneath the coverlet, for-ever; and with another part she did not in the least want to. One thing she was certain of: demon lovers were not to be taken lightly. Her instinct in this respect at least had been confirmed.

Sylvia broke her pose, got up quietly and moved towards the

door. Posy sighed and flopped as noisily as possible on the bed. Sylvia turned. "I thought you'd gone to sleep."

"Not really."

"Oh. Well, everything all right now?"

"Yes thanks. You don't need to stay with me."

Sylvia smiled. "I suppose I've got to return to the fray sometime." Nevertheless she went back to the chair and sat down again. Posy was flattered, especially by the frankness of the last remark. That was the thing she liked so much about Sylvia, even if she was often curt, even though she usually tried to avoid her, when she did talk it was without the condescension older people generally used with her. For that matter, in recent weeks Sylvia had been quite approachable, and great fun to talk to. "It's freezing in here and dark as a . . . I don't know what . . . a vault of some kind. Why don't you move to another room?"

There were good reasons for not doing so, but at that moment Posy didn't choose to give them. The urge for real and proper confession had come suddenly upon her. She said, "I didn't tell you the whole truth a few minutes ago."

"I know," Sylvia said in a tone of finality. "Could we just leave it at that?"

"All right." She sat up cross-legged on the bed. "What's teaching really like?"

"Teaching? Oh . . . like anything else." She looked faintly wary, the way she had used to look most of the time.

Posy said, "I certainly never had a teacher like you."

Sylvia smiled again. "Be glad of that. I was very tough I'm afraid."

"Oh that isn't what I meant. I don't think I'd have minded that." She was in her way an expert on teachers, having gone to five different preparatory schools ("Preparatory for what?" she had asked one of the headmistresses), all of them expensive and all of them bad. The last one, Miss Bench's, had been the worst. There they had tried to teach her little things to say at cocktail parties about the atom bomb and T. S. Eliot and Pablo Picasso. She had felt as though she were a dog being trained to speak by people who she was quite sure were not fit to be her masters. This was exactly what she had told the psychoanalyst and exactly why, like a little dog seeking a happier environment, she had always trotted away from one school after another, most quickly of all from Miss

Bench's. "You liked teaching though, didn't you?" It was not the first time Posy had asked this.

"Yes. Very much in fact." Sylvia sounded grudging. "But it left so little energy for anything else. If one wanted to do anything else. If one were so foolish as to want to do anything else."

"Like writing books?"

For an answer Sylvia said, "Oh, art's a silly business. Isn't it odd how the more lunatic forms of endeavor always seem the most alluring?" She stood up again, determinedly this time. Slyly, quickly, Posy reached out and removed the shade from the little lamp on the table beside her, and now, as Sylvia turned away, the added light made her aware for the first time of the still somewhat obscured figures on the wall behind her. She peered at them. "What is all this?"

Posy leapt from the bed. "My brass-rubbings!"

Sylvia moved closer to them, pacing a little to the right and left. A whole procession of men and women seemed to be trooping along the wall in some dimension of their own, stretching the length of the one long wall, turning the corner, and continuing on as far as the windows. "Is there any way of seeing them better?" she asked.

In seconds Posy had switched on the two remaining light fixtures and snatched the shades from them. A considerable flood of light now billowed up toward the wall, causing the figures to loom with almost intimidating grandeur upon them. "What a startling effect you've created," Sylvia said. "How surprisingly impressive this all is."

Leading the procession was a tall knight whose limbs and torso seemed to be pressing with enormous power through the elaborate chain mail armor in which he was clad. A great sword hung from his waist, and in the crook of his right arm there rested a lance. His hands were hidden behind his shield. He seemed to be standing on a lion, and behind his hooded head, peering out sideways, was another and much smaller head, bearded, hook-nosed, leering. "What on earth is that? The devil bursting out his pate?"

"No. A decapitated Saracen. It's not coming out of his head really; it's sort of behind it, an emblem. He's a crusader, thirteenth century. The lion at his feet is supposed to mean he died in battle. It doesn't always mean that, but it's sort of complicated to explain."

"Oh." Sylvia ran her eyes slowly along the wall. Posy was beginning a detailed, an erudite account, in an oddly authoritative
voice, the voice she would have perhaps in a few years' time, the
voice she would surely use with her children. Sylvia saw that
except for the knight all of the figures had assumed various attitudes of piety, one figure even kneeling and most with hands conventionally folded together in front of them. There were, however, two rather startling variations. The woman next to the
knight had thrown her hands spread-fingered and palms outward
in front of her, as though she were warding something off, and
down at the very end of the line, crammed in narrowly next to the
windows, was a shroud-draped skeleton which looked more as
though it were waving than praying.

Pointing still at the crusader with the sure gestures of the expert,
Posy concluded, "In fact, it's the most complete representation of
chain mail among all the monumental brasses of England."

"Is it?" Then Sylvia said, "Savages mostly."

"Who?"

"The crusaders."

"I don't think *he* was." Posy was troubled. "At least not entirely."

"You don't? You know his story then?" There was a touch of
awkwardness unmistakably developing. Before Posy could answer
Sylvia moved quickly down the line. "Perhaps you'll tell me about
him sometime. But where did you find all of these, these people?
Were they all lying in a row some place?"

Posy smiled. "I got them from all over. Different churches in
London. There are hordes of them in All Hallows by the Tower. I
started out there because that's where I saw this girl doing a
rubbing—the one who agreed to let me learn by helping her—
that's where she was working." Posy stopped. She had learned not
to try to explain the ardor that had possessed her when first she
saw one of those beautiful forms appearing as though by magic on
the great sheet of paper, that still possessed her whenever she
herself was at work on one. If only there were some way she could
make a life's work out of brass-rubbing. But it was quite impossible
she knew.

"Then it really is just chance that you've arranged them in this
way?" The first four figures consisted of the knight, the distraught-
looking young woman, a slightly frowning gentleman in vaguely

academic gown, and an imposing woman with an amused mouth who had clutched in the bend of her right arm a very elegant and stylish shepherd's crook. These were followed by various attendant lords and ladies and finally by the skeleton.

"I make all sorts of arrangements out of them. It's fun."

Sylvia gave her a sharp look which she did not understand. She went on hurriedly. "After I got my job I went into the counties too. Kent, Surrey, Oxford. I had some trouble there. The worst trouble I had, though, was with him." Again she pointed to the crusader. "Margate Parish Church. Do you know it?"

"I'm afraid not. What sort of trouble?"

"I got caught during a communion service. It was very humiliating." There she had been stretched out practically full-length beside him in that funny little chapel to the right of the altar, unaware of anything else; then, when it was too late, trying to get the paper detached without rattling it, giving up, climbing into that niche that rose from above the crusader's feet. Everything the priest was doing had looked so peculiar and unfamiliar to her from where she stood. It had been fascinating, but not exactly reassuring.

"What do you mean 'caught'?" Sylvia asked for the second time.

"Oh well . . . I . . ." She had just remembered the name of that chapel. Furthermore there now seemed to her to be a troubling, if vague, similarity between what had happened then and what had just happened downstairs. The last thing she wanted to do was to tell Sylvia about it. That priest's astonished and, as she had thought, wrathful eye upon her, catching her out in that niche just as he was lifting the sacramental cup. She said firmly, "It worked out all right. He asked me to tea afterwards."

Sylvia laughed. "Posy! Who did?"

"The priest. The vicar. At Margate Parish. I went there a lot after that. He was the one who introduced me to Mrs. Dartley."

Sylvia shook her head. She pointed now to the woman with the crook. "I suppose she's an abbess."

"Yes. Elstow. Bedfordshire. She's sixteenth century. You can tell that by the barbe . . . and lots of other things. She's the Renaissance." She pointed to the frowning man. "He's sixteenth century too. A don, and in minor orders. From New College. Why do you suppose they call such an old place new? They kept running me out of there. I never had the right permissions, or something."

"You should have tipped the porter."

"Oh, was that it? Well, he was the only one I got. And *she's* from the very end of the fifteenth century, but she's not English. She may be Burgundian. There's a lot of argument about it. But she's some sort of foreigner. She's the Renaissance too."

They both stood before the figure of the woman with thrown-up hands. She differed from the other figures in still another way. While the rest of them stood facing straight ahead, her body was turned slightly to her right, in her present setting towards the crusader, and her head slightly to her left.

"She looks rather indecisive and trapped."

"It's that fancy hairdress. It was called the Butterfly. It didn't show up except in semi-profile."

"Somehow I don't think that quite explains her, do you?"

"No." Posy lowered her eyes, then raised them to look directly at Sylvia. She said shyly, "She looks as though she had to make some kind of decision."

"And couldn't, evidently, manage it." There was an embarrassed silence. Sylvia stepped back. She said briskly, "It's curious how little sense of repose there is here. Perhaps that's because you have no bishop. Why don't you have a bishop?"

"Oh but I do have one, rolled up in the closet. An archbishop of York, very decadent looking. But this time, since I had the abbess, I didn't think I needed him. I've got lots of others in the closet, especially lots of burghers. A wonderful wool merchant and his wife, both fat, kneeling on woolsacks."

There was a rapping on the door. Posy bounded to it and let Marshall in. He had the cat under one arm and a flute under the other. He handed the cat to Posy. Sylvia began to laugh. "Oh this is too much for me," the words spilling out under the laughter. "You two, somehow; I can't explain it. Just think. You at least aren't rolled up in a closet, or hung on a wall. Not yet. Oh forgive me." She stepped quickly between them, put an arm around each at the waist, stood so for just a second; in the next instant, before they could say a word, she was at the door. She said, "I leave you in good hands, Posy." She shook her head. "You are quite a little allegorist." She looked now as though she were going to cry.

As the door closed behind her, Marshall said, "What's her trouble? I thought you'd be the one who needed cheering up."

"Shhh," Posy said.

Twenty-one

Sylvia got only as far as the main staircase. There she sat herself down in a state of great dejection. When the sound of flute music began coming along the corridor towards her she listened for a moment or two, dully. A mere and trivial tootling it seemed to her, an annoying burden of meaningless noise, like everything else. She leaned back against the curving bannister. What nonsense music was really, what nonsense all art. But then, what nonsense life was too. What did any of it matter? Distance, that was what she wanted, just as when she had put New York behind her and, later, Munich; distance, and not the same old muddle of involvement. It was time to leave Kilchberg.

Sylvia shut her eyes, but was annoyed to find in that darkness the stubborn image of the figures she had seen on Posy's wall. What a lot of rot, she thought. There they were, however, moving towards her in great confusion, stepping, leaping, mincing, stumbling off the wall, pressing and weaving around her, waving their silly hands at her, encircling her, moving their lips in mute speech. *No*, she whispered, sitting up very straight and opening her eyes. No. No thank you, no. Just leave me alone. She folded her arms and looked about her. Splendid! The house seemed deserted. Behind all those vague doors a variety of lives were ticking away, but one did not have to know about them. So much the better. Or was it? As she regarded all that emptiness she could feel the old, prime fury, the passion of despair, beginning to stir in her again. She thought helplessly of the weeks that had just passed. Had they been permitted her then, those happy dedicated hours of work, that simple, spontaneous participation in life itself, only that she might be made to suffer a keener deprivation and find herself driven again by the ravaging *no* that lurked always at the edge of human experience? It was not right, it was not fair. Those great long corridors seemed to intersect precisely at the point where she was and then continue emptily on past her, as much without ending as beginning. It was a terrible old house, she decided then, barren, unpeopled, cold. She shivered, closed her eyes again, and waited, but this time there were no images at all, not of anything. She leaned her face against the bars of the bannister, stretched her arms wide out beside her and closed each fist around a bar, her

mouth pulled open into a tooth-bared grimace. And then her body
went limp; hands sliding down from the bars, she slumped weakly
against them and was still.

Later, when she tried to reckon how long she had remained
there in so evident a state of collapse and was unable to do so, she
comforted herself with the thought that at least no one had seen
her. Yet one person had: Benjamin Knox, on his way to his audience with Mrs. Dartley. He had hesitated, there on the bottom step,
and almost gone to her, but had then changed his mind and hurried
along to the back stairs, making his way safely up by them. Thus,
as it turned out, it was Marshall's flute that roused her. When at
last she became aware of its persistent music she lifted her head
and began intently to listen. It sounded so different to her now. It
was very beautiful, and the skill with which Marshall played was
astonishing. It made its own world, that music, there was no denying it. She could not quite recognize who the composer was, but
Anton would know, or Lily. She must remember to ask them.
Surely, somewhere in the house, they too were listening. Oh, but it
was lovely. Small wonder that she had apprehended nothing of
that music before—when the self was in flight there was no hope
of reaching beyond it into something else.

Sylvia sighed, pulled herself together, and peered furtively
around. How could she have been such a fool? Some things at least
were clear now—that even behind the walls of the Villa Kilchberg
the tempo of pursuit had quickened and that there was no help for
it. How little control was possible really. That was what one had
to keep relearning, even if one also believed, as she knew herself to
believe, in the possibility of choice. What did it matter then that he
from whom she had most particularly chosen to run and who was
yet the most difficult to escape was once again within these walls,
come too, she was somehow sure, at a time when tests were to be
laid most heavily on them all? The music was rising in a series of
impassioned and plaintive notes. She listened. Somewhere was an
ideal world in which a boy leaned back against a tree, pipe to lips,
subduing for a moment all the darkness in nature. If only it might
be so. She thought again of St. George, and of his destiny, which
she already saw as blasted, ruined, and as connected in some nameless but inevitable way with her own. Now the flute found and
took a mysterious climactic phrase, held and sustained it, bravely.
Then there was silence.

She waited, listening still, but she knew there would be no more. Even as she sat there a quite different sort of music began. The other was gone. Well, why not, after all? One had one's insights, even one's little visions and high moments, but they had shockingly little to do with one's outer life, which mostly, she had discovered, went on in the same old confused and imperfect way. She, for example, would now get up and go look for Bingham, no matter what. She glanced through the bars of the bannister, and there at the bottom of the stairs, staring up at her, stood Ernest Campion. She thought of running, but he began to mount the stairs with long, swift steps. She waited for him, curious, composed. He stopped a little below her, lifted one foot to the stair on which she sat, and leaning forward brought his face close to hers. She returned his gaze, catching too the outline of his body, surprised, thinking: *Now what has he to do with Greek games?* Still but taut in that arrested forward motion, his left arm extended behind him and parallel to the angle of the body, his right brought forward, bent at the elbow and pointing up across his chest where it ended in a loosely held fist, he looked as though he were about to run a foot race or whirl a discus. Now he shook his head slightly at her, gravely, gave her a look of tempered impatience, and sat on the step below her. He did not reach for her hand, but held his own out toward her, flatly halfway. She shrugged, then took it. He moved up beside her, and they sat there, hands clasped, silent.

At last he said, "What's going on with you?"

"Nothing. Everything. Better to stay out of it."

"I can't. I'm in love with you."

"If you are, you're a fool. Very unwise. I'm not like other women. I don't like entanglements."

He ignored the offense she plainly meant the word to give. "One would never know it," he said.

"And that's such a silly phrase, What do you mean by it anyway? *In love*," she said angrily. "Something humbug no doubt. That's what it usually is, something humbug. What *do* you mean? Do you feel the way Tristan did?"

"No," he said. "Thank God."

She frowned, looked at him suspiciously. Then she said, "Well, that's good, that's a relief." She did not, however, sound particularly pleased. "Women are such hypocrites," she added vaguely.

"But you're not?"

"No, I'm not."

"What does that mean? That you've never been in love?"

"Certainly I've been in love. Twice."

"Only twice?"

"Twice in the perilous way."

"And that, what does that mean?" he persisted. "That you were nearly in danger of getting married?"

"Oh, marriage. It seems to me I'm always in danger of that. I've just been lucky and managed to escape so far. I told you I'm not like other women. I've no taste at all for commercial arrangements. No, I meant two times in the Isolde way." She laughed unpleasantly. "There, you see. The very fact that it was two times and that I'm still alive proves what a delusion it is."

"Or perhaps it proves something about the way a very imaginative person handles a severe attack of sensuality."

She gave him a shrewd, appraising look, then said thoughtfully, "Oh, I don't know. It really does seem like more than simple sensuality when it's happening. It's more like a madness. Isn't that what the Greeks thought? Now that I think about it, I suppose it was only once, not twice. I hope it never happens to me again. I'm sure it won't. Do you like talking about love? Most men don't, and I don't blame them."

"At the moment I do."

"There ought, there really ought to be something in between madness and mere commerce."

"My view exactly."

"So you say. Besides, ought isn't is."

"Are you so sure?"

"Well," she said, "No. But on the basis of observation . . . And I've been a little in love fairly often. Sometimes it's hard not to be."

"When one is loved, is admired. That's encouraging," he said.

She did not respond. Then: "What you said before. You meant that you can live without me, but you'd rather not?"

"I'm quite sure I can manage to live without you." He paused, watching her closely. "But I also mean something considerably stronger than just your 'I'd rather not.'"

"Oh?"

"I'd suffer greatly."

She frowned.

"Let me try to take care of you," he said.

"Take care of me?"

"Yes. Why not?"

She was furious. "I don't want anyone to take care of me. There. You see. All you can think of is an *arrangement*. I'm not a horse, or a factory, or an automobile, or . . ."

He was laughing at her. "I ask you to marry me and—"

"To marry you?"

"Yes, and you react as though I'd made some especially disgusting, some aberrant advance to you. I know you're a free spirit, my dear, emancipated and all that, but isn't that a rather old-fashioned attitude to take toward marriage?"

"I don't care what kind of attitude it is. No one ever takes care of anyone—except parents of children, sometimes, or prison warders. And as soon as someone says they're going to take care of you and you agree, you give them the right to rule you. I don't want to be ruled. I hate power struggles, which is what, if a woman doesn't want to be ruled, marriage turns into. I think power struggles are degenerate."

"And have you always been able to keep yourself free of those just by not marrying? A remarkable accomplishment."

She glowered at him but said nothing.

"Let's try each other for a while. I won't insist on making an honest woman of you. I even find it amusing, the way you've turned everything upside down. But let's try. If it doesn't work, we can just go away from each other."

"I did try that once," she said.

"But not with me. Try again."

"You don't even know me," she said. "I'm willful, cruel, ruthless, as ruthless as any man, I've tried to make that plain."

"I've overestimated your intelligence, it would seem."

"What do you mean?"

"Your knowledge of yourself, your picture of yourself. You've just drawn an extremely partial and incomplete one. One that is designed to deceive. Who? Just me, or yourself too?"

"My God, you're stubborn." She sighed. "Do you know anything about artists? About the kind of *liberty* they need, scrabble for, scheme for, and die without? Any man who falls in love with one is a fool. It goes against nature, a woman wanting to be free.

Or against history at any rate. And that almost amounts to the same thing. Changes are so slow that one can't even see them. Someone else sees them. Later. After one is dead."

He was not even smiling now. "Maybe that's the kind of woman I'm attracted to," he said, and before she could reply he laid a hand gently over her mouth, and when he took it away they exchanged a long kiss. Afterwards she shook her head sadly at him, though she did not move from his embrace.

"It's still true," she said. "Any man who falls in love with . . . oh never mind. I've warned you. I'm an odd breed of fish."

He nodded. "Yes, you've been very gentlemanly about it. If your breed of fish appeals to me I'll have to take my chances."

She pulled back a little now and looked at him slyly. "Who's this Elsie Crone? A relative? A spinster aunt perhaps?"

"Crown, my dear. Elsie Crown. No, not a relative, not by blood at any rate. She's an actress."

"Oh she is? I don't like actresses."

"Why not?"

"I'm jealous of them. They don't have to think, they only have to do what others tell them, and to be instinctive. And they can show off without anyone thinking it bad taste."

He was amused.

"Is she very good?" she asked.

"As an actress?"

"Certainly. I'm not interested in whatever other talents she may have. Nor in your private life."

He thought. "I think she might have been extremely good in a country with a classical tradition of theatre, France, or Germany, where the grand style was permitted. As it is, she's never quite right, somehow."

Sylvia said, "I take back what I said. I don't envy American actresses. It's terrible the things they have to play in most of the time." Quickly then she got to her feet. "I've got to go now."

"We'll talk about this again?"

"Why? There just isn't any Papagena in me."

"But far, far more Pamina than you care to admit to. That is exactly why we'll talk of this again."

A brief, surprised look of admiration crossed her face. Then she shrugged. "Maybe. I love you too, Ernest. A little. But it doesn't mean a thing. It doesn't mean anything will come of it. Or that it will change anything else, all that I've said to you, and other things too."

He bent over. Once more they kissed.

"Are you protecting him in some way?" he asked.

She was caught a little off guard. "Why do you ask that?"

"Something about the way you were with him just now, about the way you moved beside him during all that stupid confusion. By the way, how's Posy?"

"She's fine. Quite recovered. You know what girls are like at that age, always just on the edge of hysteria. It takes so little. She'd overheard part of a ... conversation. And then you belted her one. But she's fine."

"Good. *Are* you protecting him?"

"No, of course not." Her face was becoming closed. "It would be quite impossible to, anyway." She started down the corridor.

"Are you going to him? Now?" he asked after her.

She turned around. "Yes."

"Why?"

"I simply must. I even want to. I even choose to. I'm sorry. We're alike in some ways. I can't explain it." Then her eyes widened, and she said, "And I love him too."

Twenty-two

Benjamin Knox stared at the ugly little wooden mask, the round empty eyes, the huge deteriorating nose, the wide mouth studded with a few jagged teeth and twisted down on one side in a lewd growl. He took it to be a death's-head, and found it vaguely satisfying that such an object should be hanging on the walls of Mrs. Dartley's room. At the same time he had difficulty controlling an impulse to stick his tongue out at it. "Folk art?" he asked her.

"Here in the mountains one is close to the truth in nature."

"I don't follow you."

"Old pieces of tree trunk and the like. Broken, worn, weathered. The result is this ... now what shall we call it, Mr. Knox? This parody. In the forest. I imagine it's quite startling to come across one. I must ask Faustine if she ever has. They appeal greatly to the mountain people. And why not? Such people don't lie to themselves nearly as much as we do. Consequently they aren't nearly so afraid of things. When they find one of these unpleasant faces they frequently sell them to tourists. The braver sort of tourists, I should think, or the exceedingly stupid. This one was a gift, however. I find it a convenient reminder. Come along. Sit down. Drink something."

She rattled among some bottles on a sideboard. He had been admitted to these chambers for the first time and he looked about him now with growing disappointment—when a child enters the wizard's cave wonders are expected. But except for the death's-head and, near the windows, a sort of platform on which there was a massive work table heaped formidably with papers, magazines, and newspapers there was nothing much out of the ordinary here. At the very least he had thought to find it filled with relics and mementos. Everything was plain, simple, even agreeable. He had miscalculated again.

"Kirsch," she said, handing him a glass. With a tip of the head backwards she consumed the liquor in her glass, and then watched while with an effort he managed a good swallow. "Good," she said, "very good," and tapped him on the shoulder. She climbed onto the platform and began searching intently through the stacks of papers. He watched, hating himself for wanting to be liked by her and for going ahead with a program he already knew would be a failure. "Waifs, strays, failures, orphans, n'er-do-wells, and a tyrant," he had said to Bledder in a rare burst of unsullied language after the first evening at Kilchberg. Yet only this morning, at breakfast in Zürich, when Ralph referred to Mrs. Dartley as a "phony" Knox had lashed out at him so angrily that he had choked on a piece of toast.

She said, "It's so important to grow old gracefully. Once I slept in a bedroom that had a bad print of the Botticelli Venus on the wall. Such a long time ago. And another time I remember a little statue of Pallas Athena. That was a more difficult delusion to free myself from. How naïve the belief in science, the exclusion of old Triton, has made us, don't you think?" She continued to search among her papers, which were becoming noticeably disordered. "Symbols! Ha! We march through a forest of them, they cling to us, even if ironically. A pity that technological advance has trained us not to see the forest, isn't it? So dangerous. How can we wonder at our depravity?"

Of course Ralph was probably right about her. That prattling she was doing now, while pretending to look for something, making him feel he ought to understand her when chances were she was only playing with words or filling up time; whichever it was, he felt she was being unfair to him. How she loved to hear herself talk. Yet as usual she had aroused his curiosity. It reminded him of her readings, of which he had thus far heard two. One, in the form of a letter to *The New York Times,* had been an attack on the American government's "misleading and therefore immoral" doctrine of liberation of the satellite countries, and the other had been some queer and complicated and very fragmentary thing about what she called "otherness." As nearly as he could tell it was because people couldn't or wouldn't imagine otherness that everything was out of whack. He struggled now to keep himself from asking what symbols might have attached themselves to him. She said, "I know you're happier when you're in motion. Please feel free to move about. I must, I simply must find something. Forgive me." She looked wild for a second or two, then, as though remembering, put her glasses on and began shuffling frantically through more papers.

Benjamin Knox determined not to move. It was impossible for him to say exactly when or how or why his attitude toward Mrs. Dartley had undergone a change. In the beginning he had pushed ahead with the program simply because he felt that everyone at Kilchberg was against it. He wasn't used to this and it annoyed him. Then there was the matter of paying off Mrs. Dartley, in every sense. He had come to Kilchberg prepared to offer her a sizable fee, knowing that it would be useful if it were artfully leaked in New York that *The World at Large* had made a generous contribution to the worthy if unrealistic causes and activities of an eccentric old lady who had once sat with the great and had now lost all her influence with them. But when *she* had brought up the matter of fees and had then made her oblique reference to an incident in his past which she assumed he wanted kept secret he had chosen to let her think he was giving in to the implied threat. Of course it had shaken him a little, but not enough to keep him from turning it to his advantage. In time he had even found that the little agreement had given him a sense of moral superiority to this woman who seemed somehow to have set herself up as a judge of the moral worth of people like himself, and hence it had also given him a sense, if not quite of power, then at least of being able to hold his own with her. The trouble was that in the last few days he had found himself seriously attempting to devise ways of getting across to an audience the importance of Mrs. Dartley, as though she really did have an importance. But what was it?

She leaned forward suddenly, said to him as though she were interrupting herself, "I'm worried about Posy. She has immortal longings in her. One would hardly guess it, but it's true. When her imagination is seized she's swept away so easily. She's had no proper education, you know; her mind isn't trained to recognize limitations. In another era I dare say she'd probably have been religious. Now what do you suppose would have been better for her, the church, or her brass-rubbings? Because they're really all the poor child has found to believe in, to correspond to her instinctual self. If anything ever catches her fancy the way the brass-rubbings have I'm afraid she might do something quite foolish." She frowned, and then returned to her search.

Knox thought it better to say nothing. Her view of Posy amazed him. She belonged to the idle rich whom he both admired and hated, and that was that. Spoiled, petted, protected, pretty and dumb—he had known hundreds of such girls grown slightly older, fashionable women in their thirties who were just clever enough to realize that it was a good thing to be able to get Benjamin Knox to accept an invitation to one of their parties and who were not always averse to going to bed with him. He smiled. Choo-choo-train evenings was the way he referred to these private encounters with them, the reason being that they reminded him of how, as a boy, at night in that tiny house that was never painted, that was cold in winter and hot in summer, listening to the trains that passed all too near, he had longed so often and so bitterly to hop one of those trains, to be steaming away from there, faster and faster. He had even developed the rather nasty habit of always, afterwards, making some smutty remark to these supposedly well-bred women that had to do with trains and the sexual act they had just performed with him.

As for Posy, the only foolish thing he could imagine her doing would be marrying and divorcing several times and dropping a confused child or two along the way, as her own mother had done—Bledder had checked that out for him. Was it possible that Mrs. Dartley was right in seeing something else in her? He doubted it.

What was she looking for? She was now taking a bunch of old letters from their envelopes. As he watched her a strange glow of pleasure started up in him. It had nothing to do with the memory of choo-choo-train evenings. He had just realized that Mrs. Dartley had spoken to him as he had often heard her speak to Campion. He would have to get a grip on himself. It reminded him of the childish delight he had felt earlier in the day when she invited him to stay on that evening for dinner; it reminded him too of the eagerness he now felt driving out to Kilchberg and the depression that overtook him on the way back to Zürich. Why should he feel so at home in a place where there was so great a difference between himself and everyone else, a place where the measurements of success and failure which he regarded as normal simply did not apply? They were the ones who were not in step, yet he felt himself the outsider. They all took him for granted now, courteously, yet he did not feel at ease. And why should he care? It seemed to him an incestuous sort of house, with everyone related to everyone else, and no one following any of the usual rules of behavior. None of them was actually related, he knew, but ever since the first night he could not rid himself of the notion that they were. Now to add to the general confusion which his contact with Kilchberg had aroused in him there was a very specific worry, for with the arrival of Elsie Crown he felt himself being inextricably drawn in while remaining still the outsider. He said, "I'd better tell you that I know Elsie Crown."

Her glasses were teetering on the end of her nose. When she snapped her head up they fell off. "I gathered that. It's not really very surprising that you should. You're a television person and she's an actress."

He suppressed the anger he always felt when she used the phrase "television person." "I thought I ought to tell you that it might be rather awkward, my running into her here."

"Awkward? Awkward? What does that matter? The whole place reeks with awkwardness. Whatever you've done to Elsie Crown or she to you cannot possibly be so bad as some of the things people are doing to each other under this roof at this very moment."

There it came again, that feeling of profound uneasiness. Like all her mysterious pronouncements, the remark she had just made seemed designed both to close him out and draw him in. Why could he not get his hands on things in this house, in the detached, impersonal way he was used to, impose on them a perfect, mechanical control and ignore what could not be controlled? He said, "Anything that would be useful to me?"

"Now who knows that, Mr. Knox? Who knows that?" By now the table looked like a litter pile. She shoved at the unruly papers and made a clear space for her elbows. "I can't find what I'm looking for," she said wistfully. "Well, there's nothing to be done. I'm wasting our time." She paused. "I've been brooding over certain matters. This afternoon I made some decisions, one or two of which concern you. First, I must tell you that I'm not going to take the money we agreed upon."

He was immediately wary. Did she want something more from him then? He shrugged. "That's up to you. But you might as well. It's all arranged."

"I thought perhaps if I didn't take it you might not try to humiliate me."

So she had guessed that too, the clever old . . . witch. Yet he felt let down that she was giving up the game so easily. "Oh I don't blame you," she went on. "I treated you very badly that first day, especially when I referred to . . . that other matter."

He wanted no favors from Gwendolyn Dartley. What he had done was so trivial measured against a world in which every day people did a thousand worse things, usually with the tacit approval of society—he couldn't possibly take it seriously. "You mean your finding out about how during the war when I was in prison camp I stole chocolate?"

"My information didn't extend so far. I only knew that a charge was made but never even formally processed for lack of evidence."

He was forcing himself to sit still. "I've never lost any sleep over it. A thousand worse things happened every day. They still do. Out in the real world, I mean."

"Oh I agree entirely. And your fellow prisoners weren't starving, were they? I'm sure you thought of that when you found your way of pilfering the Red Cross rations, or have thought of it since. 'If 'twere gorgeous to go warm.' "

He felt a furious need to defend himself, but kept control. "Gorgeous? Warm? It wasn't exactly cosy in that camp."

"Ah? That is the point. But never mind. I'm tired of fine moral distinctions myself just now. Frankly, I was surprised that you didn't laugh at me when I mentioned your love of chocolate. But I suppose it could have been troublesome—it's the sort of issue hypocrites love to make a fuss over. What I really want to say to you is that it was contemptible of me to use it. I am sincerely sorry. I beg your pardon. I'm not a very nice person, as I'm sure you've noticed. But then, neither are you. It's a meager concept, being nice, but I suppose if one lacks any of the grander qualities one ought to try at least to be that. I've always failed at it, alas." She held up her glass. "The kirsch is over there."

He got up, filled her glass and set the bottle beside her.

"I suppose you had quite a dossier on me when you came here?"

"Yes," he said. "Standard procedure."

"Yes. Just like the secret police. A world of dossiers. What progress we've made. It's such an interesting century. Take the sort of work you do. People will voluntarily submit to your grillings for the sake of something called publicity. Now isn't that very odd? The willing victim sits there waiting for you, or someone like you, to ask the most personal and often very partial questions, among which there are certain to be a few surprises, things you know that the victim doesn't know you know, or will use if you do. The result, when you're very lucky, is, I suppose, something like a confession. Do you suppose it all started in Russia in the thirties? If so, it has certainly turned into a popular sport in our decadent West. The age of meaningless confession. By the way, how were you going to do it?"

"Get you to confess?" he asked. He did not care for this turn in the conversation either. He remembered the plan he had long ago worked out in the event there was ever trouble about the chocolate stealing, how he would go through the motions of soul-searching and public contrition.

She laughed shortly. "Oh no, no, no. I don't think you expected to manage that. Not that I don't have some sins worth confessing. But not to you. How were you going to make a fool of me?"

Despite himself he grinned. "I hadn't figured that out yet."

"Good," she said, and for a second he felt he had her respect. "When I agreed to let you come here to interrogate me, perhaps even to judge me, I thought I should like to know about my interrogator, I thought it fair. Not that in the general sense Freud wasn't right about self-betrayal oozing from every pore anyway." She looked thoughtful, then added gently, "Which is why I suppose pity is always called for," hesitated again, then went on quite briskly, "I allowed myself to think only of my desire to keep this place running. Now I feel differently about that. Things are coming to an end here, things are changing. Surely you feel that?"

"No I don't." The idea of Kilchberg coming to an end depressed him.

"Well, they are. It's just as well. No matter." Again she became gentle. "You did not ever think that I would deliberately harm you, did you? You had taken my measure correctly in that respect?"

"No, I didn't think you would harm me," he said reluctantly. He found himself tempted to tell her that they had been going to pay her the fee anyway. But he decided it was better to hold that back; it was still the only real weapon he had with her.

She poured another kirsch. "In a sense this left me free to blackmail you. It was a game for both of us. I hoped, as I've told you, that there would be some money for me in the ordeal. I needed it. But I did not connect that hope with what I had learned about you. That idea, I'm sorry to say, grew spontaneously out of our first meeting. You provoked me greatly. That ruse of yours about my novels. I knew enough of your methods to see it as a test run, an attempt to get the victim to reveal a side of the personality he usually keeps hidden. Well, as you know, I decided to give you what you wanted, to show you just how unpleasant I can be—it isn't hard for me. But, Mr. Knox, the point is that you *had* gotten to me, precisely because I knew that you were perfectly aware of how painful it was for me to be reminded of those bad, bad books. That at least should please you. Does it?"

"Not now." He shook his head. He did not really understand all of what she was saying or what was happening to him. Surely when he was outside of that room it would all seem ridiculous, but he could not keep from saying, "I'd better tell you that we were going to offer you money anyway. Please take it."

"Out of the question. And I still have not told you what really provoked me. What you said to me was not quite enough. No, it was your very cruel and unwarranted treatment of Ernest Campion. By what right did you, *a pilferer of chocolates* . . . oh it is funny, funny and horrible, and you do not see it at all . . . at all . . ." She gave in to an ugly, choking laughter. He felt nothing, waiting numbly for her to finish. Suddenly she was in control again. She said quietly, "Ernest Campion should have been born to a life of great service. It has not worked out that way. As it is he sometimes takes on himself the most modest and unassuming tasks—I must tell you that he has no illusions about what *I* am accomplishing. He has lost his occupation, yet he conducts himself as though something might after all matter. I find this uncommonly admirable. Those of us who seize every opportunity so brilliantly, often so ruthlessly . . ." She stood up. "All of this is an elaborate way of saying that I have decided to let you out of our agreement—not just the money, the whole undertaking. You have no taste for it, really. I have caught that. Nor have I. Let us call a halt. Events may interpose themselves in any case."

He was on his feet. "But you can't call it off now."

"Certainly I can."

"Certainly you can? What kind of talk is that? The tapes are set in London and Paris, in New York. The rest of the technical staff arrives tomorrow. Weeks of work have gone into this."

"Which as we both know is absurd and of no consequence. I questioned you most particularly about that on your first evening here. Even by then I had my doubts. Run one of your substitute programs. No, this will not make any difficulties for you."

"Not of that sort. But . . ."

"But what?"

"But I hadn't expected this. I—" He did not know how to explain the reluctance he felt at abandoning the program.

"It can't possibly make any difference to you." Her voice was bored.

"It can and it does."

"Why?"

"Why?" Damn her, he did not know why. Yet he saw himself in that instant as a servitor, all but wringing his hands. Why was she smiling at him?

"Mr. Knox, if I thought that this one little program really mattered to you in some vague but important way that I am failing to
see ..."

"Let's say it's a challenge ... a professional challenge."

She sniffed. "Why say it if it isn't true? What a horribly meaningless phrase! Do you always run in a crisis? No, no, please; let us
drop it."

"Mrs. Dartley, you have a reputation for fairness."

"I do?"

"Yes, and right now I'm standing here in front of you—"

"Hopping and loping around in front of me in another of your
splendid suits."

"Hopping and loping then. And asking you . . ." He stopped.
Why could he not simply say: asking you, please, without being
able to say to you why, asking you please not to cancel this program, please to trust me. But he could not bring out these words.
Nothing in his experience had ever worked that way. By God, she
was not going to get away with it. An idea came to him, and with
it a decision. "Mrs. Dartley, I happen to know that you want your
citizenship back. I happen also to know that this program could do
you a lot of good in Washington."

Now it was he who stood still and she who paced, circling
around him. He thought she would never stop. At last she climbed
back up to the work table. "And by implication if I do not do this
program it will do me a great deal of harm?"

"I didn't say that."

He could not doubt that there was pity in that steady gaze she
was directing upon him. He felt both angry and afraid. She said,
"Under normal circumstances what you have just said would absolutely prevent me from going ahead with this stupid program. It
would also probably cause me to write revoking my request for
citizenship. But what you have just said also shows me the exact
extent to which these are not what is generally meant by the term
normal circumstances, or times. Will you forgive me if I say—and
I have no actual right to—that you have a way of making judgments about things you don't in the least understand. You have
also reached a position of considerable power. That is an unfortunate combination. I wished to spare us both a pointless struggle. I
am intent, Mr. Knox, on preserving certain things which seem
valuable to me and which for you have no meaning at all. I am old,

and very tired, tireder than anyone knows. But I see now that I cannot spare myself."

He said, "Are you doubting my ability to handle the program objectively?"

"*Objectively?* Oh Benjamin, Benjamin, Benjamin." Her use of his first name struck him like a series of small blows. How he hated her, but how he also wished that he understood. Suddenly he remembered Sylvia Grierson at the top of the stairs, crumpled up as though by pain. Perhaps he ought to have followed that first impulse and gone to her. "Why will you not see? Is it really that you cannot?"

"If there are any assurances that will satisfy you," he said thickly.

She shook her head at him sadly. Then she said, "I see now that I have been unfair to you. Yes, this program does matter to you, otherwise you would hardly have done to yourself . . . what you did. We are both still in the dark as to why it should matter to you and in what way, and for the present we shall have to remain so."

"I didn't mean . . ." he began.

She gestured at him to be silent. "It would have been very hard for you to go at it in another way. I see that. What I am trying to tell you is that I will do this program."

"Thank you," he said shortly. He had got what he wanted. He could not help but feel that he had also lost something. "Then we go ahead as planned."

"We do. But I must ask one thing. Perhaps we could call it an assurance. Keep your obsequious Mr. Bledder under control."

"Ralph? Keep him under control?" He actually laughed, and a wonderful sense of relief went through him. This was the sort of eccentricity on Mrs. Dartley's part which he actively enjoyed. "Ralph works for me. Or rather for the network. He's first-rate at his job, but he knows exactly what it is. He's gone as far as he can go and he appreciates that fact."

"I do not like Mr. Bledder."

"Well, I'm not sure anyone likes Ralph, but he's very useful to me, to us. It would be really hard to run an operation like this without men like Ralph. He takes care of all sorts of details."

"I do not like petty bureaucrats who have been given the power to do the dirty work of their superiors. They follow the rules you give them much too obediently. I will take my chances with you, Mr. Knox. But I do not like invisible adversaries."

He laughed again and moved jauntily towards the door. "Well, don't worry about old Ralph. I'll take care of things."

He was pleased that things were ending on this note of absurdity. Just as he opened the door she said, "Oh Mr. Knox, I've been meaning to ask you what word if any you've had from Andreas Greifenberg's widow?"

The word had been a categorical refusal, but he could not bring himself to admit this to her. "Nothing definite yet."

"I see. Well, you must keep on hoping."

Her face was quite expressionless. The last he saw of her she was pouring herself another kirsch. He went along to the main staircase, but Sylvia was of course gone.

Twenty-three

George Bingham was seated at Sylvia's desk, reading the manuscript pages she had left there. "You haven't any right . . ." she began.

"To learn more about my rival?" he said. "Or one of them at least." He was cheerful, almost tender, standing now before her.

She sighed and sat down on the bed. How like him to refer at the earliest possible opportunity to that last passionate statement she had flung at him in the music room, the most terrible of all the terrible things she had ever said to him because the truest. It was his own peculiar form of honesty, she recognized, his way of saying: perhaps it is death it's all about; if so there's nothing I can do about it. And behind this lay the old, unadmitted-to challenge: Is there anything you can do about it? He held some pages toward her. "It's the real thing," he said. That too was like him, deliberately to use some common phrase when feelings were most involved. In this instance, then, in spite of the phrase, she should feel joy, for she trusted his taste, his judgment, more than she cared to admit. But she felt nothing. As she had feared, her book, held in his hands, had only the most distant sort of reality for her. She stared.

It was true that some hands, like some faces and bodies, were simply more beautiful than others. His were. What incredible power their grace belied, what tasks they had known she did not wish to consider.

He came and sat beside her. "Who was playing the flute?" he asked.

"Marshall. The boy who . . . *the cat-tamer*. Remember?"

"He's good. And the eavesdropping girl?"

"Just a girl. One of the guests. Like me. But don't worry. I'm sure she didn't understand any of the impersonal things we said."

"I don't like slobs."

"Posy? She's not a slob."

"She's got the manners of one. Didn't anyone ever tell her it's impolite to spy on people?"

"*That from you!*"

He laughed and reached out for her. But she eluded him, angry, remembering Posy's pilgrims, puzzled as always by that enormous contempt of others which could spring from him like a devil, that lack of charity. It disturbed her the more keenly because behind it—how well, alas, she knew this from her own life—lay an untempered mania for perfection which must absolutely be struggled with if one did not want to end up alone on the polar icecap. But he would not stoop to this struggle, and if he made mistakes in consigning human beings to certain absolute categories in the scheme of things it did not seem to trouble him. "Posy's a little foolish at times, but not a slob," she said. She was still watching his hands. "She's even quite imaginative."

"So it would seem."

She remembered then one of those tracts which Mrs. Dartley had read them the week before. All crime, she had said, personal or collective, is based on the failure to imagine otherness. It had shaken her to hear so neat a formulation made of various vague but obsessive ideas of her own. She would leave it to others to decide, Mrs. Dartley had said, whether or not even under the best of circumstances the spiritual apprehension of otherness—any and all otherness—would lie equally within the power of each, whether or not perfection as doctrine was even worth arguing about. She would also not attempt to deal with those more mysterious demons which made it so difficult to see, to feel, to act beyond the self, but

only with the social ones. She had then gone on to talk rather mean-
deringly about the impediments of tradition, outmoded social
structures, vested power interests, and lying officialdom. It had all
been rather thirties-ish and therefore something of a letdown, but
the first part of what Mrs. Dartley had said now seemed painfully
connected to one great source of the anxiety which St. George
perpetually aroused in her: his willfull rejection of those great gifts
which were in him, his misuse of them, his deliberate turning away
from the reality of others. She was looking at him now as through
a veil of sleep. Indeed, a weariness so great, a fatigue so physical,
had come upon her that she could hardly keep her eyes open. Like
a somnambulist she said, "I suppose that Posy has a soul too. Or
whatever you want to call it. Underneath all that silliness there's
something else that matters. Just as I suppose that when you have
your hands on a man's throat there's more to you than murder—
you still have a soul too."

The blood sprang to his face as though a blow had been laid
across it. Her words came back to her now like a slow, sonic
boom. She could not believe she had spoken them. She felt at once
sick and frightened and confused. Something was begun that could
not be stopped, though both would try. "Forgive me," she said.
Inexplicably, that sense of kinship with him was suddenly stronger
than ever. She got up and stood facing away from him.

"You can't turn your back on me," he said, lightly.

"Why not?"

"Because you're my *Doppelgänger*, my bright one, my good
one, my angelic *Hexe*, my shield."

"No," she said firmly. "No more, at any rate. That was really a
great deal of nonsense, harmful nonsense." Her mysterious perception of his comings and goings, which had been real enough, had
led them both into talking as though she were some kind of protective spirit hovering always near him. "That was just another
game; it pleased us both. It was flattering to both our egos. And
another thing—all this becoming all sorts of other people and
things. One can't do it really, except in visions, in art, maybe.
There's such a difference. It's so important to know this. I haven't
any magical powers at all. Except maybe as an artist. As a human
being I'm terribly limited."

"You're me," he persisted.

"Oh no I'm not," she said. For a brief period in their history she had got the fixed notion that if she had been born a man she might have been frighteningly like him. "There's a difference. There always has been. And not just because I'm a woman. I don't know what the difference is, but it's there. It's real." He was always trying to usurp her existence.

He said, "I'll leave you if you want me to. Do you?"

She shook her head sadly. "No, I don't." He had drawn her again into the exclusive reality of his own world of struggle and sorrow. The atmosphere of all those months in Munich came back.

He made no attempt to hide his relief. "It was stupid of us to fight over an eavesdropping child."

"That's not what we were fighting over. Mrs. Halász was right, wasn't she? You had met, hadn't you?"

He nodded. "I thought you never wanted to hear another word about things like that."

"Oh I don't *want* to, God knows." It now seemed to her incredible that there had actually been times when they had been gay together about his clandestine activities, some few intimate moments when the sheer fun of deceiving, the double-game, the playing with identity, all of which were important factors to him, had charmed her too. There was no denying the fact that somewhere inside the perimeter of terror there were also magnetic sites, and that for all her attempt to stand on the safe side of that perimeter —could anyone do that, really?—there had been times when she had been drawn irresistibly toward them. Calmly she said, "It was her son, I suppose. Mrs. Halász said something about a party he gave. Was he part of the apparatus?"

"No he wasn't."

"But it was her son, wasn't it? Why?"

He answered in the casual, clipped tones she knew so well. "He might have been a good contact. Someone in England suggested him. Someone in our organization did a poor job of checking it out."

"You did approach him then. He refused. Why?"

"The usual reasons."

"Family?"

He nodded. "And there were a couple of particularly vulnerable aspects to his situation. He wouldn't have been much good to us anyway." All this time he had been holding her manuscript. Now he laid it gently on her desk, one hand resting on it for a moment, then outlined against it as he neatly flicked it into perfect order. She was both moved and disturbed by this, and felt driven on.

"Do you know what happened to him?" she asked. "He's dead."

"Yes, I know."

"His wife and two children have been sent off somewhere, no one knows where. His widowed sister too," she said passionately. "Mrs. Halász and her husband were shipped to some muddy little village near the Roumanian border. He died there. Finally they let her move back to Budapest. And then, after Mrs. Dartley made every possible effort from here, they let, they let her come."

"You don't need to tell me what's going on in places like Hungary." His voice was harsh. "How would you like to live that way? You damned well wouldn't. Do you think anyone does? That's an unpleasant little picture you've got, but don't think of doing anything to change it. That might be risky. If you'd seen some of the . . . Can we talk about something else? Can we drop it?"

"Yes," she said. There was silence between them. They had nearly begun again the familiar, useless round of conflict. She knew what he would say, knew too with the usual sense of blank despair those facts he would remind her of and that could never, she knew, be wished away: mass-deportations, spiritual and physical violation, unspeakable daily fear and terror, these, the facts of life in countries like Hungary. To justify them at all was impossible. To justify them in the name of an abstraction was obscene. It was right, it was proper to oppose a tyranny of such dimensions. But how? His way? Had he the right to decide for others, as in effect he did, that their lives were not worth living? And wasn't what he was doing not only dangerous, but in the long run naïve? How could the meddling of secret agents make things better? The collecting of information, yes, that she could understand in a corrupt and warring world. But this notion of a holy mission? Worst of all was her conviction that his own motivation sprang in part from obscure sources, that there simply existed in him as a person some deep pull toward the life of risk and danger and violence he had chosen, something that had little to do with the human issues at stake and that enabled him to act without asking whether or not good could possibly come from it.

He said now, as though to answer the question about consequences which she had kept herself from putting to him, "We don't intend harm to come to people like the Halász'."

When did the I get conveniently lost in a monolithic we? She would never free herself of the paradox of his nature. And what of herself? Was it not true that in spite of everything the primary luster of his daring, his personal courage, was attractive to her? It came to her then that in any number of earlier eras she might have loved and admired him simply and without doubts. But the warrior-hero was then a potent figure, of broad and public scope, not someone who slunk around in the shadows. Besides, everything was changed, irrevocably. What could a hero of the old sort do against the new forms of terror? She had once seen a newsreel of the Polish cavalry in 1939, charging, foredoomed, the German tanks. How stirring the beginning of that charge had been, she'd had to admit this to herself later on; for a few seconds it had been impossible to feel anything but brave horses, brave men, heroes all, admirable. The tanks had been nothing like this, but only terrifying, remote, depersonalized, slow and certain machines of destruction. She had lifted her hands to cover her eyes, but just as she did the objective eye of the camera itself swung mercifully away from that final clash. No, the old ethos was gone, had no place now. Preferable though it was to the manipulation of mass power, bearing within itself as it had, for the elite few, an ideal of honor, to cling to it now would be disastrous. Something new might come— did not have to and perhaps would not—but might, new ideals to shape that inchoate world into which she had been born, transformations of the old valorous virtues. But the old way—at best it was the Polish officers, at worst, perhaps, an unwitting making of the self into an instrument of the new terror.

St. George was taking a small box from his pocket.

Sylvia said aloud, " 'Gone are the heroes of Greece,/Gone the warrior-aristocrats . . .' "

"What?" he said, frowning.

"Nothing. Sorry. They're the beginning lines of a sort of poem. Mrs. Dartley made them up, one day when it was raining and we were all restless. A game. Each of us had to make up two lines in turn. It went on and on."

"It doesn't sound like very impressive poetry."

"I suppose not."

Now he caught her off guard, saying, "You and Ernest Campion have become friends. I've kind of expected that. Sooner than this, in fact."

"Have you?" She felt suddenly as though she were going to cry.

"His penitential qualities were bound to interest you." There was no irony in his voice, no contempt, and he was looking at her steadily, almost with shyness. It was an expression she had never seen on his face before. "And your passion for saving souls him."

"You're talking foolishly," she said. "That's all over with for Ernest, past. You hardly know him. And I have no such grand notions about myself. If I ever did have you've certainly cured me of them. Besides, no one can save someone else."

"Can't they?"

She did not reply. Then he said, "Are you going to marry him?"

"No, I don't suppose I am." It was all cut off now, whatever it would inevitably be.

"Good." His tone was cheerful.

He would like nothing better than to keep her sitting in a tower somewhere, a *princesse lointaine* but one who awaited his convenience. She changed the subject rapidly, feeling a great weariness. "Don't worry about Mrs. Halász being here. I'm sure she'll reveal nothing."

He shrugged. "A lot of funny coincidences have been happening lately." He paused, then went on in that forthright way that characterized his reaction to anything that seemed to threaten him, "Coincidence is the word we use for patterns that we can't ignore but feel are outside our power to control. Only fools think coincidences are trivial or accidental."

She said, "Sometimes I think everybody knows everything about everybody else anyway, that one can't hide a thing really. I suppose most of the time there's a sort of tacit agreement not to notice—that's what keeps things running. Or if you do notice, then you pretend to your self you haven't."

"That's good manners."

"It's more than that. Reciprocal kindness. And recognition of the fact that one understands so little. Maybe everyone in this house actually knows all about you, for example."

"I doubt it."

"Oh I don't mean specifically that you're a . . . what you are. But that you have secrets that have nothing to do with AMPERE."

"I brought you a gift," he said. From the small box he took out a medallion on a silver chain, swung it lightly in the air.

"Beware of Greeks bearing gifts," she said. He handed it to her. "What does it mean?" she asked. It was silver, cast in it: an owl on some sort of branch, five stars ringing the owl, a crescent moon.

"I'm not certain. It caught my eye. I thought you'd like it."

"I do, very much. Very much. Thank you."

He took it from her and fastened it around her neck, his hands resting for a moment on the top of her breastbone, near her throat. She looked at him fully, for the first time really since he had come, searching his face. Something about him reminded her now of the way he had been the night of the snowstorm in Munich. A horrible sort of fear began to possess her. "You're thinner," she said, reaching up, touching his cheek. "You don't look well." He was leading her to the bed. They sat down side by side. "Have bad things been happening?" The words felt heavy and foolish on her tongue. But there was worse to come. There was a question she would not be able to prevent herself from asking now, since she herself could no longer hide from one particular bit of knowledge, knowledge she had always had, even that night when she took upon herself the weight of his body, knowledge she had deliberately chosen to suppress. It was the key; once it was in place there could be no more deception on either of their parts. Guilt, fear—these were not phantoms. These were real, as palpable as the flesh.

Sylvia and St. George had their arms around each other, holding each other as two children lost on a cold mountainside might do. She said, "That night in Munich . . . the snowstorm night." She named now the exact date of the visit, as though to be sure there were no misunderstanding. "Shortly before that, perhaps the day before, probably the day before . . . you had killed a man, hadn't you?"

His eyes gave her the answer, eyes suddenly sick and full of pain. There was nothing of deception there now. They rocked slowly back and forth on the couch, their faces pressed together, side by side. He laid one hand on her breast, and she placed one of her own hands upon his. How different were the colors of their skins, hers so much lighter. And their faces together so, profile to

profile, his on one side, hers on the other; for one swift instant she
saw them from a great distance, saw some royal Egyptian pair,
man, woman, husband, wife, brother, sister, clinging together.
Then the distance closed. At least I know now, she thought; at
least I know.

Twenty-four

For a few seconds it appeared that both Sylvia and the swaying
burden above her were about to crash to the floor together, but
then she regained her balance and managed to finish lowering the
smaller of her two suitcases from the top of the wardrobe to the
floor.

Like everyone else she had been dutifully filing into the drawing
room for a reading when suddenly she had remembered about the
journal. Without a word even to Mrs. Dartley she had turned,
pushing her way out among the chairs, and rushed back to her
room. Of course it had to be there. But was it? In the bad old days
she had always been so careful to check on it, and now weeks had
passed without her even remembering its existence. She smacked
her hand wildly against the inner lid of the suitcase. Yes, it appeared that it was still there. With the usual sense of humiliation
she began to pull at the fabric-covered lining. Disgusting, disgusting, she thought, a degrading film-version parody of his own degrading work. But what else could she do? She could not leave
such pages just lying about. She had hold of them now, hesitated—
how pointless everything was—and at last hauled forth from behind the lining a sheaf of torn-out notebook pages. She got up and
stood very still in the middle of the room, holding these pages in
her hands, not looking at them, uncertain of what to do. Her hands
were shaking a little. Downstairs the other guests at Kilchberg
were gathered, except for her, listening by now to Mrs. Dartley—
even the intruder, even St. George, Bingham, whatever you
wanted to call him, even he. Sylvia Grierson had never felt so
alone.

She tossed the notebook pages onto the writing desk. They

landed neatly in order, as though they had been carefully placed
there. She sat down and leaned forward. Scrawled across the
top page was the title she had once given to this sad record—
The History of an Agon—in a large, ugly script hardly recognizable as her own. A good title, she had to admit, a painfully apt one.
She was shocked to see as she turned through the first few
pages without reading, that evidently she had once decorated the
margins of some of them, much as medieval monks had illuminated
sacred script or nineteenth-century ladies had hand-painted roses
and violets along the borders of their writing paper. Only, the
border she had invented, in Greek letters, repeated over and over
again, was formed from the words *Bios* and *Thanatos*. Seeing this
now in the light of what had sprung out of her that afternoon in
the music room was frightening. Then she had always known
everything, but had lacked the courage to make conscious truth of
this knowledge. She began to read.

Enormous relief at one thing. Though it's as I expected, it's good
to know. *They* came to him first, they being the government.
(Has government replaced the gods, usurped the role of fate?)
He didn't tell me more than this, only adding that he doubts it
would otherwise have occurred to him. (What is his life, his
soul, to them?) It is quite easy to imagine how it all happened.
No doubt they're always looking for likely victims, checking
through records, especially war records. His must practically
have leapt into their hands. Astounding physical courage, I'm
sure. I think too from something he almost talked about once
that there was one particular event during the war, in Italy,
something that showed not only courage and judgment under
stress but *an incredible will to survive*.
   He said once, "My friends are all dead." It shocked me. I
knew he meant the men he had been in the army with. I waited
for him to explain, but he changed the subject. Thought about
this a lot later. Something a bit melodramatic? The world is
quite literally peopled with the survivors of so much violence and
terror—with most of them you'd never know it. Adaptability of
life, need for the species to go on? Yet if a man has fought
bleeding body to bleeding body for his life and had to kill, kill,
who knows how many times? Who can say what that survival
may cost?

Then too he would be so perfect for them in other ways. His having lived abroad so much, all the languages, the highly trained mind, the knowledge of so many different things. And the job with AMPERE would be a splendid cover. The first approach was probably only to ask him to do some very small thing, make some simple contact, leave a message or pick one up. Would he not do this for his country? All of that. Difficult to refuse. But fatal not to. From that first step the rest would follow, all too easily, as *they* must know.

I said to him. "Sometimes I think that for all the anonymity what you're really trying to do is impose your personality upon history."

He said, "Personality's a luxury I can't afford to indulge in." This is not true.

I hate myself in this new role, The Waiting Woman. These vigils I keep for him when he is away—I am not Penelope! How am I ever to get back to my own work if all my psychic energy is secretly being diverted? I have gotten this absurd notion that his safety depends somehow on me. As absurd as his notion— unstated but implicit—that the West will collapse, the Turks take Vienna, if he doesn't keep racing about spying on people.

I make light of this here, and I'm glad I can still occasionally see how comical it all is. Yet it is very dark and very real at other times. A spell is at work. Sometimes I feel as though my own reality is being usurped, or at any rate that all those powers that make me an artist, powers which in the past I had neither to control nor obey but simply co-exist with, are going awry. I can almost feel the magic being subverted.

Even when I can manage to stop feeling as though I'm a sort of double double-agent (talisman going with him), I find it difficult to resist trying to understand rationally what he is.

How Id (note that Id for I!) dislike this journal, for instance. The idea of keeping so self-conscious a record has always repelled me as being at best narrowly narcissistic, at worst an elaborate self-deception about one's capacity for art. Yet I know I must go on with it, because I have the hope that if I get a little down here I might be free of him for a time and able to work. How ironic that I came here to be free of entanglements, to be free and alone supposedly (all that scrimping and saving and

finding a place where it's cheap to live), only to get involved
with him. At least I knew my way around in the old labyrinth.
Isn't there something to learn here, something too obvious for
very very intelligent stupid people like myself to see?

Oh, why did he have to tell me at all? The aloneness getting
unbearable? Quite likely. (I read once in an *Illustrierten*—what
higher authority?—that this bearing everything alone is where
the first cracks appear.) A form of boasting even? A little, I
suspect. For some time, though, I thought it chiefly the aloneness, and I must admit this aroused a very strong sympathy in
me. For him to tell anyone, to break security in this way—especially for a man who is I think quite high up in the organization
(disgusting word)—this breaking of security is a cardinal error.
He could do nothing riskier. Is it some horrible urge he has to
add still another element of risk, of danger, to an already perilous situation? Trust me! How can he? Look at what I'm doing
now. Besides, he isn't supposed to trust anyone! This risk of
trusting, then—is it only another symptom of his . . . disease? Or
is it a need no human being can free himself of? If so, is it
possibly redemptive?

A week since I've looked in this notebook. The last word, above,
strikes me hard. Yes, what he is doing is contemptible. No matter what, I'm sure of that. Yet I cannot quite believe that he is
only the sum of his actions.

My work goes so badly.

"Why not climb a mountain, ski, race cars?"
"Too simple-minded." He laughs.

But I remember now that when we were in the Vorarlberg
together earlier this month I learned by chance that the slope he
went off to by himself one afternoon was in so dangerous a
condition that everyone had been warned away from it by the
really expert skiers, who left it alone after one of them had made
a trial run.

In other respects our little trip, our little holiday, was far from
what I had hoped it might be. The change of scene had no effect
on him at all really.

"You're as much of an outcast as I am," he said last week.
"Why?"

"Because you're an artist."

"But that's my worry. I'm not hurting anyone, not trying to run the world."

But when I was alone this little exchange plunged me into depression because it reminded me of how at home I do sometimes feel an outcast, a pariah, or some sort of nameless criminal. To judge by the reactions of most middle-class burghers when they learn I'm a writer there is nothing that would please these people more than to hang me, burn me, and then, just to be sure, scatter my ashes to the wind. I don't really fool myself about why I'm here.

The next time St. G. came we talked a little about this, and I said that I seemed only to have to walk into certain rooms to bring out the savage in the great American middle classes. I expected him to make fun of me (it would be easy after an admission like that—paranoia, persecution complex, etc.), but instead he said, "The trouble with savages is that when they vaguely sense a life being lived at a higher level than their own their natural instinct is to want to destroy it." Very flattering that, and it would be nice to think it the whole story. It isn't! But it did touch me, especially since he doesn't usually find it easy to say anything nice.

I said, "I get the feeling they think I'm dangerous."

"Baby," he said, lapsing into that way of talking that I hate, "you are. You look harmless, but you're lethal."

"Well if people are rude, cruel to me . . ."

He interrupted with the familiar, cynical laugh. "You see too much. Too much about yourself. And too much about them, things they don't want seen, not even by themselves. I ought to know. You're a witch. Primitive magic. They think maybe you're going to make an image of them . . ."

"But I don't do that, not in the sense you mean."

"They're too stupid to know that. What do you expect of slobs?" (One of his favorite words: slobs. To him they're a blot on nature; to me a problem.)

He also said something about how women aren't supposed to be that smart, and that if they are they're supposed to be horse-faced, and that if I looked like a horse maybe they'd be able to forgive me a little bit.

"I still don't understand why they're *afraid* of me."

He looked bored. "You've got a mind that's always ticking away like a time bomb and they're afraid it'll go off while they're around."

A fine situation!

Am I to beg the world to forgive me for having a mind, or let it go unused? Or explain that if I lack grace, as I often do, they will just have to remember that dogs walking on their hind legs lack grace too?

Am I to hang a warning sign around my neck that says: "SHE WRITES"?

St. G. tonight: "If the head of the CIA is a respected member of the community, in fact a very desirable person to have on your guest list in Washington or New York, why can't I be?" But when I tried to follow this up, to talk about all that it means, we ended by fighting bitterly, and he took refuge, deliberately to annoy me, I'm sure, in all those meaningless phrases they've taught him, along with all the other horrible things they've taught him—how to kill, I suppose. I can't stand it.

A bad time. A unique event: we spent an evening with friends of mine, Jeff and Polly. They're touring Europe in a kind of late 1940's version of a 1920's version of innocents abroad. This in 1956! They haven't changed a bit since graduate school days; in fact, Jeff still is in graduate school and Polly of course had gone in for ceramics and has a little shop in the Village. St. G. was charming to them, but later, in another context, when we were alone, lashed out about them with incredible violence. Well, they are silly, even seedy, I suppose, with their determination to be "different" (of course they aren't at all), but I like them. Besides, they're not afraid of anything, so they're not dangerous. Beneath St. G.'s controlled charm with them I sensed at the time that they made him uneasy—because their lives are "messy," not highly controlled? It reminded me of the way I am with my own natural enemy, the bourgeoisie . . . I've noticed too that when he and I are out in public together he seems always to be searching for some flaw in my behavior, holding me to some impossibly high standard, as though any imperfection in me will somehow reflect discredit upon him. And I suppose the same thing applies to my friends.

I said, "How *can* you cut yourself off so completely from the normal?"

He lashed back with, "How can you?"

"Me?"

Then a series of cold, cutting remarks about how most women of my age are settled down, raising a family, etc. I interrupted as quickly as possible, for both our sakes. I said my remark had nothing to do with his not having "settled down." And I asked him to leave. Which he did, promptly.

But oh, it cannot be, it cannot be, that what I am serving is no higher than . . . it cannot be that this will of mine to create in my own way is at root no different from his drive for . . . his attempt to escape from the inescapable cycle of things. No. I don't believe it. There is a difference. Why does he want us to be so unnaturally alike? However odd my life, I have not hardened my heart.

Well, suppose a woman wanting to be an artist is only a dog walking on its hind legs. Why not? However "unnatural" we think the dog (and *do* we think that, do we really?), even however funny sometimes, we respect it too. So with all unusual striving. Men fly but have not wings or feathers, the laughter of centuries safely behind them now. Why should a woman in whose head unheard melodies chance also to sound not follow where they lead and still survive? What's "natural" is all too often only what those with interests to protect decree. A human being—*any* human being—walking on his hind legs is funny too. Like cathedrals, we defy gravity, all of us. Foolish word, defy. We come to understand a law of the universe, we come at last to live at a higher level with it.

My relationship with him has somehow brought together all the indissoluble conflicts of my life. I am not yet ready to face all that I must.

Survival is not enough. I had a dream about him the other night. He was on a ship. Suddenly the ship was blown apart and he was flung high into the air. Then he was all alone on the sea—I knew it to be icy—swimming, round and round and round, in ever-narrowing circles. I woke up to find that I was close to tears.

A letter from what the newspaper would call one of the "hot spots" of the world. In it a piece of writing paper folded over, and inside that a small piece of red paper shaped like a heart. You could see a pencil mark or two around the rather unevenly cut edges. He must have drawn it himself, then cut it out. On it in his hand the name of the place, and the date. He must have been very lonely, even perhaps in a very difficult situation. Or am I getting as cynical as he? And yet, never mind, the form that loneliness took. Oh, why is he at such pains usually to put down the tender, gentle side of his nature? What has happened? The man who once intended to give his life to Bach, to Mozart? Caparisoned now with vile and secret weapons, leaving behind him in his trackless wanderings not melodies, heard or otherwise, but bootmarks.

Dirty dregs, remains of snow. Still. Will spring never come? And if it does, what? My work continues to go badly.

The demands on his intellectual and physical energies must be enormous, especially since he really does go on working for AMPERE too, in order not to arouse his colleagues' suspicions there. I gather that one or two of the highest-ranking men in AMPERE know the truth. He hasn't told me this, but it's obvious; someone has to arrange "cover" for his other assignments. How nice to know that AMPERE can be trusted! And that AMPERE and the U. S. government understand each other so well!

But somehow it is all so life-denying—his life, I mean. Why would anyone want to turn his energies into a constant combat, a sort of meaningless testing of his prowess against . . . what?

He's safely back and seems not the least bit the worse for wear. Though something he said indicated that I wasn't wrong in thinking he'd been feeling rather desperate when he sent the belated valentine.

"Someone has to do it."

"But why you?" A shrug. Then a comment about his having a really pretty odd combination of talents. I suggested, half joking, that he might have made a good actor. "Actors don't act," he said. "*Im Anfang war die Tat*," I thought but did not say, since the mood was light. We went through a whole list of possible occupations for him: law, teaching, journalism, science, AMPERE itself, government service. etc., etc. (I omitted anything connected with art, for obvious reasons), but he rejected them all with a series of contemptuous remarks. Contemptuous and, I must admit, unpleasantly convincing. Still, I got an image of some spiritually deprived loony who goes to a concert and hearing a violin sonata can think only about cat intestines and horsehairs, or who listening to a singer keeps reminding himself— and others—that singing is after all only organized screams and moans. These things are true, yes, but out of them come other truths, beauty for example, and meanings of a very much higher order. It is as though we were to think only and exclusively of our spinal cord, the primitive snake in all of us, or of the horror that in one sense underlies all our actions. Original sin, yes; it is always with us. It should not be forgotten. But neither should it be *worshiped*.

About high-placed government officials, elected or otherwise, he said, "If you think some of the things I do are reprehensible you ought to know some of the things they do. At least I have to take direct responsibility for my actions, mostly in my own hide. If I make a mistake, I've had it, or someone in my outfit has. And who do you think sets the whole thing going anyway, who do you think dreamed me up?" I said I hoped the people who dreamed him up would never have cause to regret it. But of course he has a point, and after a time I started saying something about it being odd that someone could accept orders unquestioningly and yet be really so very anarchic, as it seemed to me he was, and he got furious. "I risk my neck for a lot of people I don't even know on both sides of the Atlantic, and you make a stupid remark like that."

At least St. G. has not tainted his mind with the notion that the Russians as a people are a vile and fallen race, nor has he gone in for any of that nonsense about capitalism as a system—if that's what it is—being divinely ordained. With his education these stupidities would hardly be possible for him. He said last night that he sees it as a simple question of who's going to dominate the world, "us or them." What they profess and what we profess—doctrines which he admits even have points in common—that's not the issue, he says. Power, pure power, is.

Can it really be that terrible, that simple? I wondered later if he were talking about complicated historical processes, or about himself. I said I thought that he had very strong notions about his own personal liberty, which he was always very frank about, that I respected this, but I wondered what he thought the limitations were. He only laughed and said, cheerfully enough, "I've noticed that artists have some pretty unusual ideas about their liberty too." Then he made some brief and just observations on Russian history, on czarist authoritarianism and bureaucracy and on how these things have been perpetuated under other names. (But why, at other times, does he try to make it sound as though it's a holy war in which one side or the other must perish?) He points out too how much espionage they engage in, how much less scrupulous they are—all of which I do not doubt. When he talks this way he almost convinces me that it's right, natural, necessary—even self-sacrificing—what he's doing.

I have stopped writing altogether. How innocuous those little words look. Yet what a catastrophe they spell out for me.

Humbug! They are all jerks, all of them, these stupid spies. Only a small percentage of what they do actually relates to these dreadful needs that the Cold War has thrust upon us, to having to protect ourselves. Sometimes I want to laugh in his face. Sometimes I do laugh. These solemn, only half-veiled references to their activities, all the risks they take, their own importance. Boasting Beowulfian Bravado. Maybe all of them have a woman somewhere to whom they come for admiration and sympathy. Oh, they are so stupid. Sometimes I think men never grow up. What dangerously childish games! Some games are suitable for adults and some are not. When he appears ridiculous to me I feel more compromised than ever. It is sordid, sordid. And I am not his damned mother.

We've had a little *Waffenstillstand*.

Not long ago I said to him that I had never quite understood about the music thing. He answered in such a strange way. He said, "I was a pretty talented kid, they tell me. My parents were the worst sorts of *Schwärmer* for music. It was one of their two great passions. Naturally they were all for it."

"But you loved music too?"

"A silly question. Sure, I still do."

"What I meant actually was why you gave it up."

"It was too passive for me, I guess. And you get a little cut off."

What an odd idea, that making music is passive. Even odder for him to talk about getting a little cut off!

I still think it all has mostly to do with his inability to bear the slightest infringement on his own liberty unless *he* chooses the limitations himself, that it doesn't matter what they are so long as he's chosen them. Thus the paradox of a man who can brook no authority but his own serving two such authoritarian organizations as AMPERE and the CIA.

I suppose that when you play a Mozart sonata—even perhaps when you write a novel—you're not really choosing the limitations. What then? Discovering them, once in a while transcending them? If this is so, then art is bound to be a long and arduous voyage. And at the wheel? Not, I think, the ego.

Must admit that sometimes I understand only too well his hatred for "authority," his refusal to submit. After all, I have only to see a policeman to want to say something to annoy him, to argue with him, anything—just so it isn't quite actionable—to make him feel doubt about his authority. How I hate uniforms. How, for that matter, I hate the police. What I most absolutely dread is the ordinary person, who has never asked a question in his life, being invested with a power he has neither the right nor the knowledge to wield properly, the small bureaucratic villain, the one who feels protected by some system or other and also fears it and is thus bound in the most narrow-minded way to implement . . . or to use it as a sanction for releasing the sick savage in himself. I always remember M.'s story about how her father had waited till nearly the last moment to leave Munich, unable to believe that some miracle wasn't going to happen, the Germans come to their senses, Hitler drop dead, etc.—hopes it would be natural enough to have. Then, early summer of 1939 her parents sent her to Switzerland, for a "holiday." A month later they finally decided they would have to go too. Her father took their passports, which luckily they had, to some little police official at some branch office for the necessary exit stamp. "You have a daughter?" the official asked. "Yes." "Where is she?" "In Switzerland." "Ah so?" He then stamped her father's passport, handed it back to him, and put her mother's in a drawer! That is the sort of "authority" I dread.

And justly dread. Still, it would be dishonest not to admit that my little secret passion for annoying policemen also has a strong element of the personally neurotic in it, the underlying absurdity going something like: Why should a uniform give some jerk the right to decide whether *I* get a driver's license or not?

Probably the only thing that's saved me from the gallows is that I've lived in a country where the laws are not very repressive. Or do I only think that because my parents had a reasonable amount of money and were the right color?

But perfect, absolute freedom—that is beyond any of us.

St. G's new nickname for me is Old Druidical, and we have got into all sorts of mysterious waters. A recurrent joke—at least I hope that's all it is—which he loves to elaborate. He has some theory about the Celts (the ubiquitous Celts!) having been part of the same group, or actually being the same tribe as the Pelasgians, who I now learn were the pre-Hellenic, pre-Achaean, whatever-you-want-to-call-it inhabitants of Greece. The Pelasgians weren't entirely killed off or driven out, he claims, and there was, as always, a good deal of interbreeding. And so because of my distant Welsh ancestors I am Old Druidical and Old Pelasgian. He is always involved in some curious attempt to make us blood-kin. With my pathetic handful of Greek it's all very confusing to me, but perhaps no one else really understands it either and one theory's as good as another. From my own brief poking around in encyclopedia the other day no two are alike. Where St. G. gets his information is never clear to me, and when I ask he laughs and says "Oral tradition, but not in graduate school."

Anyway, it seems there are points of similiarity between the religious practices of the Pelasgians and the Druids, and the chief deity was female. I suppose one of the many versions of the dear old White Goddess? The Pelasgians worshiped her and then along came the Achaeans and by Hellenic times Greece was of course absolutely male-oriented, I should say officially male-oriented, with Zeus the superior deity. The old goddess was supposed to represent the three personalities of woman (nice to

know how many there are!)—all in one, I gather. Trying to put
this in terms of my own I said she must have survived into
Hellenic times and got divided up. Aphrodite, Artemis, Athena?
More or less, he said. But he claims they never really forgot she
was one goddess, and he said that even in classical times there
was one shrine—I don't remember what he said the name of it
was, but he's been there—where she was worshiped under one
name, Hera, simply meaning Lady, maybe once Earth. He said
Athena was "the really important babe" (that odd way he has of
talking! sometimes very colloquially, all those slangy phrases,
and other times he's so stiff and formal), the closest in descent
from the old pre-Achaean, Cretan One Goddess. I said, but it
got even more changed around in Roman times? He said, yes,
they controlled the female more, and so did the Jews and
Mahomet, but that even with Rome and then the Hebrew influence coming in with Christ she survived in Italy in degraded
form in some of the little church saints. And sprang back with
the Virgin cult? I asked. Yep, he said, and added—this I didn't
really follow, but then he knows so much more about it than I
do, his studies, his travels—that Artemis was once as much
maternal as virginal, then said it didn't make much difference,
nymph, virgin, mother, crone, child, lawgiver, they were all
one and that it wasn't until the Renaissance that people decided
to "make a big show out of her as Venus," mainly because of the
painters. By this time I was fairly lost in all the names and
transformations. So then he laughed and said that the Achaeans
in spite of their own male-ethos culture, warriors and all that,
had been attracted by Pelasgian dames, preferred them to the
subjugated women of their own race, intellectually as well as
sexually, and were always sneaking off to cohabit with them. I
said, a good thing too.

Since then I've been thinking what a dangerous idea it is, God
the Father or God the Mother, one without the other.

Anyway, for the moment it appears that he is an Achaean
chieftain sneaking off to a lair (the Kuppers' old flat!) inhabited
by a Pelasgian priestess, me. Good grief!

I said, wasn't Athena the enemy of Mars. He said yes.

Is love of him only perhaps a sort of making recompense for
what I often feel to be the cold and ruthless side of my own

nature? That side which so often now seems to remain always a little disengaged, observing? My relationship with him has led me into the most horrible fascination with myself.

As I listen, as I guess at much, I sometimes think: ah, but if various imponderables were different might I not react so? Or even if, with the power that is in me and I were a man, that creature to whom all is historically available, what he wills, might it not be easier than one thinks to succumb to temptations that are much more frightening than those of the flesh? Oh poor men, all that being so free, that ruling of the world—and all the infinite possibility for tragedy that goes with it. That playing at God!

In any case, extraordinary endowments make for extraordinary burdens.

People with greater power in them balance more precariously between good and evil than others, perhaps?

I have heard my first *Ariadne auf Naxos!* A marvelous work, a masterpiece. I was overcome. When we drove to Vienna I didn't know this was the reason for the trip. Later he said, "In the first act you were the Composer, weren't you, and in the second act Ariadne?" I suppose he was right. We talked about what Strauss's "real" reason was for having the role of the Composer sung by a woman. I said that if there was just one "real" reason, it was probably purely aesthetic, that above all he loved writing music for a certain kind of soprano voice, certain combinations of these voices. "And most tenors are such slobs," he said, "it would be kind of hard to find one who could express that much idealism." We agreed too that it was a nice psychological touch, a comment on the artist's "feminine" sensibility—his term. Then he said "All artists are spiritually androgynous. Good ones. They've got to be."

But sometimes I've wondered if one of those yielding, submissive, spongelike women might not be right for him. When I made an oblique reference to this he was quick to understand. There was such a woman in his life, for a long time. He admitted he had liked the absolute devotion, but it didn't work for two reasons: he was soon bored with her conversation, and he felt "an odd blurring of distinctions."

He reminded me, almost arrogantly, of the Pelasgian goddess.

Why should my relationship with him have made me so aware of myself as a woman, almost in some very primitive and there-fore unnerving way? I never thought about such things at all in the past, not even when I had better reason to than I do now. This ridiculous sense of femaleness, *trapped* femaleness—all the odder since he certainly hasn't made me very happy as a woman. It is as though some special obsession of my own, something at the very root of my existence and being, finds a reverse, a mirror-image in his person, or in his life.

Exploration of one's opposite? Opposites imply each other. That only by exploring that opposite, which is a part of the self in any case, a sort of shadow cabinet, one comes, paradoxically, through the full circle of the self?

The only thing he has ever said to me that could possibly be called an endearment: "You're so soft, so soft," escaping him in a kind of moan during an embrace, as though it had been torn out of him against his will and through gritted teeth. And then as though he hated himself for this afterwards. How he drew back. What great cold distances he set between us for a time after that, more even than usual.

About men and St. G. Maybe because the history of the world is so largely a history of men and their actions, that he both arouses and in some way satisfies my curiosity. At times in an almost completely impersonal way.

Yet I can't pretend to being all that detached about him. If I were, he wouldn't have the power over me that he has. (Tonight is another vigil night.) Alas, I do care for him, and care about him, even if I don't find it makes much sense.

Once I went to night court after a party (such ideas of fun some of "the nicest people" have). A woman and her husband—he had just smashed her face in. She had called the police, wanted him put behind bars, cursed him, made her complaint. Then as they started to take him away she began weeping and begging the judge to let him go. "I forgive you, Lennie, I for-give you," she kept crying out. When he was hauled off, the judge, who remembered them from another time, took the sort of liberty with her that people often do with those they consider to be their inferiors. How could she explain her attitude, he asked, a man who had repeatedly beaten her, etc.? She sniffled and said, "Your honor, I guess I just like his looks."

Who knows?

There are times when I find myself almost believing that what he is doing is noble, all the more so because the need is not obvious, as in war, and see him as self-effacing, painfully alone. If he dies I won't even know for the longest time. And if he dies I will be the only one, outside of those secret official circles, who will really know the truth.

No, no, no—it is ignoble, there are, there must be worthier forms for the expression of his will, for the shaping of his powers. There are too many consequences to others along the way, simple people who ask only to be left to live, even many no doubt who would choose the craven way of life on any terms; rather a hungry belly than no belly at all, rather a spirit shaped by tyranny than a spirit unhoused by flesh. And who can dare blame them? Not I. But he . . . when I said something like this to him he replied, "Others will always make the choices for these people."

St. G.: "Artists are pretty devious too."

Me: "No, we are not devious. We are intricate."

There's no doubt that what he is doing feeds his ego enormously. I made a sort of list for him, superficial admittedly, a sort of manual of the pleasures of spydom. It amused him greatly.

Twice now he has told me where he was going on a trip, supposedly for AMPERE; once to a place in South America, once the Near East. Each time, about two days after his arrival, public events of such importance have occurred as to occupy the headlines of the newspapers of the world for some time, and though I know nothing in detail about what really is going on in such places, I'm left each time with the conviction that he's on one of the two wrong sides. It's so clear that we support the most selfish men, the most backward elements, in these areas—anyone in fact who is guaranteed to be "anti-Communist," whatever that is (and surely "Communist" in such areas has for most men chiefly to do with wanting to live better, more freely?). Once, along different lines, I pressed him on this; to my surprise he agreed that those officials we support are contemptible, corrupt, suppressive. His solution? To let them know there *are* strings attached to U. S. aid, *to order them to be more democratic!*

It will get worse and worse, the CIA. I am certain there is a slow but inevitable corruption in such work.

There is, I suppose, a hierarchy of spies, just as there is of everything else, and I'm sure he is fairly high up in it. Some guesses: his work is largely organizational (and largely, despite forays elsewhere, in Europe, especially eastern Europe), but there can be no hard and fast line and it's obvious that he's also "in the field." Even there his specific tasks are to make decisions and do further organizing, not to murder or carry out sabotage himself, but he has been trained to do these things and every little "field trip" must bring him near the possibility. That's a fair thought to . . .

Yesterday a conversation which began lightly enough and then as usual turned into a struggle. It began with my recalling how often people I know, especially in New York, used to tell me I "ought to do something about things." They would say this to me with a special animus which they never directed towards anyone else, especially not themselves. Nor would they ever say what it was I was supposed to do or about what, and they didn't like it when I asked them to be specific. It was quite all right for them to sit in their living rooms talking about how bad things were, but not for me to, it appeared. For a long time, I told St. G., I thought it had to do with the fact that I was teaching, but then I realized that behind all the talk about teaching was something else: that I was a writer, or trying to be one. St. G. said, "Americans, Jews, Russians—they all have a weakness for thinking of art as evangelism." Perhaps, I said, but that wasn't what I meant; there seemed to be some even stranger notion at work, that the artist is somehow *more responsible* for everything than others—a version of the attitude of the burghers, who think that the artist is *more to blame* for everything, and that while both attitudes were unacknowledged, grudging tributes to the

suprarational powers of art, both, I thought, were very unrealistic.

"Don't you think art deals with morality?" he asked.

"Oh yes, but not in any simple-minded way, not like calender
wisdom. The moral dimensions of art work very mysteriously, I
suppose."

"You mean that reading *Hamlet* never instructed anyone in
how to vote but that one's general conduct may in some way be
affected?"

I said yes, more or less, that was one way of putting it,
and only later realized that this was a mask conversation,
at least for him. Somehow we got talking about action, and
something I said angered him and he said, "Oh I forgot, you're a
real little liberal, aren't you?"

I knew very well what he meant by the term, used in that
sneering tone, and it infuriated me because *he* knows very well
I'm *not* that kind of "liberal," people with their machine-
punched mentalities, no different in that way from their opposites among the illiberals, having in common with them a passionate desire not to look at the object itself, heads filled with
stock responses, their minds never engaged by whatever is really
happening. But I managed to say nothing. He'd been referring to
some particularly ghastly things that have been going on in the
Baltic states, and he lashed out with, "You'd cry for help soon
enough, all of you, if it were happening to you, and you
wouldn't care what the cost. But safe in New York or London
you can pretend these things don't happen, can't you? Or you
justify them. 'Excessive measures which in time will be amelio-
rated.' Disgusting hypocrites, all of you."

This reminded me of something I heard Mrs. Dartley, Gwendolyn Dartley, say at the party Stefan took me to last week—a
rare event for me these days, to go out socially. Of course I'd
never met her before (she's quite something). She was talking to
an American foreign correspondent about the race problem;
evidently she's been writing some articles about it or letters or
something—that wasn't clear. I didn't hear what he said, but she
said, "Ah yes, our barbarous south, our hypocritical north."

Calmer, we went on to agree that the self-righteous attitude of
a lot of official liberals isn't very nice but that compared to their
equivalents among the illiberals they look good. We talked

about the coming presidential campaign and for a little while made quite a surprising little domestic scene between us. Very pleasant.

Last week at a party in London he got into an argument with some man—St. G. called him a waterfly—about why he, St. G., did not think we should disarm unless Russia did too. The man persisted, followed him about, "bleated" about what he called our higher, moral duty, etc. The usual nonsense, I guess. Finally St. G. said to him, "Are you telling me that if I were right now to knock you down you wouldn't do anything about it?" No he would not, replied the waterfly, and continued to follow him about yapping. And so St. G. turned around and did knock him down.

I felt sick when he told me this, the sort of sickness you only feel when someone you love reveals something horrid about himself. (Later I had to admit to myself that along with this feeling went a faint sort of sympathy with him, though what intemperance, what pride—that is frightening). Then it seems that the waterfly sprang up, rushed at him, and began clawing wildly at him, and St. G. had to pin his arms behind him. What a scene, ugh.

I remained calm throughout this story, and then asked if the waterfly had won his respect by fighting back. He said, "On the contrary. If he'd stuck to his beliefs, or meant them, then I'd have respected him."

"You changed the circumstances," I said.

"That's right. If he had still done nothing then he'd have been a hero of a higher type than anyone I know."

This answer of his shook me. I had been ready to break with him. I found myself ensnared again.

There is, oh somehow there is nobility in him, greatness, lost in him somewhere. And yet his own life! It is as though he feels there is no way back for him now. Too proud, too proud. He is driven by private demons; that I cannot give name to them does not make them less real. Submit, submit to the imperfection of things.

The struggle continues. "I *enjoy* my work."

"Nice for you," I said.

"You're not going to try to get me to give it up?"

"No, not for my sake, if that's what you mean."

Great variety within a strict form. *Chess*. Power too. Of course he enjoys it. But for all its resemblance to a game, its uses as such are wrong; there are consequences in a world of human beings. He has closed his mind to consequences, though he thinks, or says he thinks, that he is defending his own right to be free. Free? He is less free than anyone I have ever known! No, not quite closed his mind. If he had he wouldn't suffer so much. And he does suffer, he does. No man of his general qualities who makes love so poorly can fail to be in some state of spiritual distress.

All this talk about "idealism." I said that my guess was that with very few exceptions most of the people he has to deal with in the Soviet bloc are the worst sorts, mostly people who will do anything for money. I could see that it's true. Then I shocked him. I said that if I were in a country where I hated the regime I'd keep as far away as possible from foreign agents, I'd never trust them, but that if I were really a brave person I'd work from within to try to mitigate things, until or unless a good natural opportunity for throwing things over came along.

"You're really dangerous," he said, and meant it.

A curious conversation about Freud. He said it was interesting that Freud has been taken up most enthusiastically in America, a country with no very great traditional culture, perhaps because people can't live without something that will explain "all the things that are really kind of hard to explain." I said that was what I had against Freudians, their having turned Freud into a doctrinaire system, that no system has all the answers. Besides, I said, most people who thought they were "Freudians" had insight mixed up with dogma and science with religion.

Then I didn't think Freud "explained everything"? I laughed, said he knew I wasn't that naïve. This amused and somehow pleased him. I added that naturally one couldn't talk this way about Freud around people who hadn't even begun to accept him, but that he had his biases too and he did leave out a lot. St. G. sensed a subject with personal implications for me (I thought at the time it could as well have worked the other way around)

and he began to tease, asked if I rejected the notion that all
artists are neurotic. I said no, certainly not, but pointed out that
not all neurotics are artists, ho hum and *tout au contraire*. I felt
as bored as I sounded, and he goaded and goaded in a variety of
clever ways until I lost my temper (which was what he wanted)
and said that one of Freud's two great weaknesses was his envi-
ous attitude towards art, that it scared him, especially music,
which he actively disliked—something worth thinking about,
the more so since he lived in Vienna, of all cities the city of
music—and that you had only to read his essay on Leonardo to
see how disingenuous and limited Freud could be and even ill-
informed and how incapable of experiencing the reality of art. I
said that even his admiration for Shakespeare was so tinged with
jealousy that he could never credit the Stratford bourgeois with
having written the plays and passionately supported a man
named *Looney* in ascribing them to Oxford, since Oxford at
least had Norman blood and Freud had always thought Shakespeare's face looked more "Latin" than English! I said a lot more
than this too, and suddenly St. G. burst into laughter, great
waves of absolute laughter. I'm not sure I'd ever heard him laugh
before and certainly there had never been anything like this
complete abandonment, his head thrown back, the most free and
pleasant deep laughter. I thought, for once making a fool of
myself has been worth it. He grabbed me in a sort of quick and
trusting bear hug, the only spontaneous gesture I think I've ever
seen him make. Then he poured us both second drinks, and
asked if I thought ideas could exist independently of the personal
organism that conceived of them. I said I wasn't sure of what he
meant by that but if he meant did I think ideas referred us to
more than sense phenomena—then yes.

He said, "But since most people don't have what you could
really call ideas, but only a collection of opinions and of . . .
verbalized . . . desires and dreads . . ." He broke off at this
point.

"Not very well verbalized usually," I said and got up and was
going into the Kuppers' kitchen to bring in the cold supper I
had made earlier, and, practically out the door, I said something
like, "One thing I'm sure of at least—ideas and neurosis aren't
simply interchangeable, any more than art and neurosis are."

Suddenly he was on his feet, pacing about the room, and

talking just as fast as I had been, about some new book that has just come out on poor old T. E. Lawrence, this one explaining him as a sadist or something like that. St. G. had had a series of fights about it when he was in New York last week (though he hasn't read it—he said that didn't matter, he was sure none of the people he was fighting with had either, they only read reviews), chiefly because he thinks it absurd that people can't see that Lawrence's ideas were important. It had infuriated him that instead of "mucking him over" they wouldn't take him seriously as a man of "great and extraordinary ability," who suffered "one betrayal after another." He went on for some time, as usual when engaged very convincing, about Lawrence, whom I'd never thought much about before. I doubt that women do. It all seemed to matter so intensely to him, and I had the feeling I was missing something.

Now, later, it occurs to me that what St. G. lacks is an idea! He needs scope for both the mind and action, an uncommonly difficult combination, and what could he not do (for good, I was about to write) were he possessed of a really important idea, one connected to the reality of now, one that would require great striving, great uses of the self. But he really doesn't have one! All that incredible energy—he has only to step into a room for everyone to feel it—and yes, the gift of imagination; no, perhaps not quite *that*, but inventiveness anyway (is this the crucial difference?). Everyday life, family, "happiness" even—how clear this seems to me now—"success"; no, none of this is enough, it doesn't begin to unburden him. And this energy, it simply has to go somewhere. Oh, how awful for him. I'm sure now that he himself doesn't believe in what he's doing, not really, not in the holy mission side of it. If he did there would be better ways. His "idealism" is synthetic! Idealism—all the good and the bad done in its name; nevertheless some men can't live without it. He needs to believe. In something. But he doesn't, he can't find it. And so everything he does is perhaps just an expression of *nihilism*, the old horror.

Or so it seems to me at this moment. Tomorrow I'll probably see him differently.

I must do something to get myself out of this. What does he expect of me? I can do nothing to help him. And this love between us—if love it is—is nothing to found a life on. We get

nowhere. I am suspended in that same meaningless in-between
world that has claimed him. I'm imprisoned in a void, given but
scraps of life, and these days no scraps of art at all. And what
about *my* androgynous spirit, my "man's mind," as intellect is
called? As useless now as all my sensibility? Can either be free to
work creatively without the other? No. Would any free man
tolerate my present bondage? I do not think so. What a delusion, thinking one is "emancipated." A New Way to Discover
Old Woes, my little history with him.

Three days in London. As meaningless as all our holidays.
Wanted to phone friends but somehow couldn't bring myself
to.

Spring has finally come, even to the Kuppers, who go about
singing. My rooms look out onto a ruined courtyard, most appropriate. But some shrubs have started growing back, and there
are a few damaged trees. Most of the tenants have planted vege-
tables, and a few impractical, beauty-loving souls even some
flowers. Spring should restore me—it always has in the past. But
it doesn't seem to be working this time. The sap stirs not, or all
too little. I stare for hours out the window, mostly bird-watch-
ing, or so I tell myself. Pleasant enough, after the years in New
York. But I'm not writing a line, except in this stupid notebook. Just now I was staring away, feeling . . . nothing much of
anything. And then, so swiftly, a black bird of some kind swept
down into the courtyard and out again. It made everything
different somehow. It seemed to be a reminder of something.
But what?

He has been away for much longer than usual. The first night
back he began, to my amazement, to talk about his parents, and
some early memories, not in the very generalized way I'm used
to but a more purposeful sort of telling. I learned more about
the Greek line in the family. It comes through the maternal
grandmother, who was well-born to a proud family that never
quite accepted her having married a non-Greek. This "non-
Greek"—a phrase St. G. used often—was a German who'd come
to Greece to dig. "A gentle enough guy, but kind of mediocre as
far as talent went." They moved to Berlin, he went to work for
his father, a merchant of some kind; after the First War the

family lost everything in the inflation, the grandfather died, and then to everyone's surprise the grandmother went back to Greece, to her family. St. G.'s own mother, who had never had any contact at all with her Greek kin, went to Switzerland after the war ended to a language school; she was planning to be an interpreter. There she met St. G.'s father, an American, they married in Geneva and moved to America, and then when he was about two to Paris. (He said, "They were in love with each other. Not just fond of each other. And not just well-adjusted to each other. In fact, I guess they weren't very well-adjusted at all. They fought a lot. But they were passionately in love." I wish I could have fathomed the expression on his face when he said this, but I can't be *sure*.)

He remembers especially two visits to his Greek grandmother. The first was after his father lost his money and had to give up his European office (which didn't make money anyway, he just liked living abroad) and move the family back to America—they sent St. G. to Greece for half a year. I suppose he was about thirteen. He remembers how fond his grandmother was of the Germans, how she reminisced about life in Berlin. This puzzled him because he was still young enough to have trouble with the idea that his very own grandmother could have been so fond of the "enemy," and then the shock one day of realizing that for that matter the grandfather he had never seen had *been* the "enemy." He also remembers his Greek great-grandfather, who was still alive, and his hatred of the Turks.

The next and last time he visited his grandmother was after the Second War, 1947, she was over seventy by then, and had lived through the German occupation, the Germans' starvation policy and other brutalities, and she was all confused. She had the Germans and the Turks mixed up. She would stare off towards Asia Minor. "You," she would say, using a Greek nickname for him, "may some day take Byzantium back from the Germans for us."

This story made me unutterably sad, but I hid this. He seemed in some way relieved to have told it, and we went on to have what for us was quite a gay evening.

St. G. on spies: "Most of them are only technicians or acrobats." Said in such a way as to leave me in no doubt that *his* role is a superior one. But then he told me about jumping—he's had to learn that too—about before the parachute opens, about free fall, about how much he likes it. He was strangely inarticulate. What picture did he have in his mind? What did he see that he couldn't tell me about? A god leaping in the sky? A man daring a forbidden element? Or was it something quite different?

That name I've given him, St. George, no wonder it startled him. Because of course I didn't know about the Greek connection then, nor that he likes to see his present occupation as heroic. I wonder if the accident of the nickname hasn't played its role a little? Certainly it must have had something to do with him thinking I have—what is his phrase?—special powers. Always used ironically; still, it's beginning to annoy me very much. I try not to use the nickname any more, though it's become so habitual it's hard not to. Just plain *George* doesn't come easily to my lips either—not for him, it never did. Mostly now I call him Bingham, which he tells me is what his mother took to calling him after his father's death, and which he prefers to his first name.

St. G. says what he wouldn't like about being a writer is that you give the right to any slob to think anything he wants to about you. I said that just by being born anyone at all gave that right to slobs.

"You're a real little toughie, aren't you?" he asked.

"Yes, about as tough as a daffodil. Anyway, it's all an academic matter as far as I'm concerned."

A slow blink came over his face and then an extremely guarded expression. This is one of the two subjects we never discuss: my not writing.

One can get inured to almost anything. I see that looking back over this notebook. But for reasons which I can't find I feel some sort of change coming. For a little while recently it almost seemed that some sort of reconciliation, between us and, oh everything, was possible. Now I think not. He's returning to the old themes. I feel my inner resistance growing. Though I don't *do* anything about it.

He talks again about the war. Not in any self-pitying way.

I remind myself often that this did happen to him, to his flesh, and to his spirit. Yet I think too that he came into the world with his nature intact, like all of us. What the war did was to trigger, to release, certain forms of the self that might otherwise have lain quiet throughout his life. And wounded beyond cure certain other forms?

Thinking about policemen again and suddenly—isn't he a sort of policeman, the worst sort, the secret police? Supra-legal? *Eheu, Eheu.* One can hate policemen (and even think how nice it would be if they could become obsolete, like a species left behind by social evolution) without doubting that law forms the great social basis of civilizaton. What if, in a country where the concept of legality, especially as an instrument for social justice, is always being threatened by those who believe in "taking the law into their own hands," who are so deluded as to think they are fit to do so . . . ? One thing I know: such people do not hate policemen. They envy them. They want to *be* them.

Disgusting that my mind should work associatively from him to such thoughts. And unfair to him. But should government itself, that which lays claim to legitimacy, create a group that is above the law? (It is really *below* the law!) And give it powers that I cannot think will always be easy to limit, or control? Or is the CIA perhaps that face of government which is always there but simply never seen? Or almost never. Its hidden, darker self?

A great struggle is beginning again between us. Probably there are new assignments in the offing which he feels some reluctance about, scruples even, but which he will end by accepting. There is always a mounting tension in him before one of these undertakings and then, when it is accomplished, a brief period of release.

Impossible to say any black thing to him that makes an impression, that he has not already been prepared for and in some formal, almost ritualistic way got rid of. When we talk of his present life . . . how to explain this? As though one were to have a long conversation with a butcher about the realities of his trade and have him nod in acceptance at every point and at the end have him say to you, "Well, time to go slit up some lambs now."

What if all life, like war, is at root wholly irrational? I sometimes think that, without knowing it, this is what he has decided to believe, and having decided he now aims simply to stand strong and intact and unreflective among the horrors.

The other night, in answer to some remark of mine, he said, "That's like putting a tiger down in the middle of the jungle without any teeth."

"But we are not tigers."

"I'd rather be a tiger than a lamb." (Especially disturbing in light of what I'd written above, just a few days before.) "And so would you," he added.

Is it true what he says? I'm a good fighter, no denying that. But at any cost? Doubt it. Not because I'm virtuous. Because I'm proud. Here pride has its good side.

I said, "We are men and women. Perhaps with tigers and lambs roaming around inside us, but we are not they."

He said, "Touch a certain combination in anyone and a wild beast will spring out."

"Yes, that's true. But it's nothing to *boast* of."

For some time I've noticed that I haven't really wanted to listen much to music, that even Mozart sounded "different"— impossible to explain this. Now something horrible has happened. I went to *The Marriage of Figaro* with Stefan, and I thought I had gone mad, had to force myself to stay in the theatre. It all sounded as though devils were shrieking and clanging, especially the overture, as though absolutely nothing remained or had ever been there from the beginning except an underworld of unleashed demons. *What is going on?* Now I shall have to stay away from music too. By the end of the evening it was just sounding "unimportant." Why bother, I thought.

Depression, guilt, disorder, sloth!

How I have struggled with this nameless enemy, this dark shadow he brings with him, only to be whirled again and again into the vortex of despair. *I am not writing!* My work my work, my *heilige Kunst!* Gone! Stolen! Usurped! That in the end my pursuit of art should have turned out to be nothing but a pursuit of furies!

And then, I am a woman—by what right my pursuit of art in the first place? *Yet I am also my art;* I am nothing otherwise. And my deep feeling, which nothing he can ever say or do will

change, that we owe our coming hence not only a dying but
that we are meant to give something back to life as well. A man's
life a proving, a woman's a garnering? I do not know. But this
unbearable idleness! What am I doing sitting here, idle, solitary?

Is it possible that what passed for freedom, even before St. G.,
what I thought I had and must preserve at all costs, including
not only acts of denial but also acts of cruelty, was perhaps a
delusion? And all of this, and a million other things, leading here
to the Kuppers' flat!

But oh, the spiritual trickery on his part, the almost deliberate
attempt to transfer to me the guilt he feels and does not admit
to, as though I were a pool into which he could plunge and come
out sinless. His love-making that night in December, the first
time—has it ever been different? Was it me he slept with? Not
love, not lust even, but a blind and desperate and *reluctant*
plunging, an exorcism?

I see how tempting it would be to seize only on the last point,
his love-making, to make it explain all. Very curious, one's un-
willingness to accept the fact that a number of things can be
true at the same time.

We quarrel bitterly now when he comes. We both want to. If I
were he, I would not come back—some of the things I say to
him! If I were I, I would not let him come back.

He seems now, very subtly, to be distorting some of those remarks I made about Freud, as a way of smoothing over or excus-
ing to himself the dilemma in which he finds himself. This really
strikes me as dishonest.

I said that beyond Freud, beyond all explanations of the way
we are, there is simply a point at which we exist, like it or not.

What did I mean, he asked.

I said that the fact that the old established sources of moral
authority had been thrown over, mostly rightly because they
were so false, or perhaps once weren't but had certainly degen-
erated into official lies long before he and I were born, that
none of this meant one didn't still have ethical decisions to make,
that possibly now each one had almost to be a creative act.

What did *that* mean? he asked, sneering. He knew very well,
so I picked as insulting (to his intelligence) a way of explaining

as I could. I said, "It's like having red hair. It's all very interesting to know why one has it. But one has it. One has to live with
it. You can buy a wig, or dye it black. But you've still got *red
hair!* You live with it, or in spite of it, or maybe you transcend it,
if you happen not to like red hair and wish it had been naturally
another color."

He laughed. Nastily. "I'm afraid I don't get it," he said.

"Don't you? A pity. I mean that we can pass beyond Freud
but not beyond good and evil. I mean that in the final analysis
we exist independently of all the forces that have shaped us. Not
to accept this is not to be . . ."

"What?"

"Responsible, I suppose. Among other things."

He said, "Thanks for the lesson in ethics."

I said it really had to do with more than ethics and told him I
wanted him to go away and not come back.

Without another word, but with a look I cannot forget, he
left.

This final break I have made with him (am going to make, will
never make?) could only be made on ethical grounds. But
there's a higher ground than ethics, which makes it impossible to
break with him. I see that now.

He has come back. We go on as before.

As though by agreement we fight in shallower, therefore safer
terms. I said, "If you really want to be a lone hero why don't
you work for a rapprochement between us and the Soviet
Union?"

"Some spy you'd make."

"I suppose that would be treason?"

"You might call it that."

"I meant, really, work openly."

"You're naïve."

"It's going to happen anyway," I said.

"What is?"

"A rapprochement."

We fought. He talked a great deal of nonsense about "their"
system and "ours" and I got nasty and said he reminded me of a
smalltown businessman; then he got nasty, referred to things he

knows about that I don't, forced me to admit that I think life
behind the Iron Curtain would be unbearable and that to me
Bolshevism is a nightmare of quantitative abstractions. But then I
said, "Nevertheless I believe in it."

"You believe in *what?*"

"In the attrition of time. Things change. New generations
come along. And sometimes we outlive issues. If people like you
don't get us blown up first."

Bestirred myself enough to go to the Pinakothek. Thought looking at paintings might help, that concrete specific world of truth
through flesh and palpable object. Or at least that's Rubens'
world, and for me the Pinakothek is above all Rubens. But
things didn't work out the way I'd hoped, chiefly because of
The Murder of the Bethlehem Innocents, the *Kindermord*. I'd
been wandering around enjoying myself and then I went into a
room and it was as though I'd never seen the *Kindermord* before, or rather as though I'd seen only the familiar Rubens
splendor and not the uses to which it was being put in this
canvas. It was an unnerving experience, quite unlike the falling
angels, the boars, lions, tigers in a frenzy, *The Last Judgment*
itself, Rubens' familiar "terrible" subjects. There in the *Kindermord* was a revelation of the most awful and precisely *human*
terror imaginable. I think it was that woman in the center who
caught me first, the one in purple, being supported by a servant.
Her face and body are so peaceful, unlike those of the women
around her (is she in the eye of the storm of horror being unleashed on the canvas?), but her hand, curving up toward the
dead baby held next to her face, is curving into a *claw*. And
that baby—the deadest-looking baby! That grayish-green skin.
And the skin of her own face—it is exactly the same color. And
then the violence, the movement, the *surprise;* these richly
adorned women plunged into a reality which none of them
could ever have imagined as existing, let alone happening to
them. But the most terrible thing of all is that while their
struggle against the murdering soldiers is heroic, it has also
turned the mothers into something as beastly and savage as the
soldiers—patrician lips curled back over teeth that slash and snap
like fangs, manicured nails ripping into eyeballs; they *become*
their persecutors; or most of them do. It appears that this action

will go on being repeated forever, this murder, this terrible tearing of the flesh . . .

And the babies, the children themselves, the murdered innocents, all those pink fat Rubens cherubs one is used to, with their
angelic faces and curling hair and plump pretty rumps, the
beauty of the Babe incarnate, all in death now, their skins turning a variety of death shades, very real that, *actual presence*, as
always in Rubens—is that why he isn't admired much today?

I glanced at *The Madonna of the Flower Wreath* hanging just
across the room, and there are the live cherub-children, the real
flowers in the wreath incidentally, and then back to the *Kindermord* and all that slaughtered beauty. Rubens, among other
things, mocking his own sensuousness, his own highest gift, or
even perhaps letting it slip that behind this too, this love of life
and beauty, lies the knowledge of evil? Well, one is never surprised at this in Rembrandt and never allowed to get very far
from this knowledge. But Peter Paul Rubens, that splendid,
happy, successful, incredibly sensual, flesh-loving, flesh-celebrat-
ing, high-placed man of the world, that really quite "correct"
and blameless life—and with visions like this flowing out of his
paintbrush! Somehow for a few minutes I felt, oh more of a
malingerer than ever. I tried hard then to concentrate on
Meleager and Atalanta (oh, what Rubens could catch between a
man and a woman) and on *The Abduction of Leukippos'
Daughters*. But I couldn't. They also reminded me of too much.
A couple next to me agreed that Rubens' women were "too fat."
I headed for the Dürers, which I always deliberately leave till
last. But just before I got to them, I turned and left the building.

An amazing thing. This morning Frau Kupper came to the door,
very excited, muttering something about a "great lady" who had
come to see me. I didn't really understand, we got into a language muddle, and the next thing I knew Gwendolyn Dartley
came sweeping into the room. She only stayed a few minutes
and was, on the surface, very brisk. Invited me to come stay at
her villa in Switzerland, more or less indefinitely. Talked about
the mountain air, said I mustn't think I'd be under any obligation,
especially not to her, that there were always half a dozen or so
people staying there, a big house, one could be antisocial if one

wished, that at the moment I would find among others a fellow American more or less my own age, etc. She said I didn't have to decide now of course, left an address card that had a map of how to get to the villa printed on it, and was gone again almost before I had time to thank her.

Amazing . . . At the least this will force me to face up to the fact that I have to make a decision before too long. What I really should do is get a job in America and go home. Face this wasted year, the not having written anything, be quite open about it with friends. Will have to anyway, eventually. Or take that part-time teaching job at the university here, scrimp along as usual, and hope one day to write again. But the issue isn't really *where*. If I go to New York the same little drama will go on. He's even told me that if I go back to New York he'll arrange things so that he'll be there almost as much as he's been in Munich. "A few more hours on a plane, that's all it will mean," he said. The truth is that as long as I'm still bound to him writing is out the window.

Anyway, Mrs. Dartley's arrival, her offer—they've reminded me of the fact that there *are* choices. If one has the energy and fortitude to make them.

Almost the month of my birth, a not too reassuring thought at the moment. The time of the twins, of the *Zwillinge*, of Gemini. I sit here longing for a change, and not in my usual way able to find it in the season itself. I remind myself that my birthdate marks the beginning of the last high arc toward the solstice of summer, which comes but a week later, and entertain myself with all sorts of wishful notions about how my own spirits are sure to rise then too. But I doubt it. The truth is that after that longest, brightest day it's all down into darkness again. No, if April doesn't catch one up, then by June one has been left too far behind. What silliness. A writer who doesn't write has to do something with pen and paper. Odd how thoughts aren't quite real to me until they've been put down on paper. All sorts of cabalistic numbers here beside me, as I waste time in my now customary fashion. One thing strikes me—I wonder why it never did before. The night St. G. came to me, during the snowstorm, now nearly half a year ago, that night was precisely to the very date equidistant in the time of a calendar year from my birthday—in other words its complete, its exact opposite.

We were to have spent the weekend in Salzburg together, some chamber music we both wanted to hear. As so often happens, at the last moment something came up and he left town. I left a note for him at the hotel, saying, among other things, "I am not Penelope. She sits elsewhere."

When next we met he professed, or feigned, great distress at my reaction. I was perfectly free to come and go as I wanted to, and should know better than to count on him, he had no right to expect anything of me, etc., so long as he remained so involved with "his work"—which in time he would give up—he knew he could at the moment offer a woman very little, etc. I saw no point in trying to force him to the truth, to remind him, for instance, of his reactions to those few times when, having had other plans, I was not willing or able at the last moment to change them for him, or how sulky he was when Maggie arrived from the States and I spent two weeks traveling around with her, or how outraged the night he actually saw me in a restaurant with Stefan.

A standard little domestic struggle, almost a relief after some of our struggles. What struck me at the end of his little speech was how *bored* I am with the whole thing. Bored, bored, bored! How wonderful. If only I can go on being bored there is hope. Really annoyed with myself too, in a quite simple way—I am a fool with him, I do on the whole play Penelope!

I said to him, trying to be light, "Oh I understand very well. You're just a wandering Greek."

He was *pleased*.

A perverted Odysseus!

A terrible quarrel, which ended so unexpectedly that I cannot even remember what the quarrel itself was about, or how it led to that shattering remark with which he concluded before slamming out of the room: "You and your longing for *goodness*," he said.

I was absolutely stricken, numbed, afraid. I must have sat without moving for half an hour after he left. If it is true, what he said, then what a lifetime of misery I am doomed to, for I do

not even know how to begin achieving goodness, and I think it a
condition which my arrogance, my vanity, would most absolutely prevent. If there is such a longing in me and he has detected it, then . . . I am not going to think about this again. It
would immobilize me utterly. But I am still *afraid*. If I "long for
goodness," doesn't that put me in some special relationship with
evil too? One thing I am glad of, that he left in that way (what
had I said?). Perhaps this time he will really stay away.

Damn him! Today a letter addressed in his hand. I open it. Inside
a slip of paper. On it, printed in his hand the word: MALO.
Ironic, many-leveled, reverberating. How incredibly clever he
is. Almost as an afterthought he has written at the bottom.
"Sorry. Back on the 10th of June. A free week, I think. Or at
least a few days. Italy together?"
    And I am left with that *Malo*.

I have the telegram from Mrs. Dartley in answer to mine. I leave
for Zürich tomorrow.

The Villa Kilchberg. An extraordinarily pleasant country house
run by a benevolent autocrat—the most obvious description. But
what is it really like? I have the feeling that it will be a long time
before I can answer that, not perhaps until it is over with. My
mood of high drama mercifully dissolved upon arrival. No cries
of sanctuary, sanctuary, no banging upon gates which at the
very last moment swung open to admit me to a safe embrace and
closed to against the assaults of my enemy. In short, my arrival
created no stir at all; they are used to comings and goings here. I
was met in the village of unpronounceable name by one of the
other guests, Ernest Campion; he was driving her old and beauti-
fully-kept-up Rolls and is evidently the "fellow American" she
mentioned.
    I stay very much to myself (one can do that here), having no
desire at this point for any further involvement of any sort with
anyone, adhere to a very strict discipline, so many hours a day at
my desk, etc. Not that it's working. But it helps keep up the
illusion that there is hope and that I have not fallen into what
looks like a permanent lethargy of the spirit—a lethargy that is
sometimes interrupted by what I can only call passing seizures of

rage. The weather? On a postcard home I would write "glorious." And so it is. But I hardly stir out.

One thing at least: no great need to go on recording things here. A good sign? I hope so. I don't think about him often, not consciously. But when I do, when I am off guard, then *soulsickness*. It is far from finished. One can change one's sky, but not one's soul, or one's shadow either—to alter Horace ever so slightly.

He has found me out here. Of course. Typically, instead of writing ahead to ask if he might come or at the least saying he was coming he simply appeared. I have been extremely unkind to him and had I been he under the circumstances I would have left within a few hours. Instead, he stayed on for three days. I do not think his pride will permit him to come to Kilchberg again.

For some reason Ernest Campion interested him, much more than anyone I've ever seen him with. Usually he is so indifferent to others as to make them feel vaguely demeaned. As for Campion himself, he seems to be an old hand at guarding against intrusions into whatever his own private world is, but he has a much gentler way of doing this than St. G. A man who seems to me to have been battered about a lot, hurt, yet who in spite of himself goes on trusting. He and Mrs. Dartley are certainly funny together. And close.

My breaking of that circle, I think it has given St. G. some sort of relief from the tension of the conflict too. He seems to me now more the way he was when we first met, and he seems also to have suppressed, if not resolved, any doubts he had about himself or what he is doing with his life. From something he said I apparently have made the same impression on him!

Masks! One could keep searching behind them forever.

No wonder St. G. was interested in Campion. I have learned a little of his story now.

When Mrs. Dartley is bored or secretly upset about something she can't talk to us about she forces us all to play games ("When the natural healthy game-making instinct goes dry it must be artificially supplemented, as harmlessly as possible," she says).

Most of them are her variations of classic parlor games, or sometimes, luridly, entirely her own invention. The other day we
were all herded into the big drawing room. Then it began. One
of us would be sent out of the room, and the rest of us would
decide what his occupation was (she calls this The Occupations
of Mankind Game); he would be brought back in, seated in the
big chair in the middle of the circle we'd formed, rather like a
tribunal of some sort, and then on the basis of the clues *we* gave
him he would eventually guess as to *his own* identity! (A damned
unfair game!) If he was right, that is if *he* saw his identity as *we*
did, he was allowed back in the circle; otherwise he had to go
out again. I thought at the time there was something not just
bizarre about this but wrong, backwards. Campion, I remember,
protested furiously, but Mrs. D. was adamant and said something
about how that's the way things are now, and besides, she was
experimenting.

When it was Anton's turn to go out, someone, Marshall I
think, decided he should be a master spy. I said I didn't think it a
good choice and suggested jewel thief, but I was overruled.
Anton came back in and sat in the chair—all smiles because he's
usually very good at this sort of thing. Clues are supposed to be
ambiguous, and each of us was to give one in turn. I don't
remember who gave what (except mine), and there were seven
or eight of us there altogether—including two visitors, someone
from the Jung Institute, and a Dutch diplomat, I remember. But
some of the clues were: remarkably developed powers of observation, ultimate loyalty not to one particular faction or group or
even to yourself but to the occupation (my clue, and I could see
that the others didn't think it particularly good), mastery of role-
playing and disguises, unnaturally keen senses, someone who is
dreaded by society in general and by officialdom in particular,
someone who sees through complicated materials to hidden
truths, etc. By the end Anton's smile had nearly taken over his
face and he was squirming to answer. He said in a very self-
satisfied way, "Too easy, much too easy. It is so obvious. I am a
literary artist!"

General laughter, and then grumbling and squabbling. Anton
was put out at being told he was wrong, complained bitterly,
muttered something about the criminal and the artist being but
two sides of the same coin anyway. I must have shown very

great distress, because Ernest Campion said suddenly, *"Bilge,"* in a very cool but edgy voice (I had the feeling he wanted to say something else); then he said to Mrs. D., "Gwendolyn, your games, which are never based on rules that can be rationally comprehended anyway, your games sometimes go too far"— here his voice got for a second quite loud— "and I for one have had enough of this one." He poured himself a large whiskey and pulled his chair out of the circle and began talking to Marshall.

Recurrent and undeniable anxieties about St. G. again, for the first time in a long time. Little by little I'm putting them down *—with reason.*

G.D.'s favorite game, of course, is Playing Pontiff, but it's a role she puts on and off, and with me she's always left it off—until yesterday. Anton had been teasing me as usual and I was responding in a sort of whining way. Suddenly she said to me, "My dear, if you're afraid of what you're in touch with, the dark side, then give it up now."

Marshall is a perplexing boy. He is often silent for hours at a time, but sometimes he says startling things for one of his age. The other day, talking of his parents and their friends, i.e., of the particular social group he comes from at home, he said suddenly, "Babyish men and manipulating women."

Anton tells me a strange story about him; I don't know whether to believe it or not. That just before Marshall left America there was a great and final blowup with his father in the course of which there was actually a physical struggle over the flute (one gathers the usual methods, bribery, threats, etc., of trying to get him to do what his father wanted him to had failed), with the father trying to wrest it from him, threatening to break it.

I really find this a litle hard to believe; it sounds too much like the sort of story Anton likes to make up. But who knows? People like the Sears family are often given to acting out unwittingly some pretty hair-raising psychodramas (these are the people, needless to say, who "don't believe in Freud"!).

Anton also maintains that Marshall could not bring himself to play his flute after he ran off to Europe. Not, at any rate, until he came here to Kilchberg (he and Posy are certainly additions

to the household—not that I spend much time with them), and
that at first he used to take his flute and climb up into the
pastures and play it there. Anton claims that once when he was
visiting at a little chalet near here he heard, amidst the cowbells,
which are so musical, what he thought was a shepherd's pipe. It
was very far away, and he thought he was hallucinating. Then
he walked a great distance along a path (can't imagine Anton
walking far . . . yes, for music perhaps) till he came to a place
where he could see one of those high meadows, like a misplaced
green sea (my image, not Anton's), and way up, all by himself,
Marshall wearing Bermudas and playing Pergolesi!

A very pretty story, even if it mightn't be true. I do know
that in the last few weeks Marshall has been doing a great deal of
practicing, usually out in the gardener's cottage in order not to
disturb the rest of the household. I peeked through a window
once and saw him there, surrounded by the most extraordinary
collection of *hats*.

Sylvia laid the notebook pages on her desk. There was only one
page still unread, and it contained the last entry she had made in
the *Agon*, made the night after the dinner for Knox, or to be more
exact, the night after the encounter by the pool with Campion, an
encounter that now struck her as astonishing not in that it had
happened at all but in that it had not happened sooner. The truth
of this had leapt out at her from those very few entries she had
made since coming to Kilchberg. But what difference did it make?
As she had said to Ernest with such deliberate, cruel honesty at the
top of the stairs, her loving him "changed nothing." She could
never deny Bingham, nor turn her back on him. The silent dark
struggle in which he was engaged would always touch her, reach
her in some fatal way.

Downstairs the reading had evidently come to an end. Some sort
of music-making seemed to be taking place now. She went to the
door and opened it. Yes, an impromptu concert of some kind, but
impossible to say what—it was muffled and far away. Quickly she
closed the door and went back to the desk. She turned to the last
page in the journal, where handwriting, syntax, and style all indicated how drunk she had been when she had scrawled those last
lines. She read quickly.

Came here and set up all those rings of defense. Just like him. Stupid. Not my style, really. Behind them intended to practice the sleight of hand of my calling. No good. Why? Art not sleight of hand. Also there's life, good old, miserable old life. All that getting involved. Messy. Substance-devouring. But re-plenishing too. Ought to have known myself better. Broken dialogue. Involvement, detachment. Must repair. Dancer, dance, and *danced*. Meant to be torn apart, just like everybody else. No special privileges. On the contrary. Art duration . . . But as for him, as for St. George, George Bingham, Esq., *Georgie Peorgie* Bingham, someone else can bear his damned burden of guilt for him . . .

Drunk she had been that evening, overwrought, and without any question experiencing a sudden and long-awaited release. Nevertheless it humiliated her, this last entry—its superficiality, however inevitable, even necessary it may have been at that mo-ment, its banality. And that so obviously contrived false bravado at the end. She could hardly forgive herself. She picked up a pencil and drew several heavy lines through what she had just read. There was a little space left below these scorings, which had run far down the page. She now wrote there: *The dark side of the moon, a necessary journey*.

Now she took all the notebook pages and threw them in the fireplace grate, found some matches and, striking one, set fire to several corners. At first the pages began to burn slowly; like every-thing else at Kilchberg they were evidently a little damp. But she took the poker and with the judicious lifting of a page or two they soon began to burn quite grandly. She bent over, watched page after page curling back, being turned by the flames as by some impassioned reader. For a brief second or two she could read each page as it appeared; indeed, the writing seemed for an instant, before being consumed, to stand out more clearly than ever in that heat. Consumed by that which it was nourished by, she could not help thinking. *Bios, Thanatos* now appeared, and in their turn were also transformed.

When at last the grate was filled with ashes she turned, washed her hands, put on lipstick, used a comb, and went downstairs.

Twenty-five

Sylvia stood in the entrance to the drawing room, aghast at the scene before her. There in concert together were the other inhabitants of Kilchberg, playing and singing what sounded like something by Monteverdi. *"Ich bin der Phönix, du die Flamme,"* were the words that had greeted her before being obscured by the somewhat desperate efforts of other voices to maintain the madrigal. Phoenix! Flame! Who among them dared presume so? What was this all about? Another of Mrs. Dartley's conjuring acts? And the piano moved in from the music room. How intent they all were. Marshall's flute, clear and strong, seemed somehow to be leading them, but Anton Hrubick, scraping away on the old cello, was bringing forth a quite respectable sound from it, and there at the piano, half smiling, half frowning, diligently bending to the keyboard as though his life depended on it, was George Bingham. Impostor, she thought, impostor. But then her heart turned; he did seem at that moment to belong there.

As for the others, they, peering over the shoulders of the instrumentalists, they were singing. It was Lily who carried them here, her old and trembling soprano sure of line and rhythm, joined by the breathy pipings of Posy; then came Mrs. Dartley's strong and tuneless alto, followed by the lusty mouthings of an evidently delighted Benjamin Knox and the careful baritone of Ernest Campion. Only the faintly ironic expression on his face suggested that all was not perhaps as it seemed. She stood still and listened, trying to catch at the words. *"Du bist das Licht in das ich fliege . . ."* Another chorus was beginning now, and with it a new sort of confidence seemed suddenly to spur them all on. Sylvia had the clear impression that they had already made a number of determined efforts to get through this song but had not managed to and now felt that some crucial point had been safely passed and they would make it this time. Imperceptibly they had picked up the correct beat, and the parts seemed to flow into one another as they were meant to. *"Tödlich Los, dass ich, dass ich dein Licht gesehen!"* rang out now, followed by what seemed to Sylvia to be a quite unnecessary number of repetitions of something that meant: But you too pay the price . . . But you too pay . . . But you too . . . And then at last they were coming to the end, for the music slowed and swelled, the singers all intent on making a particular effort, tremolos and vibrati filled the air, and one after the other they intoned the last phrase: *"Dein Leib muss leuchtend selbst vergehen,"* Marshall inventing a number of decorations of his own along the way but joining the others in the final, resolving note.

There was a good deal of laughter now and some bravos, words of congratulation, a joyful milling about, a certain unmistakable gaiety. Sylvia struggled to overcome the irrational resentment she felt as she moved among them. Evidently the text had been translated for them before they began, but Posy and Knox now demanded that Anton go over it again; "all that moth and flame business," as Knox put it. With considerable relish Anton began:

> *I am the Phoenix, you the flame,*
> *From which, though burned a thousand times,*
> *I trace my descent . . .*

He grinned at Sylvia, and she moved away, all her resentment returning.

It was true that dinner had gone off surprisingly well. It was even possible to say that in contrast to the ludicrous melee that had taken place in the hall before dinner everyone had been at his social best. Anton had refrained from teasing; Lily Halász had been supremely tactful with Bingham and had drawn Knox into a conversation that enabled him to talk about the celebrities he knew and that had therefore made him feel valued; Bingham in his turn had said just the right things to Posy and he and Campion had conversed easily with each other, finding an acquaintance or two in common and then discussing at great length the deciphering of the Linear B—such great length, in fact, that Sylvia had been almost annoyed. Certainly no one looking at Bingham would have guessed at those painful moments of revelation that had taken place only a short time before in her room. How artful he was. But then, looking at her would anyone have guessed what she herself had just been through? How artful then perhaps she was. Oh, but one had to be. How many different dinner parties were perhaps preceded by scenes of private violence and anguish. The social effort to maintain form, how necessary that was, how impossible life would be without it. Then too, people were more flexible than they liked to admit. Her only difficulty during dinner, for example, had been in not being able to look directly at Ernest.

Anton was finishing his recitation in a loud voice:

> *But you too pay the price,*
> *But you too pay the price:*
> *Your body itself*
> *Must glowing spend itself.*

but Sylvia was not listening, thinking still that yes, on the whole, the dinner had been a tribute to one of the minor values of civilization. She felt her resentment fading. It was just that she had not quite been prepared for that happy little family scene when she came downstairs. Never mind. It was never possible to predict the course of any social gathering, least of all one of Mrs. Dartley's.

Mrs. Dartley said to her, "Ah, you've returned to us. A pity that you missed the best part of the evening. I don't mean my reading. That, I'm afraid, was a failure. As usual. But the heavenly music we have all just been indulging in. We missed you."

"Thank you. But it was no loss, my not being here. I sing very badly."

"Do you? Do you? But what has that to do with it?" She took Sylvia's arm and began walking with her. Sylvia felt a certain reluctance. The wine that had been served at dinner had been a Nuits St. Georges, to her the one barbarous note, and even if it was only chance she nevertheless held Mrs. Dartley responsible. That stupid nickname. As far as she could remember she had slipped and used it only once or twice at Kilchberg, a long time ago, but that, she was sure, had been enough. It was probably quite common knowledge at the villa now.

Mrs. Dartley was saying, "Marshall finally agreed to play for us tonight, and he did, most beautifully, most generously. It is really to him that we owe the Monteverdi. What a lucky thing. I did want something special for tonight, Lily's last evening with us . . ."

Sylvia started and felt shame. Lost in her own struggles, she had completely forgotten that Lily Halász would not be there after this night. Mrs. Dartley seemed aware of her distress, for she did not pursue this subject. "Though it was a remark of Mr. Bingham's that gave us all the idea. He was telling us about the Monteverdi cycle that's being done in Lucerne. Then Marshall remembered that he had uncovered a great cache of old music in the gardener's cottage, stashed away under the hats. Among it a considerable amount of Monteverdi, though the text is in German, as of course you noticed. He and Posy skittered out for it, and it struck me as such a good idea, something we could all join in."

At this moment Giovanni appeared bearing a great bowl of wine punch. It gave off a delicious and at first almost overpowering aroma, its incense seeming to fill the whole room, a mingling of . . . what? Exotic bark, seed, root from Asia, bloom and fruit from the southern slopes of the Mediterranean? Fired according to the ways of the passionate north and served forth near the high Alps. Sun, earth, the grape, held in memory against the long nights of winter and consumed in the hope of returning summer. Sylvia smiled at herself. It was surely the punch Mrs. Dartley had referred to so often in recent weeks, the one made only for special occasions, from a secret recipe, a recipe concocted, she had said, by Bob Dartley and Andreas Greifenberg when they were young men traveling together before the First War. She sniffed again; a decent wine probably, cinnamon perhaps or cardamon maybe, orange peel, lemon. Mrs. Dartley left her and went to oversee its placement.

Marshall had just finished putting his flute away. She said to him, "What did Mrs. Dartley talk about tonight?"

He smiled but shook his head slightly. "Something about bullfighters and adventure and glory." He paused, seemed to be making a concerted but useless effort to answer Sylvia more completely. "I tried to listen, but I couldn't follow very well. It was about archaic man, or maybe anarchic man. I don't remember which."

Sylvia laughed. "Never mind. I'm sorry I missed hearing you play just now. But before dinner. I wanted to tell you. I haven't heard anything so beautiful for years. There was one thing in particular you played . . ."

Before she could go farther George Bingham came up, and Marshall with a few words of apology left to take his flute upstairs. She and Bingham stared at each other. Then she said, "A new role for you tonight."

"Maybe it's my real one."

She ignored this. "How did you find Mrs. Dartley's reading?"

"A little confused. But interesting."

"What did she talk about?"

"About heroes. About how the hero's lot is not a happy one."

Sylvia waited, but he said no more. His expression looked faintly pleased. Was this the man who had all but wept in her arms a few hours before? She said, "Ernest Campion still interests you, doesn't he?" She had seen them talking again after the Monteverdi.

"Sure. More than ever now. That shouldn't surprise you. Besides, he's a nice guy."

"Yes he is. I thought you didn't have a very high opinion of nice guys."

"You're wrong," he said. "It's only phony nice guys that get me down."

He took an envelope from his pocket. Marshall had come back in the room and had joined Posy. Bingham said, "Since we aren't going to use the Lucerne tickets I thought I'd give them to them."

He waited a second or two, as though expecting to be praised, and when she only said, "Why not?" he lowered his eyes in the characteristic way that signaled hurt or annoyance and left her.

Lily was standing alone for a moment and Sylvia stepped across the room to her. Lily smiled, saying, "I'm afraid we were all very bad, very bad. Quite amusing though. I haven't enjoyed myself so much in . . . a long time. The boy is gifted, Marshall, oh he is gifted. He is already almost a virtuoso. And he has only studied under the most ordinary people, people of no reputation at all. I have never heard of one of them." She shook her head with disbelief. "But his sense of music. It isn't only the sounds he brings forth from that flute. It is his general sense of *music*. Perhaps he should be a conductor. But then, perhaps he will have more *joy* from life this way. He's young. Perhaps time will decide for him, then? But it was all a far, far better idea than the Strauss songs."

"What Strauss songs?"

"*Morgen* for example. Anton began with that. I told him I hadn't the mood." She looked at Sylvia as though to say the last thing in the world she would ever do would be to turn this evening into a sentimental occasion; it did not suit *her* idea of good taste. But what could you expect from someone as erratic as Anton? How could you expect him to understand the delicate nature of social situations? Sylvia nodded in agreement, thinking what an unbearable scene it would have made, those two old people, Lily and Anton, the words to *Morgen,* the melancholy, unan-

swerable music. How right Lily had been. She suspected too the
timely intervention of Mrs. Dartley.

Suddenly Lily reached out, touched her, said, "You must tell
your young man not to worry."

Quickly Sylvia's eyes swept the room and lighted on Campion,
who was approaching. Then, although she knew she had betrayed
herself, she turned her head belatedly in the direction of Bingham.
Mrs. Dartley would have said, no, no, your *other* young man, or
something like it. But Lily Halász, though she had quite plainly
taken it in and though her violet eyes brightened still more, only
said, almost apologetically, "It is so easy to be mistaken about
identity today." She tottered away.

Campion said, "Hello. We missed you. What did you think of
the concert?"

"It was lovely. And surprising somehow." She was struggling to
be at ease with him.

He said, "What's happened to your face? You've actually got
something like a high color."

She said, "I've been standing near the fire."

"Why?"

"I've been burning something."

"What?"

"The past."

"Is that good?"

"I don't know. I hope so. One can't of course do that really. It
was only a symbolic gesture. The future . . . well, it obviously
grows out of the past, doesn't it?"

"But perhaps a good future." His eyes did not leave her face.
She dropped her own.

"I hope so. But I don't know." She changed the subject. "What
did Mrs. Dartley talk about this evening?"

"I think," he said slowly, "that she was trying to say something
about . . . about the need for a new kind of individualism. Something about old patterns being either broken or outmoded. Something about the old anarchic sort of individualism . . ." He stopped.
"It was extremely complicated, and not at all clear. Not one of her
successes. She began with an apology, said that these were old ideas
she had jotted down a long time ago and only unearthed today,
that they needed work. They did. But it was something about

there no longer being any place in society for the old anarchic individualism. Except an underground life, which was dangerous. She said it would be fatal to abandon the Western belief in the individual, but that it must be redefined. Then, instead of doing that, she abruptly ended the whole thing with a garbled reference to how Dragan had in one sense been living only to practice medicine again."

"Oh."

Campion smiled nervously. Suddenly he pulled an envelope from his pocket, thrust it at her, saying, "Read this, please. Later. Don't be in a hurry to answer," and left her.

Benjamin Knox came up. "I was afraid maybe you were sick," he said.

"I'm all right. Thanks. How did the taping of Lily go?"

"Wonderful, wonderful. She's a brilliant, wonderful, very grand, very brave old lady."

"Yes, she is, isn't she." It seemed to Sylvia that he meant what he was saying, somewhat overdone though it was. She felt too that he was making some special effort to be friendly with her, even to be solicitous.

Leaning close to her, he said, "Between the two of us, I hope our Mrs. D. doesn't pitch things quite so—ah—high during the show. I have to admit that I couldn't follow her too well. From what Campion tells me it wasn't one of her better nights. One thing seemed clear—she came back to it twice—that the way out—that was the actual phrase—didn't lie in hiding or losing the self in one of the great group systems of our times—her phrase too. But the way out of what? There you've got me." He laughed. "Does it make any sense to you?"

"It might," she said, thinking back on what Campion had just told her. What a chaos of disordered insight Gwendolyn's mind must be, how painful to live with that.

Knox looked down at the envelope which she was holding in her hand. "What have you got there?"

"I don't know," she said. "But I'd better put it somewhere. Excuse me."

Just as she reached the door, however, Anton came and put an arm about her, squeezed her with surprising strength and propelled her back into the room. His short, rounded little body must once, it occurred to her, have been capable of considerable passion. "No,

you are not to run off again! I will not allow it. It is too good
having you back. And I must chide you, for you have missed one
of our hostess' most brilliant readings. All about the individual
who makes his life a contest with death. Now why? Why would
anyone do that? Because death is the one thing we can *never*
conquer. Ergo, for a certain kind of adventurer, the adventurer of
the will, it is the only worth-while challenge, the ultimate in struggle. Hence the phenomenon of those who seek out what they fear
most. Could we say that? Yes, my dear I think so. To 'cheat' that
ultimate victor from time to time, to *choose* to do this, to enter
voluntarily into a situation in which Death may be the victor, one
day will be, but then to wrest, to seize from it a temporary victory. What euphoria then, eh? What a dangerous narcotic?"

She forced herself to laugh. "Oh nonsense, I'm sure she said
nothing of the sort." What had Gwendolyn said that had started
Anton ranting so? It must have been something, for though the
style, the obsession even, was his, it clearly had its origin in Gwendolyn's reading. She was very glad she had not been there for it.
Oh, if only things could become simple again. She saw Posy approaching. "Behave now," she said to Anton, "or you'll frighten
the young."

At that he bounded forward, seized Posy in a dance embrace,
and the two of them, as though they had been practicing for days,
did a quite remarkable although brief series of dances that went
from the waltz to an apache and ended in the cha-cha-cha, both
laughing and panting when it was over.

There was considerable applause from the assembled group and
then all eyes turned toward the door. It was as though Mrs. Dartley, who was presiding over the punch bowl like some bright spirit
who promises great favors but does not dispense them lightly—she
had not yet begun to ladle out the punch—it was as though she had
given some signal, and in the door came Celeste, carrying the most
elaborate and miraculous of chocolate cakes. On the top it said,
"Our Lily." They were all gathered around the table now. Mrs.
Dartley swirled the ladle in the punch bowl, its silver gleaming;
once, twice, a ringing, musical sound, the candlelight shining on
them all. It won't last, this moment, Sylvia thought, it will break
apart again.

Then, as though to confirm this, Mrs. Dartley said, ladling out
the first of the punch glasses, handing it of course to Lily Halász,

"I still think it annoying that you are leaving at such an unearthly hour in the morning."

Lily laughed, raising her glass now to all. "I knew exactly what I was doing, Gwendolyn. Mornings are dreadful at best. Especially when there are good-byes. No, this is my kind of good-bye. Much more civilized, much to be preferred. No rushing around. No *fussing*."

Gwendolyn Dartley continued filling punch glasses. It was clear that though she respected her friend's wishes, though she had planned exactly the kind of evening she knew Lily would enjoy, she had not yet reconciled herself to the fact that Lily had decided to go at all. She said, "Well, you won't escape me tomorrow morning. I shall be up to say good-bye to you. Whether you like it or not. And now let us drink. And let us eat this great cake."

Twenty-six

George Bingham, who stood now in the shadows of Sylvia's room, had not often made love to her, and when he had it was as though he sought only to drive out some alien spirit and not, at the least, to enjoy himself. Beyond the spasms of the flesh his inner being remained on guard, in control, even, it almost seemed, despising the flesh for its insurgent ways. He loved, but dared not give greatly over, as though to feel too much might be dangerous, might make him vulnerable, the possessor perhaps of a fatal heel. When, lying beside Sylvia in Munich, he did turn towards her with thumping heart—those great pumpings and primings of power which in the beginning had set off so deep a response in her but which in the end she had come to dread—it was the fearful turning of a man in mortal peril, a man who had already had to fight his way silently towards her through cruel barriers, who came towards her then in the embraces of the flesh abruptly, cruelly, entered her always with a dark rush of fury, engaged in a swift and violent struggle inside her, and was gone.

Only once had it seemed it might be different—he turned to her while he still half slept. But when she moved her body closer to his and, sighing, reached out her arms to encircle his shoulders,

AMOUNT PAID   BALANCE

————————————   ————————

————————————   ————————

————————————   ————————

————————————   ————————

————————————   ————————

————————————   ————————

clasping her hands lightly together behind his neck, he started violently back, like a creature at bay, and without a word dropped on his pillow, his body turned from her.

What she had suffered then was not just the bitterness of sexual longings aroused only to be denied but, worse by far, the over-whelming sense of her own helplessness, as though she were being whirled and whistled down the unseen empty places with all the howling winds of war in her ears. The childish sex lore of her times in which she was so well-versed, the clinical phrases devised by an ailing world, what did they matter or avail, what did they explain even of the anguished and sorrowful conflicts he bore within him? What did it mean that for such a man as this loving should be the impossible risk, that her woman's body should re-main for him somehow an unattainable mystery, not to be known really, not to be trusted; what did it mean that his own body, which nature itself had also designed for the actions of love, yet feared . . . *Oh what had they done to him?* The tears had sprung from Sylvia's eyes as the last phrase repeated itself over and over in her head. She had cried quietly, letting the tears flood her pillow, and as she wept she had accepted what by then she had long known, that she could not release him, that she did not know, would perhaps never know, what it was that might release him. He was lost, and not only to her. She must save herself surely, she must leave him. But then she had thought, what if the miracle was that the yearning for love had survived in him at all? Then what would happen if she did leave him? It was the old dilemma in a new form. Cold and shivering beside his stonelike figure, she had lain there arguing with herself till morning, and mornings and nights had followed each other. They had gone on as before.

When, alone in her room at Kilchberg, after the party for Lily, Sylvia heard the soft tapping at her door, she thought it must be Campion and was half pleased and half annoyed. She had not yet read his note, for reasons she would have found difficult to explain, to him, or even to herself. Instead, she had placed it carefully on her desk, propped up against the manuscript, where it would be the first thing she would see when she sat down to work the next morning. She would read it then, turn to it before working; she would give to whatever he said in it that part of the day when both for thought and feeling she knew she was at her best, the first hours of waking, before either defenses or deceptions or conflicting realities could come between her self and her knowledge of her self.

But on the other side of the door stood Bingham. He said, "I wanted to tell you how much I've missed you."

"Oh."

Campion, when he had got to his room, had been too restless for sleep and had decided to do a little work on the Greifenberg papers. But he found he was able to concentrate on them only in the most indirect ways. He thought of how often he and Gwendolyn had fought over who was to do the Brief Life which she insisted should introduce the finished volume. He had no intention of being hoodwinked into that; she would do it or else. Nevertheless, he had sometimes amused himself thinking up opening sentences. "Andreas Greifenberg, who cuckolded my father . . ." was his favorite; he had even said it to Gwendolyn once, but to his surprise she had not found it particularly funny. It was only very slowly, he realized now, that he had come to understand how special her attitude towards Andreas really was, and only fairly recently that an accumulation of small remarks had caused him to see that they had been something more than friends, that they had probably been lovers for several years before his mother made her appearance on the scene—those recurrent comments about how in many ways Dragan had reminded her of Andreas, the references to the many visits Andreas had made to London during the time she was living there alone, to the meetings with him on the continent. It seemed so obvious now that he felt he had been dull-witted. Something she had once said even suggested to him now that a marriage had been projected, or perhaps just taken for granted, but somehow put off by two people who were also greatly absorbed in many impersonal matters as well.

And then she had also had that attachment for his mother. It could not, surely, have been pleasant for Gwendolyn, the way things had turned out. He wondered if all women were capable of such magnanimous, such generous behavior as she evidently had been, such an acceptance of what she had once called "the surprising untidiness of things." He greatly doubted it. He remembered too how he had come to see what all along he had been meant to: that if Gwendolyn had been able to forgive Andreas and his mother, then surely he could.

Not that he thought Gwendolyn had intended anything so specific as that when she first got him started on the Greifenberg papers. It would never have occurred to her that others might have difficulty with the surprising untidiness of things. It had seemed to her in the general sense *appropriate*, or so she had indicated when he had said to her: Why me? Above all, he knew, she had wanted Greifenberg's papers straightened out, put in order, made ready for the world, "served as they deserve to be." Knowing her own impatience with detail, her inability to concentrate for long on any one effort, the way her mind darted off in a variety of directions, knowing in fact that she had done little more than shuffle through them and fret in the eight years they had been in her hands, she had been desperately anxious to pass these papers on to someone else. But her own emotional involvement had been far too great for her to find the idea of turning them over to an outsider tolerable, however well-qualified. "And what if your hypothetical scholar and I didn't get on, Ernest? And what kind of scholar, exactly? No, no, no, far too likely to lead to muddle." Ill-prepared as Campion had in the beginning mistakenly thought himself to be for this task, he had accepted it; he had been chosen.

He reached now for those badly typed pages on which Gwendolyn had finally put down the week before (after long postal exchanges with Stefan Zimmerman and Andreas' widow) what she called "Notes Toward a Brief Life of Andreas Greifenberg." She was still maneuvering, he knew, but he was not going to be outmaneuvered. There was no question in his mind, nor evidently in the mind of anyone else, that this part was up to her. That opening sentence—". . . offspring of wine merchants, shepherds, army officers, and other assortments of humanity . . ." When he had asked her what in the world the purpose of that was she had replied cryptically, "To show that Andreas was Andreas." To show you that I will make it so bizarre that it will not do, he had thought. The rest, however, had turned out to be surprisingly conventional; she had evidently attempted a sort of standardized academic style, though at one or two points a more familiar voice sounded through. He read now the overly long description of Andreas' two years in Marburg and Heidelberg, then the years at Leiden and at Oxford, the travels with Dartley before the First War, and then rapidly skimmed what followed:

A small but adequate private income enabled him to remain
independent of the university world as a young man, which was
fortunate, since he had early conceived a detestation for German academic hierarchies and perhaps for most professors as
well . . . many examples of that just independence of nature
which never failed him . . . refused all of the postwar simplicities . . . bitterly critical of his own country and of those forces
which even then he felt . . . nevertheless he also considered the
Versailles Treaty to be . . . economic ruin and collapse . . . in
1921, for example, speaking in England at a meeting which had
been organized by Bernard Shaw to protest the continuing
blockade of German ports . . .

His greatest energies were of course devoted to the art and
culture of ancient Greece, his life's work . . . with the publication, in 1925, of *The Kleophrades Vase Painter,* a foreshadowing of . . . Berlin in 1927, following on a great personal tragedy
which he had suffered a short time before, and for the next five
years he divided his time between museum work there, further
extensive travels in Italy, Greece, and Anatolia, and two visits to
America, including an important two months' stay in Boston . . .
that astonishingly rapid series, *Exekias* (1930), *The Berlin
Painter* (1931), *The Theme of Dionysos* (1932), *The Munich
Painter* (1933), *The Theme of Pallas Athena* (1934) . . .

He had been the Director of the Glyptothek in Munich for
only two years at the time of his resignation in 1934 . . . of the
great exodus of German intellectuals when it began in full, that
he wished them well in their attempt to carry the truth abroad,
where, in his view, as letters to Gwendolyn Dartley indicate,
there was little more interest in the truth than in Germany. He
himself elected to remain . . . and continuing to turn down
offers from museums and universities in England, Holland, and
America . . . to the small village of Alterbrunnen, located near
an edge of the Black Forest and within a long walk of both the
Lake of Constance and the Swiss border, and there . . . until the
time of his arrest . . . could of course have crossed into Switzerland (happily, he had friends at the University of Zürich and at
the Jung Institute) at any time during this decade . . . There is
even reason to think that he received several hours' warning in
July, 1944, and would have had time to attempt . . . but at the
last moment refused on the grounds that . . .

It has often been asked why he was not taken into custody sooner. He may have been protected by a brother who was a high-ranking party member and whom he had refused to see for years. If so, it was without his knowledge, and it is much likelier that his retirement from public life to so obscure a residence made him no longer of any interest to a regime which . . .

In Alterbrunnen he learned carpentry from the Zimmerman family and eventually built with his own hands the small chalet in which . . . both the large private library (containing by then a number of "forbidden" books) and that vast collection of photographs of antique art which he had been making since his student days and which filled several large trunks . . . began and brought to completion the great work, *Attic Figure Vases*, which, whether regarded as art criticism or cultural history or, as many now believe, primarily a work of speculative thought, is making so great an impact on the contemporary world of letters. The original manuscript of *Attic Figure Vases* was taken across Lake Constance one dark night in 1943 in a small boat rowed by Stefan Zimmerman, then a boy of sixteen . . .

Andreas Greifenberg had begun his university studies in architecture. At the height of German military victories he made careful drawings of plans for redesigning the interior of the Glyptothek in the event that it was hit in the bombing raids which he felt certain would come before Germany lost the war, and expressed the hope that the great collection of Greek art which the Glyptothek housed might be removed to underground storage places in the country in time to prevent its destruction too. These plans were enclosed in a letter which reached Gwendolyn Dartley in England and are included in the present volume. One wing of the new Glyptothek, the rebuilding of which it is estimated will not be completed before 1965, is to be named for him. His general plans are not, however, being followed, save with respect to the room that will contain the Kleophrades . . .

He in part supported himself in Alterbrunnen by doing wood carvings, which he also learned from the Zimmerman family . . . a great nature lover, then as always, and in his spare time carried out a number of experiments in flower breeding and viniculture. Although these were amateur undertakings they have been found to be not without value . . . portfolio, chiefly water colors

of birds and occasional sketches from life, derive interest simply
from being by his hand . . .

In 1943, Andreas Greifenberg, who was then fifty-five, married Anna Reimer, some thirty-one years his junior. The daughter of a Protestant pastor who had once carried on a correspondence with Sigmund Freud (a debate that was amiable,
courtly, and shrewd on both sides) and who later lost his pulpit
when . . . It was she who after Andreas' murder in Dachau
protected the manuscripts from which the present volume is
drawn, until she was able to forward them to Gwendolyn Dartley, as Andreas Greifenberg had expressly requested her to do
. . . The volume itself seems to fall naturally into . . .

Here Campion laid the notes aside and touched one of the card-
board boxes which contained the Greifenberg materials themselves. For a moment his mind, almost against his will, came up
against the reality of the work itself, impersonally, as though its
author had never had the slightest connection with his own life.
He could not feel as confident as Gwendolyn did about having
found the divisions for the book that the author had intended.
Moreover, he felt that the Greifenberg papers had been in spirit
durchkomponiert, though as a practical necessity Greifenberg had
broken much of it into misleading and seemingly disconnected
fragments and had also clearly meant certain letters to Gwendolyn
to be an integral part of the whole. How could one describe its
totality? On the one hand it was a study of a new class, the criminal class (often referred to as the Dorians), and of what happens
when such a class seizes power and assumes authority—in this respect it was minute, detailed, impressively circumstantial; there
had thus far been nothing like it, Campion was sure. At the same
time there emerged behind the Dorians the monumental context
of the past, above all in Greifenberg's presentation of that imperial
century and a half which, with passionate speculative skill and
exact knowledge, he delineated as *The World as Manchester* and
which he showed as having produced, even by 1917, the insepara-
ble phenomena of *man-as-mass* and *the-state-as-crime* with the former tending inevitably to take on the psychic nature of the latter.

On the other hand (except that, again, if it really was
durchkomponiert, to make these "hands" appear as anything but
reflective opposites was false), the Greifenberg papers were an

account of a massive spiritual—hence moral—regression. They were therefore in a sense a study in psychology, the clinical history of a psychic epidemic. His belief that disturbances of the psyche were the disease of our times was quite specific, as was his analogue with the Black Death, the Bubonic Plague, the other great and hideous mass afflictions which had swept Europe in the past, his comparison of racism to the inflamed and suppurating buboes of Plague, for example, with the cause lying deeper, "in the festering sores of the spirit," all the more infectious for not being admitted to, recognized.

Campion frowned. He very much doubted that the latter would fall on sympathetic ears. He thought of other things about the Greifenberg papers; of how, even as Andreas attacked what he called the corrupting German addiction to idealism, one could feel how he wished to rescue, to restore idealism itself, but in some more chastened form. The German metaphysical flair, the love of broad concepts, of the *idea*, which was his heritage—this was powerfully there, but tempered in an extraordinary way. Campion was certain that even if he had not known Andreas' story, his youthful stays in England and Holland, his travels, he would have guessed at something like it, for the permanent influence of these experiences was there too: the modulating, tempering force of English rationalism, the enlightening traditions of Dutch humanism. And over the whole broke the sharp clarity of the classical world, as it really must have been, it seemed to Campion, not filtered through the peculiar haze of the nineteenth century, but as strong and unrelenting as the summer sun on the Cliffs of Attica. He paused; the last phrase had been Gwendolyn's, but in quite another context; he could not remember what.

He thought then of the letters to Gwendolyn, of the one which she rightly insisted must end the Greifenberg papers, the one in which Andreas spoke of his regret, his sorrow, at having to give up those further studies of art which he had intended would follow *Attic Figure Vases* (he himself had regarded that work as only a prolegomenon), and of the necessity he felt for turning to a work which he could earlier never have envisioned undertaking, a work for which he felt himself badly prepared but for which, ironically, it appeared he was better prepared than most. For the first time Campion felt moved by the suffering person who had worked away at Alterbrunnen on those papers. For the first time he let

himself feel what it had cost Andreas to face the full horror of
what was happening in the country of his birth; he had made it
perfectly clear that he thought Germany was delivering such a
blow against herself, against Europe, as to take generations to recover from. The civilizing skills of trade and commerce, the great
gifts of music, poetry, science, and thought—he had said in another letter—these had also been Germany and now would be
forgotten, and for how long to come? He could envision no easy
rebirth, he said, not of the spirit. In murdering Jews and Slavs
Germany murdered too a secret part of herself, as she would discover. And with what heroic bitterness Andreas had penciled at
the bottom of that last note to Gwendolyn, that if she thought it
right to bring his papers before the world, he wished them to bear
as epigraph a quotation from Jane Harrison, to whom, as a youth,
he had paid several visits of homage in Cambridge. Only one word
needed to be changed to make it exact; for "reading" she should
substitute in brackets "thinking." "Savages," the original went,
"save for their reverent, totemistic attitude towards animals, weary
and disgust me, though perforce I spend long hours in reading of
their tedious doings."

Abruptly now Campion got to his feet and closed up the boxes
with Andreas' papers in them. These things that a desperate man
had written, a man sick with loathing for his own country and able
only by the most heroic effort—yes, Campion admitted how much
he admired that—to hang onto his belief in himself and in those
values to which he had devoted his life: they all meant too much
perhaps, and too little. It would make no difference in history, he
was sure; history would move on through its inevitable acts of
cruelty. But it had been worth doing in itself. With every reason
for despair, and more than most men, Andreas Greifenberg had
persevered. If nothing else, his papers were the record of a mind
engaging itself at its own highest level, an unconscious counter-
statement of belief in the continuing presence of the life of the
mind, an unwitting triumph of the spirit.

Campion began to pace the room. What did it matter now,
anyway? The important thing was life, was that life itself should
go on. He had never felt this more strongly. In a few more weeks
he would be finished with the Greifenberg papers. Gwendolyn
and Anna Greifenberg could then decide what to do with them,
make the arrangements for publication as they chose. Parts of it

were bound to raise a stir, though no doubt the wrong things in
the wrong places. Germans would be likely to cling to those sec-
tions that discussed Nazism as part of a European disease, Americans and English to seize on Andreas' castigations of his own countrymen. So it would go. But his own part in it was finished. It was
time for him to find work more suitable to his skills, though he
knew very well that those new directions he now had in mind and
which seemed so possible to him were indirectly the result of his
work on Greifenberg's papers. He and Sylvia would be going
away soon, back to America—here he caught himself up short.
While with a part of himself he could no longer believe that they
were not meant to join their lives, he knew too that much was still
working against it, as George Bingham's sudden arrival had all too
unpleasantly reminded him.

He thought now of the note he had written Sylvia. It was as
simple and honest as he could make it, though he had allowed
himself a flourish or two. Was she perhaps at this very moment
reading it? Or at any rate thinking over her answer? They were
not children. Whatever the tie with Bingham was, whatever the
love she felt for him too, Campion did not, somehow, doubt his
own chances. He felt an almost irrepressible desire to go to her—
now, at once, in the middle of the night, to find his way to her
through the dark corridors. Was there any real reason why he
shouldn't? Moving towards the door, he could think of none.

George Bingham, standing on the far side of the room from Sylvia,
said, "I've got something important to talk to you about, something I decided on my way here. Maybe that's why I came even."

"Yes."

But suddenly he did not seem to have any speech. Silence filled
the room. At last he said, "Never mind. It can wait."

"Why should it wait?"

"Never mind," he said. There was another long silence. Then he
said, "Is your bed too narrow?"

It was already turned down for the night, and she herself, standing beside it, was in gown and over it the robe she had pulled
around her before answering the door. "Too narrow for what?"
she managed. To her dismay something of the old complex of
feelings from the early days stirred in her.

"For me."

He moved a step or two forward, but he was still half in among the shadows. He stopped, and seemed to her a marble figure. But now with simple, unself-conscious gestures that took her utterly by surprise he removed his jacket and began loosening his tie, like a warrior discarding his armor. She did not quite know what she felt. He seemed different to her, and at the same time as wholly lovable as at the beginning, as powerful and remarkable a man as she had thought him at their first meeting. But why now? she thought. It was as though no terrible struggle of any sort had passed between them. Oh, why now? He moved slowly towards her out of the shadows, across the great distance that had separated them, a warrior-god whose armor had fallen away at last, leaving a god-man of a purer sort, vulnerable, tender, proffering, as she had never before known him, as she had given up believing he could ever be. Oh but why *now?* In the next instant she was lifting and holding out her arms to him.

Campion had circled the house several times, but the only light burning was in Gwendolyn's room. Sylvia's window was quite dark. She slept then, Sylvia. It was as well that he had changed his mind halfway down the corridor. The fresh air had helped him a little, the getting outside for a while. He felt less restless. He reminded himself that in only a few hours he would be taking Mrs. Halász to the airport and meeting Elsie. He wished he had not, in a moment of anger, committed himself to bringing Elsie here. But it was too late now, and she could be counted on, at least in every respect that mattered. A needless worry. It was time he slept too. He cast one last look up towards Sylvia's room. Then he went back into the house.

Soon night, the bedfellow of all, enclosed his limbs too.

Twenty-seven

Elsie Crown's eye makeup was streaming down her face along with the tears. She was shrieking in Hungarian and pounding violently on the glass wall. Ernest stood by helplessly. "*Itt vagyok, Itt vagyok. Nézzen ide,*" she cried.

They were standing on a sort of walk that encircled the large In Transit room on the floor below them. There, enclosed by the glass wall, as though they were zoo creatures, men and women stood in line to have their passports stamped. Once they had passed beyond that glass barrier into the room or until they had been given permission to cross through it into the terminal, they were in another dimension; they could still be seen but could neither be touched nor communicated with except by a sort of vague and primitive sign language. It was a most ingenious arrangement. Ernest had barely managed to say good-bye to Mrs. Halász at the *Eintritt* doors—not without feelings of misgiving—in time to get around to the other side and greet Elsie, whom he had already caught a glimpse of and who came flying up the *Ausgang* ramp into his arms.

"Darling," she had said, laughing at the lipstick mark she had left across his mouth, one hand firmly anchored to his coat lapel, looking him over sharply, "you've changed. Yes, you have. Behind all that dignity you can't quite hide it. What have you been up to? Ah come now, no point pretending. I know you too well. Remember? Ah God, what a pair of outcasts we were. I've had a miserable flight. Across the aisle, this oil man from Texas. He kept waving a damp cigar stub in my face. 'Honey, now wha'r youawll goin by your lil ol lonesome?' Everybody was his honey. And in the seat next to me a little girl of eight or so with a sign hung around her neck. Do you know when I left Budapest after the war for the refugee camp they did that to me? At my age it made me feel silly. This little girl kept eating and eating, all the way across the Atlantic . . ."

He had disengaged himself and begun to move her slowly along the walk. He knew from experience that it would be a few minutes before Elsie could calm down and he did not attempt to say much. He wanted to try and locate Lily once more before they left. "How are things in New York?" he managed.

"You miss nothing. Noise, dirt, craters like bombs. No more tennis courts at Columbia, only buildings now. Everyone is still going to a psychoanalyst. Everyone knows someone who can do something for him. Nobody cares what it is. The theatre stinks, of course. One good thing—my father was picketed by some of his tenants. They marched up and down in front of that fancy Fifth Avenue building he lives in now with beautiful placards telling the

whole world that he had turned the heat off in *their* buildings. But
that's a long story. Everyone I know is working for Stevenson,
naturally. He hasn't a chance. You should read the papers! No,
you shouldn't. I am sick of it all . . ."

He did not really hear what she was saying. Staring down into
the room he had spotted Lily. Her passport had just been stamped
and she was standing a little to one side, laboriously putting it
away with her stiff fingers. She seemed about to walk on into the
Departure room; then she hesitated, turned around and looked up.
He could feel his face shaping itself into a forced smile, and he was
just lifting his arms to signal her when Elsie began to scream.

Now he grabbed her forcibly by the shoulders and spun her
towards him. "What are you doing? You're making a scene. Have
you lost your mind?"

"Take your hands off me," she said. Her face was wild and
anguished. "I've got to make her see me. I've got to make her
know I'm here." She jerked herself out of his grip and began
beating on the glass again and crying out. Down below Lily Halász
was still looking up, a puzzled, half-whimsical expression on her
face. "Oh God, she doesn't recognize me," Elsie cried, and with a
shock Ernest realized that it was Lily Halász she was talking about.
"It's me. Iza. *Iza!*" she shouted. He had the most extraordinary
sense of everything closing in.

"Quick, Ernest. Your handkerchief. Give me your handkerchief. Quickly."

Automatically, he obeyed. Elsie did not wave with it but began
swiping harshly at her face. "I couldn't have changed so much, oh
no, I couldn't." The words rang against the glass. Black, green,
bright pink smudges appeared on the white cloth. The plainer face
of Elsie was emerging. "It's my hair"—she wailed then, tensing the
fingers of her left hand into a sudden claw, as though she would
tear it to the roots—"it's another color." Ernest kept his eyes on
Lily, who was no longer amused, who was staring intently up at
this unmasking. Then Elsie let the handkerchief drop and flung
herself into a frantic pantomime of playing the piano while transforming the expression on her face into one of haughty defiance.
Lily Halász dropped her purse, one hand went to her mouth, then
she clasped both hands before her breast and slowly opened them,
fingers extended, palms open toward Elsie. Her lips moved in

soundless speech. A strange long low moan came from Elsie. Then
a sigh. "She sees me. She knows me. Oh thank God, she sees
me."

A small crowd had begun to gather around Elsie and Ernest, and
an official was approaching them. Now that the screaming and
pounding had suddenly stopped he hesitated. Ernest gave him a
look that was meant to be reassuring and he nodded and walked
away from them, like one who was accustomed to such emotional
outbursts and who preferred to leave well enough alone. Ernest
glowered at the others and they too began to move away. He put
an arm about Elsie. She was crying quietly now and had her face
pressed to the glass. She looked disturbingly like a child. She and
Lily were sending small signals to each other, not so much waves as
timid and intense beckonings. Elsie spoke a constant stream of
Hungarian and English, but in a soft and whispered undertone.

Ernest pulled her closer. "Was it Lily's family . . . ?"

"What do you think? Who else could it be? Yes. Mrs. Halász.
She is the one. Tante Lily. She played the piano through the air
raids and the bombardment. And sang. And talked to me. Oh
God." Then, taking her eyes off Lily for a second, she turned to
him in surprise and asked, "But how do you know her?"

"She's been living with us at Kilchberg. She's an old friend of
Gwendolyn."

"But why, why for God's sake, didn't you tell me that?"

"Tell you? How was I supposed to know you knew each other?
All you ever told me was that some family in Budapest had taken
you in, that you hadn't wanted to leave them." He felt angry with
Elsie, as though, against all logic, he somehow ought to have
known and therefore now had to defend himself. "Surely you
remember that. It was the one thing you could never bring yourself to talk about."

She was speaking in Hungarian again, through the glass, and was
not listening to him. He said, "She's going to London to live."

"What?"

"To London. Some relative, I think."

The reality of Lily's departure seemed only at that moment to
strike Elsie, as though until Campion had put it into words there
had been room for no reality other than the one of having found
her, of being recognized by her. Now she clutched at him. "But

she can't go now. It's impossible. I won't allow it. You must do something. Oh please, Ernest, do something. I don't want her to go. Don't let it happen."

He looked at the *Eintritt* doors. He would never get past the guard there without passport and airplane ticket. Perhaps if he could find the official who had been there a few minutes before. There was so little time left. "I'll try," he said.

But instead of releasing him she now clutched him the harder. "Look!" Down below a woman in some sort of uniform had come up to Lily, was leaning over and talking to her, making gestures towards the flight room, all but leading her away. "No, no, no." Elsie was pounding on the glass again.

"Stop it, will you?" He found himself making futile gestures now, trying to tell Lily that she should not leave, that he would do something, that she should not go with that woman. Lily was looking bewildered, a helpless figure, he suddenly saw, dropping his arms. "It's too late now," he said to Elsie, who had both hands pressed flat against the glass wall as though striving with all her might to bring it down. "You can see her in London."

Lily, resigned, nodded her head toward the flight room, then waved at them, as though to say it was not important, threw her head back and gave the short laugh, as she had done so many hundreds of times in her life when she had failed to make a bid in bridge, blew several kisses at Elsie, and then followed the uniformed woman into the room beyond.

"I come to London!" Elsie shouted, but Lily, who in any case could not have heard, had already disappeared.

Campion led Elsie out into the terminal. She sat down in a chair and wept. People were staring at them as they passed by. Her face, swollen and red, was somehow more childlike than ever. "You can go to her in London," he kept saying to her.

The last time he said this she pulled her mouth down in a nasty expression of disbelief. "All my life. Comings. Goings. Never meeting. Always these walls. It's no good. Why beat on them?"

"Because they're there."

"Fool. Goy."

"Because you're you."

She made a disgusted gesture. Then she said, "Is there some place where we can watch the plane take off?"

He hesitated, reluctant to prolong the painful scene, but he knew how different he and Elsie were in this respect. "Come on then."

They went out onto a balcony from which they could look down at the planes and the airfield. A file of people was marching towards a plane, Lily among them. She seemed to be walking unsteadily now, head down. The woman in uniform was still beside her. She helped her up the ramp. At the very top, just before she vanished, she turned around. Elsie waved, and shouted, "I come to London!" but it was plain that Lily did not see or hear her. "Good-bye. *Isten vele, Isten áldja.* Good-bye, good-bye," Elsie shouted into the damp wind and the roaring of machinery.

They went back into the terminal. The old cynical expression he knew so well came back to her face. "Do you know why I came here?" she asked him. "I was on my way to Budapest. I wanted to find out if she was still alive. I wanted to see her once again."

"Be glad that's out," he said flatly. "Warsaw's simmered down but there's fighting in Budapest it appears."

"What? Since when?"

"Last night, this morning, it's not clear yet. No doubt there's more news by now. Lily didn't know. I left Gwendolyn huddled over the radio at Kilchberg. It looks as though your arrival coincides with an historic moment."

"I'm sick of historic moments," she said. "More killings. More lies afterwards. There are your historic moments. Where's the bar around here? Take me to the bar. I want to drink a great many drinks."

"You can't do that."

"Why not?"

"Because I've got some things to talk to you about. I'll buy you a cognac, one, but that's all. Then we've got to get back to the villa. The retinue's altered considerably, incidentally, since your last visit, except for Anton . . . and me of course."

Twenty-eight

Mrs. Dartley was a frightening apparition to awaken to. She stood a few feet back from Sylvia's bed now, looking like an asylum inmate who had somehow got loose and would at any second begin to howl. She was wearing a man's dressing gown, opulent but frayed and so short-waisted on her long torso that the belt tied just a little below her bosom. Beneath this she had on some indeterminate and fusty garment, the hem of which was unraveling and hanging several sloppy inches lower on one side than the other. Her hair was not even combed—it stood out around her head like Anton's—and lipstick had been applied with such evident haste that it appeared she had two mouths, a pale one twisted down at the corners as though by pain and, fluttering over this, another one, bright, red, and faintly smiling. Her hand on Sylvia's shoulder a moment before, shaking her out of sleep, had been, even through the silk coverlet, cold and damp. Sylvia braced herself.

"Can you get the keys to Mr. Bingham's car?"

"His car? Did he come in the car? I didn't see it."

"So much for sense evidence. It's in the garage. Can you get the keys?"

"Yes, I think so."

"Will you do so? Will you then drive with the greatest possible speed into Zürich for me?"

"Yes. Certainly."

"Then hurry. Get up. What are you waiting for?"

Sylvia opened her mouth to explain but could find no words. Beneath the coverlet she had no clothes on. She hesitated.

"Are you naked? I've seen naked bodies before. Try to hurry." She stomped to the window and took up her stand there, eyes firmly on Sylvia as though she feared that if she did not watch her she would go back to sleep.

"Splendid, splendid, I knew you were not a sluggard," she said as Sylvia left her bed and moved quickly, smoothly towards the armoire. She looked very white against its dark wood, swiftly crouching, bending, lifting arms in the brief nymphlike postures of a woman dressing. "A pretty sight," Mrs. Dartley said. "A pity to waste it on me." Then she added in more agitated tone, "And ill-suited to *this* morning." Even as she spoke there were changes.

Sensuous lineaments were broken at the curve of the waist, flowing softness was bound and modified, absolute woman yielded to the severities of a breastplate. Sylvia stood now, child of her times, in half-slip and strapless bra.

"Will you tell me what has happened?" she said to Mrs. Dartley.

"Revolution. In Hungary. Budapest has arisen," her voice trembling.

Sylvia's first reaction was: but what has this to do with me? Yet the phrase was hardly formed when it was swept away by another: would the terrible barriers actually fall? A mood of almost wild exultation seized her. She had not known until that moment how much she cared that tyranny might still be overthrown, that men might still be free. She had trained herself, being helpless to do otherwise, to ignore and accept the facts of oppression; yet these facts had in some mysterious way limited her own spirit too. Could one perhaps even believe again in the possibility of a just heroism? Her heart leapt and pounded, and she thought of St. George, but this thought it was necessary to push away, to deal with later, for it brought with it all the painful and complicated questions which the world of action posed. She reached a hand towards her best town dress, but now she changed her mind, stepped out of the slip and hastily pulled on a pair of trousers. One did not do that in Europe, wear trousers, except in the summer at resorts. But at this very moment were not women of her own age in Budapest dressing so? She felt a great need to perform this slight, vicarious action. Over her head she pulled a heavy sweater.

Mrs. Dartley had filled the sink with water. She pointed to it. "Wash. But don't splash. I want you to listen carefully."

Sylvia did as she was told.

"This is the message I want you to deliver: 'The opinion of an outsider . . .' No; change that. Let us start all over again. 'The opinion of a sympathetic, outside observer: if there is no sign of outside interest, probably in the form of a significant diplomatic move, within a few days, then expect none. Abandon hope.'" She paused. "Have you understood that? Can you repeat it?"

"Yes I think so." She did repeat it, word for word. "Where am I to take this message?"

"Do you know a place called the Öpfelchammer?"

"Yes." She had been there several times recently with Ernest.

They always sat upstairs in the small room where students gathered, having an occasional go with them at *Gaudeamus Igitur,* seated beneath photographs and other mementos of the great Swiss poet who had once lived there.

"There is a man who goes there every night, to the little upstairs room. His name is Rudi. It is impossible to mistake him. He is a short, very slight man of about fifty. A crew cut. A moustache. Wall-eyed."

Sylvia remembered him. He was a well-known figure, a comic figure, a favorite of the university men who, with a certain condescension which she had found a little unpleasant, seemed to have adopted him. It was he who every twenty minutes or so insistently began a round of *Gaudeamus.* "Does he have a very high, squeaky voice?" she asked.

"Yes. That's Rudi. You know him. Good. He's a bookkeeper in a bank. I shall write that address down for you. But I hope you won't have to contact him there. He lives out along the lake, on the other side, near Küssnacht, and you will never have time to reach him there. If he went home last night he will already have left for the bank."

"But if he—?"

"Don't interrupt. Go first to the Öpfelchammer. When he drinks too much the family often puts him to bed in their quarters. We must hope we are in luck and that last night he did drink too much to make it home. He always makes it to the bank, however, no matter how drunk he has been the night before, and he is due there an hour from now."

"And I'm to give this message to *him?*" Was that why Ernest had taken her there, and had he during the course of the evening made contact with the clownish Rudi?

"Yes. He has ways, sometimes, of getting messages through quite rapidly."

"And the people who run the Öpfelchammer, am I to assume they know about this, or am I to be circumspect?"

"*Extremely* circumspect. They know nothing. They are burghers."

Sylvia nodded, but the whole thing now seemed to her ludicrous. Was Mrs. Dartley actually paranoid enough to think that she was going to have an effect on a revolution taking place in Hungary?

Mrs. Dartley said, "I see from the expression on your face that you are wondering what it is I expect to accomplish. You have a right to wonder and I will tell you. Nothing more perhaps than to save the lives of a few friends. I have felt too, I have felt ever since this terrible division of Europe took place . . ." She was obviously, Sylvia suddenly saw, struggling to keep herself from crying. "I have felt that it was an obligation, a holy obligation, *just to stay in touch*. It is more of an obligation than ever now. Hurry, my dear dear Faustine, hurry. Take his great chariot, and hurry. I shall wait for you downstairs."

They left the room together, Mrs. Dartley making rapidly for the stairs and down them with a sort of stumbling motion that made it look as though she would lose her footing with every step. Sylvia knocked softly on the door to Bingham's room. Without a word he let her in. They exchanged a brief, somewhat stiff embrace. Over his shoulder then she saw a breakfast tray on the table by the window, and beside it a book. Evidently he had been placidly drinking his coffee and reading when she knocked. It was plain that he did not know what was happening. She felt an odd, unnatural advantage over him, made the more confusing by the new tenderness between them. She felt too that she did not *want* him to know, not yet at any rate, what was going on in the outside world, for by now the fact of revolution in Hungary did not seem so simple to her as it had, and the last thing she wanted was to consider him in relation to this fact. He was leading her towards the table. "No. I can't stay. I want to know if I may borrow your car."

"Do you want me to drive you somewhere?" he replied. Like herself, he was dressed in slacks and sweater.

"No, no, I don't." She had a mission to accomplish. She would be as single-minded as he. Yet for some reason she could not look at him very directly. "I want the keys."

He nodded and turned to fetch them from his coat. As he handed the keys to her he said, "You've never driven it."

"I've watched you," she said, and turned and left him. She had an almost claustrophobic desire to be out of the villa and on her way. She raced down the stairs with the joyful lightness of a twelve-year-old, vaguely aware of his having come after her a few steps.

Mrs. Dartley was at the door, holding it open. Out they went.

She handed her a slip of paper, presumably with the name of the bank where Rudi worked on it. Sylvia stuffed it into the pocket of her suede jacket. "Am I to give the message in English?" she asked.

"Yes. He affects not to understand it well. But he does. An unusual man. I shall tell you about him when you get back."

"And shouldn't I tell him who it is he's to get the message through to?"

"No," Mrs. Dartley said shortly. "Rudi knows what to do. Now hurry."

They had reached the garage, the doors of which were already open. "I *will* hurry." She hesitated for just a second at the sight of the terrifying sports car, then flung herself into the front seat. The engine started with a great roaring sound, which, as always, made her feel nervous. Then she took a breath, closed her eyes, and managed to shove the gearstick into reverse. The gears engaged and the car was backing smoothly out. Suddenly she felt very sure of herself. She spun the car dashingly around past Mrs. Dartley and hurled both it and herself out of the driveway and towards the road. She caught a vague glimpse of Mrs. Dartley in the mirror, standing with one hand in salute at her forehead, presumably to shade her eyes as she watched the car on its way, and one foot lifted and resting on an ornamental rock—an old, disheveled Nike.

By the time Sylvia turned onto the highway to Zürich, having taken the small road that led down to it with a daring and skill she would not have imagined possible for her, all doubts had been put down and she was in a state of near-euphoria. It was impossible for her to imagine anything going wrong; an accident, for example, was unthinkable. She was perfectly alert and in control. She swung around a small Mercedes, flashing between it and an oncoming truck. Nothing lasts forever, nothing lasts forever, she thought joyously. Not even the monolithic state, not even tyrants, or horror. How exhilarating a refrain: nothing lasts forever. Except herself. She was the exception—the power she now felt told her that. Was that how St. George felt, she wondered, slamming down into a lower gear as she overtook with one beautiful sweeping arc a dawdling Simca. She laughed aloud—I'm playing at you, she thought. And why not? roaring past a tiny Fiat with two startled faces in it. What fun it must be to fly a plane. She must ask him to teach her to fly sometime soon. It was absolutely seductive, the world of danger, if it was anything like what she was feeling now. What could one not do? And there was a terrible, perhaps irresistible urge to go always a little further, to pit one's self against ever-vaster forces—she could feel that too—once one's head was turned by the notion that the self was invincible. What could one not dare? How far would one not go in pursuit of the illusion of perfect freedom, the most corrupting illusion of all?

She reminded herself that she must not become too intoxicated by that domination over space and time which she now felt she had. But it was difficult not to be. She leaned with the car, taking the next curve at even higher speed, eyes steady against the on-rushing wind, aaaahh, now straight away again. The motion of the perilous journey itself seemed everything; fine distinctions, moral doubts, were easily lost, and purpose became irrelevant. But she did have a purpose, she reminded herself, and she must keep her head, not only to protect her own life but because of that purpose. Involuntarily her foot eased a bit on the accelerator . . . *it is a holy obligation just to stay in touch* . . . These words brought a slight change. She found herself with the thought that somehow it must not, whatever happened, must not be like the war years, when one lost all sense of right and wrong and talked or permitted others to talk terrible nonsense about those abstractions into which the enemy of the moment had been turned. She did not understand why this thought had come to her or why she could not follow it to a conclusion; some connection was missing, some simple thing that ordinarily she would have no trouble with at all. A slight tension was coming over her arms and shoulders, interfering a little with her handling of the car, threatening the rhythms of the journey. But how ridiculous! That obligation to stay in touch was exactly what had sent her on this mission; surely hers was an action she could not doubt, could not hold back from. It was pure and purely good—no harm could come from it. In this she was certainly luckier than St. George. As she leaned confidently to the wheel again, relaxed, giving herself instinctively to the flow of power, pressing down on the accelerator, swinging out and passing at one bold clip on the narrowing road a truck and a car, blasting away on the horn, she could feel nothing again but the pure joy of danger, of having passed beyond the usual limits. It was only this wild journey itself that really mattered.

She sped on now, faster and faster—no authority would ever catch her or bar her way—around the turns and dangerously into the streets of suburbs in which it was no doubt true that ordinary mortals innocently unaware of the fierce engine that was bearing down upon them might be going about their usual tasks. Alas, alas, for them. Was this what men felt, in war, in battle—even, for some, in the conquest of women?

A fierce champion, Sylvia Grierson drove on to the noble goal of the Öpfelchammer, her hair helmeting her head like that of some warrior-goddess, the medallion of St. George thumping against her breast.

It was thus that she looked to Ernest Campion and Elsie Crown when the two cars passed each other. It was impossible to mistake her, even traveling at that dangerous speed, head back and so pale against the shiny blackness of the amazing vehicle at whose wheel she sat. Campion had seen the car coming from a distance, in its erratic, certain path, and had automatically slowed down. She hurtled past them. But from the expression on his face at that moment and from the way his head swiveled back, Elsie knew. Turning deliberately around, leaning even out the window of the Rolls, she watched the darting vehicle until it disappeared. "So," she said, a long, meaningful tone. "That is Sylvia Grierson."

"Yes," he replied, glowering, speeding up slightly.

She began to laugh, then stopped herself. "It will be interesting to meet her. I look forward to it," she said. "If she lives long enough."

Twenty-nine

A task had been found for Posy, and every morning now she set out for the pool to feed Mrs. Dartley's pet fish, Mrs. Dartley having become convinced that after the activities of the summer it would be unkind to leave it without any attention whatever during the long winter months when no one went near the pool. On the face of it, this was ridiculous, and it was Marshall's private opinion that their hostess had invented the whole thing simply to give Posy something to do, just as he had begun to suspect that his chair

duties, which until recently he had taken so seriously, had the same
purpose. He could not quite be certain, however, at least not about
the fish. They all remembered how unpleasant things had become
that time a visitor remarked, seeing it surface, as it happened in the
ordinary, quick fly-catching way one expected, "Well, well, well,
a good six-pounder."

Mrs. Dartley did have special attitudes towards it. Posy had
asked once, "What's its name? Doesn't he have one?"

"No, I'm afraid not," was the reply. "It seems somehow, oh a
little presumptuous to name the creature. Or at least for me to."

But Posy had done so, secretly, after she began the feedings, if
that was what they were, confiding the name only to Marshall.
Felix, she had called him, following a simple alliterative instinct.

Queer fish was a term that really applied to Felix. His history
and habits were extraordinary and everyone at Kilchberg soon
became familiar with them, learned how the first time Mrs. Dartley had gone for a swim in the pool he had seemed to cavort along
beside her, how thereafter he never failed to respond in some way
to her presence. Mrs. Dartley had only to remove her shoes, gather
up her skirts a little, and wade a few feet into the water—a sight in
itself—for Felix to appear. He would rub against her ankles and
calves, and circle about her in a most mysterious but endearing
manner, eventually following her in to the very water's edge—
even the most cynical and doubting of onlookers would find themselves curiously moved by this spectacle. And disturbed. It was as
though they were being asked to re-examine all their preconcep-
tions about nature itself, and especially about the relationship that
existed between themselves and other living creatures.

Posy was always most punctual about her morning rites, and the
fish was too. By the time she arrived at the pool it would be
leaping in marvelous arcs out of the water, expressing, if probably
not a specific hunger, then surely some anticipatory joy. There
would be a faint rippling sound, perhaps more imagined than
heard, then that always surprising leap, that sudden upward thrust,
the felt impact of the breaking of the barrier between water and
air, the striving, propelling, somehow painful motions of the
caudal fin, and the final serene instant of high achievement. "A
Nijinsky of a fish," Mrs. Halász had once been heard to murmur.
And indeed it was a little like watching a dance of some sort, that
parabolic rise—and plunge.

Marshall had got in the habit, whenever he didn't sleep too late, of helping Posy to collect the bits of bread from people's breakfast trays and trudging along with her to the pool. But this morning the atmosphere in the house was so distracting that he quickly forgot about the fish. Passing Mrs. Dartley's room, sleepy, wondering if anyone would be driving in to Zürich later on—he had decided to go to Hug's and with the last of his funds buy the music to all the Vivaldi flute concerti, study them, work, get busy, it was high time—he was suddenly assaulted by a loudly tuned-up radio and the unmistakable tones of an American voice coming from it. The door was half open, and as he stood outside it there was a sudden rage of static. It subsided into the formal rhythms of the BBC, but before he could catch more than a puzzling word or two it was switched into silence and Mrs. Dartley herself swept out of the door. She placed her hands on his shoulders. It even appeared for a few seconds that she was going to lean her head against him. Instead, she gave him a gentle sort of shake, her expression woebegone. "The accidents of birth . . ." she said slowly, "of time . . . of place." All sorts of shapes seemed to stir behind her obsidian gaze.

Marshall stood perfectly still, waiting. He did not understand what she was up to—she had never touched him before, nor looked at him in that way—but he was not in the least embarrassed by the faint, rocking pressure of her hands on his shoulders or by the searching gray eyes that roamed and darted over his face. Suddenly she changed, lifted her hands to her head and gave a swipe or two at her hair, attempting to smooth it down without much success. She said, in her more usual way, "Forgive me, Marshall. All sorts of quite dramatic and heart-breaking things are happening. I've been very upset. For a moment, seeing you, I thought how fearfully easy it would be, you in quite a different setting, I mean. I must get control." She touched her cheeks. "Febrile." She started for the staircase. "There's a revolution going on in Budapest," she said, and started down.

He followed her into the drawing room. There Anton Hrubick, his face looking almost drawn, was standing beside the little radio that used to be in Mrs. Halász's room, moving the dial, switching from station to station, flooding the room with a variety of tongues. He had popped a button on his shirt and his round little

belly was showing through. Occasionally he interpolated comments on the broadcasts. "They know nothing new." "They have
not yet admitted . . ." "Prague continues to lie."

Marshall could feel a strange but constant beat of excitement in
himself. It was odd that something happening so far away should
seem so important; yet it did seem so to him. He made no effort to
find the reasons for this. But he knew that this was something to
remember, that it was by no means over yet, that years later he
would say of this beginning: Yes, I was in Switzerland at the time,
staying at the house of Gwendolyn Dartley, when the first news
came. Aloud he said nothing, but in his usual way listened, waited,
bided the inner time. Posy, looking small, perched on a cassock,
was on the other side of the room, as silent as himself. He tried to
catch her eye, but could not.

Benjamin Knox arrived then, in a frenzy. Since he understood
no language but English—and that, Sylvia Grierson had once unkindly remarked, was debatable—he and Ralph Bledder had not
heard the news until they were a few miles from Kilchberg, when
they had tuned the car radio into the Armed Forces Network. His
greatest, his most urgent need, volubly expressed when he entered
the drawing room, was to use the telephone. "Show him, Marshall," Mrs. Dartley had ordered. Marshall took him into the hall
and stood for a time watching while Knox alternately banged
away at the telephone with a finger and cried out his frustration.
"Get me London," he would say, "Get me New York," "Get me
an international operator," "Operator, operator, this is an emergency." In what sense could what was happening in Hungary be
taken as a personal emergency of Mr. Knox's? Marshall could not
follow this. Watching him, he felt vaguely annoyed.

When Marshall went back into the drawing room he noticed a
familiar object on the floor beside Posy, the square of insubstantial
green scarf in which for some reason she always chose to carry
Felix's food. Ever since the first morning, when, scavenging among
the trays in the kitchen, she had pulled the scarf from her head and
put the bread scraps in it, she had politely declined Celeste's offer
of a pan or dish. "Oh no, thanks, this'll be fine," she would say.
Looking at it now, bulging and knotted at the corners, Marshall
remembered for the first time about the fish. Mrs. Dartley saw
where he was looking. She took a few steps away from the radio,

peered more closely, lifted her eyebrows and said to Posy, "What have you there? Your worldly possessions? Are you running away from us? That looks like a hobo's bundle, but wrapped in such a fancy bandana. For a hobo. In fact, *you* look like a hobo, a little crepe de Chine hobo." Posy's eyes were vague and gleaming; she hardly responded at all to Mrs. Dartley's speech, only smiled a little. Marshall tried again to get her attention, and again failed to do so. She looked as though she had gone to sleep with her eyes open and was having curious dreams. Mrs. Dartley frowned slightly and went back to the radio. Ralph Bledder, who had come in with Knox, had as usual disappeared to his lurkings. This at least was how Marshall assumed he spent his time when he wasn't at Knox's elbow. With Posy, much to her amusement, Marshall referred to Bledder as The Lurker.

George Bingham came quietly into the room, paused for a second, taking them all in, nodding sightly to everyone, then moved toward Mrs. Dartley. Marshall would have liked to be able to enter a room with such command. No one spoke. Bingham put his hands on a chair and made a gesture toward Mrs. Dartley, silently asking for permission to move it. "Certainly," she said. He moved the chair nearer to the radio and sat listening for two or three minutes, his face composed but his eyes darkly glimmering. Then there was some slight change, perhaps an infinitesimal relaxing of the body. something at least that conveyed itself to Mrs. Dartley. It was as though he had learned all he needed to. Mrs. Dartley pulled her chair nearer to his. They were confronting each other. Marshall heard her say, "What will happen? *There*, I mean?"

"Too early to say," he replied. "It depends on how long it goes on."

"And war?"

He merely shook his head in a noncommittal way.

Anton abruptly turned down the volume of the radio. The voice of Knox, still involved in his telephone struggles, could then be heard, coming into them from the hall, boyish, petulant, complaining and important—unbelievably at odds with the atmosphere of the drawing room. Anton put a finger to his lips; something of the old, familiar teasing look came back to him. Then he said to Bingham, "I am going to switch to Radio Moscow now. I myself don't understand Russian. But now that you are here . . ."

"Yes?" Bingham asked, his tone polite, interested.

"Well, I only meant that since I seem to remember that you do understand Russian . . ."

"That's right, I do," Bingham said in the same tone. "Though I don't seem to remember having mentioned it to you."

Anton shrugged, amused but serious. "Nor do I. In fact, I don't believe that you did. But perhaps it was some quite different thing that you said, on your former visit, that gave me an impression . . . I have been trying to remember for weeks what it was . . . it appears I never will. But at least I know now what it was about, what I have been trying to remember . . . this idea I got that you understood Russian, an idea that disappeared into my capacious unconscious, there to nibble at me annoyingly every once in a while, waiting to emerge at the right time. Ah, well, so, now it is very fortunate for us that you are here just now. We have already heard what Washington has to say; now we shall learn what the other cat with the big whiskers is up to, or if it is still not ready to jump."

"Go right ahead. I'm interested too," Bingham said, smiling.

Posy had moved to the doorway and was signaling to Marshall. He went to her and she stepped into the hall. "What's the matter?" he asked.

"Nothing's the matter. I almost forgot about Felix. I thought maybe you wanted to come with me. It's all right if you don't."

"Of course I want to come. It's just that you looked peculiar."

"Don't be silly," she said, avoiding his eyes.

Children of a political age, they nevertheless, being young and American, understood little of those great forces and ideas which, having sprung into being long before their births, had passed inevitably into the forms of power and applied abstraction, and now held the world in deadly conflict. This was as well for them, for their ignorance of dogma left their hearts free to be moved, and their hearts were moved, purely so. They did not particularly hate Russians, nor love Hungarians, but they knew that weaponless creatures like themselves did not rise up against their masters, offer flesh and spirit in contest with the steel and fire of tanks, unless their suffering had been great beyond endurance. Indeed they were exactly the right age for responding to the uniquely human plight which was the reality behind the news coming from Hungary, and which had broken through to them so surprisingly. As they walked into the out-of-doors each knew that the other was feeling something in kind. They were glad to be away from their elders, with whom they suddenly felt they had nothing in common at all.

Yet the strong emotions which had been stirred in them were hard to put into speech, and they talked instead of themselves, hoping perhaps to find some analogue in the experience of their own short lives. Both had been small children during the Second War. It was still as far from them in psychological time as the First, and that was as far from them as the campaigns of Peloponnesia. Korea was closer, but for Marshall it was associated above all with his first conscious awareness of being different from his family, with the first phase of rebellion. He remembered especially his father's tirades at the dinner table; it was always there that his father chose to deliver himself of his judgments on the state of the nation: the President of the United States was a traitor; he was sending American boys off to die in a foreign war; Americans had no business being in foreign wars; but the President was also a traitor because he was "soft on Communism" and would not "let MacArthur drop the bomb."

What had bothered Marshall most, at the age of fourteen or so, was that his mother always seemed to him, in those quarrels which did not so much break out between himself and his father as lie corroding under the surface, not only to be taking his father's side but also to be echoing his opinions with a sort of added venom. "Smoothing things over, dear," was how, if pressed later, she would describe to him what it was she was trying to do. But at what cost, he had asked himself often—at the cost of truth, of justice? In the end he had been forced to discover that these concepts, at least as they applied to anything outside the home, simply did not exist for her. And his sister and footfall-playing brother, they were always somehow mocking him, always winning his father's—even he felt, his mother's—approval. How often, at the dinner table, he had wanted to jump up, race for his flute, and march back into that dining room piping at them the highest notes he could manage, drowning out all their stupid talk.

No, there was no help in that memory; Korea had been for him as much of a personal muddle as for the world it had been an historical one.

Posy remembered quite different things about Korea, an atmosphere for those close to her of immediate, high drama, almost an excuse for making life more interesting. This had bewildered her, since for the first few weeks she herself had felt only great waves of panic and fear. Ned, her mother's husband, was a lieutenant commander in the Naval Reserve. He had made several quick trips to Washington to see some friends and was soon called to active duty to what seemed to be a very important and faintly mysterious desk job in the nation's capital. Everyone felt it would be better if for a while she went to live with her father and his wife. She preferred her mother and Ned really, but she had nothing against her father and Pam and she liked the fact that there was an infant half-sister in their house. These two households had always confused her, especially since both of her parents were always telling her that she should decide for herself which of them she wanted to live with but she never really saw very much of either of them, no matter how it worked out. She had only been with her father for a few months when someone in his London office died and he decided to take over there until things were straightened out. Then she was put in a school near Washington and could spend her weekends with Ned and her mother, and although they were mostly out at parties she nevertheless did prefer this arrangement. Ned was always fun to be with, more than her father, more really than any father she'd ever seen. In fact, he wasn't really like a father at all. Still, she had nearly died of grief when her mother had divorced him; she had suffered much more than at the time of the divorce from her father, although that, she realized, was only because the first time she had been so young she could not really remember what she had felt.

Korea, it was all bound up with this somehow, and it would always be that sick feeling in her stomach when she heard a siren, pictures in newspapers of bearded half-frozen men and starving slant-eyed orphans—and Ned and her mother having a good time.

Walking in the air of Kilchberg, Posy and Marshall exchanged these memories gently, knowing that what was told by each was not usually told—indeed that neither had spoken to anyone before of such personal matters—and that what was left unsaid was still a reservoir of pain, though eased a little by the exchange.

"Do you know what I bet my mother's friends in New York are doing now?" Posy said then. "Organizing cocktail parties for the brave Hungarians."

"What do you mean?"

"Oh, it's the sort of thing the people I know do. Any excuse for
a party. Everyone will pay ten dollars, or more likely a hundred
dollars, to come to someone's apartment and drink martinis, and
the proceeds will supposedly go to Hungarians, and it will be
written up in the *Times* and they'll all feel very good about it."

"That's disgusting," Marshall said. There were times when his
own background, western, mercantile, Puritan, caused him to re-
coil instinctively from what in the vocabulary of his parents was
the east, the Mysterious East, for rich though the Sears family had
become, they had lost neither their belief in respectability and
other middle-class virtues, nor their secret envy and hatred of
Cavaliers. Not that Cavalier was a word in their vocabulary and
not that it was that simple. The people they specifically hated,
regarded as The Enemy, and illogically lumped together in a perfection of ignorance and provincialism included: Jews (except for
those who were socially prominent in their own community);
Catholics and other foreigners; artistic types (alas, the Devil had
thus ensnared their own younger son); Democrats and Socialists
and Communists (these were practically the same); old families of
wealth on the Eastern Seaboard (F.D.R. was to blame for this);
members of labor unions; educated Negroes; professors; Wall
Street (Eastern money); and anyone rich or poor who did not take
the profit motive as a sacred and unalterable law of human nature.

Marshall had of course broken from all this, and had even
learned to pity his family, to regard them as people simply left
behind by history. But that gay and strenuously pleasure-seeking
world which had in some mysterious way produced Posy nevertheless still called for an occasional quick adjustment on his part. In
his family hypocrisy was always serious, solemn; "duty," "self-
sacrifice" were the words that disguised desires. While the natural
elegance of his own nature caused him to hate this, he was not yet
always at ease in an atmosphere where little pretense was made
about motives that were not particularly enhancing to the image of
the self—or rather where pretense took the form of a more elaborate artifice, a more light-hearted, self-mocking and formal game
than he was used to. In this case, however, remembering the radio
broadcasts, his own feelings as he had listened to them and his own
feelings now, he felt no need to justify or correct his reaction to

what Posy had just said. "Cocktails for Hungary" was, in the truest sense, disgusting.

Posy agreed with him, and went on talking. "People will use words like 'perfectly dreadful'—I can just hear them. And lots of the men will pass on all sorts of inside information. Like the time I heard someone telling Ned about Eisenhower and the basket."

"What about Eisenhower and the basket?"

"After the heart attack. Someone, a publisher, on *Time* or the *Times*, I can't remember which, said that what had really happened after the heart attack was that he'd been carried downstairs in a basket. I've always wondered what kind of a basket, and why a basket. Like a kitten, do you suppose?"

Marshall did not suppose so, but he said nothing. They were not far from the pool. He said, "I wonder why Mrs. Dartley asked Mr. Bingham those questions. What do you think he knows about what's happening?"

Posy looked evasive. "Quite a bit, I think."

"Really?"

Suddenly Posy stopped and seemed to catch her breath; her eyes had that same vague look to them they'd had in the drawing room. She had turned so pale that Marshall thought she was going to faint. The two young people turned and faced each other. Posy said, in a strange and trembling voice, "What do you suppose it's really like there now? What if *we* were there instead of here?"

For an instant images that neither had ever seen seemed to hover between them, the sights, sounds, smells of demolition, the flashing of faces, their own among them, in foreign streets, a running up staircases and into doorways, and being separated and lost and alone with a great indifferent rumbling coming toward them. They had performed a fatal act, the act of the imagination. They were afraid, but full of a high longing. Marshall shook himself. "Posy," he said, and took her hand.

As they came within sight of the pool, they saw, as always on other mornings, the fish in its dance, the enspiriting gay leaps. They stood for a moment, hand in hand, wishing to prolong the moment, not yet touch it, glad that it was there, perpetual and reassuring. And then an object spun through the air and landed with a violent splash near Felix. It had come, apparently, from the side of the pool which they couldn't see. They looked at each other, puzzled, not certain that it had really happened. They rounded the last turn in the path, and the pool and all its surroundings lay revealed to them. There, to the left, and on the other side, stood Ralph Bledder, his face as indefinite as usual, his right arm slightly cocked, his left swinging slightly at his side in a closed fist. He did not see them. Now he took a few steps to his left, his eyes on the pool. Quickly he transferred an object from his left fist to his right, lifted his arm, cocked it, squinting. At the same instant that Posy and Marshall understood and that Felix surfaced again, a dazzling, silver leap, at that moment wrist and forearm snapped and a rock hurtled between the leap and the sun, so swift, so near that it seemed impossible that it had not pierced his body.

Marshall shouted, "Hey! Cut that out. What do you think you're doing?"

Ralph Bledder moved his head slowly until he was looking at them. For the first time his features seemed to be trying to express something—mild surprise, or perhaps puzzlement, at having been shouted at. He and Marshall stared at each other across the water. Then Bledder relaxed his left fist and several small rocks dropped from it to the ground. He put both hands in his pockets and continued to stare back at Marshall, who turned his eyes for one quick second to the pool and saw that Felix was still there, alive and circling. Then he looked again across the pool. Ralph Bledder was now walking away in the other direction.

"Why, that dirty . . ." Marshall did not finish his sentence, nor did he sprint after Bledder as he had intended to. A small sound from behind arrested him. He turned and saw that Posy had seated herself on the damp, brown grass and was weeping. He dropped instantly beside her, and took her in his arms.

Thirty

Sylvia had been in luck. The owners of the Öpfelchammer, though plainly surprised and curious, had led her directly to Rudi. She sat now, a cup of coffee in hand, looking out over the rooftops of Zür-

ich, Rudi himself waiting attention on her. She had delivered her
message.

"Yes. Well. Good. So. Very well. I understand." That was all he
had said, and had stood there with his watering absurd eyes, one
looking in one direction, one another—in this respect, it occurred
to her, well cast for the role of spy. But otherwise how could so
modest and physically ill-put-together a man be of any value at all
in such an undertaking? Again that feeling of the whole thing
being absolutely, unrewardingly absurd came back to her. Then, as
though he had read her thoughts, he had said in that squeaking
voice which sometimes came to an abrupt halt, could manage no
words at all, and simply squeaked away as though he were trying
to utter words that existed only at a frequency rate too high for
either of their ears, "I'm quite—squeak, squeak—efficient." He had
managed to convey a faint note of pride, but not of vanity, and
had stood a bit straighter, if that were possible, in the dark gray
double-breasted suit and the stiff collar, a picture of clerkly correctness. Then he had leaned forward, surrounded by a gentle
cloud of alcohol which was modified somewhat by toothpaste, eau
de cologne, shoeblack, and coffee. "You've come in a great hurry.
You must have coffee. Yes, you must."

"But is there time?"

"Oh my, time. I'm always so careful about that. No need to
worry. None. But there. To satisfy you. Yes. See." He took an old-
fashioned timepiece from a waistcoat pocket, consulted it, waved it
in front of her. "You see, I knew. I have exactly eight minutes
before I must go to the bank, go to—squeak, squeak—work. Yes.
Coffee."

Before she could protest he was out the door, and she had hardly
seated herself at the little table when he returned with a lovely cup
and saucer—faïence, she noted, and as different as possible from
the plain and heavy mug he had been using. "Still warm?" touching the pot, "yes, still warm. Always twice as much as I need.
Here. See." With the shaking hands of the alcohol-dependent he
poured the coffee, and set ceremoniously beside her the sugar and
milk.

She drank now, and then said, "I came by car of course. Won't
you let me drop you off at the bank?"

"Oh, goodness, no. Very kind, it's very kind of you, but it's not
the best idea. No. It wouldn't do. I always walk to the bank,

always, when I stay the night here. Leave at the same time, buy the same newspaper at the same stand. Routine. I believe in it. Very important."

"I see." It was not clear to her whether the importance had to do with his secret activities or with his own need for order. She felt that he did not intend her to know which it was.

"I've seen you before, here. Yes, you come to the Dichterstube, the only really pleasant part of the Öpfelchammer I'm afraid. That is, lately you have. A good place to drink in? One can be free. Even in these clothes." He batted at himself and squeaked once or twice. "The wine's cheap too, but good. Hard to find that. You know the words to *Gaudeamus*, my favorite song. Good. Most Americans don't."

"Some of us do." She hesitated. "I like the way you get everyone to sing."

Rudi blushed. "I haven't much of a—squeak, squeak—voice, I'm afraid. Too bad. Nothing to be done about it."

She did not know whether to attempt a polite contradiction of what was so painfully true or not. She sipped the coffee, then said, "You sing with a lot of spirit."

"Do I? Thank you. Perhaps that counts a little. University students, they sometimes resent it when—if you're not, not yourself a university . . ." Here there were more squeaks, and at last he said, "But not here."

"Why should they resent it?"

He did not answer, but turned to another table, as though checking something. There were laid out a Homburg sort of hat and a worn brief case. He turned back and said, "You remind me of someone I knew once."

"I do? Who?"

"A little girl. I admired from afar. Needless to say. In school. I was eight. Yes, eight. She was very kind to me. Once. I'd—well now, let's say I'd had an accident." Again came the squeaks. Sylvia knew at once that what he meant was that he had been beaten; she could imagine all too easily the torments he must have suffered as a child: the squeaking stammer, the poor fishlike eyes, the badly coordinated movements, the waddling walk, what an easy target he must have been. Now he went on. "All my books, pencils, had come out of my knapsack . . . scattered about on the ground, the street. So to speak—squeak-squeak—she helped me pick them up.

Found one of my pencils in the gutter even, wiped it off on her handkerchief." He paused, as though deciding at last to tell the whole truth. "She cursed my assailants. Not really curses. She was a child too. But a child's version of cursing. Very good. And gave me her handkerchief. A bleeding nose, you know. She said I should keep it, the handkerchief. She ran away then, crying. I did keep it. A souvenir."

Sylvia felt very awkward. "What happened to her?"

"She went away." He did not reach for his watch, but she knew without being told that it was time for them to go.

She stood up. "Shall I give Mrs. Dartley any message from you?"

"Why, give her my greetings. Yes. Please. That would be nice of you, nice. Say *Grüss Gott* from Rudi."

Puzzled that there was nothing more, she said, "Oh, very well. I'll do that. She was very upset. You know how she can be."

"Why no, I don't. We have never, never met."

"You've never met?" She could not hide her astonishment.

"No, no, certainly not. I've seen her from afar, of course. Often. A very great lady. But not a good idea. We have, one could say we have often corresponded. For years. In a way."

"I see." The door was open. She asked then if perhaps he would rather have her wait a few minutes until he was gone. He answered quickly, but she knew that he'd had a half-second's doubt. "Why no. Not necessary. I am, just now, about thirty seconds early. Time in fact to see you to your car."

They went down together and onto the street. He seemed struck with admiration, almost with awe, at the sight of George Bingham's car. He touched it, stepped quickly back. "New, yes, but some custom touches. Yes, a special order, certainly. Yes, certain aspects of the style, they have been kept from other eras." He stepped still further back. "My goodness. For a prince, this car. Oh yes, a prince of some sort or other." Then, very quickly, he shook hands with her, bade her a good day, and was off. She watched him go, his limping little walk, feet turned out, the Homburg now squarely on his head, the brief case swinging from his left hand.

As she turned toward the car, the memory of the wild trip in suddenly filled her with such belated and unfathomable terror that the calves of her legs began to twitch and tremble. She looked down the street again, but Rudi was gone. She had to force herself to get into the car. A man came out of a nearby shop and walked by close to the car; a very ordinary-looking person, she noted, he didn't look particularly Swiss, he didn't look particularly anything. At last she managed to fumble the car into motion. At the first cross street she saw Rudi in the distance—he now had a newspaper under his arm—and she saw the man who had come out of the shop turning to walk in the same direction. Taking deep breaths, still trembling, she concentrated on trying to get herself and the car back to Kilchberg.

Thirty-one

As Sylvia crossed the terrace she saw through one of the windows Campion and the woman she supposed was Elsie Crown. They were talking and Elsie Crown had a brandy snifter in one hand. She did not notice Sylvia, but Campion did. He stopped talking and raised his head toward her, but she lowered her own and hurried past. She had driven back to Kilchberg so cautiously that other motorists had honked, shouted, and shaken their fists at her; nevertheless her whole body was quivering and exhausted.

She found Anton alone in the drawing room, turning the dial on a small radio. "She's waiting for you upstairs," he told her.

Mrs. Dartley, greatly changed since Sylvia had last seen her, was working at her guild table. Calm and in control, brushed and neat, she looked as she stood up to greet Sylvia almost the picture of an English country gentlewoman, except that the cut to her tweeds suggested Paris more than London. "Very very well done. I'm most grateful to you," she said when Sylvia had made her report.

Was that all there was? Her fatigue was suddenly turning into restlessness. It reminded her of the way she had felt whenever as a child she had been confined to bed by an illness and heard the voices of other children playing outside her window. Before she could stop herself, she said, almost petulantly, "But what am I to do now?"

"Do? Why nothing. Wait, my dear. Wait." The cat that had appeared the day before was curled up against her old green typewriter. She reached out and stroked it; it began to purr. "I owe you an apology, by the way. For having disturbed your usual working hours."

"Oh that. It doesn't matter."

"Doesn't it?"

Instead of answering, Sylvia said, "How did you know I work in the mornings?"

"It's been fairly clear that you've been most energetically at work for some weeks. You've been more cheerful. That is for you you've been cheerful. And since you've been spending your afternoons sloshing around in the mountains and woods and your evenings doing whatever it is you do with Ernest—till last night, that is—it wasn't difficult to conclude that you must be working in the mornings." Mrs. Dartley smiled, just in time to prevent Sylvia from making the indignant reply that was on her lips, and quickly went on to say, "What did you think of Rudi? I'm always so curious about him."

"I thought it surprising that someone who seems to be as . . . that he should be able to . . ."

"Function adequately? I'm surprised at you. You don't usually confuse appearance and reality."

"*I don't?*" her voice bitter, self-mocking.

Mrs. Dartley ignored this. "Is that all you have to say about him?"

Sylvia had gone to stand by the window. She stood staring down at the empty grounds and gardens. "I really don't know how to describe my reaction. It's just that I would never have suspected him of being able to elaborate some intricate method of . . . communication."

"Of course. But think what an advantage that is. Do you know that we have never met. He prefers it that way. I've *seen* him. Naturally. Quite often. But we've never spoken. Yes, he's an easy person to make fun of. Such a mistake."

"He seems a considerate, a gentle person."

"People react so differently to horror. A great many really don't react at all. Perhaps that's fortunate. Life and all that. Rudi was with a Red Cross team in Spain during the Civil War. And then of course there's his own life. After Spain he decided to lose himself in meaningless routine. Where better can one do that than in a bank? In the late thirties, however, he became quite adept at getting money out of Germany for Jews. Oh he was extremely clever I'm told. Since he had to outwit both German and Swiss authorities. During the war he began to transmit messages across closed borders, entirely personal messages, oh unimportant little things that saved a few lives, allayed anxieties, nothing so grand as political or military things. That was when I first learned of him, through Dragan."

Was the world, the *banking* world, of all things, simply peopled with good-hearted Rudis? All Sylvia's confidence in the little undertaking in which she had had a part was seeping away. She said, "I can't imagine there being very many Rudis scattered about."

"There aren't many," Mrs. Dartley replied sharply.

Having begun, Sylvia persisted, "But it doesn't make any sense to me. Through *banks?* How? How could a bookkeeper manage to get any kind of message across any kind of border?" Her tone was decidedly contemptuous. She stared moodily out of the window, as though to say the whole thing was a matter of indifference to her.

There was a silence. Then Mrs. Dartley said, in the tone she would use with a stubborn and ill-tempered child, "You can hardly expect me to describe this in detail. Rudi used sometimes to act as a bank courier, before the war and occasionally during the war. He made a number of friends, clerks like himself, people who did simple jobs, in a number of countries. They corresponded. Naturally enough. One day he thought it would be entertaining to see if he and a few of these friends couldn't send messages back and forth, in code, using the ordinary banking reports." She paused. "In many ways Rudi has a very intricate mind. Accountants often do. He devised a method of sending the messages. Greetings from Rudi, your friend in Zürich—that sort of thing. It worked very well. It really wasn't very difficult for him to begin, one day, using these messages for more serious purposes."

"But what *sorts* of messages?"

"Oh use your head, Sylvia," Mrs. Dartley replied, impatient at last. "And your imagination. You're supposed to have that, aren't you, as a writer? A family that is separated, confirmation of important news, nonpolitical things—or at least things that in the old days would never have been considered political. *Need* I go on?"

"No." It was clear now, it made sense; it was even, Sylvia supposed, admirable. It was impossible of course to explain to Mrs. Dartley why at that moment she nevertheless felt the strongest sort of opposition to such intrigues. She knew she had been rude and she said, "I suppose that was how you got Lily out," meaning to make amends.

"That is *not* how I got Lily out. What is the matter with you? That was done officially, after great and repeated efforts were made, and it was only possible because of her age. It was, however, through Rudi's little system that I learned what conditions she was living under and that she wished to leave. At least at that time wished to . . ." Here Mrs. Dartley seemed to sag a little, her eyes misted. "Many of these messages, of which there are not many now—there are only a few of Rudi's contacts left, they have died or—"

"Natural deaths?"

"Yes. If old age can be called natural. Or they have been transferred to other jobs when the banks changed hands. Many of these messages, as I said, do not reach their destinations, do not reach those they were intended for." She hesitated again, her voice having sunk half an octave, always with her a sign of distress. "I suppose one could even say that sometimes they are little more than symbolic gestures."

"Like the revolution itself?"

"*What do you mean?*" Mrs. Dartley's voice turned her around. She seemed to tower over Sylvia, her eyes burning now with controlled rage and power and some terrible but magnetic force, eyes, Sylvia felt, that could perhaps be seen in the dark. For the first time since she had known her she felt afraid of Mrs. Dartley.

She said weakly, "I meant that, however much one hopes otherwise, I don't suppose the revolution will succeed, reach its intended goal."

"*Are you so sure?*"

Sylvia did not attempt to answer. It would be pointless to press this discussion, and now when it was too late she saw that it would only give pain to speak of what Mrs. Dartley was already too aware of: the incredible power forces that could and no doubt would be brought into play against the revolution.

Mrs. Dartley returned to her former manner, and her eyes again seemed misted over. "I was about to add that, even so, symbolic gestures can be important, perhaps more important than one knows. At any rate that is my impression."

"Was today's message a symbolic gesture?"

"It was not. It was not meant to be." Again Sylvia had annoyed her. They could not seem to find the accord that usually prevailed between them. It was, Sylvia knew, her own fault, something in her own situation that was driving her to behave so badly, so coldly. Mrs. Dartley swung with long, angry steps around the room. "I have never seen you like this before, so cynical, untrusting, closed," she murmured. Then she sighed and said, "Today's message was quite different from any that have been sent before. I was uncertain as to whether we should or not. It was Rudi who urged it finally. He and I have discussed the problem—through an intermediary—for some time. We agreed at last that if certain events occurred it should be sent."

"And it is destined for?"

"It is destined for an old friend of my husband Dragan, and of mine too, a woman who has been in and out of prison for some years. Our hope is that she is out now, or soon will be. If they succeed in establishing a liberal coalition government she is likely to be part of it. Her voice will carry weight when judgments are made. If things go badly I should not like her to lose her life. She is a *friend*. Is this so difficult for you to understand? Furthermore, if the worst happens she may be able to prevent a few other deaths. That is all."

Sylvia nodded. "I'm sorry" was all she could manage.

"Never mind," the other said curtly. Then, "Your black sad mood has personal causes, I don't doubt. Usually I can count on you to lift my spirits somehow."

Sylvia whirled, "Mrs. Dartley, is it Ernest Campion who carries these messages to Rudi for you, who acts as your intermediary?"

"Ah, so that's it, is it, that's it? Or part of it. No my dear, Ernest does not carry these messages for me. He doesn't even know Rudi, or of his existence. On that score I can reassure you, at any rate."

"Then who is your intermediary?"

"Anton, of course."

"*Anton?*" The court jester, the fool, the cynic, the old man who believed in nothing but inevitable damnation, making himself the courier for these touching and hopeless gestures against the darkness? Only with a great effort could she control the emotions that welled up in her then: irrational relief that it was not Ernest, that their evenings together at the Öpfelchammer had been exactly what they had seemed, something private, domestic even, between themselves at least, not a mask for something else, however decent that something else might be; abashment that she, who thought always that she saw so much, should have seen so little about Anton—even her insights the night of the dinner for Knox had not carried her far enough. Of course; no one could rail so passionately at the horror who did not nurse some secret belief in the good. Ernest had said that night that he believed in enlightened despair. So it appeared did old Anton: one acted for the good as best one could. Not that the ideal way ever came. There were always risks; one had to accept that fact. Otherwise one simply sat and waited for death. But this ability to act for the good, it depended without any doubt upon one's awareness of the existence of evil, its great power.

Mrs. Dartley had been watching her. She smiled for the first time and said, "Ernest? How could you have thought that? He has no talent at all for being devious. His ways are quite different—open, straightforward—which makes life difficult for him. And even makes him a little intolerant. But for old wretches like Anton, like me . . . Ahhh!"

Mrs. Dartley obviously felt better. So for a moment did Sylvia. Mrs. Dartley said, "And after all, if one can't trust one's friends whom can one trust?"

Sylvia turned back to the window. Down below, having evidently just come out of the house, looking up at the sky for a second, was Bingham. The first full realization of what she had done seized her then, and was followed in the next instant by a depression more frightening than any she had ever known. She had slept with a man whom she now quite clearly knew, watching him stride across the empty garden, she did not want to link her life to, but who, given their history, would have every reason to assume she did. It now seemed to her a wholly irrevocable act, one that would alter her life in some absolute fashion. She thought of Ernest Campion's letter lying unopened and unread in her room. There could be nothing for them now. She had lost him, and would perhaps lose other things that also mattered, and there was no one to blame but herself. Loving Ernest, a love which she knew could have glowed by both day and night, she had again taken onto her body the body of George Bingham, and she had done so willingly—very willingly, she forced herself to recall. Why? She did not have the answer. Furthermore, for the first time he had made love to her not as though she were somehow a . . . a castle perilous toward which he was fearfully, reluctantly drawn. No, he had made love to her with ardor, a consuming, quickening ardor to which she had responded. Some great change had been upon him, there was no doubt of that—it had communicated itself to her even as he stood in her room, even before he touched her—a change that had perhaps brought him to her this time in the first place. They had acted out, at Kilchberg, the might-have-been of their early days. But the reasons lay beyond her. Why not then be grateful and let it go at that? Because the cold and certain knowledge was growing in her that those moments had come too late, and were perhaps already gone, leaving her to bear their memory and face their aftermath in her own life. She watched him now, disappearing at the other end of the garden. She was aware of the fact that Mrs. Dartley was standing beside her and had also been watching Bingham out the window.

Mrs. Dartley said, "It looks like rain. We can hope it will be gentle at any rate. Like some of us, twice-blessed."

"Pardon?"

"Rain I said."

"Oh. Yes."

"Have you met Elsie Crown yet?"

"No."

"You must."

"Naturally. But while I still have these awful old clothes on I think I'll—"

"Go for a walk?"

"Yes."

"Why not? We shall have to get through this day somehow."

Sylvia went to the door. She turned and said, "I nearly forgot. Rudi sent a message to you."

"Did he? What was it?"

"He said, say *Grüss Gott* from Rudi."

Mrs. Dartley smiled. "Did he? That was nice of him indeed." She reached out and switched on her radio.

Thirty-two

Sylvia found Bingham easily enough—indeed, he seemed to be circling the house waiting for her. The first thing she said was, "What do you think is going to happen?"

"I don't know," he said, steering her away from the house and along one of the paths. How different this news had already made him from the way he had been the night before, or even in the very early hours of the morning, when, with unconcealed reluctance, he had forced himself to leave her. His glance was cold, formal, almost resentful. His touch on her arm was not a lover's. She could feel a kind of controlled tension emanating from him as they walked in silence, familiar to her from those periods in the past when, she assumed, he had been in the midst of trying to make a decision about some doubtful mission or other. Finally he said, "This isn't our baby, though we'll probably take the blame for it. It's obvious that we've been caught off guard."

The bitterness in his voice puzzled her. She knew at once, however, that this was a day when he would speak of a number of forbidden subjects; as always when he was in such a mood she found his honesty more mysterious than his customary evasiveness. Nevertheless, she felt somehow a little less burdened. "I'm glad," she said.

"*Glad?*"

Of course, you fool, she thought but did not say. Glad for your sake. Would you really want to have this on your head too? And glad also for the sake of those who were now suffering the agonies of revolution. Sometimes he angered her beyond belief. Would he never understand his own littleness? And that the urge to lead captivity captive could only come from within?

Abruptly he said, looking straight ahead, "How would you like to live in London?"

She stared at his profile.

"That was what I wanted to tell you about last night. I'm thinking of changing my occupation. I thought it might interest you."

"It does," she said. The fear she had felt when she caught sight of him from Mrs. Dartley's room now deepened. If he did make this change she would not be able to deny her own role in it.

He said, "I've been thinking about it all summer. Ever since you ran away, in fact," trying to make his voice light and still looking straight ahead.

She listened while he described the new undertaking. He would be acting for one, maybe two if he could be certain there was no conflict of interests, of the big continental industries. He named a north Italian firm. They were the ones who had come to him. He had an idea himself about one of the Greek shipyards that was going into something new. His office would be absolutely independent. It had something to do with the expansion of the Common Market. He would *answer to no one*, really . . . Of course; he had every right, especially now, to assume that only his present occupation formed the barrier between them; all of her words and actions had implied that. And she herself, she realized now, had never considered what he might be like in another context, stripped of the trappings of the specially damned, placed in a more ordinary world, faced with more conventional choices, or with what her own reaction to him would then be. Even now she did not quite believe that it would come about. But if it did . . .

She stumbled over something in the path and he again took her arm, coldly. It annoyed her and she pulled away. He went on talking. He would be free to use his own judgment, he said. That too was understood. He would do the thinking, the planning; a legal staff would work out details. He would still do a lot of traveling. Much of the work would involve government negotiations. "I'll have my own plane. I won't even be bound to airline schedules. How about that?" She saw in an instant that uncertain future he was sketching out; it was one in which she could imagine no natural place for herself. It would always be power that would attract him, power for its own sake, even if in some quite conventional form. He would find new ways to express the old chaotic energies that sprang so violently from him; they would depend always on risks of the most senseless sorts, for himself, and especially for others. There would be questions he would never ask. She saw them one day arguing over economic manipulations as they had argued over the CIA. Yes, and now he spoke of money. It was logical, she thought; the amassing of great wealth was a form of aggression he had not yet tried. But even that she did not think would happen. It would be too banal, too simple for him. For all the jauntiness of his speech during these last few minutes she knew suddenly how great a struggle was going on in him, for nothing

would ever suit him quite so well as the CIA. Yet if he did choose
the new life—if it could be called that—she was bound to stand by
him, at least for a few months, at least until the break was really
accomplished, months that would be quite enough to lay her own
life and work in ruins.

She said, "I'd like living in London, I think." The words were
out. She was glad that he wasn't looking at her face. Perhaps he
knew too; perhaps that was why he didn't look at her. All he said
was, "Good. I've given everything but my final word on it. I
wanted to talk to you first." Suddenly he did turn his face to her;
it seemed changed, struck into some kind of expressionless mask.
She was really almost afraid. How brief, no, how illusory then, his
transformation of the night before had been. Above all, how illusory for *him* as well as for herself. He said, "If what I think is
going on right now in some conference rooms in Washington *is*
going on, then there's not a thing to hold me back."

She understood then nothing. She said, "I don't follow that. Just
before you came here, where were you? Just before. Not London
or Milan, I think."

"No."

"Budapest?"

He laughed now, seeming more like himself. "No. The news this
morning didn't exactly surprise me, though."

"It didn't surprise Gwendolyn either."

"She's a smart woman, our hostess, and a realist. Actually, anyone who was interested in middle Europe, who had any judgment
at all, and who read the papers knew it might happen. You could
even say it would happen eventually. And after Poznan Budapest
was certainly one of the logical places. History picked that city out
a long time ago. If you had any way of getting any inside information, if you even just knew about what was going on in the Petöfi
circle, for example, and I'm sure she must have, you couldn't be
too surprised. There were all sorts of minor disturbances all summer, and what we call widespread psychological resistance. That's
a nice term, don't you think? The Party was just losing control.
By the way, did you get hold of the funny-looking little Swiss
guy?"

She stood completely still, one hand on his chest. "My God,
you're not using Mrs. Dartley too?"

He seemed offended. "*I'm* not using her. So far as I know, no

one is. We know about her, if that's what you mean. Someone had
the bright idea once of trying to plant things in her mail—some of
her correspondents do seem to be pretty clever at getting mail out
to her, and from some very unusual places—but it was too complicated. It was a new guy who suggested it." He smiled, almost with
admiration. "Do you know we never have broken that little Rudi's
code? Not that it matters. We know what they're doing, what
kind of messages go through. They're not important."

It sickened Sylvia to realize that even Mrs. Dartley was not in a
sense her own mistress, that she too was in the power of the very
forces against which she was always railing. It did not bear thinking about. She said, "But if you know about it perhaps they do
too?"

He shrugged. It had started to rain. He said, "Shall we go back
to the house?"

"No, I don't care. I'm a mess anyway."

They walked on. He said, "Maybe a few people will learn something from all of this. Those clod-heads at Radio Free Europe, for
example. Do you know anything about the stuff they send out?"

"Yes." It seemed to her extraordinary that both he and Mrs.
Dartley should have a common distaste for this group, that "officially unofficial instrument of policy," as she had once called it.

"I've been agitating since July to have some pressure brought on
them. I've nothing against the ones who do the broadcasts; most of
them are refugees, and you've got to understand how they feel.
But the guys at the top, the ones you see and the ones you don't,
who for reasons of their own set policy—they're disgustingly irre-
sponsible."

She looked at him wide-eyed, thinking perhaps this was his idea
of a joke. But he was perfectly serious. He apparently did not see
the slightest connection between those broadcasts and his own actions, or between the guys at the top in Radio Free Europe and the
men in high government office who for reasons of *their* own had
elaborated that liberation policy—one had better call it a kill-
yourself-for-your-own-good policy—which he, among other tasks,
had been trying to implement.

He said with sudden passion, "At every meeting we've had in
our organization, all summer long, ever since Poznan, I've talked
and talked about how we had to make a choice. I've been trying to
drive home to them the way things are now, that the United States

had to face up to what might be going to happen and know what it was going to do."

She said quickly, "These are political decisions, aren't they?" not knowing what would come from him next—she felt extreme confusion—and wondering if he were not perhaps at last feeling how little real power or scope he had, how little choice, what a peripheral role he had been playing.

"Yes," he answered, with unmistakable contempt. "I've done a few things I wasn't supposed to. I've gone outside the outfit a couple of times. I've talked to some of the ostriches. I told them they'd better be prepared to back up their own policies, that if they weren't then they'd better lay off the propaganda and a few other activities that we're supposed to carry out for them. They're playing around with dynamite and don't even know it." He paused and added as an afterthought, "And people's lives."

Oh, how she had misjudged him, how unfair, how unkind she had been. She wanted to leap for joy. And she was not bound to him either, what nonsense that was. She could say to him as she could to any other man, I just don't think it would work out for us. The decision he was now in the process of making had to do with her only incidentally. He had reasons enough for pulling out, good ones. Things had changed in a way she could never have foreseen, and perhaps he would even find in his own way, some day, that good form the search for which he had too despairingly abandoned. Had he not at last become the spokesman for the very truths he himself had fought against, had again and again driven down into his own unconscious, where they had so terribly hurt him? She was about to speak when he said, "We've lost three good men in the last six weeks."

"What?"

"We've lost three good men in the last six weeks. On missions that ought never to have been undertaken if we're not going to be backed up." A cold, scowling expression moved over his face.

"From your . . . outfit, you mean?"

"Yes."

She waited, struggling against the doubt that now engulfed her. Perhaps he would go on, say more. Surely he had seen more than that, had had more than that in mind when he had made his rounds at the State Department. Then he said, "No one would listen to me. They put me off with the usual phrases."

She could not speak. That was what was really driving him then: they would not listen to him. It was worse than she had known, much worse. She could not speak. They came to a fallen tree. He sat down and drew her down beside him, whether tenderly or not she was too numb to know. The rain started to fall more heavily. She could hear it falling on their bare heads, and on the earth around them.

He turned her so that they were looking at each other. The faunlike expression flitted for an instant across his face. He laughed then, almost shyly. "Who knows," he said. "Maybe I'm just losing my nerve. Maybe that's the real reason I'm pulling out."

"Where were you before you came here?"

The slow blink of lowered eyelids, slowly opening then on what seemed to her almost blinded eyes, so veiled were they by whatever it was he was feeling. "I was in eastern Germany," the forthright, blunt voice he always used when it cost him something to answer. He hesitated, then, again almost shyly, "I told you that a lot of funny things had been happening lately." Then, "I broke another rule."

"You what?"

"I broke another rule. There are all sorts of rules in this game. It's a good idea to follow them. It's absolutely required. It's dangerous not to. I ran into some trouble in . . . the place where I was. I didn't do what I was supposed to. I let a man go."

"Why?"

"I don't really know. I wish I did."

"Oh darling," she said. She understood it all now, only too well. But she had to be sure. "Do you mean that you did *not* kill a man?"

"Yes," he said. "To be precise. That's it."

What kind of a world was it in which a man had to confess that he had *not* killed a man? And what was she ever, ever to do? His eyes said clearly: because of you. They perhaps even said: it is your fault; it is my connection with you that has so unnerved me, that has made me weak, capable of mercy, of feeling. He would always, she knew now, find ways of making her bear for him things which he could not. He believed in only one kind of strength; deprived of that, he was left unbelievably vulnerable.

She shuddered inside her coat, under the rain. Out of the silence he said at last in his usual voice, "I'm going into Zürich now. And from there probably to Munich. There are a couple of things I've got to find out. I'll be back some time tonight or tomorrow. If things are the way I think, we'll leave then."

"Will we?"

"I thought that was understood."

"I suppose it was. All right then." How clearly, how bitterly, she saw it. Through all that had been spoken there had been for him, as always, a reservation. If by any chance they *did* listen to him there would be no going away, no London. To her horror she realized that this was her only hope, the only thing she could cling to, even though it meant, in effect, her wishing him to go on with his old destructive life. She at least would be free then, for if they parted now they would not, she knew, meet again. Or would she be free of him? She remembered the night before.

Suddenly she sprang to her feet. "We're getting soaked," she said. "We're not far from the gardener's cottage." Before he could answer she began to run. She ran as fast as she could, slipping on leaves, letting branches whip into her face, not even once looking behind her. She arrived at the cottage panting, wild, and afraid. On an instinct she peered in one of the windows. Inside she saw Marshall and Posy clasped to each other in a passionate embrace. She drew back. When she turned around she saw him coming towards her, a neat, a methodical, a relentless trot. "Have you gone crazy?" he asked.

"We've got to go back to the house," she said.

"What's the matter with the cottage?"

She laid a finger to her lips. "The young in one another's arms," she said. "You'd never understand."

Then, thrusting her hands into the pockets of her coat, the rain running down her face, her shoulders slumping, she began trudging sadly away.

Thirty-three

Without a word Sylvia left Bingham in the downstairs hall and turned for the room where she had seen Campion, entering just in time to hear Elsie Crown say, "Well, did she spring full-blown from the head of Zeus or something?" Then they both saw her.

"Hello," she said, overcome by the awkward certainty that they had been talking about her, thinking, no, I issued forth from my mother's womb, like anyone else. So strong was the desire to utter these words that for a second she thought perhaps she actually had. Instead she had acknowledged Ernest's introduction and moved toward the fireplace, trailing water, soaked, like some creature that had been hauled up from underwater depths and was still baffled by its new environment.

Elsie Crown said, "Here. It looks as though you need this more than I do," and handed her the brandy snifter.

"Thanks." She drank and then put the glass down and began trying to wriggle out of the wet, clinging suede jacket. Suddenly Ernest approached and with rough impatient gestures jerked it off her, held it out with distaste and dropped it as though it were a dead animal on the polished bricks. She looked at him at last and murmured her thanks. Elsie Crown, who appeared to have had a fair number of brandies, laughed and said, "We passed on the highway, I think."

"Did we? I had to do something for Mrs. Dartley. In a hurry." She now felt very annoyed at the condition she was in and began wiping at her face and shaking her hair. "Do you think, do you think maybe I could borrow a handkerchief?" she asked. She knew that what she should do was to go to her room and change, but she did not want to. She wanted company, she wanted Ernest. Elsie Crown, leaning against the mantelpiece as though the first-act curtain had just gone up, looked superb, and far too much at home. A middle European of some sort, Sylvia had seen at once, one of those unadmitted-to mixtures that flourished in that part of the world: Germans, Slavs, Magyars, Jews—who knew what permutations? Sylvia had never believed that anyone did. Ernest, who had been going through his pockets, was now looking embarrassed. Elsie shrugged and went to her purse. "God, what a day. A day for borrowing handkerchiefs. A day for white flags." She pulled out a large man's handkerchief, streaked with lipstick, and offered it. "If you don't mind the smudges. Good respectable American smudges."

Sylvia began mopping at her hair, which the damp and rain had turned into a wild, Medusa-like tangle of curls. There was nothing she could do to tame them now and she gave up trying. She knew that the other woman was appraising her as she stood before the fireplace, and with her unkempt hair she felt at more of a disadvantage than ever. Elsie said, "Where did you get those slacks?"

"These? Oh, in Munich."

"You look marvelous in them. You've got the figure for them. I haven't. Too hippy."

"Everybody looks good in these slacks," Sylvia said. "It's the cut."

"Not me. I'm just not built for it. No matter how much I diet, how thin I get. It's a drawback in America."

Ernest Campion said, "One never knows what women will talk about," shaking his head, but at the same time obviously relieved.

Sylvia handed him the handkerchief. "I guess this is yours."

"I made a scene at the airport," Elsie said simply. "Just the sort of thing Ernest hates. But I couldn't help it. Something unexpected happened." Her eyes filled with tears and she grabbed the handkerchief back and began daubing at them.

"You're not going to start again. Please," Campion said, looking back and forth between the two women as though, again, he did not know what to do with either one of them. To Sylvia he said, "Mrs. Halász, Lily. Elsie knew her in Budapest."

"What? Did you? When?" Sylvia said. "During the war, the siege?" But there was suddenly such an atmosphere of recollected pain in the room now that she stopped. Too much was still happening. Too many edges of reality were grinding against each other. Elsie was nodding. But we're not at all alike, Sylvia thought; we don't look a thing alike. She said to Elsie, "Mrs. Halász still talks about you." She did not say, She still loves you very much, but later on she would find an indirect way of saying just this to Elsie Crown; later they would talk. Here at least was something one might help put to rights.

With a grim expression on his face, Ernest was pouring another brandy. Then in the silence there was the sound of a car engine starting. He walked to the window and said, "Is he leaving?"

"For a while."

"Do you mean he's coming back?"

"Probably."

Elsie Crown tried not to look at them. She got up, saying, "Ernest told me that you and Tante Lily spent hours and hours together. I'm going to ask you dozens of questions. But not now. Now I have to unpack. And make some plans." Suddenly she seemed very different, aggressive, amused. "Where did you say that shit probably is? Oh, I forgot. You can't stand me to use bad language."

He said to Sylvia, "Knox."

"Yes, Benjy. Benjy-mine. Only not mine, thank God. Got to find him and make peace with him, though. So long as we're both here."

Ernest said, "He's had a rough morning, according to Anton. He got in touch with New York too late to stake out claims on Hungary."

"That would be like him." Something now seemed to amuse Elsie very much. As she went toward the door she said, "Women have to be content with such small triumphs don't they? *Hickory dickory dock*," and exited, laughing.

Sylvia said, "What did she mean?"

"I've no idea."

All the personal horror which had for a few minutes been put down engulfed her again. She and Campion stared across the silence.

"What's the matter?" he asked. "What's happened?"

"I haven't looked at your little note yet. I haven't even opened it."

"That's all right," he said evenly. "I told you there was no rush. I can wait."

"There isn't going to be any answer. None at all."

"What? Why?"

"I'm not the woman you thought I was. I'm not the woman I thought I was."

"What are you talking about?"

"I'm going away. And you should be very glad of that. It's true what they say about women. We're all whores."

"And all men are killers?" he replied quickly.

She was the one who was taken aback by the exchange. His remark had brought a faintly shocked expression to her face, while his face had not changed at all. But she did not respond. She wanted to convey to him as unequivocally as possible that it was over with. "You understand what I'm saying, don't you? Must I be absolutely precise? I've betrayed you, to use an old-fashioned term. I've already betrayed you. Is that clear? Now you know. Surely you're not going to be enough of a fool to stand there and say that you'll forgive me?"

"No," he said curtly. "I'm not. Will you excuse me?" Without looking at her, he turned and walked out of the room.

Thirty-four

By night time a palpable atmosphere of tension and disorder had settled over Kilchberg. Sylvia Grierson had been little in evidence, and when she was she and Ernest Campion made painfully obvious efforts to avoid each other. Benjamin Knox made similar efforts to avoid Elsie Crown, but without success. She was intent on stressing the fact that they were "old friends," as she put it—only, he knew, to make him nervous and to annoy him.

Knox did not trust Elsie. He remembered her as being capable of doing or saying almost *anything*. The first night he had slept with her he hadn't been very nice afterwards. He hardly ever was. Of course he might have been a little nicer if he had known she was just a kid who'd had to start from scratch the way he had. But someone had told him, and she had somehow indicated as much herself—at any rate he'd had the distinct impression that she was the offspring of an old New York banking family. Crown was just her stage name; her family was old-fashioned and didn't like the idea of her becoming an actress at all—she had let this bit of information drop casually into their conversation. He had to admit she'd been good at putting on the society babe act; even the slight continental accent had seemed to him typical of the sort of affectation picked up by girls who'd been sent abroad to school for a couple of years. Any way you looked at it, he had been taken in, which was bad enough but far from the worst of it. The worst had been the next time he slept with her. Precisely at the critical moment, the movements of her body beneath him, which he had naturally taken to be ecstatic, had suddenly turned into deep, belly-shaking *laughter* (for the first time he really understood that term) and she had said in a loud stagey voice, "Hickory dickory dock,

the mouse ran up the clock." Even now he felt cold shudders at
the memory. It was like being back selling used cars in Zanesville,
making the pitch for them on TV, with New York and all his
success still ahead of him. Then she had gotten up and dressed, still
laughing like a madwoman—he'd been afraid his valet would
hear—and repeating that damned hickory dickory dock thing in a
louder and louder voice—she would not be shut up—emphasizing
first one word and then another, but usually *mouse*, and finally
she'd had the nerve to say to him as she put her coat on that
"Anglo-Saxon *nursery* rhymes absolutely fascinated" her and that
she had quite a collection of them by now.

Not that he hadn't had his revenge; a few months later he had
the chance to damn Elsie with faint praise and keep her from
getting a job he knew she badly wanted. But even that she seemed
to have gotten wind of somehow. She'd been very blunt about it
when she came to him earlier in the day at the villa and suggested
they both forgive and forget. He was certainly willing—for some
reason he didn't want Dame Dartley knowing anything more
about him than she already did—and he'd been very smooth about
the whole thing with Elsie. But, no, he did not trust her and he was
perpetually uncomfortable in her presence.

Gwendolyn Dartley stayed upstairs in her room, the news from
Budapest continuing to be alternately alarming and hopeful. Sometimes, when she got hold of a Hungarian station, she would sum-
mon Elsie and have her translate for her. At one point she came
downstairs for a few minutes. Knox, who had spent most of his
day on the telephone, had learned that the 7 P.M. TV news relay
was going to show some film strips taken in Budapest by an Austrian tourist who had managed to bring them back over the
border. Everyone gathered around for this. Anton started to talk
but was shushed. There was the usual difficulty with the set, all
those unnerving ripping static sounds and wild, formless shapes.
To Sylvia they seemed a crowd of evil, or at least frightened and
confused spirits, caught in the air betwixt heaven and earth. Suddenly they faded into an almost subliminal picture of an announcer,
whose words they couldn't catch, and then into some shaky scenes
of Budapest: a tremendous mass of people standing before some
official-looking building; crowds of men, women, and youngsters
running across a huge square; bakery workers standing in the
doorway of a bread store, grinning at a tank which was manned by

Hungarian workers and which had the Hungarian flag with the Soviet star cut out hoisted above it. The whole sequence lasted scarcely more than a minute, but it seemed a very long minute to everyone. Afterwards Mrs. Dartley rose and disappeared. Knox prepared to go into Zürich, revealing as always some curious reluctance about leaving, and Posy and Marshall asked to ride in with him. Something about them seemed quite different to Sylvia, but perhaps that was only because of the scene she had glimpsed in the gardener's cottage.

Sylvia left too and was soon followed upstairs by Elsie Crown. They had not yet had the promised conversation about Lily Halász. Elsie Crown took in the disorder in Sylvia's room, the clothing strewn about, the open suitcases, the general desolation of impending departure, but made no reference to it. As they talked, Sylvia forgot for a time about her own situation, even forgot to listen for the sound of a car pulling in. They got on well, although Sylvia occasionally caught a slight edge of hostility being directed at her—because of Campion, she assumed with inner bitterness.

Beneath Elsie's clever, self-assured manner she felt an acute unhappiness, and she also got the impression that Elsie was a woman who had not been lucky in love, or perhaps one might better put it not lucky with men, and that this mattered crucially to her. She appeared to lack that special narcissism which enables many women to flourish amidst the contradictions of the theatre world regardless of personal unhappiness. Somehow or other, when they were not discussing Lily, Elsie had a way, probably without knowing it, of causing the conversation to veer oddly towards sex. Not quite personal things, for which Sylvia was duly grateful, but almost; and the general subject itself seemed a kind of expressionist shorthand on Elsie's part, a way perhaps of handling some enormous need to show herself as loved.

When she left, Sylvia thought, not for the first time, how different she was from many women. Being loved as though she were merely an object of some sort had never been her aim in life and never would be. But love itself, in all its forms, what an extraordinary thing it was, really; the link to life, the link to death. She felt her whole life, her whole soul in its deepest stirrings, to be inextricably, mysteriously involved with this fact. But the pursuit of love, that seemed to her pointless. Love descended upon one, sometimes cruelly, with a great flapping of terrible wings, as it had upon poor Leda; and sometimes gently, in a wondrous golden rain; and even, most blissful of all perhaps, came sometimes to rest upon one like the Dove of the Holy Spirit in an Italian master. Sylvia yawned and caught herself; the latter was surely blasphemous. She snickered and mentally withdrew the image.

Ho-hum, it had been a long and miserable day; she was dead tired. Bingham wasn't going to come back tonight, and that at least was a relief. Perhaps tomorrow simply wouldn't come. What good did it do to have *views* about love, or even about sex, when one got so entangled anyway? As for Elsie Crown, something about her definitely made Sylvia think of her as a miscast, hapless maenad, when probably all she really wanted to do was to make someone a good wife— the right one of course. How she wished life were that simple for her. She yawned wildly, and this time flopped into bed. Her bed of sin, she thought; only that seemed a word both too grand and also irrelevant. In fact, at the moment the whole idea of "sin" of any sort had no reality at all. That was nice. If only it could go on being that way tomorrow. Probably it was better to try to be superficial about the whole love thing, to regard it as a foolish but mildly amusing game, as if one were living in a Fragonard. What a pity she always had to take everything so seriously. But she always had, and no doubt she would again tomorrow. The present illusion of it not mattering that nothing mattered, that nothing made sense, was very nice. Sleep lapped delicately around her as it had in childhood; soft, reassuring, rocking her slowly away, without fear of the dark, without worry about tomorrow.

But Elsie Crown had never read about maenads, though she felt the hectic strongly enough; nor did she have a store of literary and pictorial references to draw on to give her even the temporary illusion of distance from the heat she felt in her body, the near-throbbing between her legs, and the heaviness in her heart. She had not quite been candid with Ernest that morning at the airport. It was true that she had been on her way to Hungary to try to find Mrs. Halász, but she had also wanted to see him again before conceding her life to the love of a man whom she herself did not really love. Whatever vague hopes she'd had were out now; she had known it the moment she saw Ernest, and the rest of the day told her why. He was hopelessly gone on Sylvia Grierson. Her

own choice was exactly what it had been when she stepped on the
plane in Houston; it lay between marriage with a man who would
be "good" to her—rare enough in her experience—and going on
with a life that with each passing month disgusted her more. Sylvia
had been right about her. She longed for nothing more than to find
the right one, and her search took the form of promiscuity. "Why
do I do it? Why?" How often had she asked herself that? And she
had no answer. Was it the sheer love of cock? If that was so, then
why did she feel so used afterwards, and often so badly used? At
the same time why did she only feel she was alive, worth something, when she was about ready to climb into bed with someone?
The only time she had felt her sensuality to be truly a gift from
nature was with Ernest; the only affair she had ever had that had
not left her feeling demeaned afterwards had been the year with
him, and given her nature when that ended her only alternative
had been the bitterness of trial and error. Somewhere along the
line everything had got very confused for her. Should she be
grateful for small favors, the fact, for example, that Ernest still
valued her as a person? That was something, she supposed. But it
was not enough! She lighted still another cigarette and thrashed
about her room. So near to him, and yet so far! She dreaded the
night, and she dreaded tomorrow.

Ernest Campion stood outside the villa looking up at Sylvia's room
and remembered with bitter irony the thoughts that had gone
through his mind as he had stood there only the night before. Ever
since morning he had thought of Sylvia as a jigsaw puzzle that had
come apart. She had previously seemed to him all of a piece, but
that was an illusion; there had just been all those invisible lines
holding together a nothingness, a contrivance of light and shadow.
    As a child he had once been given a reproduction of the Mona
Lisa cut into a very difficult jigsaw. He had finally got all the
pieces together and left it alone on a table, only to find when he
came back that some stupid adult, Nathalie probably, had decided
to straighten up and had swept it away into the hundreds of little
meaningless bits again. He had forgotten about that until today:
the fury, the sense of loss, of enormous injustice. And then he had
lost interest. He had refused, stubbornly and absolutely, to try to
put it together again. And today he had refused to try to put
Sylvia together again. And yet, he realized now, she *was* together

again; all the fragments had somehow mysteriously rejoined while
he was not looking. She was still there, real, whole, and unlike the
Mona Lisa very much alive and very much more to his taste, a little
different now, it was true, but not really changed. No woman he
had ever met had touched so deeply his inner being. He had made
up his mind; he was going to marry her. Somehow. He loved her
and he believed in her. And he knew that she, whatever might
happen, whatever appearances to the contrary, that she loved him.
That was reality. He could not be wrong about it.

Thirty-five

By noon of the next day a general deterioration had set in. No one
seemed to know what to do next, except possibly Posy and Marshall, who were nowhere to be found. Sylvia expected Bingham
back at any moment, and yet with every moment that passed she
was also more inclined to hope that he had gone off somewhere on
a sudden mission and would not be heard from again for months.

Elsie Crown seemed about to fly apart; she smoked and talked
constantly and looked hollow-eyed. She and Sylvia had grown
rather wary of each other, and it was beginning to cost an effort to
go on being polite. Several times during the morning Sylvia had
felt like saying: Elsie Crown Go Home! Especially when she got
going on "J.A.," which was evidently the "in" way of referring to
Jane Austen. The spring before Elsie had had a job acting in a five-
day-a-week soap opera and this had left her free to take several
classes in the evening division of one of New York's great academic factories. There, in a freshman English course, she'd had as
her instructor a young man who was writing his dissertation on
Jane Austen and who had devoted the term to what he called "the
canon," thereby turning Elsie, at least, into a perfect Jane-ite. It
seemed a little incongruous to Sylvia, this passion of Elsie's for Jane
Austen, an inconceivable ideal for her to have hit upon. It was Box
Hill this and Lyme Regis that and Frederick Wentworth all over
the place and the theatricals at Mansfield Park and what R. H.
Chapman had said and dear proud Emma and her Daddy and the
Great Crescent at Bath until Sylvia thought she would scream. At

one point Elsie said to her, rather nastily she thought, "Do you write like Jane?"

"Of course I don't. How could I? How could anybody? *Today?* I haven't even read her for years."

"You haven't?" Elsie said, incredulous, then added with sudden scorn, "You mean you don't feel in her *debt?*"

A little stunned by the non sequitur, Sylvia said shortly, "Why should I?"

Elsie lifted an eyebrow. "Every woman writer owes a spiritual debt to Jane Austen."

"Who says?"

"Donald Jeffries."

Sylvia controlled herself. "Who's he? Should I know him?"

It appeared that she should—he had been Elsie's instructor in the English course. Sylvia was tempted to say she didn't even like Jane Austen, anything to put an end to the conversation, which had a lunatic atmosphere to it, like everything else happening that day. Campion banging on her door in the morning, for example. That was how her day had begun. She had pretended to be asleep until he made so much noise that she decided the whole household must be out there with a battering ram. Then she had told him to go away and had refused to open the door. "You little fool" had been his parting words. "I'll see you tonight."

Elsie went on haranguing her about the juvenilia, which she had to admit she hadn't read. "You mean you haven't read *Lady Susan?* Hmmm," shaking her head. "What, you've never looked at *Sanditon?*" "Well, of course I thought *everybody'd* read *The Watsons*. I mean, really . . ." Sylvia felt this was some kind of masked competition into which she was being forced against her will. Or perhaps she was just the victim of an elaborate leg-pull. At the same time, whatever other uses Elsie was making of "J.A.," her enthusiasm was quite unmistakably genuine. Sylvia could not bring herself to deny Jane; she did like her, of course; she did, she supposed, feel in her debt, for that matter, even though she didn't "write like her." She was relieved when Anton's appearance on the scene at last brought about a change of subject.

Anton and Elsie liked each other, and both being pessimists, or affecting to be, agreed on nearly everything, which made conversation difficult for them. At last they had settled on Wagner, whom Elsie of course, like most Jews in her generation (and most young Germans and Americans too, and for the same reason, though you could not tell Elsie that), detested. Sylvia suspected that she wouldn't know the difference between Wagner and Mahler, but hadn't said so. Anton, naturally, had suddenly become Wagner's champion. Sometimes he would lecture Elsie about how she must develop a taste for late Romantic music, and go on in great detail to emphasize its excellences, completely contradicting everything he had used to say in arguments with Lily Halász. Sometimes he tried other tacks. As Sylvia slipped away she heard him saying to Elsie, "Tell me, my dear, tell me, now just exactly where in his music do you hear this anti-Semitism most strongly?"

The rest of the day Sylvia hid out in her room, feeling cut off, as though she were a child being punished for bad behavior. She could not work, of course. Towards five she had a very bad moment when a car pulled in. But it was Ernest in the Phantom. She immediately locked the door—which turned out to be quite unnecessary, for though she waited expectantly for over an hour he did not come. She skipped dinner and played with the soup Celeste insisted on bringing up to her. Later she sneaked down to the drawing room and peeked in. The Young Lovers were still missing (Sylvia felt she could now rightly use that term for them), and so was Mrs. Dartley. Elsie Crown was at the center of that group of men, Ernest, Knox, and Anton.

By now Elsie was very drunk, or fancied herself to be. She believed she was a heavy drinker, but actually it took very little to bring about a personality change. How much of this, as the psychologists would say, was culture-conditioned by a background that held drinking to be a dirty goy habit and how much had to do with chemical intolerance was not for Elsie's friends to say, though they had often wondered. Sylvia accepted what appeared to her to be a fact: Elsie was drunk; and decided on the spot that she did not really approve of women drinking too much—although of course it was a little different when she herself overdid a bit. Elsie, leaning again with one arm on the mantelpiece (a trifle unsteadily, but nevertheless impressively, rather like Lady Somebody-or-other), all authority, bright-eyed, seemed to have Knox in a state of advanced intimidation. It was at him that her remarks were particularly directed, and Sylvia listened in awe as Elsie, a stubborn, fanatical expression gathering on her features, propounded some incredible theory about what she called womb envy.

"So what's so far-fetched about it? If women can have penis envy, is there any reason why men can't have womb envy? How do we know men don't have? We don't. Do you know why we don't Benjy? I remember you thought you were such a great big ... Freudian. I asked Mr. Reed that once too. He taught that other course, the one in modern literature, if that was what it was. Everywhere for him there were phallic symbols." She paused for effect, as she always did after using a Jewish locution, Jewish speech rhythms being neither more nor less "natural" for her than Hungarian or English. She had once complained to Ernest that she didn't really feel she had a native language of her own. Now she went on. "He was shocked. I'm all for phallic symbols, I told him, but how come he never talked about female symbols, I wanted to know. Do you know what he said, that bastard? He said my remark was a good example of penis envy. He was a real stinker. Anyway, why don't we know whether men have womb envy or not? Because men don't know anything about women, not any more. Freud was a man." This concluding and double non sequitur sent a ripple through the gathering. Campion, who was looking both amused and embarrassed, said, "I don't quite follow that."

She ignored this and with a mulelike shake of her head said, "It's just as logical for men to have womb envy as for women to have penis envy."

"Elsie," he said, "*logic* has nothing to do with it."

She began again and Sylvia fled, a little disappointed that no one had noticed her hovering but surely half visible near the doorway. There was no question about who was in command at Kilchberg now: Elsie Crown. It was not a role that particularly suited her, Sylvia thought, and it seemed to her ridiculous that Mrs. Dartley went on staying in her room in that sulky fashion, as though it could make any difference to what was happening in Hungary. They all cared just as much as she did about the revolution, but they were trying to carry on. After all, it was her house, and she ought not to let her guests run wild. Sylvia was lonely. Her room seemed more cell-like than ever. It struck her all at once that she was jealous of Elsie Crown, which was disgusting, since she was usually not jealous of anyone. It also struck her that she had been abandoned, twice-over. Two men had threatened or promised their presence and both seemed to have changed their minds. Very funny. After ten minutes she went downstairs again, this time

entering with nods at everyone and going to the bar cart to make
herself a drink so that she could stand with her back to them until
she got better control of herself. Anton was in the midst of making
a speech, and again it was Knox who seemed to be its chief recipi-
ent. On his feet, bounding around the chair in such a way as to
make it impossible for Knox to move, Anton lifted his hands from
time to time into small angry fists, like a baby.

". . . in three hours' time, my dear Knox. With what? With the
clothes on their backs and what they could carry in their hands.
It's perhaps to be forgiven me if I say to you again that I *don't*
think you understand. What I said. These were the so-called
Sudetan Germans. But this was PRAHA! A city of culture! Do you
understand? It was mostly women and children by then, many of
the women as Czech as me, they had married German soldiers.
And the others from a German-speaking minority whose families
had lived there for centuries. Ja, but now *zum Fenster hinaus*. Just
like the Jews in Germany, or by us too. So we stood along the
streets of Prague while they were driven out; we laughed, jeered,
shouted at them, *spat*. I stood there too. I, Anton Hrubick. I lifted
my fists against these people. I even spat once. I told myself later,
well, it's bad, not very humanitarian—most of them hadn't done
anything—kicking them out, driving them across the border, but
not so bad as some of the things the Germans had done, I reminded
myself. Which was true. We weren't killing them, at least. Not
nearly so bad. So. Good for us. Ja, good. I'd been a soldier under
Franz Josef. But I was always a good Czech. A nationalist. Then I
was a Masaryk democrat. A nobody piano teacher. Paying too
much attention by far to politics, which I now hate. And then the
Germans came, the swinish Nazis. Prague wasn't all that unfriendly to them as you may have heard, Czech Prague too. If they
had not been such ignorant fools . . . fortunately they were. *I*
hated them, and went right on giving my music lessons as though
nothing had changed, I am not ashamed to tell you either fact. I
am not very heroic. Are you, Mr. Knox? Then the Germans are
driven out. Then we drive out with curses and blows these women
and children and old men. We are very pure, then, we think. Ja
good. And I think perhaps the Communists were right after all—
we need something all new, from the beginning. If *I* could have
stood on a corner and spat . . . So I was not unfriendly when they
made their coup. You were right about that. And then the new

defenestration. History repeats. Only the dung heap was not there this time. Except perhaps in the minds of people like me, who were perhaps to blame. But how blame? So you see you are a little late in telling me that you are interested in my history. I could do you no good at all. If I don't understand, do you think you could? And one morning three years ago I got up sick, tired of being cold and of my old clothes, yes, but out of everything I had ever seen or done what I most remembered was my driving out those German Czechs. It was like driving out myself—my part of the world, that was what it was, mixed, good mixed, and I was doing the same thing the stupid Nazis had done. I went along the hall and found the W.C. and leaned over it and vomited. If I remember correctly I nearly lost my balance and fell in. And then I decided to try to get out, to live somewhere in simple peace and comfort, and forget all that. I was lucky, and I had my good friend Gwendolyn. But you tell me, you tell me, that in a place called *Zanesville* you understood all about those things? Forgive me if I tell you that you are . . . you are . . . are . . ." Whatever words Anton had been looking for he did not find. He lifted his small fists again, struck one against his forehead, and left the room.

No one spoke. Knox shrugged, to cover his embarrassment. Sylvia felt sorry for him. No matter what he'd said, it couldn't have been that bad. She sat down beside Knox. "Anton's obviously in a state about Hungary." She was about to elaborate when Elsie said in a muffled voice, "What if the world is only a sick ovary producing distorted forms of life and we just don't know it?"

"*What?*" Ernest said. "Why these anatomical obsessions?" he added in that precise, almost stuffy way Sylvia had come to enjoy so much. He had been standing by the window, a little apart from the group until then. Now he joined their dejected little circle, sitting down beside Sylvia.

"I believe in taking an interest in a man's work," Elsie said. Then, to Sylvia, "Don't you?"

"Sometimes."

"What's that got to do with it?" Ernest asked.

"Doctor Beau. Have you forgotten already? That's not very flattering, darling. My rich widower who wants to marry me? My famous Texas surgeon. There's a kind of ovary that goes kerflooey and all by itself starts producing life. Of course it's sick and produces a tumor too and that's where they find all these little bits of

hair and fingernail and teeth, all these nastily misplaced unpleasant
little things which the little sick ovary's been dreaming up all on its
own."

"Very unwise of the ovary," Ernest said. No one could tell
whether Elsie thought what she had been saying terrible or funny
or both.

Knox said, recovering quickly from the blows he had taken,
"He must be a fascinating conversationalist, Doctor Beau."

"Oh *Beau* never talks about these things. I poke around in his
books." She paused, squinting her eyes, then went on. "Beau talks
about . . . let's see, mostly about plays and operas. He's gone on
theatre. And sometimes about the dangers of socialism. And sometimes about skin-diving. He likes that too. And he talks an awful
lot about me too, which is *real nice*. As he'd say."

Knox said, "Beau? Bow? As in bow ribbon? I'm leaving." He
struggled always with the desire to prolong his visits at Kilchberg,
even though he was usually miserable there. The excuse he had
been using with himself tonight, when he had been particularly
uncomfortable, was that he wanted to ask Mrs. Dartley something
and would hang around for a while in case she decided to come
downstairs again. Now, once on his feet, he hurried to be gone.

Elsie, Sylvia, and Campion sat on in silence, clinking ice cubes at
each other. "Is his name really Beau?" Sylvia asked.

"His name is Beau as in Beauregard Charles de Vere."

"Oh."

They heard Knox's car pulling away. Suddenly Sylvia felt that
everything was going to be all right. It was late. Bingham couldn't
possibly be coming now. She was aware of Elsie's eyes moving over
her, and then over Ernest. Elsie seemed to have drooped a little,
but she said, "Shall I tell you about my other course? Somebody
has to keep the conversation going. Let's see. I'll tell you about a
useful critical tool." She laughed mysteriously. "A useful critical
tool is being alert to meaningful ambiguity. That's a very good
tool, in fact. Let's see if I can give you an example. Suppose . . . I
marry Beau, sweet Beau Ho Ho; well then you could kind of say
. . ." Then to the tune of *Alexander is a Swoose* Elsie Crown sang
out, " 'Half goy, half yid,/Elsie's favors are forbid . . .' *That* is a
meaningful ambiguity. Do you get it? Forbid. For *bid*." She
laughed again, this time harshly.

All the sympathy Sylvia had felt for her the day before came back with a sudden rush, as she realized that the other woman had in part been desperately trying to entertain them, and if the only way she could do this was by parading before them her personal miseries . . . well, it wouldn't be Sylvia's way, but then. It was exceedingly generous of Elsie, really. Now it was Sylvia's turn to look away, for she realized that Ernest had moved towards Elsie with tenderness and was gently remonstrating with her about having another drink.

And then all three of them heard the car, the heavy, dark sound of the engine, coming toward them in the night. Sylvia felt nothing. She stood up and started out of the room. Ernest Campion stood up too and came after her. From behind he put his hands on her arms and stopped her. He said firmly, "I think Celeste and Giovanni have probably gone to bed. It's late. Why don't you let me go to the door?"

She looked back at him, knowing that Elsie was staring at them both, and then she too said firmly, "No thank you, I'd rather you didn't. It's for me."

The last thing she heard as the room faded away behind her, as she moved toward the sound of that engine, was Elsie Crown saying with unmistakable bitterness, "So what's so great about Jane Austen? Will someone please tell me that?"

Thirty-six

"I've resigned," George Bingham said.

"Now? Of all times?"

"Is there something wrong with that?" he asked quickly.

"No, no, of course not," she said. For a second it had been as though they had reversed positions. His urgency, his tension, she saw, were terrible.

He said, "A couple of weeks ago in Washington one of those desk-chair heroes in the State Department reminded me that my job wasn't to make policy. I told him that I thought the guys who took the risks had a right to say something about policy, especially phony policy. I should have pulled out then."

"I don't understand entirely," she said.

He ignored this. "We're lying low now, pulling out. Larger considerations." She began to understand. Of course: he himself had been taken in, had been used by vague powers above him, and he now knew this. His suffering this knowledge had visibly harrowed him. "What better time for me to pull out?" he said, and put his hands on her shoulders, pressing her flesh painfully. He tried to smile. There was a false, wintery jauntiness in his voice. "And let's not forget there's an election coming up." He sounded as though he considered this to be a personal betrayal. Nothing about him made sense to her—and everything did. "I've been to Munich and back since yesterday." What she understood above all was that he was a man undergoing the agonies of an enormous disillusionment.

"Do you mean you're free?" she asked.

He looked over her head now, away from her. Sometimes his very cheeks scowled. Such a strange expression, uniquely his. "I think there are times when you've got to stand up and be counted," he said in the old forceful way. Sylvia did not pursue this; she had a vague sick sense that whatever he meant might be something more than "diplomatic moves," that obsessive phrase that kept recurring in Mrs. Dartley's comments on Western reaction to the Hungarian uprising.

"You're mad," she said.

He laughed. "I'm out of it. Come on. Hurry up. How fast can you pack?"

"Do you mean now, tonight?"

"Don't bring too much with you. We can send for the rest of your things later."

"I don't have much anyway."

"Good. The trunk isn't very big."

"You do mean tonight?"

"That's the idea."

"But where are we going?"

There was only the slightest pause. "Greece," he said.

"Greece? Not London?"

"No. Greece first. A holiday. I haven't had one in years. And we've never had a real one together. Don't think I don't know that. Come on, hurry up."

She saw that he had just in that instant decided on Greece, knew absolutely that when he arrived at Kilchberg he'd had no idea of what even the next day would bring him, of where he would turn, except to her. Suddenly she asked, "What about my book?"

"What?"

"My book. The one I'm working on. The one you spied on. My *manuscript*. Remember? Shall I bring it along?"

"Sure. Whatever you want."

"Whatever I want?" she repeated. And then it was as close as the next breath she would take, almost saying to him: No, I will not go with you, not to Greece, not anywhere, this is not my responsibility, this is not even real, what you are doing, this is not even what you want. But she could not say this. She could not turn her back on him, on that need, whatever it was, that drove him now to make a fierce entreaty of a word that did not often cross his lips: "*Please.*"

"Of course," she said. "It won't take me long. Ten minutes. Come back for me then."

"Good. Just a small suitcase, remember," he said.

"Right. Mozart can just go hang."

"What? What does that mean?" he held her back from him, searched her face across the confusion that rose between them. "What does that mean?" he repeated, as though she had broken some rule, touched on things that should not be touched on, and just when he had thought all was well.

She was embarrassed and confused herself, and felt tears in her throat. "I don't know what I meant," she said gently. She kissed him on the cheek. "I really don't. Something silly. Let's forget it. I'll hurry now."

When he came to the door she said there was something she had to do first. She would meet him at the car. It almost seemed as if she and Bingham were alone in the house now, as though everyone else had disappeared. She waited until he had gone along the corridor with her suitcase. Then she went to Mrs. Dartley's room, and rapped on the door. She felt the most painful shyness about facing Mrs. Dartley, but no matter how unpleasant the next few minutes were going to be she could not leave without saying good-bye to her. She thought of Bingham waiting for her outside; he would already be impatient, circling about the car. She stood there for what seemed a long time. Perhaps Mrs. Dartley had also disappeared. But then the door opened.

She followed Gwendolyn Dartley in. The room shocked her. It

reeked of some kind of heavy oriental tobacco, and even perhaps of cat urine. It was in a state of great disorder. Newspapers were flung and strewn about everywhere—Mrs. Dartley was probably the only woman in the world who subscribed to some of the world's worst publications as well as most of the best—and it almost seemed that if burning ash were to drop from the cigarette Mrs. Dartley now removed from her mouth the whole place would go up in flames. "I've come to thank you. And to say good-bye," Sylvia said.

Mrs. Dartley stared at her standing there in her shabby coat, clutching her purse to her, but did not break her silence. "I'm leaving," Sylvia said.

"So I see. Would you care for a drink?"

"I don't think so, thank you."

"I don't think I do either. Well?"

"I've much to thank you for. I wanted you to know how grateful I've been . . ."

"I do know. You have thanked me. Have you anything else to say?"

"No."

"Are you waiting for some last words from me? I have none for you."

Sylvia lowered her head and turned toward the door. Then, as though it were costing her a great effort, Mrs. Dartley said, "Are you saying good-bye to anyone else here, leaving a note for anyone, doing anything so normal as that?" For the first time there was emotion in her voice.

"No. I lack the courage."

"Your Mr. Bingham. Is he in government service?"

"Yes. No. He was."

"So I had thought."

"But he isn't . . . he didn't . . . he isn't involved in what's happening now."

Mrs. Dartley snorted. "Of course not. Though not from lack of trying. People like Mr. Bingham and his colleagues are never involved in the great moments. Oh, they can manage a military coup in Latin America now and then, or the Middle East. But the great moments, no. *They* are not the movers and shakers." She paused and then seemed to change her mind about something.

Sylvia said, "I wonder if it would be all right if I left a few things here for a while. My manuscript, some books, a suitcase. I'll arrange to have them picked up later."

"Perfectly all right." Mrs. Dartley got to her feet. "You must send me a copy of your book, Faustine. When you have finished it."

"If I ever do you mean?"

"Ah well, what difference does it make whether you do or not? So long as you are in love with this pseudo-dragon-slayer of yours."

Sylvia faced her. "The situation is much worse than that, Mrs. Dartley. Thank you again. Good-bye." She turned and left the room, half ran down the stairs and out to the car.

Ernest Campion, unseen, stood at a corner of the dark garden, watched George Bingham close her into the car, watched the car whirling her away. He walked back to the house. He found Mrs. Dartley in the doorway. She had been watching too. She said to him, "She'll be back."

"I don't care whether she comes back or not."

"Oh yes you do. And so do I."

He walked on past her. "She has left us a hostage," she called out softly after him.

Thirty-seven

No sadder pair of runaway lovers ever flung themselves into the night than George Bingham and Sylvia Grierson. Not until they had turned onto the highway south of Zürich did they even speak. Then she asked, "Where are we going now?"

"Milano," he replied.

It did not occur to her until much later, until they reached the St. Gotthard in fact, that he intended to drive them straight through. By then she was slumped indifferently into the seat, her body accustomed to the motion of the car. In the beginning the speed with which he drove frightened her terribly. It was not like him to use a car with such barely controlled violence. And then a moment simply came when her fear subsided, and she relaxed.

What did it matter, after all? Soon they would be among the southern lakes, or they would not be. She understood what was happening to him only too well. *He could not drive fast enough.* Having made his decision—as it appeared he had—it was necessary for him to act on it at once, to place himself with large and violent gestures into a new context.

They hardly spoke, for which she was glad, both of them accepting his need to concentrate on the road as an excuse for their silence. Once, passing more slowly through a town, he asked her if she knew that Milan had once been a part of the Byzantine Empire. She told him no, and he began to describe certain events in the history of Lombardy, and finally when he came to the name of Frederick Barbarossa to speak of him and of the one-time greatness of Hohenstaufen power. But she hardly responded and he fell silent again. Another time he said, "Getting married's a complicated thing in Italy. I know the consul general in Milan. How about that? It'll have the added advantage of taking place on American territory."

She said, "There's no rush, is there? Perhaps we could wait till we get to Greece?"

He turned slightly towards her, taking his eyes from the road for a second, then without comment bent again over the wheel. With every kilometer that passed she felt more certain that she had left behind her the true center, that place where all somehow worked toward balance, toward wholeness.

The architecture was beginning to change, the houses were becoming Italianate; the air, even the late-October night air, had a southern quality to it, and the flowers were more exotic blooms— the south Swiss illusion of a Mediterranean world. It changed nothing.

They had slowed down some for the mountains and the pass, but he was still driving too fast. Turns, curves, rock walls, chasms came and went. She slept, waking from time to time to the sudden radical skimming of a curve, the high shriek of tires, finding herself thrown against his arm or against the door. When she looked out at these moments, spinning trees and sky surrounded her, vague and confused in the moonlight. The moon she had given up looking for, that only made her dizzy; for while its light remained, diffuse, ironic, the moon itself seemed also to be engaged in some wild and frantic chase across the sky. No sooner did she glimpse it than it would career away. She felt that they had no destination at all. Milan, Milano, Mailand—*kennst du das Land?*—these were only names for a place that did not exist.

But then they were at the border, which was quickly passed, and coming down into Como. She sat up and pulled herself together. They entered the city of the Lombards. He slowed down now. The great industrial slums passed her windows. She remembered the area of great villas where the rich businessmen and members of government and the professions lived. Once he had taken her to dinner in one of those villas. They glided through the empty streets and were now in the familiar central part of the city. She saw the Principe e Savoia, where they usually stayed, but to her surprise he did not make the turn. He said something about their trying a new hotel this time. When they came to it she saw that it had evidently been built for the view. It was on a rise, modern, a skyscraper of sorts, but except that it was made chiefly of glass it resembled nothing so much as an Assyrian tomb. It was almost dawn.

He went in and returned with a sleepy night man who took the luggage from the trunk. At the desk they handed over their passports. "You look beat," he said.

What did he expect? "I suppose I do." She remembered suddenly that she should be getting her period soon, before the next day was over probably. No doubt she did look terrible. But still, aside from that, what, what did he, really, expect her to look like under the circumstances? He, amazingly, did not look the least tired. On the contrary, his face was smooth and somewhat high-colored; the pallor and tension that had marked him when he arrived at Kilchberg were completely, almost disturbingly gone.

He picked up her suitcase and both keys. "Which is which?" he asked the porter, then handed him the key to his room and pointed to his own suitcase. He spoke rapidly in Italian: The porter was to take the suitcase to his room and wait there for him; he would want him to send some telegrams for him and take care of one or two other things; he would be there in a few minutes. The elevator door closed on them.

When they got to her room he looked it over. It met his approval. Sylvia went to the window and pulled at the curtains. They moved back ponderously, as though they were unveiling a mystery, but instead they revealed only the familiar outline of a

large, industrialized city which might have been anywhere. Dawn
had come now, and a not very enspiriting one. What was the point
in having a view in such a city? Where were the Alps? Where the
fertile, gardenlike valleys of the Po, now ever more encroached
upon by the iron city? Perhaps a few days a year one might be
able to glimpse the high peaks, and a wavering bit of green. But
how often through that factory haze? The view out the window
reminded her of New York, uptown Manhattan, looking north and
east toward the factories and huddled dwelling places of Queens
and the Bronx, towards the roads and toward the bridges, beneath
which ran rivers where once the sturgeon had leapt and the trout
and along whose once-wooded shores the wild fowl had abounded.
What was the point?

Now they looked at each other. "Sleep as long as you want to,"
he said. He did not move to touch her. A strange phrase crossed
her mind: *Chi tocca muore.* "I'll probably be out most of the
morning. Good night."

"It's morning," she said. "But good night."

Thirty-eight

Sylvia slept until nearly noon and awoke to that confusion which
customarily follows some rapid alteration in the circumstances of
life. Above all, time and space she suddenly perceived to be without substance. She lay in bed attempting to dispel the perception,
telling herself, Yes, I am in Milan, in a hotel—I've forgotten its
name, however—I'm a day older than I was yesterday, not that
that means anything, and it is October, the twenty-something-or-
other, anyway a Friday. These were the starting points, but they
did surprisingly little to help. She felt too that she was still balancing on the edge of bad dreams, that in her sleep she had entered a
world of deeper, and of darker, truths which she now wished to
forget. Vague apprehensions remained, the atmosphere if not the
exact images. She thought for a second or two of how nice it
would be to awaken in another way, to reach out her arms and put
aside for a moment the anxious weight of the lonely and finite self

in a dimensionless world, to feel beside her another body. But whose? Ah, whose?

The telephone rang. Out of bed now, bare feet on the carpet, shivering a little, she was listening to Bingham saying in familiar phrases of apology that he was not going to be able to make it for lunch.

"You're not in the hotel now?" she asked.

"No. I've been sort of busy today."

"And didn't you sleep at all?"

"A couple of hours. I've had some things to take care of."

"What sorts of things?" She heard the strain in both their voices.

"Plane reservations. Things like that. Just let me handle this, will you?" A pause; then, as though he himself did not know why he had said that, he asked, "How are you feeling?"

"Fine. Are we leaving today?"

There was the slightest hesitation. He said, "No. Sunday probably. I've left something for you at the desk. In an envelope. Be sure to pick it up, will you?"

In the mirror her face was oddly composed; the wild-eyed desperate look she had expected was not there. She bathed, dressed, pulled back the curtains from the windows. No Alps of course.

Downstairs, at the desk, she was handed a large, overstuffed envelope. She opened it carefully; inside was a great deal of Italian money, more than she had ever seen before, and a little note that said, "I guess trousseau's too formal a word. Vacation clothes? How about that?" Would clothes work the transformation that time and space had not? It was absurd to think so. As for Bingham, it was . . . she searched for the word . . . thoughtful of him, kind, but she knew him too well not to realize that it was something else too, and she smiled. It was true that she had become almost shabby in her dress; the two years of fanatical saving for the year of "freedom in which to write," the penurious bitter ironic year itself—certainly there had been little money for adornment. Even those few good pieces she still possessed from more affluent days had passed some subtle turning point of fashion that made them look not quite right. Bingham did not even know how beautifully she could dress, what elegant tastes she had when she was able to indulge them, what effort it cost her to live without nice things. Now it appeared that these nice things would be hers again. What a pity that it didn't seem to matter more. Yet her vanity had been nipped at and she would certainly show him.

She asked the desk clerks to give her the names of some shops. Smiling, helpful, the two young men fell at once into intense discussion, asked her questions, looked her over, argued with each other, agreed, fell to arguing again. She left them and wandering over to the newsstand bought several papers—Mrs. Dartley's habits were catching—and began skimming the front pages. Impossible to tell really what was going to happen next in Hungary. She remembered how Gwendolyn had brought downstairs with her the evening before a number of clipped-out newspaper photographs, all of them taken in Budapest and all showing working-class people engaged in street fighting or massed together in huge protest demonstrations or lining the streets and cheering young men riding about on captured Russian tanks. "Look," she had said, "You must come and see all the fascist and imperialist agents. Now how do you suppose they've managed to disguise themselves so well as proletarians, and wherever do you suppose they found all those thousands of costumes?" Sylvia folded up the papers. One thing came through certainly, unless even the Poles and Yugoslavs among the foreign correspondents were lying: a vast number of ordinary Hungarians seemed to believe they were fighting for freedom and were quite willing to risk their lives in the process. *"Ecco, Signorina . . ."* And she, the voice of one of the desk clerks reminded her, was about to set off on a shopping expedition.

The two young men now handed her a carefully worked-out list and began going over it with her point by point. *"Va bene,"* she forced herself to say, *"Va bene,"* and *"Benissimo,"* and *"Grazia tante"* again and again. But when she started out of the lobby they called after her; most of the stores would be closed now until two, had she forgotten? Besides, she had not yet eaten, they told her— they seemed to know everything. *"Bisogna mangiare, bisogna mangiare, Signorina,"* and they smiled, as though to indicate what tender and good care either one of them would take of her if but given the chance. It was pleasing, but she only laughed, shook her head, thanked them again, and slipped away. She could not possibly face food, or the prospect of being hovered over by waiters.

Off on the other side of the lobby she found a small and pleasant room, agreeably furnished like someone's garden house and, except for an elderly couple sipping away at pink syrups, deserted. There she sat down, ordered *caffe latte*, and tried to read the papers. A little later, looking up across the rim of a cup, she saw an American boy of about twenty standing in the doorway. He crossed the room—something about the way he walked reminded her of Marshall—and sat down near her. A student, she was sure; he had that look to him, the freshly laundered suntans, the button-down, the Shetland pullover. He opened the book he had with him, and when the waiter came said, *"Una Coca-Cola, per favore. Con ghiaccio."* Despite the Italian, his voice at once suggested home to her, overpoweringly so. A sudden, painful longing for her own country came over her, and the desire to go home, the desire at the least to be with one of her countrymen. There was no reason, after all, why she couldn't talk for a few minutes with this boy—she was old enough to be the one to begin the conversation.

"You're an American, aren't you?" These were the words that were on her lips as she leaned a little in his direction. But then she stopped. He was a Negro. Was that how she had known he was American? No, it wasn't, not at all; his being a Negro, of course she had also seen that when he stood in the doorway, at once, without attaching importance to it; it had meant no more to her than the way he walked or his sweater, one fact of many. But would he believe that? She still hesitated. Would he believe that what she had seen was a young man, a middle-class American, a student? Or would he think she was condescending, favoring him with her good manners, or worse, attempting to prove to him (to the self really), as so many did, that she was one of the enlightened ones, a goodnik? How often she had observed that proud, aloof look on the faces of Negroes in conversation with white people, who were usually too caught up in a sense of their own magnanimity to notice. And how understandably sensitive, how quick to know when they were being patronized, Negroes were, how quick to catch the smallest false note, of which there were still so many, to know when their jokes were being too heartily laughed at, their opinions too readily agreed with, the white man or woman showing them an elaborate deference they would never show to another white person. It seemed to Sylvia most unlikely that this young man, for example, would guess that it was she who at this moment stood in need, who had almost turned to him in the hope that a few minutes of speech might in some way have eased the mysterious burden from her own heart.

Almost, but not quite. She leaned back against the couch. It was too late now; she had lost the moment when it might have been possible to have spoken, to have acted, without self-consciousness, to have been what still at root was most natural for her to be, spontaneous. All this searching after motive, this doubt, this holding back, this being trapped in categories—how murderous it was. There simply was no trust any more; that was the real horror. And what was life without it, even if all history itself was but a record of betrayals?

She stirred the last of the coffee, thinking of Bingham, of how the ultimate risk is trusting, of how he could not really manage that. He had come as near as he could, perhaps, with her. And now her own energies were burning so low that she wasn't even up to the little risk of a possible social misunderstanding. She cast a quick glance at her young compatriot. No, she was too nervous to speak now. Perhaps it was not an important loss, but it was a loss. It was bitter to find that old barriers one thought put down had so many cruel and unexpected ways of reasserting themselves—to acknowledge the truth, which was, after all, that if he had been white she *would* have spoken to him. She had an extraordinary sense of personal failure; at the same time a sense that some personal failures were not entirely one's fault. She placed money on the table and stood up. As she left the room she thought she saw the boy glance up from his book and look after her, wondering perhaps in his turn if she too might not be an American? For some odd reason she found herself thinking suddenly of the barricades which had been thrown up in the streets of Budapest.

She hurried out onto the street, deciding not to take a cab but to walk. Her head had begun to ache fiercely, and the air might help. Besides, walking would pass the time until the shops opened. In her purse she carried, still unread, the letter which Ernest had put in her hand so long ago at the farewell party for Lily. At the last moment at Kilchberg she had been unable to destroy it and had thrust it into her purse. She felt she no longer knew herself even a little, or understood in the least her own actions. Coming here with Bingham had made her miserable, as she had known it would; refusing to come, letting him leave Kilchberg alone, bear alone what he and no doubt his colleagues must surely regard as his defection—that too would have brought misery. Somewhere, obscure, unfathomable, it seemed to her a question of honor was

involved. Or was that an elaborate self-deception? Was she trying
to find high motives for low or confused actions? Or did she
perhaps quite simply feel that after the love-making she now "belonged" to him?

It was still something she did not really want to think about, that
at this point in their history he had at last carried them into that
world of touch, of feeling, of closeness to another human being
which had always before been so painfully alien to him, as perhaps
its corollary had also been, the final moments, beyond will, beyond
control, the regenerative little dying itself. What was it about the
sexual act, the coming together in the flesh, what was its deepest
paradox? It was not just that when it was a pleasure it was also sad
but rather that . . . that the antonyms of life and death played so
profoundly on one, upon the eager little animal body and the
perplexed little panting spirit both. For her at least it was so. She
existed and she did not, and she did not know which was sweeter
and which more bitter or whether it was closeness to another living creature that made one know that when the moment comes
one dies alone or whether it was knowing this that drove one to be
close to another living creature.

But not just any living creature, of course—that too was part of
the mystery. There were affinities or there were not—that was as
good a phrase for it as any—and they did not in her experience
come all that often. Sylvia admitted now to the full irony of the
year with Bingham and saw that, despite all the disappointments
and the struggle, there had been something inevitable about the
night they had spent together at Kilchberg, and that she herself
had quite unconsciously desired it to happen. At the same time, she
felt certain that it would not happen again, that all that it implied
would never be—for which fact, although unable to regret really
the night of love itself, she also felt herself somehow grateful. But
if this was true, then what in the name of all reason was she doing
with him here?

She plodded along the streets of Milan. The recollection of the
night in Bingham's arms had brought with it not the slightest
erotic ripple. Instead, her only emotion was one of vague anxiety.
It was absurd that she could not rid herself of the feeling that that
one night was going to change her life. And yet she did not feel
quite so depressed as she had in the hotel. The air was helping her
head. Perhaps so relatively frank a colloquy with herself was help-

ing too. Still, what a fix to be in. Anything, it appeared, could happen to anyone, and one was often most humbled where one's pride was most involved, one's image of one's own virtue most precious. That she, who prided herself on her *integrity*, who in the past had even said no to affinities when they collided with that . . . She could not rid herself of the notion that she had betrayed Campion. But that was absurd too. Wasn't it? She had given him no promises; he had no claim on her; she was a free woman. She had been out of her mind to tell him she had "betrayed" him. And yet that, she felt, was exactly what she had done. It was really ridiculous probably that she could not be more casual about sex.

She snickered now, remembering suddenly a rejected suitor telling her that she acted as though she thought she would be going against the categorical imperative if she went to bed with him, in fact as though she thought she *were* the categorical imperative. It had been a very clever remark, so clever that she had almost been goaded into telling him the truth, which was simply that the idea of going to bed with him didn't appeal to her. But if you liked a man in other ways that was the one thing you would never say; it inflicted too much pain and bewilderment. It was kinder to let him think whatever he wanted to about you.

She remembered too this same suitor's final approach, this one not nearly so clever; after all, he had said, they were "only bodies." She had never been able to decide what had offended her most about this, its cynicism or its naïveté. She knew very well that she was not a woman for whom any reasonably acceptable and interested male body—and there never seemed to be a dearth of these—would do. Perhaps this was something to regret, but she never had. A small fear ran through her now and she thought, You are a vain, proud, spoiled woman, and you are going to be brought down. Hardly a comforting thought. Still, it *was* better not to lie about one's feelings; the one time she had, when she was very young, she had got into a terrible situation that it had taken her a long time to get out of. No, in this respect, at any rate, she knew something about the sensual side of her own nature. Besides, even sexual love of the most transforming kind couldn't change Mozart.

Change Mozart? Sylvia stopped and feigned interest in a shop window, trying to understand where so bizarre a thought as the last was meant to lead her. Then she remembered that once for nearly a year one of the two great loves of her life had been

Mozart; there was no other word for it really but love. And where
did this lead her? Again, to the year with Bingham. How had she
survived? She had been cut off not only from her work but also
from the small affections of daily life, from friends, from simple
pleasures and social civilities, *and from Mozart.* Oh, how she
suddenly envied those people who really believed that love was
an object, something you could buy or win or deserve even—at
any rate something you could possess, fix like a dead butterfly in a
glass case, clip and cage like a bird. They knew nothing, such
people, but surely, surely life was not so painful for them.

And she? What did she know of love? Only that it was more
nearly an image than it was an object, most often no doubt only an
image of the self, but sometimes perhaps of the dream of the
eternal, which was why it took so many forms. In the past she had
known this without having even to think about it; she had in truth
always been a little in love, in many ways. How impossible it was
for her to live without this yielding of her spirit to whatever life
offered. It was not fickleness, such a yielding; on the contrary, it
was constancy; it was a recurring gift, connected in some un-
knowable way with the possibility of art, as its antonym was, the
awareness that it was all passing, not to come again. Sylvia looked
into the plate glass window and saw in it the reflection of a mysterious, serene city, somewhere over her shoulder; it could not be
Milan surely, those gleamings, those forms.

She turned now, sadly, back to the noise and the traffic, and
walked on. Soon all the old conflicts were stirring again. She
knew perfectly well what was in Ernest's letter. It helped nothing
now. The truth was that she did love Bingham; it would not do to
say otherwise. And she did love Campion. And she had run away
with the one she could not imagine living her life with and left
behind the one she could. Could any woman be in a more foolish,
more humiliating situation than this? That she was a woman with
pride only made it the worse. And how was it possible for her to
feel, as she still did, that even now it was not up to her to force an
ending, but that it must happen through no agency of her own?

Suddenly neither man, Bingham nor Campion, had any reality
for her. Both seemed very far away, and even rather unimportant
and silly. She felt a revulsion from the whole idea of men, from the
whole troublesome mess of the sexes, from personal relations of
every sort. She would have nothing more to do with either Cam-

pion or Bingham. Even their names seemed to her nonsense syllables. She thought of all the books she hoped to write, and as she
did so a curious indifference to her own fate overtook her. Perhaps
she would spend the rest of her life alone, as she had frequently in
the past so vainly resolved to do; perhaps like the Countess
in *Fathers and Sons*, a cool and aging, but only slowly, gently
aging virgin. Well, perhaps one could not quite say that, either of
herself or of the Countess. A virgin *manquée* then.

In considerably improved spirits, Sylvia Grierson stepped perk-
ily into the door of the specialty shop which had just at that
moment opened, as though its owners had been awaiting her arrival alone.

Thirty-nine

Late in the afternoon of the same day Elsie Crown announced that
she was leaving Kilchberg. Mrs. Dartley, for reasons which she
freely confessed as being selfish, attempted to keep her. She hated
to lose the only person who could translate the Hungarian broadcasts for her. She hated to lose someone who, as she told Elsie, was
not boring. She hated too, though she did not confess this, what appeared to be a general exodus from the villa. She could sympathize
with Elsie's desire to visit Lily, but *right away?* What difference
could a few days make? And when she could not persuade Elsie
she became really pettish, at her selfish worst, scowling at Elsie
across the green typewriter and the rising mounds of newspapers,
puffing out, it seemed, like that cat that was always somewhere in
her room.

Elsie was unmoved. Her behavior the night before had left her
feeling she must get herself in hand, she had explained, though she
had refused to say more than one word, "Wildly," when Mrs.
Dartley pressed for details. She did want to see Lily as soon as
possible and then she was returning to the States to face up to
some decisions. She had made reservations to fly from Zürich to
Amsterdam the next day, the 27th. There she had some things to
take care of—her manner indicated clearly that she did not think it
was Mrs. Dartley's business to know what. She would fly to

London on the 31st and had already written a letter to Tante Lily
to that effect. Furthermore, although her Amsterdam flight was
not until the next afternoon, she wanted to go into Zürich now, at
once. She had already reserved a room at the Zum Täubli.

Campion was presented with all of this as an accomplished fact,
and with the demand that he drive her in. He had never seen her in
so uncompromising a mood or felt before such a remoteness in
her. The gay, lively, amusing, if somewhat crazy Magyar in her
had made one of its sudden disappearances. He was used to that,
but none of the familiar personality phases had followed. If she had
taken one of her frequent plunges into Jewish melancholy or wit,
or even turned to the one thing she sometimes did which he detested, a sort of forced, arch, patter-patter New York entertain-
ment-world talk. But here was a brisk, efficient, even cold Elsie.
Only her eyes told him that behind all this lay still the old untap-
pable reservoir of sadness. About what he had no idea. And he did
not greatly care just then. Those devices for cheering her up
which he had learned to employ on Amsterdam Avenue, he had
neither heart nor energy for. They drove to Zürich in virtual
silence. It had been nearly dark when they left Kilchberg; it was
completely dark and the air filled with a heavy mist, not quite rain,
by the time they arrived. Out on the lake a mysterious white sail
fluttered in the distance, impossible to understand at such an hour,
on such a night.

In the hotel lobby Elsie suddenly became recognizable. She
pranced to the desk, spoke to the clerks in her most winning way,
everything just a little overdone but charmingly so. Then she
turned to him and invited him to come up to the room. He
nodded. No doubt there was something she wanted him to do for
her, if he knew her from old. It would turn out that she had
promised the child of a friend a Swiss music box, or she had seen a
certain bracelet in the window of a certain jewelry store, but she
wouldn't be able to manage it herself tomorrow, she really was
exhausted and would probably sleep all morning and then there
would be no time before catching the plane, if he could just possibly manage to drop by and pick it up one of these days, put it in
the mail? Something like that.

There was always, he remembered, something curious about
these requests, as though she were saying to him, Do I matter
enough to you for you to want to do something for me, something

as outrageous as this, do I really? And they always were just a little outrageous. Most men would not have put up with it, she had often told him belligerently. It surprised him now that his thoughts should dwell so deeply on Elsie, on their past. Neither had been in his mind for a long time. Odd, when the rage of loss was so strong within him.

The room surprised him too when they got there. He thought it looked very expensive, and he said so, turning then to stare out the window at the Limmat.

"I've decided to indulge myself for one night," she answered.

Now she moved about the room with unnaturally hurried gestures, talking constantly, making jokes, laughing nervously. He watched in growing bewilderment. He could not remember ever having seen her so unsure of herself before. But it was a funny time somehow, for everyone who had been staying at Kilchberg. So much had been happening. He felt suddenly sorry that Elsie was going. Being with her in some way helped.

A bellboy came to the door with a small bucket of ice and soda water on a tray. "Party," she said to Campion, "party-party all the time," smiling at him. "Why not?" Then she opened her cosmetic case and pulled out a bottle of Scotch. "Tax free," she said triumphantly. "I lugged it all the way from Paris. I had to wait two hours between planes there. Did I tell you? God, what a rat race."

She was mixing a drink, the pale amber into the glass, a little soda water, one ice cube, handing it to him, his taste exactly. He recognized ceremony. As he drank he felt a welcome sensation of the familiar, of the lost retrieved. It was odd how life unexpectedly returned whole segments that once had had meaning but that had been entirely forgotten by the conscious self in the meantime. A hotel room in Zürich or the apartment on Amsterdam Avenue? Those days seemed very close. Elsie had not really drunk at all when he first knew her. A little vermouth or white wine might be coaxed past her lips; these things she thought civilized. But whiskey for women? Only for women who were pigs. The faces she had made. Still, his love for Scotch was another matter. "On you it looks good," she would say. Now of course she had a glass in hand too, but very very light in color, he noticed. "Flavored water," she said, as though following his thoughts. Her drinking was still only for others, and to annoy by remote control her

father, who thought it was final proof of her having turned into a
Schickse.

Now she had suddenly dropped the pretense which even with
him and quite possibly with herself she had been keeping up ever
since arriving in Switzerland. "Do you remember how we named
me?" she asked, laughing suddenly. "Isabelle? Isadora? Bella? Dora?
And how long did it take for us to decide finally between Elsie and
Elisa? Weeks!"

It all came back; they discussed it at length, laughing. Then he
said, "I was for Elsie all along. That sweet old-fashioned fresh
American sound."

"Much good it did," she said bitterly. "I'm still typed. That
accent. You never do quite get rid of one. Anyway, what's there
to play in but . . . ?" She did not finish the question. Then she
suddenly said, "What would you think if I married Doctor Beau?"

"What would I think?"

She smiled cynically, got up and lighted a cigarette. "You
wouldn't think anything, would you? Good wishes and all that.
Fine. I just wanted to be sure."

He changed the subject. "What are you going to do in Amsterdam?"

She lowered her eyes. "My father asked me to do something for
him. Export-import. Some new gimmick. But a legitimate gimmick," she added quickly. He nodded. He knew that for all the
railing, for all that separated her from her parents in the way of
what she so violently called *values* (she fought as bitterly with her
mother about her mother's taste in clothes and furniture as with
her father about money), she had remained in some ways a
dutiful daughter, still visited her parents regularly, and had
done so even when she lived with him, though because she had
never seemed to want him to know it he had never indicated that
he did. At her kindest about her father's business methods, she
would say he was learning fast to be a good American. At her
unkindest, she spoke scathingly of the transplanted ghetto psychology of New York, which she despised and yet understood and
which therefore obsessed her. Her father's cupidity she took to be
a personal affront, and she herself was so indifferent to money and
so generous with it that she was usually in debt to a bank, "one of
Mr. Rockefeller's banks," as she would put it.

Elsie's attitude toward being Jewish had puzzled Campion for a

long time, because it was so unlike that of the Jews he had known
in school, young men as privileged as he himself had been. On the
one hand, when she had been fighting with her parents she allowed
herself to make the most scathing generalizations about Jews, and
if he protested she would tell him he just didn't know. On the
other hand, if he appeared to sympathize too much with her she
subtly shifted into a series of stories the real point of which was to
show the superiority of Jews, or she began talking about Einstein
or Yehudi Menuhin or, quite often, Lady Harewood. In the
end he had decided that her self-consciousness was as inevitable as
it was painful and to let it go at that. He had at last, however,
come to understand Elsie's particular dilemma; she was one who
would naturally and easily have chosen assimilation in the pre-1933
world. That the inclinations she felt in that direction were
thwarted by feelings of both guilt and fear was but one more sad
reminder of the disaster that had intervened.

She sat now, still brooding in the silence that had followed her
last remarks. He said, "I suppose you still give your father a hard
time."

She shrugged and said, "Barbering was an honest trade. At least
in Hungary."

He said, "Your father's not uniquely lacking in what I think is
called good business ethics."

She answered, "But he's my father." This too was like the old
days, and though it was a subject he had sometimes found tire-
some, it now brought Campion a deepening of that sensation of the
pleasantly familiar. Elsie went on, suddenly aroused again, "Listen,
there are things you don't understand and never will. We're Jews.
When a Jew does something like that business with the tenements
. . . it doesn't matter how many goys are doing the same thing . . .
it's worse if a Jew does it. We stick out. People notice. It's what
they expect of a Jew. You'll never get it. Right now he's got a
secret partner. White, Anglo-Saxon, Protestant, the most respectable son of a bitch you'll ever meet—and a real cutthroat. They
really hit it off. So that makes my father less of a *goniff?*" She
paused, threw her hands skyward in a traditional gesture, laughed,
and saw that he was holding out his glass. She filled it again and
poured water in her own glass, adding about four drops of
whiskey.

"*Ecco, mio professore,*" she said, handing his glass to him. He started at the name, the one she had used to use for him. He had completely forgotten it. Now she began to talk away about Doctor Beau, his house, his two nice kids, the swimming pool, the easy life. "I don't dig him entirely. He's a sweet guy. But how can anyone live in the South and be that innocent? Or anywhere. I mean really. He just doesn't *see* all the bad things. Being that naïve . . . it's almost . . . not very bright. Some of his friends say the most God-awful things and he'll just smile and tell you afterwards they've really got a 'heart of gold.' Ugh. I don't like some of his friends." Campion listened, soothed by the familiar tone of harangue. Both he and Elsie had their feet up on the coffee table. He already imagined her trying to get Doctor Beau to *see*, as she had been trying to get her father and mother to see for years. "They think I'm marvelous of course, or sort of. New York. An actress. A foreigner. A *Yur-o-pe-an*. Everything they really hate but that fascinates them. Oh God, what bumpkins! In eastern Hungary in little towns we had provincials? *Oi weh!* They prefer to think of me, incidentally, as Hungarian, not as a *Jewess*, though they're just sickeningly polite about my being Jewish."

She took a breath and he said, "What about Doctor Beau?"

"He thinks both are absolutely wonderful. Especially my being Jewish. That's some sort of never-never-land thing for him; it hits the romantic streak in him. He thinks it's exotic. I don't honestly suppose he ever knew a Jew before, except maybe to buy something wholesale from or take their appendix out. He's not a bad sort of man, especially when you consider what most American doctors are like. He's not at all a bad sort of man," she added defensively. "If kindness could move hearts . . ." Then she said, "If you're wondering, darling, I think *he's* exotic. I just never met anyone like that before." She paused. "I wouldn't be talking so much if you weren't so unhappy. You are, aren't you?"

"Not at this particular moment. Go on." He felt comfortable and didn't want the atmosphere to get too serious.

But instead she clutched her arms around her knees and rocked back and forth a little. And then, staring away from him, she said in the low, different voice that was Elsie at her best, even perhaps her truest, "Have you ever been able to figure out why you never asked me to marry you?"

Before he could say something that would take the place of the
answer he did not have, she went on quickly, still looking away,
"Forget that, darling. A stupid question. There aren't any ways of
explaining things like that, are there? I ought to know. When I left
New York, what did you think, did you think I wanted to go off
and come back a great actress?"

He said, because she was serious now, "Yes. I did think that.
And I thought other things too, about myself."

"Yes, well it was true, about my *ambition*." Here she gave the
bitter, rasping laugh that was Elsie at her worst. "You know, a
childhood dream, and then you find out you're not good enough,
or something. But that wasn't the only thing that was true, not
even then." She stopped. "Christ!" and before he could say a word
she went to the wall and switched on the radio, whirling the dial
until she found some acceptable music. Haydn it sounded like to
him. She said, "And you stopped writing me. There I was touring
the whole damned country and you stopped writing me," this last
having the unexpected force of an accusation. In their other two
meetings since the New York parting nothing like this had ever
been mentioned.

"I was suffering from a disease called Begging Off," he said
cheerfully. "It covered everything."

She shook her head, lighted still another cigarette. "Most men
don't really like women. You do, Ernest."

"I had the opposite impression about men. I thought most of us
liked women inordinately."

"Fakery," she said, "Fucking fakery." Then she began to blush.
"I don't know why I talk this way," she said softly.

"You didn't used to," he said.

"I know. Anyway, it's true. They like to sleep with us. But they
don't really like us."

"Oh come on," he said teasingly.

"It's true." Then with sudden violence, "Do you know how
many men are good lovers? Damned few. I can tell you. I'm an
expert on the subject now."

He had winced. "Don't tell me," he said. "I like you," he said.
He felt suddenly responsible, and it did not seem fair. Nor did it
seem to him right that a woman who could, he suddenly recalled,
be so loving, so giving, should have known such miseries as it

appeared she had in the time since they parted. His ego was also touched.

"Oh well, I don't want to embarrass you. I know you hate that. Maybe Beau—do you know I haven't slept with him, he's got such old-fashioned ideas, my God you don't suppose he thinks I'm a virgin, do you?—anyway, maybe he'll rescue me from meaningless sexuality. I know all about *that*." She laughed, and seemed suddenly in a better mood. "I've even read about it."

"Surely not in Jane Austen?"

"No. Not in Jane. In one of those other stupid courses. In . . . lots of other people. In . . . Oh what do I care who? I wouldn't be talking this way if *I* weren't so unhappy. And if I can't say what I want to to you . . . I don't suppose I can with Beau, ever. Though he does admire to hear me talk. I skip the four-letter words for him too. He shocks so easily. The poor schmo," she added with a giggle. "Not that I won't be a good wife. If I make a bargain I keep it."

"Of course," he said, and believed her.

"And the galloping Grierson girl?"

"There is no Grierson girl. She galloped away," he answered. At the moment it seemed to him that there really wasn't.

"Oh come on. Don't kid me . . ." She shook her head again. "Funny. All the complicated situations these smart complicated women get themselves into. To me it's all so simple."

He made a movement to get up and she said, "Another Scotch?"

He thought not, he said, and did get up. A great change came over Elsie. Her bluish-black eyes glistened, her face expressed a conflict that had not so much caught her unawares as slipped unexpectedly out of control. "Does it matter if I . . . ?"

He knew the words that would follow would not be the ones she had originally intended. "If I feel sentimental?" she said. "Does it hurt anything?"

"Why should it?"

She laid a hand on his sleeve and said, "Stay here tonight." Her tone was lighter, almost gay.

"Jane would never approve," he said.

She laughed, "Oh darling, how can it hurt anyone? Especially now? Who will ever know, even? Before respectability claims me? Before then?"

He saw a devotion in her face, an absolute caring that he knew he would never see on Sylvia Grierson's. He knew at the same time that this did not change anything.

"Oh darling," she said, smiling now, laughter in her voice, absolutely sure of herself, "why not, *why not?*"

There could be only one answer. "Why not?" he said in reply.

Forty

The taxi Sylvia was riding in swept past the Duomo, its absurd and lovely spires wavering in the thin light. Sylvia smiled. Some vaguely reassuring association had started up in her. But then it was lost. Beside her on the seat were a number of packages, the fruits of several hours of abandoned and euphoric shopping. Now it all uneasily reminded her of getting ready for a masquerade ball, and the only thing that comforted her was the fact that from one moment to the next weariness or rebellion or something had suddenly overcome her and she had thereby managed to hang on to her terrible old coat for another day.

The taxi slammed to an abrupt halt, throwing several of the packages onto the floor. She retrieved them and settled back. The driver began muttering. There was some sort of disturbance up ahead, an accident perhaps. Whatever it might be, they were stalled in a traffic tie-up. She leaned out the window. She could see placards on sticks bobbing up and down and the black hats of police moving in and out of a crowd that was chanting something and marching around in a circle. The driver muttered more loudly and flung himself about behind the wheel of the car. They were in a small side street and there was no way out. She began to feel curious and told the driver she would walk on ahead until he caught up with her.

The moment she got out of the cab the anonymous shoulders, elbows, and bodies of the outer reaches of the gathering crowd began jostling her firmly along toward the center of the demonstration. She resisted and moved forward more slowly than those around her. When she got as close as she wanted to the cross street where the people were circling around and blocking traffic she braced herself against further movement; it was possible to do this, to stand against the mass of newcomers who kept pressing toward that circle, but she knew perfectly well that with even a slight increase in the emotional tempo of the crowd she would lose her footing, even if not her head, and be carried along against her will.

She concentrated on the demonstration without being able to make much sense out of it; it had something to do with Hungary but what was not clear; it almost seemed to her that these marching people might be protesting just to be protesting. She braced herself more firmly and was able to step a little aside and climb onto an iron bar that ran along one of the buildings. Leaning against the wall, she felt she could have been anywhere. Everything was merging into an indifferent but agitated mass. She felt the placards themselves could have been about any number of horrors and even written in a made-up, make-believe language, and that what she was witnessing was little more than a sort of conditioned ritual response, one that no longer had either meaning or power in it. A low humming mutter was coming from the spectators, those who had not yet become a part of the chanters in the processional itself, and a kind of rolling motion was beginning. She began to feel a little frightened, but she told herself that there was nothing really dangerous in this situation. After all, it *wasn't* Budapest. What *were* these people doing, unconsciously but safely imitating Budapest, playing at revolution? Or were they trying to participate in the only way they could, vicariously? She looked at the police and the usual antagonisms rose in her. She would have liked to go up to one of them and knock off his fancy black hat, step on his booted toes, or even hit him. They frightened her as much as the crowd; both could turn so quickly into mindless instruments of terror. Suddenly she realized that they depended upon each other, this aroused mass of people and the police, that it was impossible to imagine the one without the other. If anything needed to be changed, it was surely that.

Then she saw Bingham, his face clear and unmistakable among all those other vague faces that were gathered on the opposite street corner, his body shouldering its way lightly through the confusion until he reached a point from which he was evidently satisfied that he could see what was going on. He stood there now, outwardly casual, a spectator like her. It was strange to be observing him of all people and to go unobserved in return. At any second she expected those eyes which swept the scene so efficiently to fix on her. But they did not. All else they took in, but not her. She thought of trying to cross over to him, but decided against it. Never had he seemed to her a more powerful figure, never had she felt more deeply the force of his one abiding passion, the need to act—and never had she been more certain that he would not find the way. He was born to be among the mighty, but not the mighty of this century. The old fear for him clutched at her heart, the old deep tenderness. Solitary, motionless amidst all that movement, that senseless moil, he smiled now, and now, as she had feared, now came the small twist to the mouth which bespoke contempt. He had seen all he needed; there was nothing of interest in this scene. He turned indifferently away, and she watched his back disappearing through the crowd, and then with her excellent long vision she saw a driver holding open a door for him and saw him get into a car which he, like herself, had just left.

She was suddenly aware of being shouted at. Her cab had at last made its way to the corner and was ready to turn out of the street. The driver's voice was hoarse with anger, and he was shaking his fists at her. Two policemen were raging at him. She raced for the cab, flung herself in and sat back, her heart beating much too fast. She resolved to say nothing to Bingham about having seen him.

In her room at the hotel she found a bouquet of flowers—white lilac mostly and other spring blooms, which seemed to her very strange. She leaned her face toward them for a moment, letting the petals brush against eyelids and cheek, a curiously stirring, almost erotic sensation, breathing in their fragrance. Then she hurried to bathe and prepare herself. For what, exactly?

At seven their evening began, with drinks on an enclosed terrace on the top floor of the hotel, the factories of Milan for background. He admired her dress; it was made of a dark silk and heavy ribbon material, simple but ingenious. They were exceedingly careful with each other. Between them wavered the unspoken struggles with the self in which each was engaged. They talked of Greece, as they had done so often in the past. She tried not to give in completely to the passionate desire to go there which these conversations always aroused in her.

"We'll rent a boat for a couple of weeks if the weather's still good," he was saying. "I'll take you to an island I know. It's not one of the fashionable ones. As a matter of fact it used to belong to one of my ancestors. A rich place once. The Turks never got it. We made a deal with Venice, so much money per year in tribute, so much protection. It worked. It's poor now, poorer than anything you've ever seen. There's not even a place where I'd want you to stay the night."

"Then how—?"

"The boat, dummy. What else?" Then he said. "It's a funny sort of place. You can still find little kids who'll take you to a cave and tell you some long story about Odysseus, something they never got out of a book. It's just been passed down over the generations. And they believe it now."

"An enchanted isle?"

"No, not really." His eyes lowered, a flicker of anger. "I told you it's poor. The chief crop is sailors. The women wait, the men go off. They come back. Sometimes."

"Very Greek."

Both smiled, sadly.

"They don't quite know how to figure me," he said.

"I don't either," she said.

"I've been there three times since the war. At first they called me the American. Then I talked to them in Greek and told them some stories about the place, stories no foreigner could have known. I'd heard them from my great-grandfather. That really got them excited. The news spread through the village in minutes, they all came gathering around. They're simple people. The best, but simple, and things change slowly in a place like that. Now, to them I'm a Greek."

"What are you really?"

"Me? American. What else?" He grinned. "I get a kick out of going there. I'll show you the castle. It belonged to our family. It's a ruin now, has been for centuries, just a few walls left, some stones, filled with goats wandering in and out. Do you like goats?"

"Friendly ones."

"They're friendly." His eyes gleamed; he leaned forward. "There's just the one main coastal town now, a little place, a village. It used to be quite a port. Now they always decide to have a big celebration when I come. They have a feast. Everyone sings

and dances. They make a big fire outdoors, at night, and roast
lambs. They think the heir's come back. It's kind of awkward—
they're poor and they haul out all this food—but I've given up
trying to stop them. A Greek night, especially in spring, there's
nothing like it. It's different from anything I've ever known."

Was it really so? Did a Greek night transform him into a
reveler, the last thing in the world she could imagine him being?
Did it unmask—or free—what hid behind the beard? Would they,
the two of them, dance and sing, drink wine, give over and love
among the olive trees and the vines, along the sea-drenched shores?
If that were to happen it might all be worth-while. Or perhaps that
was not the way to put it. If that were to happen all might yet be
well. "Bacchic?" she murmured.

"Something like that. The wine's not much today—a little too
sharp, and you have to get used to the resin. It must have been
better once, different anyway. But there's a lot of it. Everyone
ends up happily drunk."

"You too?"

"Me too."

"I don't believe it. And what about me? What will they think of
me? Are women allowed too?"

"Sure. Why not? They never treated women the way they did
in Rome or Palestine. Besides, I'll tell them you're Greek. Old
Pelasgian." She forced a smile, as she was meant to. He looked
down and said, "I'll tell them you're my bride. They can't very
well turn down the bride of the lord of the island, can they?"

She said suddenly, "I want to go to Naxos, and Crete, and
Cyprus, and—"

"You're voracious," he said, amused.

"Yes." But she did not really believe that either of them would
go to Greece, not now, not together. She did not think he believed
it either.

"Come on," he said abruptly. "Let's eat." He held her old coat
for her, mockingly.

They went to the Galerie Vittorio Emanuele, walking its length,
traversing the Latin Cross, then returning to the octagonal center, where her favorite restaurant was. But she could hardly eat,
not even the beautifully prepared fresh-cooked fruits which she so
loved, the whole little apples and pears, and the cherries—wherever did they get them at that time of year?—and peaches and

apricots and plums. What mysterious south produced them in late October? Of the wine he drank, as usual, sparingly; she felt the old sense of vague disappointment when she saw this.

He said, "I tried to get some concert tickets for us. But there's no Mozart around at the moment."

"*Mozart?* Why did it have to be Mozart?" Her mouth was suddenly dry.

"Because I like Mozart too."

"Of course you do. I know that. I don't follow." Didn't she?

He looked very directly at her. "Something you said just before we left Kilchberg. I'm not Mozart's hangman. I'm nobody's hangman. I guess I wanted to show you that I'm a civilized guy."

She felt pain. "Oh of course you are, darling. Of course you're civilized. Oh I didn't mean that. I don't know what I meant. I told you so at the time."

They had floundered. She asked him if there were a piano in his room; usually he insisted on that. He told her no, he hadn't bothered to ask for one. That was another illusion he was giving up; he "played like a ditch-digger." Until he had time to practice properly he wasn't going to inflict his attempt at music on anyone again. A pity, she told him; she had thought it would be nice if he . . . He shook his head. No. He called for the check, more politely than usual. The air had turned surprisingly warm, balmy, though there was a slight mist too. They walked through the arcade, beneath that great glass canopy which, even when it rained or snowed, protected the lucky ones against the weather. They walked to Piazza della Scala and stood before the opera house. The season had not yet begun and all was shuttered and dark. No voices seemed to linger there. Arm in arm they walked. And then they walked back to the Piazza del Duomo, which was quiet now and almost free of traffic, and the great cathedral itself seemed isolated and remote, and walked on still under the neon lights running and blinking across the sky like the constellations of Orion and the Pleiades or falling, falling, falling into the blackness, like the crown of Ariadne.

"Hot chocolate?" he asked. It was the nightcap she liked best in Italy.

"I don't think so."

"Tired?"

"A little. Yes."

They got into a cab. "When *are* we leaving?" she asked.

"Sunday," he said firmly. "And I'll make it for lunch tomorrow."

At the door of her hotel room they turned to each other. He did not kiss her but pulled her slowly to him, gripping her by the shoulders, holding her close, put his arms stiffly around her, enfolded her, pushed her stiffly back, looked into her face, did not seem to know the anguish that was revealed in his own, and let her go, turning her, propelling her almost, toward her room. "Get some sleep," he whispered. "See you tomorrow."

In the room she crept quietly out of her clothes, tiptoeing about as though enemies might be listening. She went to bed at once. She slept, but some time later on she had a bad dream. A bright white light on white little houses, and the sea. Then night and flashings in the sky and a great circle of dark-garbed people on a shore. The circle broke apart, revealing a little pit of fire in the center. Its light flickered on the faces of the people, not happy, not sad, but intent, absorbed in the flames. Then the sound of music in the air, flutes, and tambourines, and something sadder. She saw an old man on the ground, playing a strange long coffin-shaped instrument. Why don't they dance? she thought. Then they did, but it wasn't what she had expected. These were only slow grave steps, lifting of solemn knees and arms, in a circle. She was dissatisfied. It is not right, she said. But to whom? It is right, the old man said. A woman beside him laughed. He frowned. Then nothing. Then a whirl of other faces in the high sad pleasure of sweet lust and the dance she had expected seemed to be beginning. Heads back now, eyes gleaming, the dark-garbed ones drew back and beckoned her to see. Beyond them she knew but could not yet see, beyond the widened circle they formed, young girls and young boys leapt, naked, garlanded, like goats they bounded she thought. Suddenly things changed. The dark-backed circle began to undulate. Something sinister was happening she was sure, something that threatened the dance. She was looking for someone, looking for someone. She was seized with panic. Oh no. She raced around the circle, trying to get through, they had closed ranks against her. Their power was greater than hers. And then she saw. Oh why? There were the lambs, all downy-white and with flowers twining their throats, and with great fearful innocence in their little eyes and great little bleatings coming from their mouths. Stillness for an

instant. Expectation. *Oh nooooooooooooooooooo*, a voice called
from somewhere. Hers? But her lips had not moved. *Noooooooooo*. Two women approached her. They spoke but she could
not understand. What were they saying? For her too? Absurd.
Obscene. False. Suddenly she had broken through. She was making
a speech—her arms raised to heaven—"Listen to me. Listen. Something's wrong. A mistake. These things don't happen now. People
don't do this sort of thing. If you think you're doing this for me
too, you're crazy. It's not what *I* want. Oh, don't you see, don't
you see, isn't it enough that we're all washed in the blood of the
womb?" And then the knife flashed, the eyes of the chosen one
started, the throat squeaked, the white down gleamed purple with
blood, and the sacrificial head fell forward.

She awoke then, slowly, uncertainly. The dream lay in fragments in her conscious mind. She forced herself to reassemble
them. She did not think she had ever had such a dream before. Her
mind sought out and found at once the multiple sources in the
events of the past few days. Her analytical powers strained like a
chained falcon—the very image crossed her mind—eager to seize
on and dismember the dream's meaning. But she held them back, as
though to prevent a profanation, and also because she already perfectly understood it. The dream, she knew, must simply be borne,
intact, whole, terrifying as it was, until it had sunk back into that
pool from whose mysterious depths it had been stirred. She hoped
it would have done so by morning.

Then she felt a second's amused relief and went into the bathroom. Perhaps her period had come and that was all. But it hadn't.
She took an aspirin and drank a glass of water. In the mirror she
surprised fear on her face. She had then the quickest, quickest perception of what it would be like to go mad; one could see too
much, be in touch with too much; one could be carried all too
easily into madness, not just despair or guilt, the familiar, lowburning diseases of the times, and not into the violence of those
crippled souls who struck out against their fellow men in a vain
attempt to murder the universe, but into that high holy madness
from which no return was ever possible. She shook her head, as
though to refuse it. A tune ran oddly through her head, a melody
of some sort, but she could not place it.

She was now extremely nervous. She looked around the room
for something to read, and realized bitterly that for the first time

in her life she had brought no books with her on a trip. In despera-
tion she picked up the telephone directory, went back to bed, and
for half an hour read through it. Every now and then the images
from the dream returned. She let them and because she did they
seemed to go away as rapidly as they had come. Occasionally she
recited aloud from the telephone directory, sometimes a whole
series of names, sometimes lighting here and there on an isolated
entry that caught her eye. *Alliata Topazia, Bigeschi della Sera
Constanza, Bigeschi della Sera Giovanni, Bigeschi della Sera Maria,
Biggi Enrico, Caliari Paola, Giandomenico Arturo, Fabbrini Bo-
cetti, Fabiani Elvira affittacamere, Fabiani professore Emilio, Filip-
peschi Palmira frutta e verdura, Filippi dottore Ilio studio com-
merciale, Filippi Marino, Filippi Pia, Filippone Vincenzo, Fillini
Ezio, Fillini Marcello, Finucci Oreste, Lancetti Giorgio, Mairani
Fausto, Maldini Sergio, Morosini Francesco, Robusti Jacopo, Sirani
Elisabetta . . .*

Towards dawn she fell asleep again, and then she had another
dream.

She was in a hotel lobby, perhaps in New York, certainly at least
in America. The lobby was crowded, swarming with people, as
though there were a convention of some sort going on. One little
group standing together were Hungarians. She knew this somehow. Then she heard a general babble of tongues. It seemed to be
an international gathering. There were so many tongues being
spoken that it sounded like the United Nations. It looked it too.
Everything was very formal. The lobby was quite dark, not entirely dark, but not well-lighted either. It was as though some odd
power failure had come over this fancy place, dimming everything. Something horrid happened then, or to her it seemed horrid,
grotesque beyond measure. A very very old man with an ancient
withered face and thin white hair hanging down like a woman's
and dressed in a bellboy's uniform passed through the lobby carrying an enormous bouquet, heavily scented, with white ribbons
streaming from it. "Flowers," he kept calling out, "flowers for the
widow of . . ." She could not catch the name; it seemed to her that
when he pronounced it the name was suddenly garbled, like a
child's double talk, or as though it were being put through a
scrambling machine. Yet she knew that the name was perfectly
clear to everyone else there, that it was only she who did not
understand it. Her sense of horror increased. "Flowers, flowers for

the widow of . . ." She remembered now that when she had entered this building the great flags hung outside had been at half-mast and that people on the streets had stood pointing at them. She became aware that many of the faces around her were contorted with pain, that people were weeping. Some of the little national groups stood huddled together, talking their strange tongues. Others trailed listlessly back and forth across the carpet. A far-off keening began, a wailing of women, somewhere, but she could not see them. She began to feel her own heart suffused with the pain of tears yet to be shed. "Flowers, flowers . . ." The old-man-bellboy was standing by her now; he looked at her, puzzled, then shook his head and passed on. Another man came up to her, an official of some sort, and stared at her with contempt. Who has died? she wanted to say to him, who is the man who has died? She felt she knew but did not know. He said to her, "The least people like you can do when a man like that dies is to ply your little trade of elegist." "But who has died?" she brought out at last. "Do these great events mean nothing to you?" he said, leaving her. "Who? Won't you please tell me who? Who's died? Who?" A group had gathered around her now and was staring at her in disbelief and with mild disapproval. She hurried across the lobby after the official. "Who's died?" Suddenly she said to him, "Bingham? Is he dead? Is it George Bingham?" The official looked at her coldly. "Bingham? Who's that? I never heard of him." And instead of relief at this answer an even greater feeling of helpless terror came over her, a deepening of pain. The voice began calling out again, the old man with the long hair passing along on the other side of the lobby ". . . flowers for the widow of . . ." and she felt that she had been on the edge of a pool of grief and that now she had slipped into its center and that it was rushing up on all sides and over her head . . .

This time she came out of the dream with a start and into absolute wakefulness, the dream perfectly clear and present in every detail. She was very cold and she sat up in bed shivering. What terrible thing had happened, or was going to? She was afraid. This dream seemed to her more a terrible prefiguration than some personal, eventually paraphrasable sum done by one's darker or more truthful self. She thought about Bingham, and shivered more violently; oh, he was involved, and all her old anxieties about him, but she could not center on him, could not be certain it was

he who was the lost protagonist. She became intent on limiting this
dream's meaning, as though if she could, something of terror might
also be contained. She thought of the revolution in Hungary, and
told herself yes, surely it was that, a foreshadowing in the sense of
the unconscious insisting on what the mind knew but would not
yet accept, that the uprising there would be put down, with force
and violence and in blood. This was enough, surely. And yet she
could not quite rid herself of the notion that she had brushed
against some awesome and tragic event that lay still further off in
the future, some other great loss, some fearful sacrifice to a thirsty
world, some high heroic and blameless life brought down. Whatever it was, when it came, if it did, she felt she would know it. She
went to the writing desk and with cold and trembling hands began
to write, for the first time in her life committing a dream to paper.
When she had finished she found the anguish aroused in her by the
dream unchanged. She paced the room. Then she added to the
piece of paper: *Death the Enemy, the fierce champion, riding large
in the land, the hewer-down of hearts, even the truest.*

The memory of both these dreams was to change subtly the day
that lay before her, though a long time would pass before she
understood this. It was a strange morning, a morning of waiting.
She walked to the Duomo, and this time when she saw it the
association that had flickered up the day before took hold; it was a
film she had seen about some poor Milanesi who swept the streets
in front of the cathedral for a living. Only the ending came back
to her, how when every hope was gone, some briefly won happiness snatched back, they were chased to the cathedral by the
wicked men who were about to seize them, and the good dead lady
who had found the young hero in a cabbage patch when he was an
infant had suddenly come sweeping down from the sky on a
broom and beckoned to them, and their brooms had become magical too and they sailed off into the sky with her, singing, and out
of reach at last of the wicked ones who stood huffing and puffing
below. No one else had liked the ending, she remembered, but she
had; she thought it had the bitter truth of all good fairy tales.

She looked up at the sky above the Duomo and had the quite
simple wish that some miracle would descend on her too, and on
George Bingham. It wouldn't, she knew, life and art being in this
respect so very different.

She walked on past stores and cafés, watching the people in them. She felt a slow deep affection for the ordinary carnal selfish man, the average sensual fellow, toting up his accounts, gathering his possessions as though they would last, having a bash at his wife on Saturday night. Perhaps after all the world could not bear too much consciousness. She thought back on Kilchberg; it seemed to her that all of them there, in one way or another, if not by choice then by chance, if not for a lifetime then for a while, had been taken out of the animal cycle of things and were engaged in some nameless striving, some attempt to live beyond the law and yet to keep the law. *Pneumatikos.* Perhaps it could not be done. Or perhaps the price was inconceivably more than one knew. You could not expect very many to want to pay it.

At noon she went to the terrace restaurant at the top of the hotel to wait for Bingham. She ordered an aperitif and drank it slowly. But he was very late, and she had nearly finished her second Cynar before he appeared. On his face was an expression she had seen only once before, the night they had left Kilchberg. He said, "Let's go down to your room," and took her arm.

When the door was closed behind them, he said, "Something's come up. I'm going to be tied up for a few days, maybe as long as a week. You go on. Take the flight on Sunday. The hotel reservations are all made."

"And you?"

"I told you. Something's come up. Something I've got to handle. People's lives are involved." The familiar, faintly film-strip quality their relationship always had at such times asserted itself. This did not make it less real. The photographs taken of real people racing across the squares in Budapest had that same quality; they had looked like an Eisenstein film, ironically enough. Nature had many ways of imitating art, which was not surprising. He had walked over to the bouquet of flowers and now he did something that seemed to her out of character and very strange. He broke off one of the flowers from its stem, looked at it as though he had never seen a flower before, sniffed it and twirled it in the fingers of his right hand. It was clear he did not know he was doing this. "A car's picking me up here."

"When?"

"In a few minutes."

"They knew where you were then, all along?"

"They'd have to. Pulling out's not as easy as turning in a time card."

"Yes. I'd wondered about that."

"I'll meet you in Greece," he said with false cheerfulness, unable to look at her eyes, this for the first time.

She said, "I don't want to go to Athens alone. Why should I? Sit there, of all places? Waiting? Perch myself in the shadow of the Acropolis like a statue?" None of this said in anger or reproach.

"Go to Delphi then. Wait for me there."

But she shook her head firmly at him. She said, "You knew about this yesterday."

"Yes. I had an idea."

"So your being through with all that lasted . . . two days No, a few hours really. Have they listened to you?"

"No, they haven't," he said. "This is something special. Something I worked up. Most of the details are in my head. Nowhere else. With what's going on now . . . it might be a good idea to drop the whole thing. For now. No one can decide that but me, it seems."

"Then it's a question of honor?" she said.

"You could put it that way."

She laughed, not unkindly, but as though it were hard for her to take this very seriously. "Then you must go." She did not understand him at all.

There was no battle of wills. He felt this and seemed almost disappointed.

"You've changed," he said.

"How? I'm always changing, and I'm always the same. Besides, I've never been so stupid as to think that your choice was between me and your occupation. Would you rather I had been? I don't think so. Your choice would be the same if I had never existed. I think you are incapable of giving up this . . . this life you like . . . of giving it up. I think you care only to be alone. Except at odd moments. And to feel power. My pride isn't offended. But I don't feel I have the slightest obligation toward you from now on."

"I never wanted you to feel that."

"But I did. That was part of my nature. And you knew it . . . and liked it. As recently as last night. Feelings make for obligations, the only kind that count really. Or at least they do for most people. I betrayed some in coming here, you know."

"Are you saying you don't want me to go when that car comes?"

"No. What would that be for either of us? We'd both be so miserable. Consider these last two days." She hesitated. "I'm saying I think that I do want you to go." She knew that later this would be the part she might not forgive herself for.

"No matter where you run to I'll find you," he said.

"Perhaps. But I'm not running. Not again. At least I hope not to."

"Don't marry Ernest Campion," he said suddenly.

"What's that got to do with it? Why should he want to marry me?" she asked, angry for the first time. "After what's happened."

"I would," he said.

"Hadn't you better pack? Or something?"

"My suitcase is already in the lobby." There was a pause. "Then London? Meet me in London. You don't know everything. London." He hesitated again. "This is my last mission," and the words startled them both somehow. He had never said that before, never in fact made the slightest appeal to her at such moments in the past. It came over her then how great his struggle had been in the last few days, whatever its terms, or however little they seemed possible ones to her, how great perhaps his struggle still was and how dangerous for him if this were so. But, oh, what was she to do? She shook her head again.

"Have you got enough money?" he asked.

She nodded. "Too much," she said. "And all the pretty clothes. The fruits of being a kept woman."

"A *what?*" He was furious.

"A joke," she said.

"A bad one."

"Yes. I'm not good at jokes. Never was." She was almost crying.

"London," he said. A command.

She shook her head. "No."

"Where are you going then?"

"Next? To Zürich I think. I left some things there."

"I'll have a ticket for Zürich sent to the desk in your name. Do you want to go today?"

"Yes."

"Does Zürich mean you're turning your back on me?"

"No. That's the one thing I could never do, will never do. How could I turn my back on you? It would be like turning my back on a part of my self. But we won't meet again, I think."

"Old Druidical," he said lamely, but could not go on. A heavy silence came between them.

"No, no intuitions, none at all. That's not what I meant. That's over with."

"It's still a great way to send a guy off."

"I'm not sending you off. But since you're going, I wish you'd hurry. Please."

He shrugged but seemed reluctant to go. Then he moved toward the door and she walked with him. There he turned. Their bodies closed. To her surprise she knew in that moment that she could hold him if she chose to. She had never thought that he of all men could be held in that way. Her heart beat wildly as they stood so, with fear for him, with love, with indecision, all mixed in that sudden perception. But it was impossible. It was not right; it would never do. One did not take such liberties with another. And she did not want all that it would mean, either. She gave herself instead to that moment's embrace, to that kiss, that good-bye. Other arms? Perhaps yes, but not his, not again. He drew back at last. "You're dangerous," he said, meaning it lightly, but for just a second a look of real hatred had crossed his face, as though she were his enemy, some alien force, not alien at all of course, but something to which a side of his own nature now belatedly, dangerously, responded, and had therefore to be put down, to be denied.

She had felt the change in him when his body moved away from her. But now, suddenly, he changed again, and she saw him as he had been that night at Kilchberg, all his beauty, all his strength, and it seemed to her unbearable, not that she should lose him, but that he should be lost.

He was standing out in the empty hallway now, had turned back and was looking at her. He still had the sprig of flowers in his hand. She wished she could remember what kind of flower it was. She knew and did not know. He evidently had forgotten he still had it. Now he remembered. "Do you want this?" he asked.

She shook her head and he tossed it onto a hall table. "I wish you'd go," she said.

"You don't know everything," he said. "You just think you do. We'll meet again."

He would of course have to think that. He reached out and touched one of her breasts. "Good-bye," she said. "Good luck. Be careful. Good-bye."

"*Ciao,*" he answered instead.

She watched him go down the corridor, a fine figure of a man, an incongruous figure among the bric-a-brac that was spaced along the otherwise empty passage. Then before he reached the end she closed the door.

Forty-one

Ernest Campion searched his mind angrily for words that might best describe the role he felt had been thrust upon him in the past few days. All this conveying of people back and forth to the airport. He peered down into the glass enclosure. He had stood in this same accursed building saying good-bye to Elsie only a few hours before, and then when he got back to Kilchberg he had found the telegram from Sylvia—sent to Mrs. Dartley, cool, non-committal, formal, the words of a guest who, arriving too early or too late, through no fault of her own, fears she may be inconveniencing her hostess. And arriving from where, exactly? The telegram had given nothing but the time. He had barely managed to get back to the airport by nine. The only plane scheduled to arrive at that hour, posted as being a little late, was due in from Cairo, Athens, Rome, Milan, which told him nothing. He noted that she had been gone almost exactly forty-six hours. It might as well have been an eternity. Then the words came to him: *Hermes Psychopompos.* That was what he felt like. It was a recognition that brought pain, that stirred up a great uneasiness in him; it did seem to him that some absolute gulf lay between Sylvia's departure and her return. And then, on the other side of the glass wall through which he had had his last glimpses of Lily Halász and of Elsie, he saw her, Sylvia Grierson, below.

He walked quickly around to the *Ausgang* doors, then took a step back and watched her, keeping a deliberate distance. She moved through the line, claiming her suitcase, intent, unaware of being watched, and then began to walk slowly up the ramp, her

every motion, her castdown eyes, clearly indicating that she had
not expected to be met. At last she looked up, and saw him and
stood perfectly still. The distance closed; he moved towards her.
She seemed very changed to him at that moment. There were
dark, bruiselike shadows around her eyes, which had gone a sort of
flat marble gray. Hers were changeable eyes, but he had never seen
them like this before. Usually a light and golden brown, they
sometimes suddenly became almost green, as though she were looking out at him from the other side of a great wave. Taking her
suitcase, walking beside her, he wondered if they would ever look
that way again. They talked only in the conventions. But when he
put her in the car a slightly defiant look crossed her face, and when
they had gone a mile or so in silence she said, "Don't you want to
know anything?"

"Not yet. I don't think so. Yes, perhaps there is one thing.
Where has he gone?"

"Off to be killed."

"What do you mean?"

"Eventually."

"Have you left him?"

"Yes. He has left me."

"You're not making any sense."

"It's very simple. He has left me. I have left him. We have left
each other. There's been a sundering."

"How final?"

"I'm very tired," was her only answer.

He reached out and took her hand. It was cold and lay inertly in
his grip.

When they reached the Münster Brücke they had to stop. A
torchlight procession was winding its way down from in front of
the main portals of the Grossmünster, Zwingli's church. FREEDOM
FOR HUNGARY, most of the placards said. Sylvia and Ernest sat in
the car while the faces bobbed and floated past them, young intent
faces mostly. They were all chanting something. The only word
they could get was *Freiheit*. Suddenly in front of them they saw
Posy and Marshall's faces, flickering under the light, in and out of
the darkness, their mouths opening and closing . . . *Freiheit* . . .
Freiheit. Sylvia began to weep. "What is it? What is it?" he asked.
"Never mind. I can't explain. Let me alone." She wept more violently, and then she flung herself on him. As they kissed, the salt of
her tears ran into both of their mouths.

Halfway to Kilchberg she said, "I can't talk to Gwendolyn tonight. Will you tell her for me? Explain?"

When they got to the villa he carried her suitcase to her room, which had been made ready for her. She looked as though she would topple. Then she suddenly began to chatter and, darting about the room from suitcase to armoire, to throw off her clothes. When he, half amused, half frightened at this wild mood that had come upon her, turned slightly away, she laughed at him. He had "seen her nakedness" before, she reminded him; he had spied on her by the pool. "Besides, it's only a body, isn't it?" she said, and laughed again, harshly, bitterly self-mocking. He stood watching, filled with anxiety for her. Naked, she flung things out of her suitcase. "I can't find my nightgown," she complained childishly, and threw more clothing about. "I'll have to wear briefs."

"Shameless," he ventured, and laughed in spite of himself. She laughed too, again at herself, but not so harshly as before. Then she stood there clad only in a little pair of pants, her arms crossed, with sudden irrational modesty, over her breasts. She was visibly shivering. When he moved towards her she said "*No*" sharply. Her eyes kept closing heavily; each time she opened them with effort, as though she were forcing herself to try to think of something. Then, her arms still crossed over her breasts, she ran around the room again. This time she found a dirty-looking white pullover of some sort—it looked like a sweat shirt to him—and pulled it over her head. He laughed again. Without a word she got into bed and closed her eyes. "Good night, I gather," he said. She did not respond. He walked to the bed and bent over her. "O thou that sleepst like pig in straw, thou Lady dear arise," he murmured, wondering from what curious source those words had come. At any rate, he had the satisfaction of hearing her go out to sleep on a small current of giggles.

Forty-two

For nearly a week Posy and Marshall had been living in two quite different but mysteriously compatible realms of experience, both equally intense. Their passionate identification with the young people who in their eyes were making the revolution in Hungary

—an identification which had apparently culminated in the march
from the Grossmünster to the Soviet Consulate—had not in the
least prevented them from pursuing passions of a more private sort.
Every day they went to the gardener's cottage, there to turn to
each other in the ecstatic embraces of first love, parting at last and
reluctantly so that Marshall might work on his music and she
might attempt, still another time, to sort through all her brass-
rubbings with the idea of "readying them for the market"—such
was her phrase for it. At some point an hour or two would also go
into Marshall's teaching her how to read music. For the rest they
scrounged Mrs. Dartley's discarded newspapers, listened to the
radio, joined the circle around the television set, and managed in
one fashion or another to get into the city, where with other
young people they sat eagerly about in cafés talking about the
revolution or milled around in front of consulates looking for
some way to express themselves. They had reached a number of
conclusions about their own futures, and it needed only the arrival
of two cablegrams from America the morning after Sylvia's return
to Kilchberg to make it seem absolutely necessary to settle on
some definite plan.

The first of these cablegrams was addressed to Posy and had
caused a small scandal in the village telegraph office, for it was the
longest one that had ever been received there. It was from her
mother and it read:

Darling, do you think you should come home? Or would you
like to stay on? You must decide for yourself. Switzerland is
probably safer than New York. Why haven't you drawn on
your allowance? Very perplexed. Or have I used it again without realizing it? It would be nice to have my baby home again.
I go to Florida with the Hargates in three weeks. Please tell
Gwendolyn Dartley how grateful I am to her for looking after
you. You never said how you met her. Did someone give you a
letter to her? I can't think how else you met. One of our nice
young senators told me at a party in Washington last week what
a fine person she is and how much he wants her in America.
That part wasn't awfully clear. It is certainly a small world
and now we all have to face that fact, and certainly the brave
Hungarians will teach us all something. There is great excitement here, as you may imagine. I had lunch at the U.N. only

yesterday. Do you remember that nice young Israeli, the one you talked French with so beautifully at the going-away party I gave for you? He invited me, and we had a wonderful conversation about you and your problems. He thinks maybe you would enjoy working in Israel on a Kibbitzing, if you haven't made up your mind yet what to do. Would you? I don't want to influence you, and Israel I suppose is even farther away, and quite hot in summers. You must decide for yourself of course. I miss my baby girl. Love and kisses, Mummy.

Posy was used to such messages from her mother, who could hardly ever bring herself to write a letter but who was nevertheless unable to accept the conventional limitations of the telegrams on which she amost exclusively relied whenever telephoning was impossible. Or rather the night letters, as she was always at pains to point out, lest she be suspected of being extravagant. Marshall, however, thought he had never heard such nonsense in his life, and he felt a great resentment on Posy's behalf. "Does she always go around talking about you with strangers?"

"Of course not," Posy said quickly. "Not with everyone. Mostly with young men in their twenties. It gives her a lot to say to them. And then it always makes them realize how hard it is to believe that she has a daughter my age. People are always telling her that anyway."

"Good for them," he said. He looked at the telegram again, slammed it down onto a table, and began to pace. "Problems. What does she mean, your *problems?*" he asked.

Posy ignored this. "It really is hard to believe. When you meet her you'll understand. And you won't be mean to her either. Nobody can be. It isn't just that she *looks* so young . . ."

He interrupted. "You'd think you were a toy from the sound of that." He gestured toward the cablegram, then, turning, saw how deeply she had colored, and hated himself for having hurt her. They moved together, looked quickly around, and exchanged a quick kiss.

Posy said, "I don't mind. Not now. I really don't. It's just her way." It was a plea that he always be kind about her silly mother, and tactful. He understood it as such. He thought of the iron-willed woman who was his own mother, of her habit of talking so authoritatively about things she knew absolutely nothing about, and in spite of everything that was weighing on his mind he smiled, wondering, if their two mothers were ever to meet, if Posy's would not in some odd way be a match for his own.

The second cablegram that had arrived that morning had been for him. It read: "COME HOME AT ONCE. MOM AND DAD." He had been expecting something like that and was almost relieved that it had come. Having not the slightest intention of showing this message to anyone, least of all to Posy, he had immediately torn it into small bits and flushed it down a toilet. A money order for a very odd sum was also included, and this of course he did not destroy. A quick phone call to an airline office confirmed his suspicion: the odd sum would cover the price of a one-way ticket from Zürich to home, plus $20. This touch was so like his parents that a most unexpected affection for them began welling up in him, along with the sense of outrage. He could almost hear them discussing it; it had probably taken them a day to decide that $20, not $25 and not $15, was the "right amount" for him to have in his pocket on his way back to the safety of America.

Now he said to Posy, "I'm talking to Mrs. Dartley today."

"Today? Even if she goes on staying upstairs?"

He nodded, and continued to pace. He was a provincial only in the sense that he lacked direct experience of the great world; he knew music and he knew his own mind, and having decided what his next steps in life should be he wanted to take them under the best circumstances possible. He had already spoken to Anton Hrubick, who, however, had told him that Mrs. Dartley was the person to talk to. He would have done so before now if she had not been so inaccessible.

He said, "What's to prevent me from simply knocking on her door and asking if I can speak with her?" He did not really relish doing this; on the other hand, he felt an almost blissful sort of confidence in the outcome, even if it did mean barging into her lair.

"Well, nothing, I suppose."

"And I'll talk to her about your situation too?"

"All right."

They were both looking out toward the terrace and were therefore in a perfect position to observe Gwendolyn Dartley, who at that moment appeared in the pith helmet, her hands full of a disorderly pile of newspaper cuttings. She hesitated, stooped and placed the cuttings on the terrace, clumsily arranged one of the long lawn chairs for herself, got into it, and then, instead of picking up the cuttings, sighed, weighted them down with the helmet, brushed a hand across her forehead, leaned back and appeared to go to sleep.

"Now?" Posy asked, half a dare, half a statement of disbelief.

"Now."

"Then I'm leaving," she said, and fled to her room.

Forty-three

Hope had stuck in Mrs. Dartley like a burr in a dog's paw—the more she tried to shake it out the more firmly it dug in. It was a small, precise, and constant pain; it made her even more irritable and difficult than usual and gave her an excuse for isolating herself from the rest of the household. Only at certain times of the day did she come down, seating herself before the television set, straight-backed, grim, uncommunicative except for a remark or two to Knox, who presided over the instrument in a proprietary way and in general behaved as though he thought the entire purpose of the uprising in Hungary was to increase his prestige as a "television person." On the 24th of October Mrs. Dartley had said something nice to him about " the medium," about how possibly it might after all, if used properly, become a force for moral good. Her remarks thereafter, however, were rather different in tone. "What would happen if the machinery one day broke down and we all went back to being little dots and blurs?" Or, "One man's magic is another man's science, and vice versa." Or, "What do you suppose would happen, Benjamin, if those of us sitting in this room stopped believing in your magical box? Would it stop working? Of course I know this is nonsense; these light waves, these patterns of form, are real phenomena, none the less so for being most of the time invisible to the ordinary eye. For that matter, what would happen if we stopped believing in ourselves, I wonder, in the reality of our own existence? Would we then cease to exist, or would our reality continue so long as some extraordinary eye remained upon us? But without that eye . . . ? Perhaps we too are only lines

and shadows, tricks in the air. Or," she added, for this was a
particularly long comment, delivered to mask the impatience she
felt at the difficulty Knox was having in getting a clear picture,
"blurred nothingness struggling to be purposeful."

Knox seldom attempted more than a friendly mutter in response
to these remarks, but to Ernest Campion at least there seemed to be
all sorts of disturbing connections between them and the scenes of
chaos that would then unfold: photographs or an occasional quick
film strip of the city of Budapest undergoing another dark night of
the soul, and even, in another way, between them and the tapings
of that large number of extremely well-cared-for-looking men
who bustled importantly about at the United Nations in New
York.

For the rest, Mrs. Dartley was silent, and the moment she was satisfied that nothing new would be coming over the set would return
to her room. There she kept a passionate vigil, listening to the
radio, cutting things out of those newspapers and magazines which
now streamed more copiously than even into the house, scrawling
off letters, and devouring huge meals sent up to her on trays, for
she was one whose appetite was whetted rather than dulled by
great tension. Every now and then she would call Ernest to her
and ask his opinion about something. Otherwise she was alone.

It had long seemed monstrous to Mrs. Dartley that after the
years of Nazi power there should have come for so many millions
from the Baltic to the Danube not respite and the longed-for freedom but terror and tyranny under another name. She was far too
sophisticated to think one could center the blame for this, and she
felt nothing but contempt for those who sought to make political
profit from so great a disaster. She still quite firmly believed in the
need for a democratic socialism in those countries which had not
yet freed themselves from a degrading, pre-capitalistic feudalism.
But what had been happening under the military occupation of the
Soviet Union had nothing to do with this or with the things in
which Dragan had believed. To her the stories of murder and
imprisonment, intimidation and exploitation and general intellectual enslavement which continually reached her from across the
Iron Curtain were a nightmarish reliving of the past, of what had
happened to Europe under the Third Reich, and for that matter of
what had been going on in the Soviet Union ever since the found-
ing in 1921 of Homogor, the first of the many death camps in the

East. Only now, men and women of supposedly liberal intelligence turned their eyes away, content with praising themselves for having opposed the Nazis.

It wasn't that Mrs. Dartley expected these people to do anything, really—she knew in fact that at the moment there was nothing of a responsible nature which they could do—but she did expect them to be less hypocritical than they were and, yes, she did, somehow, expect them to *care*. *She* cared. She had cared about the starving Armenians and, retrospectively, the starving Irish, about the Jews and about the Japanese-Americans, cared about German orphans and Greek orphans, about the Poles and the Balts and the Algerians and the Negroes, about whatever outrage might come to her attention—cared on a profligate scale and in a way that was easy to make fun of, the more so since she combined this caring with a certain blunt awareness of how little one could really expect in the way of justice, with a certain strange reasonableness before facts. Needless to say, no groups welcomed her, liberal or conservative; she was too critical, too apt to see how easily causes, even the best of them, developed into drives for power or interest, too apt to put into words what she saw. She fought therefore alone, and from a distance, and it was of no great consequence perhaps to anyone that she fought at all.

For several years now she had been fighting most vociferously against what she called "the dual heresy": that is, the official Anglo-American-German attempt to establish everything "Eastern" in Europe as bad, alien, and threatening, and the official Russian attempt to establish the same set of associations for everything that could be labeled "Western." To her these political manipulations of the truth represented the breaking of a dialogue of such importance to the life and culture of Europe that it overshadowed many of the other matters to which she also gave her attention. She lamented particularly the cutting off from the West of Poland and Hungary, countries which in spite of their position in the middle and the suffering so frequently inflicted upon them from both sides had managed to maintain their individuality and were each in a different way a reminder of how difficult it is to say what is "Eastern" and what is "Western" in the culture of modern Europe.

She knew of course that her peculiar concern with the fate of Hungary had its roots in personal as well as historical matters, in

the many happy visits she had paid to Budapest with Claude
Simon, and later in her brief but memorable contact with that
small group of dedicated people who had been Dragan's friends.
And behind this, she knew too, lay simply her love of Danube
culture, even its aspects which were "decadent" and were hence so
great a foil to the puritan element in her own character. Love of
place was, after all, like love of person; no reasons could quite
explain it. Still, it had always seemed to her a miracle that so small
a population as the Hungarians, speaking a language unrelated to
any of those in Europe, had managed to keep itself and its language
alive. Like the Jews, Hungarians had a talent for survival and a
way of producing in response to constant threat an extraordinary
number of capable individuals, though of course they were lighter
of heart than the Jews, being free of the burden of believing
themselves especially chosen and preferring insight to ethics, the
love of life to the love of law. Mrs. Dartley had not always *approved* of Hungarians (it had always astounded her that Lily
Halász remained so blissfully unaware of some things that were
going on under her nose, in her own family in fact) but she had
never failed to *enjoy* them, and she had often found much to
admire.

Ever since the Polish uprising in Poznan in June Mrs. Dartley
had been waiting for "something to happen in Hungary" and had
been certain that it would. Yet when the great events in Warsaw
in October had provided the trigger force, when the news had at
last come, when she saw the form it had taken, the October 23rd
protest in Budapest turning spontaneously into the reality of revolution, she had been caught off guard, shaken and uncertain. What,
after all, could one hope might come of this heroic attempt but a
good deal of dying? She had thought back often to that question
Ernest had put to her in September, almost as though she bore
some responsibility for what was happening. She had taken refuge
finally in what she had told Sylvia Grierson that first morning, and
she had gone on clinging to the idea that the eloquence of symbolic gestures might in the long run, like faith, move monoliths.
But when she contemplated the price in human suffering she could
hardly bear it.

By late morning of October 28th, however, Mrs. Dartley had
decided that it was time for her to descend and pick up the normal
life of the household. She considered the immediate fate of Hun-

gary to depend now upon that aspect of political action which is seldom discussed because it is so unnerving to admit that it is there, the psychological. Rulers of nations were as subject to control by the unknown and unrecognized in themselves as anyone, even those who had striven to rule out personal error and replace it with error of another kind. And nations, like individuals, often followed invisible precedents. In Hungary what had begun as an attempt to ameliorate a particularly brutal totalitarian regime had turned swiftly into a bid for complete freedom and national independence. For the moment the impossible seemed to have happened: the country was effectively liberated. It was even possible to think that the revolution might succeed—this was the burrlike hope. But the question was—what precedent would the Russians follow? It was perfectly obvious that the Soviet Union could, if it chose, bring into play at any moment a kind of force against which no one could stand for long. It would not be a simple decision for them, if they did this, or even an agreeable one, Mrs. Dartley was sure; as Gomulka himself had said, it was "politically naïve" to call these events the work of imperialist agents.

As for the West, she had waited in vain for diplomatic action, even for *words* from Washington, but it did not really surprise her that the great pseudo-preachers should fall so silent in a crisis. There was nothing to do now but wait; she was a bystander, as helpless as anyone; it was time to accept that fact, time definitely to pull herself together, to consider the influence she was having on others. What Ernest had told her about Posy and Marshall taking part in the march to the Soviet Consulate had vaguely disturbed her. Perhaps they were too caught up by all this. If so, her own behavior was at fault. One had certain obligations when one invited young people to one's house. It was time indeed to descend. Besides, it was a beautiful clear sunny day—the sort of day on which it is impossible to believe, in spite of experience, that anything bad could ever happen. The news from Hungary continued to be good, and Sylvia Grierson had come back, a fact that had a great if irrational importance to Mrs. Dartley. All things considered, she could not have been in a more receptive mood when Marshall approached her on the terrace.

"Do you think the world could use another flute player?" he asked her.

She sat up at once, swung her legs around and faced him. "Why

not? Why not?" she said, and beamed upon him. She had a secret
passion for doing things for people, but it was a passion she indulged only with discretion, having learned long before that the
line between helping and meddling was a very tricky one. Besides,
if one so seldom knew what was best for one's self, how could one
possibly think one knew what was best for someone else? What
she felt now was gratitude; Marshall was presenting her with one
of those few legitimate moments when she could act on behalf of
another. She did not flatter herself that he would not do just as
well in the long run without her, but she might, as it were, be
permitted to speed him on his way. She listened carefully now as
he talked. She felt for the young that respect which is only possible to a woman who has never brought up children of her own.
When the appropriate point came she said, "Oddly enough, I've
done a little research into the matter. The best flutist playing at the
moment is a young Frenchman. I don't know him personally, and I
am told he does not yet take pupils. Perhaps, later on, something
informal might be arranged."

To her delight he picked this up much as she had hoped he
would. Frowning, he said, "You see, it isn't technique I need
really. By my age you've got your technique; it's basic and it
doesn't change much. I don't need to study the flute as an instrument." He paused, then added, "Of course it would be fine to play
with this Frenchman some time. But technique's not what I need
now."

"No? And what is it that you need now?"

"I need to play with other first-rate musicians. I've never done
that. Mr. Hrubick—I've discussed this with him—agrees. And
repertory. My repertory's much too small. Every time Mrs. Halász
mentioned something I didn't know I felt like an impostor."

"I wonder," Mrs. Dartley said, as though the idea had just come
to her, "I wonder if you have ever thought of the Mozarteum."

"That's just the kind of thing I have been thinking of."

"Ah well," she said, "now we have a beginning."

Mrs. Dartley was happy. Like everyone else, she enjoyed having
her judgment of people borne out. From the moment she had first
seen Marshall, standing in the rain outside the concert hall in Zürich looking at posters, she had thought him a young man of quality, despite the somewhat raggle-taggle appearance he had acquired
from several months in the Greek islands. She had never regretted

thrusting at him that extra ticket she had chanced to find herself with. When he finally got back to his music after he came to Kilchberg, she had found ways of sneaking about and listening, and had decided that he had what could only be called a gift. Other opinions, Anton's, later Lily's, had confirmed this. The only question in her mind was whether he was sufficiently immodest to pursue this gift, and now she had her answer. "And what," she said, "what if you were lucky enough to get a chance to play for, let us say, Pflaumgartner, the head of the Mozarteum? Are you ready to do that? Today is Sunday. If they are willing to listen to you and name a day next week, are you prepared?"

"I certainly am."

"Good." In her heart she hated the fact that the world moved by influence, that it seemed incapable of working any other way; she had resolved that at the least she would never use her own influence except where she felt it might be justified by true merit. "You couldn't expect to start work there before January. You know that?" He did. "And suppose you were to get a scholarship, which is not impossible, so that you did not have to pay fees and would have just a bit left over, perhaps for your rent but hardly enough I think for food, how would you live? Have you thought of that?"

"I've had a sort of windfall."

"Ah you have have you? What sort? Has the munificent Sears family decided suddenly to become a patron of the arts?"

"It will carry me a few months anyway," he said evasively.

"Yes but this money—after all, Marshall, we are talking about something very important, money, a sacred trust. One must not take it lightly. At bottom almost no one does, and people use it for holds. This windfall? Surely their purpose was not to keep you in luxury while you play the flute in Austria?"

Marshall spoke. "They've ordered me home and sent some money. I'm not going, but I am going to use the money. If they want it back some day—and they probably will; my parents are the sort who loan their children money and charge interest, that's what they did to my brother, for a cause they approved of, of course—if they want it back I'll pay them. Naturally I'm going to write and tell them what I've done. In the meantime I can't worry about it. I've worked part-time since I was twelve—for money I mean. I was *taught my responsibilities*. Just like him."

Mrs. Dartley knew who "him" was, but she thought she detected the first signs of reconciliation; Marshall sounded more
amused than angry. "When I finished high school I wanted them
to send me to a conservatory. Would they? No. Mother hinted
that if it had been *piano*, which was what she had started me on . . .
Anyway, I lived at home my three years in college, and the thousand dollars I came to Europe on I earned making musical sounds
on the keys of a cash register in a supermarket. Of course that
threw them too." He smiled indulgently. "I should have banked it
forever, not squandered it on *travel*. Travel's like music; you can't
hang on to it. I think that's how they feel about it. They always
wanted to teach me the value of a dollar and to be independent—
that meant money—and I feel kind of sorry for them. They think
they're failures."

"Perhaps they did teach you the value of a dollar, though not in
the way they had expected. Perhaps they were good teachers
without knowing it. Or perhaps it is pure luck. You certainly *are*
independent. Of course what most parents mean by that is that the
offspring is doing what they want him to without being forced to
and without asking any help from them. Strange, isn't it? You're a
little different, Marshall. I wonder if it is the gift of superior
hearing that accounts for this—the same thing, in short, that makes
you a musician. And so you are going to steal their money?"

"Yes."

"Good. All I wanted to say was that I'll give you some money if
you need it. Give, not loan. I like corrupting the young."

He thanked her but said he did not think he would need it.
Anton had told him he should be picking up some small fees before
long. "And if I can go on freeloading on you till the first of the
year . . ."

Then, very casually, he told her that he and Posy were engaged.
With equal casualness she congratulated him. The news filled her
with joy, however; it seemed to confirm how good the day was.
"But what is all this worry about money then?" she said. "Posy is a
very rich little girl."

He said, "She isn't really. Not just now. When she's twenty-five
she comes into a trust fund from her father." His tone made it
clear that an event five years in the future was much too far off to
have the slightest reality for either of them. "Her mother doesn't
seem to have much of a head for figures. She's been a little careless,

and it involves Posy's allowance in some way that I don't understand. It could be straightened out, but Posy doesn't want to
bother. I think she's right. As a matter of fact, what she has in
mind is selling her brass-rubbings and living off the proceeds until
we get married." He sounded suddenly very doubtful. "I don't
know whether that's very practical or not. What do you think?"

"I think not. Besides, I should imagine Posy would hate parting
with her brass-rubbings just yet."

He nodded. "We were wondering . . . if you had any ideas for a
job for her."

"Perhaps I do. Or perhaps I can come up with some. Shall I talk
to her? Now? Before I start tracking Pflaumgartner down in
Salzburg?"

She was on her feet and extremely eager to go into action.
When they had agreed on a point or two, she left him on the
terrace and went to Posy's room. There she found her sitting
amidst her brass-rubbings, a disturbing sight at first; it looked as
though people had been blown about by some giant wind and now
lay in disorder waiting for someone to set them up and put them
together again. Soon Mrs. Dartley was saying, "Good; then since
you have no stupid prejudice against working with your hands and
since we can assume you have some dexterity, that suggests all
sorts of possibilities. But first we must decide where. I doubt that
the economy of Austria will yet bear giving jobs to foreigners,
except in music, of course. But there is Munich. How about
Munich? It's only a short train ride from Salzburg, which is of the
first importance for you, naturally. And it is an excellent city for
the moment. They are out of the cellars and not yet behind the
wheels of their Mercedes. It is a city that loves art and artists and
artisans too and it is just a little provincial, a most unusual and
happy combination. One must keep changing cities, alas. Berlin
was a great place to be in the twenties even with inflation and the
Nazis and Communists shooting at each other and causing so much
trouble for everyone. And Paris was still possible until quite recently. And New York, well, it has been impossible and possible
again so often that I can no longer remember which it is at the
moment . . ."

Posy listened patiently. She had not seen Mrs. Dartley in such
high spirits in a long time. Everything was going to be all right
now.

Forty-four

Campion had waited until nearly noon to go to Sylvia, but when he got to her room he found that instead of sleeping late, as he had assumed she would do, she had been up and working at her desk for several hours. He was both disappointed and pleased: disappointed because he had been looking forward to waking her, pleased because she had made so startling a recovery. What a strange woman she was, really, he thought. Her face, though still a little pale, was composed, the bruised look was gone, and her eyes had the old dark-bright glow. It was clear to him that it all had something to do with her work, which she now laid aside, saying, "What good timing," and got to her feet. "And if it had been bad timing?" he asked. Both laughed, a little uneasily. And if, when she moved into his arms, he felt a reservation in her, a faint but quite perceptible holding back, a something not quite conceded or perhaps not quite confided, he resolved for the moment not to ask what it might mean. It would be unthinkable to press her so soon after the journey she had just made. They made plans for the afternoon, the evening. She wanted to go into Zürich. Could they go to the zoo, or feed gulls perhaps? She sought, he knew, a connection to the past. How lucky they were to have such fine weather, she said. And where should they eat? "Under the speared hearts, perhaps?" returning briefly to the self-mocking tone of the night before. He knew what she meant: the arching gothic roof of the Zum Rüden, with its carved design which did oddly resemble nothing so much as long arrows piercing heart after heart. "No," he said, "no. Not tonight."

By the time they came downstairs Mrs. Dartley had set everything into almost intimidating order for Marshall and Posy. Pflaumgartner, interrupted at his lunch in Salzburg (after skirmishes with operators and then his wife), had first said to Mrs. Dartley, "There is a revolution in Hungary and you want me to bother my head with an American flute player?" whereupon she had put a hand over the phone and said to Marshall, "Splendid. He's in a good mood." The conversation that then ensued had sounded to Marshall more like a fight than anything else—"*Wir schimpfen einander immer,*" Mrs. Dartley remarked, as though by way of explanation —but in the end everything had been arranged. Pflaumgartner

would hear him on the following Wednesday, October 31st. Then
the whole process of struggling with operators and getting lines
through began all over again. Posy and Marshall, watching, thought
that Mrs. Dartley seemed actually to be enjoying herself. She was.
She knew very well that she was flinging herself so ardently into
their projects in part to relieve the tension she felt about Hungary,
to compensate for her helplessness. Yet at the same time what
really could be more important, she asked herself, than helping
two youngsters who were beginning a journey? How right and
natural it was to be doing this. At last the arrangements for Posy
were made too. In Munich she would visit the atelier of a stage
designer and the workshops of several craftsmen, among them a
couple who specialized in repairing baroque angels that had been
damaged in the bombings.

Mrs. Dartley was alone on the terrace drinking a celebratory
glass of sherry when Sylvia and Campion appeared. It was the first
time she had seen Sylvia since her return. She went forward and
embraced her, an unusual gesture for her. Despite her passionate
nature, she was only verbally demonstrative in public, an inherit-
ance from her northeast background that had been enforced by
her years in England. "Welcome," she said, "welcome." And then,
stepping back, "You don't look greatly the worse for wear. Fortunately, since in a sense you are the mother of us all."

"The *what?*" But Sylvia laughed; Mrs. Dartley's tone was so
gay, so light, she could not take offense.

"Only a metaphor, only a metaphor. Here," she said, handing
around glasses of sherry, in her own mind switching more than a
metaphor and thinking that probably only Sylvia Grierson could go
off with one man and return with another and still somehow manage to look virginal. She began to tell them about Marshall's plans.

Sylvia said, "I suppose his parents will be quite annoyed." All of
them at Kilchberg knew a good deal by now about Marshall's
struggles with his family. Sylvia envied Marshall his not having to
bring these people into his music.

Then Mrs. Dartley told them how she had found Posy. "There
she was, surrounded by that paper graveyard of hers. So very
touching, her brass-rubbings. With anyone else it would be
morbid; with Posy it is something quite different. But there's no
more sherry. Of this sort, I mean," she said, "I can only stand the
very dry, the Pepe. Ernest, would you?"

He knew she wanted to get rid of him. "Hurry," he said. "It will only take me a couple of minutes."

When he was gone Gwendolyn Dartley said, "You haven't heard anything special, have you? About the Hungarian situation?"

Sylvia shook her head. "No. Nothing."

Both women leaned back in the sun. Sylvia said, "I'm a little surprised about Posy. Somehow I've never thought of her as a career woman. I've always thought she'd be a decorative young matron before too long. One of the nice ones. With a taste for being honest, and a lot of feeling. A Jane Austen girl," she added.

"Oh I don't think Posy's going to have a career. This is just something to keep her busy and happy until she has children to take care of."

"That's what I meant."

"Of course," Mrs. Dartley said, rather as though she thought Sylvia thought her stupid. "What do you think the brass-rubbings are all about?"

Sylvia did not answer. She closed her eyes. She could feel Mrs. Dartley staring at her. Perhaps if she offered her a tidbit it would distract her. She was thinking about Marshall's family; she had long ago guessed that the real and manipulatory power there was his mother. It usually was these days. "*Mal de mère*," she murmured. "Marshall seems out of danger now."

Mrs. Dartley, delighted, caught her meaning at once. "That is a very serious sickness, I do agree. It has so many forms. In my day it was tyrannical controlling men; the disease was *mal de père*."

"Yes, that's what caused *mal de mère*, I imagine. It's really the same disease in another phase. Controlling, tyrannical women operate more subtly."

"And what do you think is the cure?"

"I really don't know. Not, certainly, going back to something that didn't work before. Even the boy-fathers, the playmate-companions, are better than that."

"Oh my dear, you make me realize how behind the times I am. What do you mean, the boy-fathers?"

If she went on talking Mrs. Dartley might be kept from asking personal questions until Ernest returned. "Fathers who aren't fathers but only pals. Pals with special privileges."

"And the women?"

"Matriarchs, as I've said. Terrible."

"What is to be done?"

Sylvia opened her eyes and sat up. "I suppose the only hope is a dual monarchy."

"What a wonderful phrase. You have returned to us full of wonderful phrases."

"This one isn't mine."

"Oh?"

"No. I read it in a letter I opened this morning."

At that moment Campion returned to them, bearing the Pepe. He filled their glasses. Posy and Marshall appeared at the far end of the lawn. When they saw Sylvia they waved. Mrs. Dartley suddenly got to her feet and, leaning over the railing, called out to them, "I've got another brilliant idea." All laughed, Sylvia and Campion on the terrace, the youngsters coming across the lawn. It referred to one of Mrs. Dartley's favorite stories, about the college dean with whom she had served on an international committee after the war and who had begun most of his statements with that phrase. When Posy and Marshall were a bit closer, she said, "Take the car, Marshall, take the car. Would you like to?"

"Take the car?"

"Yes, why not? It needs a good run on a highway. It's not good for a car to be used as little as the Phantom is. And it will be more fun for you both than taking the train. Enjoy yourselves. Why not? Make a picnic of the trip. If we need a car we'll requisition Mr. Knox's. Yes, take the Phantom, but be sure not to let Pflaumgartner see you in it."

"The Phantom, the Rolls, the Phantom?" he said, a young male old enough to be in love and want to marry, young enough to give a great leap in the air. He grabbed Posy's hands now and danced around with her on the lawn.

Ernest Campion had stepped down off the terrace and was walking toward them, waving a key ring. Mrs. Dartley said to Sylvia, "I haven't told you. Posy and Marshall are going to be married. I believe some time next summer is the plan for the moment. They are quite resolved. And you, are you going to marry Ernest?"

"That," she replied, "is not quite definite yet."

Then she stood up. "This weather is so beautiful," she said. "I think I'll go for a quick swim."

Forty-five

Lily Halász, balancing carefully on her high heels, rode the swaying elevator cage to the top of the Russell Square tube station. Although only five days had passed since her arrival in London she had already established a quite firm routine, one which she was determined to cling to on any day when the weather permitted. In the mornings, shortly after her great-niece Margó left for work (Lily feigned sleep until then), she ate a large breakfast, put on her one good dark suit, and left the apartment as rapidly as possible. With its drab damp walls, its indescribably bad furniture, it depressed her very much. In fact she hated Margó's apartment and could not yet face the prospect of a winter confined to those rooms. And the neighborhood, those rows of identical houses, divided into cramped little flats inside, the nervous gentility of the inhabitants, the perplexing and dull uniformity of their clothes and the expressions on their faces. It was, as Margó had several times said, "a respectable neighborhood." Perhaps that was what was wrong with it—and with Margó too—it lacked color, it lacked life.

Happily, all of London was not so depressing, and Lily had on the whole found it far more agreeable than she had expected to. It seemed to her somehow changed from the last time she had been there, in 1936, less insular, less cold and overbearing, more mixed perhaps, as though the war had left it, whether anyone had wanted this or not, open to new and quite unpredictable influences. One even saw in many of the ordinary little shops foods that had never been available before, and she enjoyed just being able to look at them. No, London was not unsympathetic to her, except for neighborhoods like the one Margó lived in. And except too, alas, for Margó herself.

Lily was particularly grateful for the London parks, and on her second day there, which was the day that Stalin's statue was pulled down in Pest, she had set out to make a survey of them. She was a good walker, better than most her age, she knew, even though not perhaps ideally steady, and she had covered a great deal of ground. But London was a huge city, and for the longer jumps she had allowed herself to take taxis, though later on, she had reminded herself, there would certainly not be enough money for such lux-

uries. (How humiliating that discussion with Margó about money
had been, Margó speaking of "the small weekly allowance" as
though she Lily were a child. Margó of course had *meant well*, but
like most people of whom that could be said she had committed
one atrocity after another.) St. James, Regents, Hyde Park, all the
great and famous places, Lily had done them all—in a way it had
been quite an exhausting tour, she had felt that in the evening, and
she did not really know why she had felt compelled to rush around
London in that way. But then there was so much that she did not
understand now—why, for example, she had even come to London
in the first place.

It was really by accident on that great day of touring (perhaps
that was what, unknowingly, she had hoped would result from it?)
that she had found, on her way home, the Russell Square area. She
had known at once that she would make this her premise. It was
not only that she preferred the small and modest squarelike parks
in this area to those that were vaster and more elegant, it was that
the whole atmosphere made her feel more at home. One heard
other tongues than English, saw other faces and other kinds of
clothing and ways of walking. And there were a great many young
people about. (There was a university nearby, Margó had told her
somewhat sniffily; she did not seem to think highly of Lily's taste
in neighborhoods and had muttered something about it having
once had a Bohemian reputation and now being just plain seedy.)
And there was of course, as Lily had discovered, that great
museum, which she looked forward to visiting often in the coming winter, and then too it was nice that one could buy all sorts of
foreign-language newspapers so easily; there was a shop on nearly
every corner.

On the whole, Lily was satisfied at the ease and speed with
which she had established a semi-independent life of her own. The
dressing up, the trip on the underground, the buying of newspapers and sitting in the parks, later in the day taking a coffee in an
espresso bar where a few of the young people sometimes reminded
her of Posy and Marshall—all of this seemed to provide her with
an indispensable purpose for her days. There were other reasons
too, naturally, for her having so determinedly sought some clear
form for her new life, something that would carry her safely
along, for she felt altogether too much had been happening to her,
and too fast: the move to London itself, the almost overwhelming

appearance in Zürich of Iza Kronfeld—or Elsie Crown as she was now called. And then the news coming from her own country, from Hungary. About the latter she felt she was holding her breath; she did not dare to think too much about what was going on now in Budapest, or to hope too much. Whenever Margó in her unfortunate emotional way went on about it she was very short with her, which afterwards she very much regretted of course. In time, she knew, there would be changes and she would want to find friends; it should not be difficult, there must be other Hungarians in London, people she could speak her own tongue with, play bridge with. But for the present, at least until things were decided, she did not want company, did not want a social life; she would wait through these days alone.

Coming out of the underground she went first to a nearby bookshop and bought two newspapers, one a London paper and the other a Hungarian-language daily. She folded them both quickly together and put them under her arm without even glancing at them. This action had become part of a ritual. Then she stood hesitantly for a moment on the sidewalk. Bedford Square, or Russell? Which should it be this morning? She decided on the latter. When she got there she hesitated again. But since it was difficult for her to get in and out of the long canvas lawn chairs, she went instead to one of the wooden benches, and sitting down arranged the newspapers under her purse beside her. She turned her face to the dim English sun, for a long time thinking of nothing, dozing almost. Then the attendant came around, and this aroused her. Paying him reminded her of one of the two letters that had come that morning, the one from an English bank. It informed her that an account had been opened in her name and stated the amount which she could draw each month. It was Gwendolyn's doing, of course. Not only that, it was a sum which, Lily had recognized at once, would even permit her to live adequately on her own should the arrangement with Margó prove utterly impossible. How like Gwendolyn that was: not just making a gift, but making a gift that was adequate to the end it presumed to serve.

Lily considered again that out of all her old friends in so many parts of the world, almost all of whom had repeatedly been guests of herself and Senator Halász in Budapest, only Gwendolyn had remembered her existence in recent years. Whatever faults Gwendolyn had, lack of generosity was not among them, nor lack of

loyalty. What a dazzler she had been when she first began coming
to Budapest with Claude-Simon to visit his daughter and that silly
little nobleman the girl had married. Half of the town had been in
love with Gwendolyn. The other half had despised her of course.
Later on, in the thirties, she had gotten so serious about politics.
And always so outspoken, which was a little awkward if you tried
to give a dinner party for her. Lily hadn't a scruple about accepting Gwendolyn's gift—at her age she certainly hoped she knew
the difference between pride and false pride—though for as long as
she stayed on with Margó she intended to draw on it only for
pocket money, concert tickets, once in a while perhaps an opera.
As for whether she could go on living with Margó or not she
would wait and see. She was realist enough to know that at her
point in life even Margó might turn out to be better than no
company at all . . . But oh, how ill-suited they were to one another.
Even being able to use Hungarian turned out not to make up for
that. And what was the good of talking Hungarian or anything
else if one did not have anything to talk about? Margó knew
nothing about music, about literature, about *people* even, and it
was quite hopeless trying to explain things to her. If only her niece
would realize in her turn how different their interests were and
not go on and on trying to explain to her about colloidal mole-
cules, reagents, tintilations, or titrations, or whatever those things
were that she did every day. How unspeakably boring Lily found
it, especially since Margó lacked completely the power to communicate the things about her work that probably *were* interesting. How could she possibly have known Margó would be like
this? She had only seen her a few times when she was a child, a
young girl. Her parents had been such gay, charming people. And
how *fussy* Margó was! What a great to-do she made about little
things. Fifteen minutes to decide what to have for supper! Half an
hour's discussion over what a laundry had done to a blouse! A
pity. And deeper things than these . . . Here Lily tried without
success to think no further . . . If only people would not go around
confessing things. Such bad taste, such a . . . a spiritual imposi-
tion.

Now, in spite of herself, Lily realized how much anger she had
been suppressing ever since Margó's confession. If people must
confess let them do it to a priest, or directly to God if they
preferred. But let them not, please, not pass their burdens on to

people who were having a difficult enough time bearing their own. All her pleas in those letters that she should come and live with her ... that had only been Margó's way of making herself feel better about what she had done. She had taken advantage of Lily's own confusions at that particular moment. What a childish, immature woman she was. Had she no idea of the pain it would cause her, Lily, opening up subjects that were better left alone? Confession! Bah! She remembered Margó's face, her stupid, rabbitlike face, blubbering with tears that very first night, the stammerings, the wringing of hands. For it was she who had given the name of Lily's son to the authorities as a possible contact in Budapest. A very nice young man from the government had called upon her, had asked her to help; she had felt it her duty. Well, perhaps she had felt that; people had odd ideas of duty, especially when it came to others; or perhaps, as Lily suspected, softening a little now, Margó had simply been afraid, suffering from the refugee's insecurity, and had felt she dared not refuse to make a suggestion. The latter was at least something Lily could understand, in a weak-spirited girl like Margó, even if she couldn't admire it. *But why had she had to tell her?* That was what she could not forgive—that and the effort it had cost Lily to get her at last to drop the whole subject.

She took a deep breath now and felt a bit better. One thing the stupid confession had confirmed: she hadn't been mistaken about Mr. George Bingham, or whatever it was he had called himself in Budapest. He had looked somewhat different of course, had spoken a perfect Viennese, and had come, supposedly about trade, with a letter from people in Vienna with whom her son had done business before the war. But it was he. And it wasn't long after his visit that her son had been arrested, that they had all ... Well, there was no helping it now. And it might have happened anyway. It had happened for no reason at all to dozens and dozens of people she knew. Still, someone walked into your life, and without asking your permission ... She had a moment's pang about Sylvia; she could not imagine a tie between her and a man who ... however attractive he was ... she must know, or guess, a girl as alert as that. Could Sylvia herself not be what she seemed? No. Lily Halász rejected the idea. There could be all sorts of complicated reasons, not necessarily to her discredit, for the involvement. His arrival at Kilchberg had certainly been unexpected, and not, she had sensed,

entirely welcome. Lily had the definite impression that it was
Ernest Campion who laid claim, not without response, to Sylvia's
affections. And a far more suitable match it would be, too. She
suddenly remembered something Gwendolyn had said once of
Sylvia: "She was not meant to fust unused." Lily remembered it
very exactly because Anton Hrubick had, as usual, made a fresh
remark which was meant to be funny and Gwendolyn had put him
down sharply and then explained her meaning most particularly.
(But really Gwendolyn ought to be more discreet in what she said;
her remark *had* sounded very odd, and all this talking in quotations
that she so often indulged herself in had its drawbacks, and so did
her bluntness; she had always had the habit of saying strange, blunt
things, and now it was growing on her; she should not let it; one's
quirks became worse with age; as one got older one had to
watch.)

In any event, Lily felt that Sylvia could be counted on. Somehow. She was a girl who in spite of always appearing to be teetering on the edge of disaster of one mysterious sort or another never
quite went over that edge. Not that she hadn't suffered a great deal
in her young life; it was clear that she had, and Lily took it as
perfectly natural that an artist should suffer. But despite her being
so driven, so touchy, so vulnerable, so—Lily struggled and came
up then with a word she had often heard used at Kilchberg by the
Americans—so *neurotic*—in spite of all this Sylvia had a great
inner strength, more perhaps than she knew, and almost a fanatic's
obsession with truth. She would be all right.

Lily chuckled. It was reassuring to think of the confusions
which life itself breeds going on and on and on. To judge by what
she had seen at the airport, when she had been able to think back
on it later, past her own emotions, Ernest Campion was, or at least
must once have been, on close terms of some sort with Iza! How
she should love to know that story, and how amusing things must
be just now at Kilchberg. This last thought cheered her up considerably.

She opened her purse now and took out the long letter that had
arrived from Iza—well, perhaps it was better now to think of her
by her new name—from Elsie that morning. She read it again,
with deliberate slowness, lingering over the phrasings, it was all so
impetuous and bold, like Elsie herself, yet also such excellent Hungarian, such a contrast to Margó's clumsy bumblings. America?

Perhaps. Who knew? But no, it had no reality for Lily. Besides, though it was kind, it would not do. What great nonsense for a young woman to think of burdening herself with an old person. An old person who wasn't even related to her! She would bring Elsie to her senses. It was nice, though, a sign of the—Lily had almost thought love—a sign of the quite unnecessary gratitude Elsie evidently felt towards her. And she was coming to London in such a short time now. At the thought of that meeting with Elsie Lily felt a little clutch of fear, of anxiety, but it was followed quickly by a sense of pleasure. No, no worry. It would be a good thing to see her again, whatever pain might also be involved.

She put the letter away and laid her hands on the folded newspapers, waited a moment, not quite admitting to herself how strongly the superstition of following exactly the same procedure with the newspapers had taken hold of her. As though not deviating from the ritual could possibly alter anything. She shook her head. And yet, since the day when she had first stopped in this park, she had not been able to break from it. On that day, having seen and bought but not looked at the newspapers, having come to the park and taken from her purse the list of concerts she had compiled the night before (after Margó's confession), having decided which concerts she could manage and which not—opera at the time seeming to lie beyond the resources of her purse, a fact to which she reconciled herself with some difficulty—having done all this, she had then opened one of the papers and read that Stalin's statue had been pulled down, that the revolution was a real one, that the news, in short, was almost miraculously good.

Now she picked up the English paper. As she did so she heard a newshawker shouting something in the distance. She listened. But it was something about Israel. What were the Israelis up to? Never mind. Briskly she unfolded the newspaper, her eyes flickering over the front page, which was covered with news from Hungary. In a second she knew that things were still going well. Then her eye fell on one caption in particular. "Ha!" she said aloud. What was this? PRAVDA REPROVED. A long quotation from the official Communist Party paper in Budapest, *Szabad Nep*, followed. Her eyes raced along . . . *not the work of underground forces or foreign agents . . . Pravda has reported falsely the efforts of the Hungarian people to . . . freedom . . . independence . . . Hungarian workers . . . the Hungarian people as a whole.* Quickly Lily folded the paper together again, her cheeks burning. If even *Szabad Nep* said that, printed that, then, then . . . For the first time Lily Halász allowed herself to hope. It set her heart to pounding, this hope; it rolled towards her like a great and almost overpowering wave of feeling. She rose suddenly to her feet, as though to meet it better, and then she felt it break upon her, and with only the smallest of cries she fell forward into the blackness that had swept in between her and the grass.

Forty-six

Emergency victims were handled in routine ways in the big general hospital to which Lily had been conveyed, and while the atmosphere was cold and impersonal and therefore frightening to those who awoke there, the system itself was quite efficient. Coronary patients, for example, were taken to resuscitation rooms equipped with the most modern of devices, there labored over, and sometimes brought back to life. The doctors and nurses who worked with Lily had even, for a minute or two, been quite pleased as well as surprised when she began to respond. The prognosis was not, however, a particularly bright one, and during the second twenty-four hours of her hospitalization—by which time her mind at least was functioning as well as ever—she was quite sharp enough to sense this. Those who attended her went through the motions with complete correctness, and they gave her what bodily comfort they could, but they did not, she gathered, really expect her to recover, and they were not especially interested in whether she did or not.

During the first night after her attack Lily had had an extraordinary number of dreams—or visions perhaps, since they by no means seemed all to be occurring while she slept—whether stimulated by the drugs they had given her or whether nearness to death itself had acted as some sort of stimulant to the roots of memory and desire would be difficult to say. A few of these she remembered quite clearly.

"Why, what ever are you laughing at, Missus?" a fat female face had asked, leaning over her.

"I'm laughing at myself for having forgotten the last lines of
Dove Sono. What else is there to do but laugh? Mozart would
never forgive me." This she had said quite firmly and then had
laughed again, for no sooner had she spoken than she realized how
ridiculous it must have sounded.

"Well now, don't worry about it. Do just be a bit still now. You
sounded as though you were humming something before."

Lily, quite awake by then, was aware of being rolled along on a
hospital cart. She looked at those great long empty corridors that
seemed to stretch out in every direction around her. They were
not reassuring and she decided to close her eyes again.

"That's a dear," the voice continued. "Not the best time to
move you, the middle of the night. But that's the way things are
now. Space shortages, you know. Now then, we're almost to your
new room."

With her eyes closed Lily found herself recalling the dream
quite easily, catching in fact a few images of it, as though a reel of
film were spinning uninterruptedly along but the light that il-
lumined it was only being switched on for a second or two and
then off again. Anyway, it was a very satisfying dream on the
whole, and amusing. She suppressed another chuckle. There she
had been (whether it had looked exactly like her or not wasn't the
point; it was she) drifting down a staircase, looking quite tall, in a
white gown and singing the Countess' aria. Appreciative faces
peered up at her from behind what appeared to be the footlights.
All was white, silver, silks, a rippling in candlelight. But then she
had forgotten the lines. How silly of her. But what was so strange
was that she hadn't felt the least embarrassed. She had simply
decided to start all over again. Oh it was good to be able to remember something upon awaking, however foolish it was. It made
her feel that things were more . . . *in order*. When she had come to
in the emergency room there had seemed to be nothing to connect
the self that was lying there with the self that had existed before;
between then and the park lay only absolute blackness. The rolling
table was slowing down now, turning. Perhaps it was only that she
hadn't been able to remember. They were bumping through a
doorway. She felt very tired again, and before they reached her
bed she was asleep.

For the remaining hours of that, the first, night, she had continued upon awaking, as she frequently did, to experience a num-

ber of strange sensations. It was as though illness, disease, had touched her at the very source of life, and brought with it a final, ironic quickening. There were memories of her mother, and most astonishing of all was one awakening to such a sense of bodily relief, such joyous unburdening as can only come after pain and meaningful labor, that for a few seconds she expected to hear cries and see Dr. Láng turn and place in her arms her first-born, her son. And whose moustaches brushed her face then? Her father's, or was it Senator Halász's? It was after this that she had fallen into an easier, a more tranquil sleep.

Later she remembered too—and this was amusing, this part she would tell, she decided, if she were ever to have the right audience —all the *pastry eating*, the recurrent scene, the taking of her favorite table at Gerbeaud's, and having set before her the *Dobos* and the *Indianer* and the extra portion of *Schlag*, a cold winter's afternoon, she knew, for that was when she had most liked to visit Gerbeaud's. For some time the memory of this dream cheered her, and she tried to make a little joke of it, deciding that her *O Patria Mia* would at least in part be a song of chocolate and coffee and whipped cream.

By noon of the second day, however, all of this was past, and Lily was faced with the minute-by-minute apprehensiveness of the sick or the dying, and by the loneliness, a loneliness made worse by being in a foreign land. She lay in a room with ten beds, each filled with a woman who like herself was suffering from some form of bodily betrayal. No one spoke much, and the women next to her did not speak at all. Nurses came and went with chilling briskness. During the afternoon Margó had been allowed in to see her, but fortunately only for a few minutes. Her trembling, rabbitlike mouth, her shaking hands and voice—all of this was unpleasant. And she had looked at Lily as though this illness were something that threatened her, Margó. When she left, Lily had the first of the great depressions. It was too much, Margó, her visit, too much; she ought not to have had to bear that too. It was then that her violet eyes brimmed with tears, then that she almost gave in and allowed herself to think of all those whom she wished she could see again, wished could be beside her, her lost family, or Iza, or anyone from Kilchberg, Gwendolyn, Sylvia especially, but anyone, even Anton Hrubick. But she did not quite let herself think any of this, only almost, for she knew that if she did, even once directly, it would be too much for her. It was like the thought, "Yes, I am about to die." This had been necessary, but only once, and then, once thought directly, it was better put aside, better expressed thereafter in indirect ways, like the answer to the question of whether she would rather die just now or not. So it was that after Margó left, instead of giving way, she allowed herself to think only of how unfair it was that her visitor had not at the least been someone beautiful, someone she might have enjoyed looking at for a minute or two.

By evening she felt herself caught by two alternating forces: an almost unbearable restlessness and a suffocating weariness. She did not complain; indeed, she tried to hide this struggle. But her condition did not go unnoticed. A young resident appeared, one she did not remember having seen before. He examined her briefly, then spoke to the nurse in tones that she could not hear. Some change was to be made in her medication, she was sure, although nothing was said to her about it. Night came and the lights were lowered. She slept and woke, woke and slept, no longer able to tell very easily which state was which since they blended disturbingly into each other. Then she was wide awake again, watching someone disappear out the door, someone finishing one of the hourly rounds no doubt. She could not sleep again. Her time sense was disturbed. She was sure that morning ought to have come. She concentrated on the window at the foot of her bed. She would watch there for the first signs of light. Lines of poetry and libretti sometimes ran swiftly through her head and then were gone, along with a great tumble of music, to which she kept time, beating her feet together under the sheet. Earlier in the day, before one of the nurses had scolded her and told her that it wasn't good for her, was against the rules, she had copied down on a piece of paper a few lines of poetry. It had annoyed her that she couldn't remember who the author was. It still annoyed her. She wanted to ask someone who had written it. But who? Margó? She snorted. How odd the room was. All those strangers lying around her, so still, so resigned, not like her, foolishly awake, wasting her strength, waiting for the morning. She stared at the window. Still no sign. Did they expect her to go on waiting forever?

Nurse Beardsley came into the room, neither kind nor unkind, a woman doing her job, but bustling, hearty, the best way, she had found, of waking up the sick. She began every morning duty tour the same way, chose one person in each ward to say something to in a loud voice and then got things underway. This morning she had chosen the little foreign woman; her bed was near the door and she had just been reading her report.

"Well, well, now how are we coming along this morning, Mrs. Halász?" letting the peculiar name trail off into an indefinite slur, not even looking at her but clomping to the window and with a bang and a clash pulling up the blinds on a gray and dirty day. Then she turned back to the room, hesitated for a second, frowned, and with an instinct developed from years of experience, walked purposefully toward the bed. She saw at once that the woman named Lily Halász had died. There was no need even to try the pulse. But it was routine. She pulled one of the hands from under the covers and laid her fingers on the wrist. Then she put the hand back under the covers. She would have to go for a screen; yes, and take care of a hundred other things too. She looked down at the bedside table. It was rather untidy: a pencil, a purse half open with things sprawling out of it, and scraps of paper, evidently torn from an envelope. She picked one of them up. It had something written on it. Nurse Beardsley could not make it out. It was in a foreign language; it looked as though it might even be *French*. She stared at the words written there, as uncomprehending as if she had held in her hands one of the tablets at Knossos.

> *De ta tige détachée*
> *Pauvre feuille désechée*
> *Ou vas tu?*

Nurse Beardsley put it down, looked at her watch. If she didn't hurry the schedule would be completely off, and there was no time to waste as it was. There would be a lot of extra work now and the other patients would be difficult too—they always were when there was a death. She would put these slips of paper with the patient's other belongings. There weren't very many, for that matter. The poor old lady.

Forty-seven

The day of All Hallows Eve proved to be appropriately phantas-magorical at Kilchberg. Sylvia felt she had nothing in focus and greatly resented the way everyone and everything had again sud-denly given in to disorder, to a kind of celebration of chaos. A radio was always blaring away somewhere in the house, as though to remind them that they were not really cut off from the violent world itself; at the same time the weather made it seem that they were. That was what was so odd. Knox, for example, had been stuck with them since the afternoon of the day before. If one stepped outside the house that white cold mist seemed about to swallow one up. Whenever Sylvia peered out a window distant figures seemed to rush forward and then, with equal rapidity, to recede to small pinpoints of unreality, and then simply to vanish.

Mrs. Dartley had ceased the stormy speech-making which she had been totally unable to control the day before. From the moment she heard the news of the Israeli invasion of Egypt she had kept up a barrage of talk, some of it wild, emotional, full of a strange bitterness, a sort of disillusionment, some of it showing a really astounding grasp of the ways of political power—she pre-dicted almost exactly how Moscow would react, even what words they would use, what steps they would take, an hour before it came over the radio; what legalistic positions would be adopted by America and Israel and England. But none of this talk helped any-thing, Sylvia felt, except possibly Mrs. Dartley herself. She was glad that Posy and Marshall, who had left for Salzburg in the Phantom, cheered by all, on the 29th, had been spared this. One after the other Mrs. Dartley had cornered the rest of them, all day long and late into the night of the 30th. "England!" She would repeat, "France!" as though the very names were curse words. "Will they never learn?" And of the Israelis, "*Arrivistes! Ar-rivistes!*" as though that word were an obscenity. She had sent off telegrams of protest to Washington, London, Tel Aviv, Paris, and to the United Nations in New York. It was not until the morning of the 31st, in fact, that she had regained her composure, and though she still listened avidly to the radio every hour or so and insisted that it be left on she did not speak much of what was happening. She seemed somehow a little different. Her usual emphatic gestures were subdued; her remarkable, faintly Edwardian posture was gone. She slouched about like an adolescent and, when she sat, slumped backward onto her spine. She wore rumpled and dusty old clothes and no lipstick. She seemed tired, worn out, but she also seemed vaguely to be looking to be entertained. At one point she had come downstairs with the cat on her shoulder and had then wadded up a piece of cellophane from a package of cigarettes and tried to get the cat to play a game with her in the front hallway, though it had ended with the cat watching her knock the cellophane ball from one end of the hallway to the other until she got winded.

Altogether, Mrs. Dartley was almost too much for Sylvia, who had been sent into a most extreme depression by the news of the further convulsions in the world, and who also had very great worries of her own. The little euphoric lull she had experienced her first day or two back at Kilchberg was over with. She was still not free to give Ernest Campion the answer she knew he sought. On the contrary, she was if anything on ever falser terms with him as each day passed, but she could not bring herself to tell him why, and she did not know what to do. She tried to keep a distance from him, using whatever natural ways of doing this she could find, but not too great a distance. He sensed all this, she was sure, and she was grateful that he had not yet begun to press her.

Gwendolyn Dartley had indeed worn herself out the day before, and now had accepted, though with great inner bitterness, what she saw to be the inevitable direction of things. It was plain to her that there had been collusion—England and France had intended to have their way with Suez, and Israel had welcomed the chance to gain some territory. It was all a humiliating anachronism. It would not work, of course. What it would do would be to deflect from Hungary the attention of the United States, for whom the Middle East was of far more strategic and military importance at the moment than middle Europe; it was certain too to make it far easier for the Soviet Union to move. Imre Nagy had just announced an end to the one-party system in Hungary, had promised free elections, and had at last appointed non-Communists to cabinet posts, among them Anna Kéthley. This was the news Mrs. Dartley had been waiting for, had expected, longed for, and also dreaded. Communism had simply collapsed in Hungary; it was at stake now, and with it Soviet power and prestige, in all of middle Europe; she did not find it possible to believe that Moscow would not act, and she could not yet quite bring herself to face what would happen then. She distracted herself therefore with small comforts, among them the fact that in England at least there had been in the last twenty-four hours a great and general outcry against the government. (There had been none in France, and she had not expected there to be.) It would be amusing too, in a gallows-humor sort of way, to watch an American government which had pledged as part of its political platform to help "liberate the satellite nations" go on trying to sidestep the Hungarian question in the United Nations until after the presidential election while leading a censure motion against her own NATO allies and Israel. Almost as amusing as listening to the Soviet Union denounce the imperialist invaders of Egypt (whom she had secretly been arming for months), while Russian troops put down the entire Hungarian nation. There were many times when Mrs. Dartley considered that the Soviet Union and America deserved each other. But in her heart she could find nothing in the situation that was amusing; she could think only of the strange agony of the Hungarian people. She could only regret deeply that America would not speak with the voice of authority while there was still time to be persuasive, and that Britain, involved as she was in a grave offense of her own, could not.

Benjamin Knox was the only person at Kilchberg who appeared to be happy. The day before, he had come streaking into the house exactly as he had the day the revolution began in Hungary: he had just heard the news about Suez, *Whooopee, wouldn't Israel show those Arabs,* he had to get hot on the wire right away. But this time he had not persisted so long in his attempts to get New York or London, and he had even seemed rather hangdog about it afterwards. Later he had sent Bledder back into Zürich in the car, to see if there were any messages for him at the hotel. And then the fog, or whatever it was, had come rolling in and Bledder had phoned to say he didn't think it was safe to drive. Perforce, Knox had been invited to stay on. Now that Elsie Crown was gone that old feeling of liking, irrationally and in spite of rebuffs, to stay at Kilchberg had come back to him. He made himself useful in a number of ways, helped Giovanni take wood around to the various fireplaces, and was even asked to Mrs. Dartley's room to give an opinion on two conflicting news reports. For once his presence seemed to be accepted as entirely natural. He welcomed the bad weather and secretly hoped it might last a long time.

Sylvia thought the weather the strangest she had ever experienced. There had been no rain, no snow, no visible precipitation of any sort. And yet when they got up that morning the trees had taken on a unique and miraculous splendor; their bare branches had flowered into a light and delicate, feathery leafing, as though they were a week or so gone into spring. Only instead of the pale yellowgreens of spring here was a white of almost absolute intensity. And instead of real leaves a frozen crystalline substance which, though it imitated nature so faithfully, suggested too— upon closer observation—a structure both more abstract and more ideally ordered. It was certainly unlike the ice she remembered from New England winters, that glittering transparent phenomenon which sometimes cracked limbs with its weight. Nor was it snow. When she asked Celeste she was told that usually it happened only in midwinter. There was a word for it too, which Celeste used, but Sylvia did not recognize it. A local word for local magic, she assumed. In any case, it was clearly the result of that great mist which had suddenly descended on them from the higher and infinitely colder reaches of the nearby mountains. It seemed mysterious to Sylvia that a mist could be cold enough to do that to trees and yet still remain a mist.

By midmorning the trees were no longer visible from the house. Nor was anything else. When one looked out a window one saw precisely . . . nothing, as though the whole house were adrift in some new and uncertain element. It was a little intimidating. Stubbornly Sylvia decided to go for a walk. Once out in that fog or mist it would not seem so absolute; one could surely see enough at least to make one's way along the pebble paths of the rose garden. But when she actually was outdoors and had walked briskly along in what she hoped was the right direction for perhaps a minute she was forced to admit that there simply was no visibility at all. She stopped. It was like being blind, really. It was most unpleasant. Going much more slowly and cautiously, she stepped on through the nothingness. She had not gone far, however, when she realized that she was probably traveling in a circle—only she wasn't at all certain that it was a circle that had the house at its center.

And suppose it didn't? What could she do about it? She had no idea of where she was; the villa could be ten yards away or ten light years. What difference did it make? She stood absolutely still, at first afraid amidst all that swirling emptiness and then giving in and simply letting it come at her and wrap around her.

She saw, or thought she saw, a garden bench a few feet from her. Perhaps it was an illusion, or perhaps the mist really had cleared for a second. She concentrated on moving slowly in that direction, her hands groping in front of her, her feet suddenly moving over pebbles. Then she touched the bench, and sat down—why she did not know. She shivered, but felt so incredibly tired that she decided to wait a minute or two before setting out for what she hoped would be the house. Of all the idiotic things she had ever done, certainly sitting on a bench in a garden in the midst of a bitterly cold fog would rank high among them. In the end she had to make a great effort and force herself to get up and, following the pebbles under her feet, move along the path. Suddenly she heard a sound in front of her; as though someone were coming toward her. It caught her off guard and for an instant frightened her unreasonably. Yet it was a fear that had also in it a strange thrill that was nearly pleasure. She waited, listened, but now could hear nothing. She started on. *Wie ein leichtes Blatt im Winde,* she thought. And then again she sensed someone coming toward her, and again stopped, and again there was nothing. But a few steps more and she and Ernest Campion met face on.

She felt a flicker of anger at having been frightened. "Oh, it's you," she said. "What are you doing out here?"

He took her arm and they walked on through the mist. "What are *you* doing out here? I'm looking for you."

"Oh."

"Well what *were* you doing?" he asked.

"I haven't a clue. Don't know. Just wanted to get outdoors."

They walked on in silence. After not many yards they came to the house. There was even a small glimmer of light coming from a window and the faint sound of music. "Were you lost?" he asked.

"I'll never know now."

"I'm trying to make some plans," he said. "Can't we talk?"

"Now?"

"Why not?"

"This evening, could we make it this evening?" she countered.

He shook his head. "You are interested, I mean just faintly

interested, in talking about the future?" he asked.

She nodded.

"All right; this evening," he agreed, and held the door open for her.

Anton was playing the piano. Sylvia and Ernest found Mrs. Dartley and Knox leaning on it as though they were a pair of nightclub entertainers. The music was *Nymphs and Shepherds Come Away*, and Anton had just begun to take it through a number of modulations. Ernest and Sylvia sat down to listen. It was quite a performance. It had been country English when they came in, moving towards Haydn or Mozart—at any rate to the music of the eighteenth century—and after lingering there for a long time it went to Beethoven, to Brahms, to Schubert, to a sort of mock Wagner (now that Elsie was gone Anton was free to hate Wagner again), and then to a blues version, and a tango, and finally into a twelve-tone rendition. Anton's expression was particularly impish during the last, and only when Mrs. Dartley complained did he return to one chorus more of the original version. Which perhaps was a mistake, for when he had stood up and accepted their admiring compliments Mrs. Dartley was suddenly inspired to verse.

"Jews and Arabs, come away,/Live to die another day," she sang out. "Why that's very good, don't you think?" she asked. "Anton, once more, please." He played the relevant bars of the Purcell while she half sang, half talked her own words to them.

Sylvia and Ernest looked at each other and were moving towards the door when Mrs. Dartley stopped them. They had been afraid of that—it was to be another Poetry-Writing Game. "A splendid way to pass an hour or two," she was saying. "We're shut up here anyway. There's nothing else to do, is there? It will be a good way of keeping away from the radio." They knew it would be wasted effort to protest; she had set her mind on it.

Usually when this particular game was forced upon them she pretended she was trying to test some sort of ballad theory, which Sylvia thought the most ridiculous of excuses. Sylvia tried to say something now but was interrupted. Everything was in Mrs. Dartley's hands. She was talking very rapidly, and organizing them. It was a pity Elsie Crown wasn't still with them. She was very good at this game. They were to be divided into teams. Yes, that was the answer. Instead of each person doing two lines at a time, as they had in the past, each *team* would do an entire group of lines, following whatever form the first team happened to lay out for them. Since she had started the whole thing, she of course would be on the first team. But now how should it be arranged exactly? At this point Knox said that he didn't know how to write poetry. "Nonsense," she replied, "anyone can manage a verse or two." She began explaining to him about metrics; not all of what she said was accurate but Sylvia did not correct her. She rang for Celeste and asked her to bring pencil, paper, and her alarm-clock wristwatch. When these appeared she covered a piece of paper with meter marks for Knox. He was obviously concentrating furiously on mastering them. Soon she got so involved with Knox, who had begun to argue over a few points, that Sylvia allowed herself to hope the project would advance no further.

But this was not to be. Mrs. Dartley whirled on them: "Well, well, let's get on with it." Sylvia would have to be her own team, that was only fair; as compensation for having to go it alone, she added illogically, Sylvia would come second, the most important position. "Now then, let us see how to arrange it finally. Ernest, you are better at this than Anton—" Anton protested but was ignored. "Ernest, you are better than Anton, and I am better than Ernest, and Benjamin, you are an apprentice. So Anton and I shall begin, Sylvia will follow, and Ernest and Benjamin can finish. For this round, that is."

"*This* round?"

Like all of Mrs. Dartley's games, this one depended in part upon rules which no one could possibly keep. Nevertheless, the rules were strictly set out. Those who were "not composing" were supposed to converse in low, quiet tones among themselves and not watch the "composers." This seemed to her "simpler" than having people leave the room. Each team was to have five minutes. She had set the wristwatch on her arm, and at her signal she and Anton marched to the end of the room where paper and pencils were now arranged on a table. They muttered together for a minute or so, and then Mrs. Dartley began to write; she gathered speed, and Anton grew impatient and snapped at her—it was typical of her to have arranged a competition within a competition. She looked at him in surprise but reluctantly pushed paper and pencil toward him, and he was evidently allowed to get in the last two lines.

Having had, as it were, a head start with the first two lines, they finished before the time limit, a fact which Mrs. Dartley talked about as though it were some stunning and prodigious accomplishment. She also thought it would be nice to make a fresh copy on a clean sheet of paper of the "model" she and Anton had composed for them before handing it on to the next team—this being Sylvia, who was eventually prodded toward the table. She sat down and slowly read the words before her. Her resistance to the idea of continuing them, of fashioning lines of verse, was so enormous that her mind was entirely empty. She was aware of being watched. "Two minutes left," Mrs. Dartley said threateningly. Suddenly Sylvia wrote, and just as the alarm went off on Mrs. Dartley's wrist, finished, stood up, left what she had written and joined the others.

Mrs. Dartley reset the alarm. "All right now," she said to Knox and Campion, "all right. *Go*." It seemed to Sylvia that Knox had perhaps already made up their first two lines. After all, they all had the model for those in their heads and it was perfectly possible that he had been secretly working away. As he crossed the room he seemed terribly eager; she even thought that she saw his fingers and throat muscles working as though he were counting feet. She watched carefully in spite of not being supposed to. Sure enough, once at the table Knox grabbed the pencil and scrawled away, looking very pleased with himself. Then he stopped writing but did not relinquish the pencil. Campion made no move to take it from him and sat there waiting, his eyes, however, running over the whole of the paper in front of them. Time was passing. Knox began to chew on the pencil, his smile a bit uncertain now. He rubbed at his cheek, the familiar shaving gesture, leaned forward and with a great, suddenly generous sweep offered the pencil to Campion. Campion took it and slowly wrote two more lines. He paused and offered the pencil to Knox, who squirmed in his seat. Swiftly Campion completed it. When he had done so he lifted his head and looked directly at Sylvia. Then there was some whispered argument, impossible to tell over what, but it was cut off by the ringing of the alarm.

Mrs. Dartley at once took possession of the paper, looked it over with cluckings of approval, and decided it should be read aloud. She did so, her voice so skillfully cadenced that while they listened they all had the illusion that those verses had been written by one person.

Jews and Arabs come away
Live to die another day
Black and white men plunge and chase
Till the final cold embrace
    All too late
    The song is sung
    The worm is sate
    The dead man hung

Nymphs and satyrs dance and play
On the moldering godhead's clay,
Nimble hooves a-thumping shake
Silted layers of mistake
    Horror lasts
    In all our pasts
    The pride of waste
    The blood unchaste

Russian tankmen press your fire
While Hungarians twist like wire
History plucks the trembling lyre
Teaching dead men to desire
    Air and Water
    Fire and Flame
    Earth to Conquer
    Love proclaim

"Why I think we have all done very well," she said when she had finished. At the moment the others thought so too. "You see what a good idea it was. It is even *interesting*." Knox had picked up the paper and was reading it over and over. Mrs. Dartley told him she could not believe it was really his "virgin effort" but he insisted that it was. Then she said, "And now? Shall we try to put it to music, do you think, or should we have another round first?"

At this there was an outcry from everyone except Knox—indeed he joined Mrs. Dartley in attempting to persuade the others to go on with the game. Anton was brought round at last, but Sylvia and Campion remained adamantly opposed. No, they did not even care if they were bad sports; they would not play. Mrs. Dartley reasoned with them, got nasty, pled, and cajoled in turn, and at last admitted to defeat with a good grace. "Then we must drink champagne," she announced. "We must drink to our little company." She rang for Giovanni and told him to bring up four bottles of the Dom Perignon '33. He returned with a tray of glasses and two bottles. "I said four," she reminded him. "There are only two left," he said. "I'm sure you are mistaken," she said coldly, "but never mind," turning so that Campion could not look directly at her.

Sylvia disliked drinking in the afternoon and took only a little of the wine. Mrs. Dartley drank quite greedily, but before the second bottle was finished she suddenly set her glass aside. "Ah, it's no good," she said then, shaking her head sadly. "When even wine fails . . ." She stood up and excused herself. She would be better off alone; she would leave word that she was not to be disturbed. Would Sylvia mind taking any messages that might come for her? "Not," she added wistfully, "that I expect there will be any. There hardly ever are any more." Knox asked if he might borrow the poem they had written for a few days; he thought he might just have a few copies printed up in Zürich, to give to friends. "Ah, you are going to memorialize us, are you? How nice," Mrs. Dartley said.

In a few minutes they had all dispersed.

Sylvia sat in her room with the curtains drawn against the outside. When evening came she would find a way of avoiding Ernest. Before long Celeste knocked at her door to say that there was a telephone call for Mrs. Dartley. When she got to the phone a voice at the other end told her it was a telegram; they had tried to send a man up with it but the weather was too bad. The message was in English, from London; they would do their best to pronounce it for her. She did not recognize the name of the sender, and she wrote it on the pad, thinking it must be from Lily's niece or cousin or whoever it was she had gone to. She knew then what the message would be. She copied it down slowly. It had an hysterical ring to it, not at all suitable to anything connected with Lily. But then people reacted so differently to death. She thanked the operator and looked down at the message on the pad. She thought: now all those singers have died in her head.

She found Ernest and told him. He closed his eyes for a second, grimaced. "Elsie," he said.

"Yes, I know. Terrible. Terrible."

"I'm not sure when she was leaving Amsterdam. I've got to try to get hold of her."

"Yes, try."

"I don't want her arriving in London without knowing."

They looked at each other. Sylvia said, "I'll tell Gwendolyn."

When she entered Mrs. Dartley's room it was worse than she had expected. Mrs. Dartley was just sitting there, staring off into space, the cat asleep in her lap. It took Sylvia aback sharply. She looked like an old lady.

"I'm, afraid there's been some bad news." How else did one ever say it?

By evening Ernest had got through to Amsterdam. But Elsie had taken a late afternoon flight to London. There was nothing to be done.

Forty-eight

George Bingham walked slowly along the outer gallery of the Munich Pinakothek. The general apprehensiveness he felt was familiar, and reassuring. A certain amount of fear was necessary; it even helped drive him toward that special selective alertness which before long now would assert itself and would enable him to pass over or cut out almost automatically whatever in his surroundings might distract him from essentials, and at the same time to take into swift account even the smallest matter that might relate to his immediate purpose and safety. For the past thirty hours every action he had taken had been exactly planned, some of it at his own suggestion, to suit his own desires or interests—the present visit to the museum, for example, the evening at the opera house the night before—but all of it within a standard and carefully constructed framework of protective devices. He had also moved a fair distance away from personal considerations, from the possibility of the inner self making some sudden and ill-timed protest, and toward the psychological point of no return. There were still resistances, not quite acknowledged, but by the time he walked out of the Pinakothek they would be gone. He would have withdrawn intact from the world of objects; he would have entered those curious secret reaches which, like some new or higher element in which he was privileged to move, very cold but very pure, were as much beyond conventional attachments and feelings as they were

beyond the capacities of the ordinary individual. He would function perfectly in the coming days, but it might as well be in an
unpeopled universe.

He bent over now to examine a series of small Rembrandt canvases. Artists were hard to figure. Here was Rembrandt painting
himself in at Calvary, standing there in a turban and watching
Christ being hung on the cross, or maybe being taken down, you
couldn't say exactly which, and looking out of the framework in
such a way as to seem to be forcing the passer-by to stop, to pay
attention, looking out, in fact, with an admonitory eye. That was a
good phrase. Admonitory eye. Bingham repeated it to himself, and
returned the stare, eye for eye. In the canvas next to that one
Rembrandt even had himself twice, the first a slender youthful
figure, ardent and awed, it appeared, by the crucifixion scene, and
the second heavy-set, an old indifferent burgher-patrician, the kind
of man you might find as chairman of the board, only sterner and
more dignified. And in the canvas next to that he wasn't at all sure
that the face of the man on the cross wasn't Rembrandt's too. He
smiled ironically. Now just how, just how would she explain that
one away, Sylvia?

He caught himself. She had a tricky little habit of being everywhere at once too, at least for him, at least if he let her. He had no
intention of letting her, not for the next few days at any rate. It
was simply bad luck that his present undertaking called for him to
spend this much time in Munich. He had tried to avoid it, but it
couldn't be done. *The Magic Flute* hadn't been the best idea either,
as it had turned out. For him there were no special associations at
all between that opera and Sylvia, and yet he had been painfully
aware of her existence from the first notes to the last. Of all the
women he might have got involved with why did it have to be
someone as disturbing as Sylvia? Someone who wouldn't even
leave him in peace when he went to a Mozart opera. It had been a
queer evening. For the first time there hadn't seemed to him anything even faintly ridiculous about the trial by fire and water; on
the contrary, he had felt he was watching some magical and important rite, something that was at last revealed to him, something
that had been there all along but that he just hadn't been able to
see, to take part in, a mystery. And it was all associated with her
somehow, especially with his last visit to Kilchberg. He had been
left afterwards with the feeling that he had barely managed to

escape some much too powerful tie with her, and the whole opera itself had seemed to pose questions that he just didn't want to think about. Well, it was really only an absurd little fairy tale with something in it for everyone, not to be taken the least bit seriously for all its musical sublimities. Artists were about as untrustworthy as anyone he could think of, which was saying a great deal. They were all charlatans.

He tapped the museum catalogue against a thigh and turned to look out the windows toward the city of Munich. In a very short time now he would be at the cab stand in front of the Rathaus and on his way. They were all illusionists, the worst kind; they played around with your soul. All that worn-out talk about the superb harmonious order in Bach, for instance. He'd used to talk that way too, and feel it. Now most of the time Bach just sounded to him like the music of a mad mathematician. It would take a staff of psychiatrists and a couple of certified public accountants to straighten it out. And if, on certain winter evenings in Munich, he had sometimes found himself feeling about Vivaldi, the only music she'd had at the time, the way he had used to feel, then it could probably be put down to the first-rate champagne he'd always brought along. They were all illusionists; you just had to learn to see through them. It was really bad luck being hooked by a charlatan, but it was all right if you kept reminding yourself not to be taken in. He walked now back along the gallery corridor, noticing, among other objects, the exposed rump of Boucher's Miss O'Murphy. He stopped for half a minute and was put in a better mood. What did anyone need with a Sylvia Grierson when, if you looked around a bit, you might find a Miss O'Murphy? That was exactly what he would say to Sylvia the next time he saw her. No one teased more beautifully than she did. But she seemed very far away to him now—a name really, an echo. You could say that he was on schedule, in more ways than one. He turned into the main rooms of the gallery.

From Milan Bingham had flown to London, where he had made a series of decisions and had spent much of his time committing to memory all the details of a complicated plan and several new identities. Then, infuriatingly, on the 29th of October, had come Suez. It was intolerable that the CIA people in the Middle East had had no inkling of what was going on there—that move in the desert had called for a lot of planning, it wasn't like what had happened in Hungary—or if they did have, that their reports had been stopped somewhere along the line in Washington. In any case, there was no excuse for it. Several of Bingham's English colleagues had had quite a laugh. He had said nothing; with their record they didn't often have a chance to laugh at American intelligence people.

For him, then, there had been another day of conferences and reconsiderations; certain changes were made in his routing and cover and he had spent the last few hours before getting on the plane for Munich the day before memorizing these. Not very cheerfully either. He had made it clear to everyone that he thought he was doing them a favor by taking on this mission at all, and he had resolved again to cut his ties with them when it was completed. What had he to do with a bunch of amateurs and politicians? He had even insisted on a couple of guarantees of a special sort which they didn't usually like to provide, since if anything went wrong it would mean the exposure of several related operations. Still, no matter what kind of precautions were taken, you were on your own after a certain point. He knew that. The most difficult decision had been taken only at the last moment and in the face of intelligence reports which indicated that despite Moscow's conciliatory tone new Soviet troops were being poured into Hungary for the purpose of intervention: Bingham was to carry out his mission according to plan regardless of what might break in middle Europe. The Russians would probably not move for several days; if he was lucky he could do what he had to before then. But no one could be sure.

Now, on November 1st, Nagy had just declared Hungary's neutrality, and Bingham read this as a desperate attempt to spell out to the world what they already knew, that a foreign power was about ready to take them over by force. His guess was that things would start to happen fast now. It no longer mattered to him. It would be just another obstacle to be overcome. Everything was in motion along the way; nothing could prevent him from going on this journey. In less than two hours he would be irrevocably in motion too. He welcomed the spiritual aloneness that was coming. It was then that he felt free. He welcomed the chance to try his wits and strength against the unknown. It was in the midst of such contest that he felt his destiny to be in his own hands.

George Bingham had passed with hardly a nod several Titians,

among them Kaiser Karl and Christ receiving the crown of
thorns. He had no interest in the unrelenting single truth of a
head. Or of a body. Or of a moment of choice. Instinctively he
had avoided concentrating on those painters who by playing most
profoundly on the senses, and hence on the spirit, most insistently
broke down the distance between canvas and beholder, whose
skills as illusionists were likely to force or entice the beholder into
some unexpected sense of connection with the reality behind the
forms. Instead he had lingered over those paintings which could
more easily, if the viewer chose, be contemplated only as objects,
even if they were more than objects, paintings which seemed to
contain fixed and static worlds within an absolute framework,
which did not move, as Titian's moved, or as most of the great
paintings of the Renaissance did. He felt himself most at ease with
those canvases in which a vast and highly detailed and complicated
design was executed in small compass—works which could carry
the mind away along with the eye into something that was finished, and not towards one particular point or center but simply
into the design and pattern itself. It was in this spirit even that he
stood before the *Alexanderschlacht*. For him it was a world seen
only from a distance, all the more satisfying for being so. He
observed, but was not pulled in. The wild array of armies, the
knightly, victorious figure of Alexander himself, gold caparisoned
and in command, the dancing horse, the lance, the fleeing Persians
and Darius in defeat, turning, his train of frightened women, ruins,
spears, plumes, fields, hills, town, sea, mountains, the stopped sun
and the volcanic clouds, the tumult in the sky as on the plain
below, a little world that just might go under . . . Bingham marveled at the virtuosity with which Altdorfer had managed to put
all this on so small a canvas, and precisely before the dark apoca-
lyptic vision behind it began to exert its force he turned away.

He came now to the Rubens collection. He did not greatly care
for Rubens, particularly his nudes. As a matter of fact, Miss
O'Murphy notwithstanding, he wasn't in the mood for looking at
naked women anyway. He made the gesture of circling the collection, past the hunting scenes and drunken satyrs and the nudes and
the painter's wives—how many had he had? He paused by the
Kindermord, remembering how hepped up about it Sylvia had
been shortly before she ran away from Munich. As usual she had
seen things that no one else did. He paced the length of the large

canvas several times and then stepped back. It was a brilliant piece
of work—he could see that—but it . . . it almost revolted him
somehow. It was too much. It was overdone—that was what it
was. Everything was touch, and terrible sound in the silence, and
. . . you could almost even *smell* what was going on in that scene.
He turned on his heel. After all, he had to watch his time. In
exactly ten minutes he was scheduled to walk out the door of the
Pinakothek. He decided to stroll back through the main galleries
once more and then return to this end, where there was still one
more room to be seen. The timing should be about right.

Now he remembered that he and Sylvia had talked about the
Brueghel *Kindermord* too. He thought it a much greater painting
than the Rubens, but she had refused to discuss them in that way.
The Brueghel, she'd said, was about a specific social experience of
evil, about what actually goes on during a pogrom, and the Rubens
wasn't about that at all; it was about Original Sin. Bingham shook
his head a little, indulgently, enjoying the recollection. How absolutely typical of her the whole discussion had been. There was
never a dull moment. The Rubens was also about beauty, specifically, which the Brueghel wasn't, although the Brueghel, like the
Rubens, was beautiful in and of itself. But both depicted horror?
he'd asked. He had pushed hard on this. Yes, she had answered, and
together they had turned that paradox in a number of directions.
He remembered it all. She had made quite a speech at one point:
the saddest and most moving thing about the Brueghel was the
helplessness of the victims, that there seemed to be no possibility
of opposing that sort of force, the Spanish soldiers in Flanders, the
police state. Rubens' vision was a little different: you could fight
back, even if you couldn't win, but he knew what that meant too.
And then she had said that the most brilliant thing in the Brueghel
was the way the artist showed who the really guilty ones were: the
officers on horseback in their fancy armor, *the ones who knew
better*. It showed, she said, what hypocrisy honor could sometimes
mask. At that they had quarreled. The officers on horseback were
doing their duty, he had maintained, and not all of them had liked
it; Brueghel had shown that too. It had been quite a fight. He had
known very well what she meant, though he hadn't admitted it.

Bingham had looked at no paintings on his journey to the far
end of the gallery and back. Now he had come again to the
Rubens and he cut quickly over to the small outer corridor and

walked the rest of the distance there, looking out the window at
the city of Munich. Thus it was that when he entered the last
room of the Pinakothek, the room he had not yet been in at all,
and first saw the Tintoretto it was as though he had crossed some
invisible border, passed perhaps through some mysterious underground chamber or, perhaps, since he felt too that he was swimming in light, passed through some chambers of the sea, arriving at
last at this new interior, entering a room in a city he had never
seen before, glimpsing beyond it, through the open door, the landscape of a new country. He saw the tiled floor, the barking dog,
the helmeted head hiding, the outraged husband lifting the telltale
cloth, the god Amor blissfully now asleep, the sea-green light
through the windows, the silks and rumpled bedclothes, and the
luminous Aphrodite herself, the still spread thighs, saw even the
title of this painting, *Vulkan Surprising Venus and Mars*. He swam
in the light, the changed air, the sea, the incredible green gold and
rose violet, the transformed elements. Then it all changed; dog,
helmet, husband, and room all disappeared and he saw only the
Venus—beneficent, patient, contained. So, exactly, had Sylvia
Grierson looked, when towards dawn at Kilchberg, he had forced
himself to leave her, one leg curving down over the side of the
bed, leaning one arm on a pillow, the other lifted to catch and pull
about her the tossed covers—that pose exactly. He stood possessed
of the sweet sickness of longing, of desire, and possessed of more
than that. With clenched fist he struck now at the air, a short
absurd gesture—and saw that he was alone. Pale and in doubt, he
turned out of the room and hurried down the long staircase and
away from the museum.

Within the hour he was alone in another room. There he began
to divest himself of those articles of identity, those tokens of existence, by which he was known.

Forty-nine

The day of November 2nd began and ended badly for those at
Kilchberg, and not much could be said for what happened in between, except for the arrival of the letter from Marshall, though

even that seemed to strike Mrs. Dartley—inexplicably to Campion and Sylvia—as being a little upsetting. He wrote about his experience at the Mozarteum in more detail, confirming what he had reported in a long-distance call the evening of the same day they got the news of Lily's death. He had triumphed, and his scholarship was only a matter of working out some technicalities—he would have definite word in a week or so. Pflaumgartner had impressed but not intimidated him, and in the letter he included a brief and amusing character sketch of him. He added that he hoped Mrs. Dartley had meant it when she had told them to make a picnic out of the trip because they had decided to drive on to Vienna. In Salzburg he had learned that the French flutist she had praised so much was appearing as soloist two nights from then with a chamber group in Vienna. He thought it would be a good chance to "hear the competition." He and Posy also thought they would like to drive back along the Wachau and look at some castles. "A plan both practical and romantic," Mrs. Dartley commented, "and therefore most appropriate to his present condition in life." But still, she had seemed a little annoyed.

In the absence of Posy Mrs. Dartley had taken it upon herself to feed Felix, and had even begun using that name for him which Posy had let slip in the course of handing over her duties. This action had become for Gwendolyn Dartley something of great importance, the only moments in her day which now gave her pleasure. She prolonged the feeding as much as possible and felt great regret when Felix had made his last leap and returned to his own watery world, for it seemed to her that some quite reassuring force of the good in nature sprang into the living air with him and put down or at least transcended all that was savage. It was therefore a most grievous and bitter moment for her when on the morning of the 2nd of November she got to the pool and found Felix floating and bobbing lifelessly along the shore's edge. She fled to the house. Did fish die? Like that? Overnight? And such a fish as Felix? These were the questions she put to her household and to which, really, they had no answers. "My poor fish is dead," she had said to Sylvia, seizing her wrist between long fingers and peering into her face as though surely Sylvia Grierson could explain. And all day, even when other matters claimed her attention, she reverted to this plaint. "There never was such a fish," she would also say, pacing through the house, not to be consoled. What could have happened? How? Had Felix perhaps been done to death, unkindly, and if so by whom?

"What have you done with him?" Ernest asked at last.

"Done? Nothing. What am I to do? He floats there still, I suppose."

At this Benjamin Knox, who had thought the whole fuss madness anyway, more Dartley Drama, as he phrased it to Ralph Bledder, made the mistake of laughing.

"You learn nothing," she said to him coldly. "I shall be glad when you are gone, out of my house, you and the vile machinery with which you have now filled it." For emphasis she pulled at a tangle of television cords.

Sylvia and Ernest looked away. "Perhaps we should do something, Ernest," Sylvia said, unable to imagine what, and saw from Mrs. Dartley's expression that this was exactly what she wished of them.

When they got to the pool, all black and viscous now under a lowering sky that threatened snow, they saw Felix. He had floated too far out for them to reach him.

"How shall we get him?"

For answer, Ernest took off his shoes and socks, rolled up his trousers, and waded in. He stood for a moment, bent over, the water around his knees, looking as though he were making some ancient gesture of propitiation, then came in to shore with Felix held in front of him. Sylvia went to meet him. They both felt a little silly standing there looking at a dead fish so tenderly; yet they were moved in spite of this. Felix was still a thing of great beauty—the corruption of death had not yet set in. He was a trout, of lovely shape, and pale rainbow stripings. And the fish eyes, in death, were a startling reminder of the fact that between fish and man the structure of the eye has undergone only the most minor of changes. It was a cruel thing, that whatever had once animated this creature had been put down or withdrawn, that the fish eyes no longer saw its world. It was unnatural too, for as Sylvia said, "The death of a fish ought, at the least, to give nourishment." There was something there that was not in the cycle. Yet had the leaping been?

In any case, as they looked now, heads bent together over the inert object in Ernest's hands, they saw that indeed some blow had been delivered against Felix; there was a wound on the side of his

head. They looked at each other. Who could have done this thing?
Impossible to think that any of the mountain people, or anyone at
Kilchberg . . . Felix had leapt towards an obscured sun, obscured at
any rate on this morning, but up, up, and up—and yet he had been
brought down. Some arm—evil, ignorant or indifferent, it hardly
mattered which—had sent through the air some deadly object and
brought him down. Why? Who? They could not say.

"What does one do with a dead fish that has mattered?" Sylvia
asked.

"Can you bury a fish?" he asked.

They both knew that they could not just leave him to rot anywhere, or take him by the tail and fling him out of sight into the
woods.

"What else can we do?"

They went to the gardener's cottage. They stared at Marshall's
music stand, at the music scores lying about, at the general and
bewildering debris of generations, and in one corner, lying a-
tumble on each other, all the hats. Sylvia rummaged through them.
She picked one up, a golden Rembrandt turban, somewhat worn
and tarnished, and tried it on, but it did not fit. She put it on
Ernest. She tried another on herself, a Dürer thing of linen veils.
There was no mirror, and they saw each other's reflections, small
and intense shapes of light, in each other's eyes. Then they took
the hats off and put them back with the others.

Sylvia said, "Gwendolyn was going to give a Halloween party.
Or so she claims. She thought that all of these hats should be put to
use. We've been spared that. What's your theory about this mysterious collection?"

"My theory? About the hats? My theory is that there was a big
costume party once. And that everyone got blind drunk, caroused,
and went off without their hats," he said.

"Mine's a little different. I think they just, whoever they were,
went off into the night and were never heard of again."

He reached out to her and she moved into his embrace. They
clung to one another for an instant, then stepped back in silence.

They began to search for something to bury Felix with and at
last, when they had almost given up, they found a cache of gardener's tools. Outside it had begun to snow. Again, as they chose a
place for Felix they felt a little silly, as though in behaving like two
children who were burying the family pet they were also laying

false claim to an innocence they no longer possessed. But again they were moved. They dug a deep basin for him in the earth, lined it with leaves, laid him in, and soon had covered the place. It seemed right to Sylvia, that mixing of elements: the watery element of fish, and the earth. The snow fell gently on.

"If you plant a fish will it grow, do you think?" she asked.

At the house they said to Mrs. Dartley, "He's laid to rest." She thanked them and to their relief asked to know nothing more, not even where. The rest of the day she spent listening to the radio downstairs, with a sort of anxious listlessness. She came to life a little at the announcement that Anna Kéthley was alive and now active again—was in fact on her way to Vienna to meet with other Social Democrats. There were rumors too of a cabinet post in the new coalition government. "A very great woman," Mrs. Dartley said, and was shocked to learn that Sylvia had never heard of her before. "Matchless integrity. Incredible courage." Sylvia wondered if this were not the woman for whom the message she had carried into Zürich had been intended. But for the rest, Mrs. Dartley had nothing hopeful to say. Sylvia herself felt, on instinct, that it was over with in Hungary, that brute force would end it all, the noble venture . . . Those new Soviet troop movements, what else could it mean, no matter how much one hoped otherwise? She could see that Mrs. Dartley thought this too, though she did not put it into direct speech. It was over with.

Anton Hrubick was gone by the time Sylvia and Ernest got back to the house. He had left for Zürich, riding in with Knox and Ralph Bledder.

Fifty

Anton and Rudi always met in a certain area along the Limmat. These meetings were purely personal, as the occasions on which Anton transmitted or received messages for Mrs. Dartley were infrequent, and when they did occur he preferred the transaction to take place at the Öpfelchammer. Of course there had been no message going either way since the day of Sylvia's race into Zürich, and to Anton it appeared that it would turn out to have been the last—things were changing. For his own part, he felt considerable relief. Physically he was not a brave man—that is, he did not like risk and bodily danger—and although there had been only the remotest, most theoretical sort of chance that his message-carrying would lead to any difficulties, it had nevertheless cost him a good deal of anxiety. He was perpetually drenched in sweat whenever he was on what he sometimes called, with a deep sense of what a ridiculous figure he cut, a mission. Rudi, on the other hand, was very different; Anton thought it most unlikely that Rudi felt fear, at least not fear of the sort he did.

For over a year now their relationship had been one of friendship, though this was not a fact that was known at Kilchberg. It had seemed to Anton that approaching old age had left him with almost no private life at all. This was a great change for someone who had always had a rather intricate and satisfying one. He regretted the loss and in a curious, almost womanish way resented the limitations which time had placed upon him. He had therefore guarded his weekly visits with the Swiss stammerer much in the way a jealous lover guards his mistress and determines to keep his friends from even so much as meeting her. They agreed on almost nothing, of course, he and Rudi, but then that wasn't unusual; it was simply not in Anton's nature to agree—in speech—with anyone. Rudi would listen for hours to Anton's long, intemperate harangues. In fact, Anton honestly wondered if he'd ever had so good an audience in his entire life, if even the stupidest and most calculating woman he had ever met had listened to him with such attention.

But the difference was that Rudi was not stupid. On the contrary; Anton had quickly learned that behind that Swiss burgher's front was a mind capable of the most elaborately complicated and sharp perceptions, despite the difficulty he had expressing himself in the spoken word. Tonight no doubt they would talk again about the Hungarian revolution, the general political situation in Europe; and also of course Anton would tell him that Sylvia Grierson had come back, which would please him. She had caught Rudi's fancy. Well, so had she caught his own, though he had a far more accurate picture of her than Rudi did. It would take a man with a peculiar sort of inner strength to live with her. Someone like himself, for example. Campion, that good fellow, seemed to have longings in that direction. Rudi, perhaps necessarily, approached all human relations at one remove; he almost seemed resigned to their remaining at a distance. Perhaps this was how he managed, behind that rather disconcerting wall-eyed gaze of his, to keep his vision fixed on the delusionary outlines of the city of brotherly love. At least this was what Anton suspected. At any rate, Rudi's interest in Kilchberg never waned; to him, all of them there were important, remarkable creatures, and Anton was always happy to expand on every little incident. He often felt himself to be a sort of go-between for Rudi in a way that had nothing to do with Mrs. Dartley's messages, a sort of link between Rudi and the world of men and women. At the same time, he felt in some way inde-scribably honored when, during the last hour or two of each of their meetings, Rudi would suddenly be free of those impediments of expression which choked his voice and speech with squeaks and stammers and long silences, and would talk as easily as other men, although so much better than most. Then, in those moments, both of them well into their wine, Anton would find himself feeling, whatever he might be saying to the contrary, that small human triumphs were still possible.

Anton crossed the Münster Brucke, hurrying a little. He and Rudi always followed exactly the same routine, as though they were a two-man club, which in a sense they were. Each Friday afternoon Anton went for coffee and conversation at the home of Professor K. up in the hills near the university. This lasted usually until half past six, and at seven he and Rudi would meet near the Stadhuis Quai, having chosen this particular spot because it was not far from the wine-restaurant in which they always dined. Be-sides, it was a pleasant spot too, especially in spring and summer when the great Linden tree on the other bank was in foliage. Rudi was usually most punctual, even if, as often happened, he was already some deci-liters of wine ahead of his friend. Anton was sometimes late, and sometimes early. If he got there early he would occasionally stroll along the quai and back, past the little boat docks, taunting the swans and cooing at the *Täubli*, which in his own mind he referred to as sea-going doves. More often, however, he simply took up his stand on the river side of the Zunfthaus zur Meise, as he did now. It was the only baroque building in Zürich, and it reminded him of Prague. Behind him was the Fraumünster and farther up towards the Lindenhof the Peterskirche; across the river the Grossmünster. Sometimes, when all the church bells were going at once, he would narrow his eyes until the city swam in a sort of haze and he could almost feel for a few seconds that he was in Prague. He seldom did this, though; it was a nice view in its own right, the old Rathaus with the Limmat flowing under the arches that were built into the river, the line of Zunfthäuser, the Zum Rüden, the Zimmerleute. It was not Prague, but it was nice.

Anton leaned on the low railing, waiting. He had arrived nearly a quarter of an hour late, having agreed to stop by a newsstand for Mrs. Dartley and pick up the papers that came in at seven o'clock, but Rudi had not yet come. It was a night laden with cold dampness. Even the falling snow did not in its usual way cheer Anton. The fine dry flakes of earlier in the day had been replaced by great, loose, wet things that seemed the antithesis of the finely constructed crystals Anton knew them to be and that disappeared, losing whatever form they had, the moment they struck the earth. He preferred to watch them disappearing into the blackened water, which would have claimed even the finest of crystals in exactly the same fashion.

The discussion that afternoon at Professor K.'s had turned inevitably to politics and to the events in Hungary. Anton shivered, wrapped in his warm coat and muffler, and was reminded suddenly of Gogol's *Overcoat*. How lucky he felt himself not to be in Budapest, or even Prague, though he was often filled with homesickness for his old city. He was too soft or too old or too something to wish himself there, despite the feelings of sympathy that had been stirred in him by the revolution. He was glad to be where he was. He liked physical comforts; he always had, and now, in his late sixties, he felt no need to be ashamed of this fact. Let the young make a new world if they were so foolish as to think it could be done, and as it appeared the young Hungarians were foolish enough to think. It was all a matter of luck, where you were born, and where you ended. As far as he could tell, the Hungarians had risen up as much because their lives were so physically miserable as because of the spiritual tyranny they had been suffering. Well, those things went together in some profound way, he believed. Economics. Bah. He did not want to think further about it. It was just something else to drive yourself mad with. Yet in spite of his attempt to tell himself that what was happening in Hungary was not really so glorious, he did think it was; it touched him deeply;

he even envied those young men, most of them working-class boys at that, and girls, and intellectuals like himself—envied them their valor.

A white whirring of wings, half heard, half seen, caught at his senses. He lifted his head and smiled. Sea gulls! *Möwen!* Crying out and circling now down to the dark water, then wheeling up again, around and around, and then with more cries to the water, looking for food no doubt. He watched them with pleasure. An inlander, from a land-locked country, he never failed to be mystified at the existence in Switzerland, another country far from the seas, of these birds. The mist had lightened a little, suddenly, as often happened in Zürich, and another light had been turned on somewhere behind him in the zur Meise, probably in the room used for the little faïence exhibition. It was sometimes used too for official receptions. How the gulls were crying! Without even being aware of it, he grew alert, his eyes focusing on that spot in the water not far from him to which, it now seemed, the birds most persistently returned. He took off his thick glasses and wiped them, put them on again, and leaned farther out—the water level was only a few feet below the quai at this point on the Limmat. It almost seemed to him that something was floating there in the water, some strange object that did not belong there. It almost seemed to him that it was a man's body. It *was* a man's body.

What one would have seen then from a distance—what indeed was seen, fortunately—was an old man, short and rather heavy, with wild white curly hair standing up about his head, gone mad it appeared, jumping up onto the low balustrade, shouting for help, throwing off his coat and muffler, appearing about to jump into the water, then changing his mind and running for a rescue hook, shouting ever more loudly, then climbing again onto the balustrade, teetering there on the edge and once more, it seemed, about to spring in, again changing his mind, and then just as help arrived losing his balance and toppling in.

They were both pulled out in a matter of minutes, Anton and Rudi. Anton was alive and relatively unharmed; he had kept himself afloat and the efficient Swiss had been most quick. He sat on the ground, heaving cries, wrapped in blankets, refusing to move from the spot. Rudi was dead, and past help. The rescuers had seen that at once, though they worked over him for a long while, and even with the inhalator which arrived with the police ambulance.

Anton from time to time muttered imprecations against the universe; at other times he repeated, "The victim of an infamous attack, I tell you, an infamous attack." Someone asked him, "Did you know him?" "Know him? My best, my closest friend?" He shook, he ranted, he cried. Never had the impotence of age more cruelly descended upon him. The old should not have to cry, he told himself, struggling to get control. No, no, no, that should be spared them, that at least. The young, yes; let them cry. Tears ran down his face until they told him that there was no hope for Rudi. Then the tears suddenly stopped. He walked over to the body. "What do you see now?" he said to it, and was led quickly away to a waiting police car.

Death had not taken away Rudi's ugliness of form or face—if anything it had accented it. His eyes, open and fixed, still stared off in slightly opposite directions, and his feet turned out too. His mouth hung open, as though still gasping for air. The striped trousers and the dark coat oozed water where he lay as hands prepared to lift him and carry him to the ambulance. Only the squeaks and stammers had at last been overcome, and the high tight collar ripped off. All that was left to Rudi was the beauty of having once been a living thing, and that perhaps was a beauty that could not easily be comprehended.

At the hospital Anton became difficult. He refused absolutely to be admitted as a patient, and there was no way he could be forced. His wet clothes had been removed and he had been put into warm hospital robes and given hot beverages and a mild sedative. He had already told his story to the police of how he had been waiting for Rudi as usual, how he had seen the body, how he had fallen in. He insisted on waiting for the report of the medical examiner; he would not leave the hospital until it had been made. Then he wanted to go back to Kilchberg. He had also asked someone to telephone Benjamin Knox at his hotel. They, the medical examiners, would not know what to look for—the fools—he told himself. And even if there was nothing to find on the body, no evidence of foul play, he had an image in his own mind—he saw a dark figure pushing against Rudi, a sudden thrust into the water. What fools they had all been, at Kilchberg, thinking that against such evil . . .

The report, when they at last reluctantly brought it to him, was just what he had expected. It was not a final report, of course.

There were many official steps yet to be taken, but there was really no question about what the verdict would be: death by drowning, accidental, while under the influence of alcohol. Anton sneered at them for this. Anyone who knew Rudi knew how much he could drink and how little it affected him in important matters, he told them. But this was the wrong thing to say, for the doctors pointed out that Rudi was well known as a chronic drinker; this was exactly the sort of end that frequently occurred, they said something too about the effect of alcohol on the lungs, on the mechanism of breathing, a depressant . . . But one of the police had suddenly become interested; he interrupted the doctors now and began to question Anton closely and sharply: had he any reason to think that Rudi had been the victim of foul play, what were his grounds, what had given him so firmly held a notion? Anton had to retrench carefully, explaining that for over a year they had met every Friday, that Rudi had always been drinking beforehand and had been completely steady, that they had spent the next four hours drinking together with Rudi showing hardly any ill effects— unless perhaps the fact that he had often stayed the night in town rather than going home could mean that he had not been quite entirely in the best of condition, unless . . . Here Anton began to feign a certain amount of confusion and to play on his condition and his age. At last one of the doctors intervened: any further questions the police had for him they could ask another time; he had been through enough for one night. Besides, someone had just come to take him home.

Knox had brought dry clothes along, some of his own clothes, and Anton was quite a sight when he had got into them. The narrow, elegant gray slacks, out of which the chunky little thighs seemed likely to burst, were rolled up a third of their length; the cashmere sweater hung and bagged and the sleeves kept unrolling themselves and slipping down over his hands; the overcoat came near to engulfing him. For a moment Anton felt so humiliated that he wished he had let them keep him the night in the hospital. But it was obvious even to him that Knox was trying hard to be kind. This "helping out" (a phrase Knox kept repeating—"I'm glad to be helping out") even seemed important to him. And for once Anton felt too weak to disregard the feelings of others. In the end he let himself be led, trundled out, like a child or mummy whose swaddling clothes were coming loose around him, and put into the

car—Knox had kept the motor running in order to have it warm
inside—and there wrapped around still once more, this time in a
blanket which Knox had brought with him from the hotel.

All the way out to the villa Anton hummed, sang, and whistled
the wildest variety of tunes. Knox did not recognize any of them,
but he was grateful nevertheless that Anton seemed this much
himself. Then he reflected that it was old Mrs. Halász who had
used to do that with music; Hrubick had only gone in for the
musical quotations when he could make a gibe or a joke out of
them. Anyway, the old boy seemed in better shape than he had
expected when they phoned from the hospital.

At the villa they were all waiting. Knox had had the thoughtful-
ness to phone ahead, and he had even told the story rather tact-
fully, so they were prepared, for everything at least but the absurd
figure Anton presented in his borrowed clothing. "You have lost a
dear friend," Mrs. Dartley said quickly, intending to warn him
against revealing anything else in front of Knox and striking in this
way, by chance, as she soon realized, on the truth, for this alone
was in Anton's mind.

Knox and Campion got him into bed. Then Mrs. Dartley took
over, displaying that absolutely stunning tenderness and capability
which self-centered people can sometimes muster up in an emergency. Everything she did was right, everything she said. She
steadfastly refused to entertain the idea even for a second that
Rudi could have met with an unnatural end, though what she
might really be thinking was not for anyone else to guess. Anton
returned obsessively to this theme, always to be put down in a new
and convincing way. Her resourcefulness seemed infinite. Her
tone of commiseration was gentle and full of sensibility, and so was
the expression of her own sorrow, as it had been for Lily Halász;
and yet all of this was somehow now being done in a way that was
meant to distract Anton, at least for this night, from what had
happened. And it did a little. At last she called everyone into
Anton's room and made them all the hot milk-and-cognac drinks.
She kept mixing them until they were all nearly drunk, and she
and Anton definitely were. A certain atmosphere of joking crept
in too, and suddenly Sylvia realized what Mrs. Dartley was doing
—she was holding a wake.

In the end Anton dropped off into drunken sleep and the rest of
them tottered off to bed. There was some concern about his catch-

ing cold after his dunking. There was greater, but unspoken, concern about what state his spirits would be left in by the loss of Rudi, for they all knew now how important Rudi had been to him.

In any case, the invasion of Kilchberg by what Benjamin Knox had once called the real world was moving ahead at a pronounced clip.

Fifty-one

Anton breathed heavily through a gathering bronchial congestion, and slept. Downstairs Gwendolyn Dartley, in old slippers and the Chevalier Levin's dressing gown, paced quietly through the night, listening to the low-tuned radio. In Budapest the thousands of thanksgiving candles which had been lighted the night before had guttered out in the windows. From these windows, towards dawn, the horizon broke with a sudden violent roar into flames. The Russian attack had begun. November the 4th had begun. Shortly after six o'clock Kilchberg time Imre Nagy announced to the world what had happened. Mrs. Dartley listened to his words being translated into English, Russian, French, and German. Then she went to Ernest's and Sylvia's rooms, awakened them, and asked them to come and sit with her.

A few minutes before eight o'clock they heard what was to be the last free broadcast from Budapest, a voice that struggled with emotion and that spoke in English: "This is the Association of Hungarian writers. We are speaking to all writers, scientists, writers' associations, and scientific unions of the world who stand for the leaders of the intellectual life in all countries. Our time is limited. You know all the facts. Up the Hungarian writers, scientists, workers, peasants, and intelligentsia. Up! Up! Up!" Hearing these words coming from far away in the city of suffering and death, Sylvia Grierson hoped she might remember exactly what it was like then, at that moment—the human, the temporal agony. At the same time she knew also that these events would be transposed, safely into history, dangerously into art, could imagine students reading about them in a textbook, could imagine a poem or an opera being composed on the subject long after her own death. For herself, she felt it to be a moment of testing, one to which she would secretly return all her life. Could it be otherwise for any intellectual, in the East or the West?

Anton appeared in the doorway, in baggy striped pajamas that looked disturbingly like a concentration-camp uniform and with a piece of flannel coming loose around his throat. "It's finished?" he croaked at them.

"Yes," Mrs. Dartley said. "And no."

Sylvia, afraid suddenly, thinking of Bingham, left them and went to her room. Campion, Mrs. Dartley and a forcibly bundled-up Anton remained by the radio. The newspaper *Szabad Nep*, in a building that was still holding out, remained in control of its teletype machine. Its messages, sent to the AP in Vienna, were quickly broadcast. "Please tell the world of the treacherous attack against our struggle for liberty . . ." "Nagy personally asks help. And diplomatic steps." It was clear that the population was giving battle, hopeless as it might be, and that the fighting was especially fierce in the huge working-class neighborhoods, in the factory areas of Ujpest, Csepel, and "Red" Dunapentele. Radio Moscow announced that "enemies of the people's regime who had tortured and hanged the finest representatives of the Hungarian people"—a new way, Mrs. Dartley said, of describing the secret police—had deceived the population. Free Radio Rajk in Dunapentele sent out calls for help to the Vienna Red Cross, to the United Nations, to Russian soldiers: "Do not shoot. You do not know that you fight against workers. We Hungarian Communists . . . free elections . . . We shall continue fighting." Radio Moscow announced that "the fascist conspiracy" was being crushed "with the active participation of the Hungarian population." From *Szabad Nep* new messages came: "The people have just turned over a tram to use as a barricade near the building . . . We are quiet, not afraid. Send the news to the public of the world and say it should condemn the aggressors." "People are jumping up on the tanks. Young people are . . ." "Help! Help! Help! SOS! SOS!" "What is the United Nations doing? Give us a little encouragement." "The Hungarian people are not afraid of death. It is only a pity that we cannot stand for long." In New York the Soviet Union used its veto in the Security Council. A meeting of the General Assembly was called for that evening. "The moment is lost," Mrs. Dartley said. "What little might have been done was not done." On the short-wave band, messages from free stations throughout Hungary were still being monitored. But one by one these voices were disappearing. Late in the morning the messages from *Szabad Nep* stopped. Benjamin Knox arrived at Kilchberg.

Everyone had forgotten that this was the Sunday when *The World at Large* was to feature Gwendolyn Dartley. It was almost impossible to imagine going ahead with this program now. Knox himself was surly and depressed. Who after all would be interested in Mrs. Dartley with the Russians having chosen precisely this day to take over in Hungary and the UN probably in session? Who would even be looking at the program? It was a very low trick, his manner seemed to suggest; it was even perhaps Mrs. Dartley's fault. In the afternoon Ralph Bledder arrived, and a train of technicians. They took over the house. Mrs. Dartley, wandering disconsolately about, seemed not even aware of their presence.

In the early evening Knox sought out Sylvia. Would she speak to Mrs. Dartley? Could Sylvia at least get her to do something about her hair? And they had to be sure she would wear the right clothes for the cameras. Sylvia replied vaguely that she did not think he need worry, and declined. Gwendolyn would pull herself together; she always did.

By now Knox's attitude had undergone a complete change. He was extremely eager to go ahead with the program. Weeks before he had decided how to handle things with Mrs. Dartley; it was all going to be light, chit-chat about personalities, the reminiscences of an interesting "character" who was something of a has-been. But Knox was not without his resources, and as he had reviewed in his mind the documentary part of the program which was already on tape he had suddenly seen enormous possibilities. He would swing the whole thing to politics, to Hungary. She would have plenty to say; sometimes, he had to admit, she even had a kind of grandeur which would make her the equal of the moment. For him, if anyone were watching, it might be a coup. The UN session was scheduled for eight. The network might cut off the last few minutes, but that would be all right. Bledder was to be on the direct line to New York and signal him when the first warning came, so that he could bring things to a climax just before the switch to the United Nations. Good fortune, he felt, had not deserted him. He even felt, somehow or other and rather headily, that he personally was taking part in an historical moment.

An hour before the scheduled start of the program Mrs. Dartley appeared. She looked superb.

Sylvia, who felt number and more afraid with each passing hour, had stayed in her room as long as possible. Now Campion gave her a whiskey and insisted that she come downstairs with him. The house was hardly recognizable. Wires and cords and buzzing pieces of machinery filled the downstairs and part of the grounds, where some sort of mobile unit had been parked, practically in the rose garden. The music room had been turned into a studio, and there was a television screen there too, placed so that Knox and Mrs. Dartley could watch themselves. They were already seated under the lights; cameramen were making their final arrangements. Next to the studio was the control room. It contained the monitor board, several very pleasant and very busy young men, two of them in earphones, and Ralph Bledder in a corner, guarding the direct line through Zürich and Paris to New York. Chairs were placed so that Campion and Sylvia could watch the large screen. Anton, now suffering from a fever, had been given medicines and put to bed. The others waited.

At last the synchronized tape began to spin, and images of Gwendolyn Dartley to flicker across the screen. Sylvia was caught up at once. The skill with which Knox and his staff had put the program together surprised her: that moving back and forth in time and space, that interspersing of Mrs. Dartley's life with the quick sharp interviews with still-living friends and foes. It saddened her too, because it was really the story of a forgotten woman, a reminder of how quickly the world abandons its celebrities. Sylvia had known Mrs. Dartley's name all her life without ever quite knowing why. She was the sort of figure who, before the war, arriving on the *Normandie* or leaving on the *Queen Mary*, always had her picture in the papers, making an outrageous remark about someone or something—a woman who, one vaguely felt, was "on the right side." But Mrs. Dartley almost never talked about the past, and now Sylvia was astonished, and touched, by all that Mrs. Dartley's eyes had seen. No wonder Knox had thought them all a disappointing lot at Kilchberg. There she was with Winston Churchill, each grinning but looking too as though each had just eaten broken glass; and there she was sitting in the garden at Riverdale with Toscanini. Knox's voice in the background, like that of an actor, caught in spite of itself the right notes. There were the husbands and a house or two she had lived in and the references to the novels and the play, and most of all there were the famous friends. What had she and Stravinsky been doing, playing a game of some sort, and of whose devising? How amused they looked. And whose smile was the toothiest and most confident at Hyde Park? And here, young and lovely and with a still hurt face, she hung on the arm of Bob Dartley, who was wearing a lieutenant's uniform.

How many Gwendolyn Dartleys were there, and which was the real one, or were they all one? The image on the screen at this instant, the one who had been that image, the one of whom there was perhaps no image at all, or the one who now sat not many feet away in another room with Benjamin Knox? Sylvia felt she had fallen into a house of mirrors. No, that was not right; into a crystal perhaps. There it was, that life, a child of eight peering out of an oval frame, a woman in her forties being thrown out of a Bundist meeting in New York. It was not a serious treatment of Gwendolyn—nothing was said of her essential spirit, nothing was shown of what was in her that united these images into the woman who was—and yet it was better by far than Sylvia could have imagined or expected.

Now came a recording of her voice, lighter, younger, broadcasting from London during the war; some comments by the former American Ambassador to the Court of St. James; Mrs. Dartley at her desk in Old Lyme in the late forties; a few seconds of a newsreel clip taken at the White House in 1948. It was all spinning out now, Sylvia felt, changing, nearly over with. And then another newsreel clip: Mrs. Dartley, the special representative of some committee or other, in Berlin in 1946, standing in the rain, addressing a crowd of ragged, pinch-faced Germans, telling them ... And then a disturbing jump to a picture of the Villa Kilchberg and, painfully, some seconds of Lily Halász. Sylvia put her head down, but heard the voice. And now there on the screen were Knox and Gwendolyn in the music room. Knox looked different; his tense manner had taken on authority. Afterwards Sylvia could never remember those opening remarks which they exchanged or how it was that Knox in his new and earnest voice turned it all so quickly to Hungary. She remembered only how the camera moved in on Gwendolyn. It was her face that filled the screen—old, one saw now, suffering, but with the marks of grace upon it, reassuring, kind even, listening to Knox. And now she was about to speak. Sylvia and Ernest both leaned forward, awaiting her words. And then the screen went black, went silent; she had disappeared.

In the few shocked seconds that followed no one moved. Then a voice from New York announced that they were "interrupting this program" in order to take their viewers to the United Nations in New York, where at eight o'clock the General Assembly would meet in special session. Several of the more important delegates, among them the delegate from India, had agreed to give their views of the . . . One of the technicians took off his earphones and turned toward Bledder. Benjamin Knox slammed furiously into the room and took Bledder by the lapels. Why had he not stood up for their rights, why had he not held out for those assurances which New York had given Knox earlier in the day, why had he not at least called Knox to the line when New York first indicated an earlier termination of the program, why had he not made them understand how important this was, why had *he* not understood? There were tears in Knox's eyes.

When Ernest and Sylvia got into the other room they found Mrs. Dartley still seated and staring at the empty screen from which she too had watched herself disappear. Now she turned and looked at them, slowly shaking her head. "No matter," she said at last.

Fifty-two

A cold wind blew round the Golden Horn. George Bingham strode past the Serpentine Column. He had made his rendezvous somewhere on the Black Sea and had returned safely to Istanbul, once the city of Constantine, once the citadel of Christ and Rome in the East, on the night of November 4th. Istanbul could not contain his unspent energy. Hungary was falling, to belated protests, betrayed on all sides. Old certainties fell with it. Istanbul was not the city to calm him. The release which usually followed a completed mission, the greater usually the greater the risk, would not come. The restlessness, the tension, even the fear were still with him. He reminded himself that if Sylvia had gone to Athens he might have got to her for a few hours. But by now she was back up in those mountains, and he was still on a tight schedule: Berlin the next day, London the day after that, and that night a plane to Washington, where on the 7th, the day after the elections, he would make his final recommendations.

"We don't journey very far into the world of feeling," she had said once, only that. He had not responded, but he had understood. Since June he had often thought of her as a protecting spirit which had been taken from him; since leaving her in Milan as a spirit whose demands, not to be met halfway, might change everything. He was drawn toward her as, after long wanderings in the icy reaches, towards a fire. But fire consumed. And what then would remain? He was not certain. He struggled. What would lie on the other side of this experience if he were to give in to it? Or had he already done so? He was no fool, and yet it did seem to him a mystery, this new world. The reality of her flesh as he had known it the last time at Kilchberg came upon him repeatedly, as did a sense of her presence in quite a new way, the woman herself, the individual—what she so insisted on being; her own sufferings, her art, all that from the beginning had drawn him to her but that he had never dared let himself feel too deeply; all this reality too had come again and again upon him in the last few days, with dangerous suddenness, exactly as the Tintoretto had done, and all of this smote him with desire and doubt. He would think about it afterwards, after Washington. He could be with her in no time then. He would hunt her down. The rest of this journey could not pass quickly enough. In a few hours he would be on the plane for Berlin. The sooner the better. He turned his face toward the Bosphorus. A disturbing phrase ran through his head. Where had it come from? A sing-song rhythm, a snatch from a childhood game, a riddle, or what? *Loser finds all.* He touched the Burnt Column and turned for his hotel.

In Berlin he felt better. Here in this city with the unimaginable differences elbow to elbow occupational doubts were more easily put down. A little even of the old belligerence came back. He made his report shortly after arriving, and decided to take a quick stroll through East Berlin later in the day. A really skilled observer like himself could learn a fair amount just now. He was going to have a lot to say in Washington, whether anyone liked it or not. At the same time he felt an urgent desire to communicate with Sylvia at once. He spent the rest of the morning, nearly two hours, searching through bookstores until he found a small, postcard-size reproduction of the Tintoretto. The colors were not very good, the light was weak, but it would have to do. That good-bye in Milano had had much too permanent a ring to it—surely there was still a way of reaching her. There had to be.

Back in his hotel room he sat looking at the postcard. Then he turned it over. The message he put there seemed really to write itself: "Sweet Venus save my soul." An odd lightness went through him when he read this over. It vanished and he was left feeling very pleased with himself. If he had thought for hours he could have come up with nothing better. He knew her so well; he knew this would please her—and catch her too where she was most vulnerable, remind her in just the right way of the one hold he had over her that Campion didn't. Besides, maybe it was even true about his soul. He signed the card simply, "Your St. G.," put it into a hotel envelope and wrote her name and address on the outside, not adding of course any return address to that of the hotel. Then he hesitated. He had taken so many little risks in connection with her, things she knew nothing about. It would be more prudent, for her sake too, if he waited and mailed this from London or New York, from anywhere in the world really but Berlin. Reluctantly he opened the envelope again and tossed it into the waste basket. Then, astonished at himself, he retrieved it, lighted a match and burned it in the ash tray. The blackened shards of ash he rubbed into dust between his hands. In the bathroom he scrubbed this off, then put the postcard, which had no name or address on it, into a pocket.

In crossing into East Berlin Bingham was not exactly breaking a rule—he had considerable autonomy in such matters—but he was going against the policy of the moment, since except for extraordinary situations such as the one that had sent him to the Black Sea a general slackening of activity had been ordered. He thought about this when he became certain that two men, ostensibly having nothing to do with each other, were following him. His first reaction was one almost of indifference. Berlin was a city where everyone shadowed everyone else; it almost never came to anything; if it did there would be no agents left on either side. The important thing was to keep your head. He led them along in a happenstance, tourist's manner for perhaps ten minutes, trying to make up his mind. Now that he considered how quickly they had picked him up he was beginning to feel uneasy, and he decided against taking any of the customary diversions. They would be as familiar with them as he, and if something really serious was going on and they were still in any doubt at all as to his identity his falling into the usual pattern would tell them what they wanted to know.

Of all cities, East Berlin was the worst to be caught in, with practically no cafés or restaurants to go into. For a few seconds a terrible fury possessed him. What was he doing in East Berlin at all? How could he, of all people, be caught in such a stupid way? What had he done or not done since arriving in Berlin that had betrayed him? Or was it something that had happened before he even got there this time? Was it a whole long chain of moments that he had not even seen that had led him here? He had to force himself to stay in the role of sightseer, for that was his only hope. The papers he had, the clothes, everything would identify him as businessman from Toronto; it was a persona he felt at home in, and he had even once spent a couple of weeks in Canada perfecting it. But now he had to remind himself of all this. It did not come easily, naturally, as it ought to. What was the matter with him? He got better control, thinking of how many times he had drummed it into his men, that above all you were never to reveal the slightest suspicion even in the tightest of situations, that they could almost never be really sure, that this was your strongest weapon. It had worked often enough in the past for him.

Yet he had to exert the most extreme sort of will power to keep himself from hurrying, had to force himself to go up to someone and ask in faked halting German for street directions, had to force himself to go slightly wrong then, to show just the right amount of bewilderment, to stop still another person and ask for directions. He knew of course exactly where he was; he had only four blocks more to go to a point where the line ran in its zigzag fashion behind the hotel, where cover would be waiting for him. But what had given him away? Now he would never know, but he was certain it was something. There was an unmistakable deliberateness now about his pursuers, an almost undisguised stalking. He was half tempted to turn and face them, but he managed not to. Was it something he had done while he was dreaming again about the damned Tintoretto? Or—the thought jolted him—was it perhaps something that he had *not* done on his last trip into eastern Germany, the one just before he had lighted out for Kilchberg? Any way you looked at it, it led back to her; though he walked now in a circle, it was she who was at the center, she who was the dangerous one. What if he had given in? What if they had gone on to Greece? With a start he realized that again he had not been paying attention, that again he had almost begun to walk too fast and to move too obviously, too directly, for the border. On the other side of his love for Sylvia lay . . . nothing, it now seemed to him, nothing at all. She was wrong, Sylvia Grierson, he knew it, knew it now with the hunters at his back. You were either strong or you were weak; there was no in-between. She was just wrong, and he was glad that he had not mailed that card, *Sweet Venus save my soul* . . .

But what a longing now came over him, what a strange lightness. He thought then of free fall, of the moment before the parachute opens, before the great tugging of the whole body, thought of the leap and the first contact with the wind as though one would be laid bare to the most unprotected quick of being and no longer minded, of the far, far out into the universe, the not caring about the next minute or whatever might come afterwards, and the fear, the anxiety, the beating heart assuaged, and the wind roaring, riding the currents now, no longer at war with a hostile universe but caught instead in its most secret rhythms, no longer master but for those moments borne in all the elements and in none. The out, out, out into space, and the wind, the giving-in, the freedom, even the serene and peaceful floating that would follow. Then, like a great parachute opening, to the familiar sound of the crack, crack, crack, the pistol shot, the white unfolding, his heart exploded.

Fifty-three

It was Sylvia who turned up the first photograph of Posy and Marshall. She had developed an aversion to newspapers, those couriers of ill tidings, but she also had a ravenous appetite for news which prevented her from staying away from them. Slowly, sadly, she had been scanning the first pictures of the refugees. It seemed to her that she had been looking at these scenes all her life, the same confusion and desperate expressions, first in one part of the world and then another, the homeless, the driven-out, the ordinary victims, straggling over mountain passes or clinging to freight cars or stumbling out of concentration camps or clotting the road fleeing east or fleeing west, people who spoke Spanish or Polish or German or it did not matter what. And then, in one of these photographs, fixed like the others in the whorl of disaster, among the border guards and other officials, the hunted soldiers, and the stunned-looking men and women with their little bundles and the shivering children—among all this stood Posy and Marshall, both in open raincoats, he reaching out toward her and she in turn reaching towards a child with a sign hung around his neck. It was clear from the expression on their faces that nothing in their lives had ever prepared them for what they were now witnessing. In the background, shadowy and mysterious, was a road marker with names on it which could not be read and which seemed not to be pointing in set and orderly directions but to be in the process of spinning, like the points of a compass that had gone wrong. Or so it seemed to Sylvia. It was probably only a chance trick of light and shadow. Or her own state of nerves. She pulled herself together and took the picture to Mrs. Dartley.

Had it not been for this photograph, the accident to the Rolls Royce, briefly noted by the wire services, would no doubt never have been picked up in the press, and those curious stories about Posy and Marshall which appeared in some of the newspapers coming into the villa during the rest of the day would never have been. According to one English paper they had been on their way to take up arms and join the Freedom Fighters—this written in such a way as to suggest that Englishmen who were protesting the Suez venture were somehow, in contrast to "these two young Americans," lacking in mettle. A tabloid stated that they had actually been in Budapest for the past week fighting. *The Daily Worker* claimed that they were American agents who had been sent with a message to the "imperialist, reactionary forces of the counter-revolution" but had been foiled by Hungarian patriots and turned back. A right-wing American paper—which counseled both isolation from European affairs and armed intervention—

implied that things had reached a pretty pass if the only way Americans could "show the flag" in time of crisis was in the "lone effort" of a single American boy and girl in whom the "true American spirit" survived. A French paper thought it likely that they had been on their way to make contact with Hungarian writers and intellectuals. A Vienna paper, with no special political interests but a love of gossip, had it on good authority that the automobile itself, the Rolls, belonged to a branch of the Esterhazy family now resident in Vienna. An English daily whose liberalism was defined chiefly by chronic anti-Americanism ventured the opinion that "it was a measure of the degree to which the world's conscience had been touched by the Hungarian people's struggles towards socialism that even two young Americans, so rich as to be travelling about in a Rolls Royce, had wished to join in that struggle."

And so it went. They felt they might have been reading about someone, but not Posy, not Marshall. Only *The New York Times* confined itself in a very small notice to a dull but fairly accurate account of what might be known. They even spelled the names correctly—"Rosanna Drummond, daughter of . . ."—and knew that the car belonged to Gwendolyn Dartley, "with whom they have been vacationing in Switzerland," although they did slip in calling them both music students.

It was not that anyone at Kilchberg believed the more fanciful of these stories which were offered up as the truth or—perhaps unwittingly—as a diversion to an uneasy world. But for a time it was a little difficult to know exactly what had happened, beyond the fact that late on the evening of November 4th the Rolls, filled with refugees and driven by Marshall, had plunged into a ditch near the Hungarian border, fortunately without injuring any of its occupants. "Death of a Phantom," the caption of one of the early reports had read. This too was far from the truth, but it gave its bad moments at Kilchberg. Mrs. Dartley, reading it, had turned her face to the wall for a few seconds, then turned back to Campion. "A proper ending, I suppose," she said, and did not refer to it again. Later in the day she said to Sylvia, in that worried, tentative way that was so new for her, "I trust there was nothing in the way of false heroics. It would be so disappointing." "Oh I don't think there could have been," Sylvia answered. But then she too found herself suddenly wondering. What had they thought, the two fair-haired ones—that world harmonies would flow from their appear-

ance at the border of the land harrowed by the knowledge of sin
much as from Marshall's flute, that the Dark Rider would be
driven away by *them?* Had they thought to sail magnificently
along the road to Budapest in the Rolls Royce, welcomed and
cheered at, casting the favors of their beauty and trusting hearts
before them, reaching out hands, and Posy perhaps waving the
little green scarf in which she had used to collect the food for
Felix? Yet no sooner had Sylvia phrased this to herself than she felt
shame, recognizing the old familiar signs of despair, the symptoms
too of that terrible anxiety which had gripped her since the morning before. Why begrudge Posy and Marshall their desire to connect? She believed in the answer she had given Gwendolyn.

In the evening Marshall at last got through to them by phone. It
was all as they might sensibly have thought it to be. Arriving in
Vienna at the time when the general population believed the revolution to have succeeded, they had quickly fallen in with groups of
students who were organizing a Help Hungary drive. Convoys
carrying food and medicines were passing freely back and forth
across the border. Supplies of this sort were badly needed and cars
were scarce. They had been sure Mrs. Dartley would approve.
One of the relief agencies gave them medicines which they intended to turn over to a Hungarian convoy at the border. But
when they got there on the 3rd things were already changing. By
the time they were able to transfer the medicines it was late, and
they had spent the night at Klingenbach. The next morning they
had been on hand when the first of the refugees began arriving.
They had volunteered the car and themselves—again they had
been sure Mrs. Dartley would approve—and had operated a shut-
tle, carrying people from the border to hastily organized reception
centers. And then on the last trip, in the confusion on the road, an
idiot truck driver . . . Marshall did not really think it had been his
fault . . . the car was not badly damaged at all . . . he would see to
it that it was put into perfect order again . . . he hoped she would
not be too angry . . . Here Mrs. Dartley interrupted him: "Never
mind about the car. Of course you did the right thing, of course."
And then she asked him if he had found time to go to the concert
and when he told her yes she smiled and said, "Ah. Good. I am
glad to hear that too."

To everyone's relief, by midday of the 6th Posy and Marshall
had lost their news value. Sylvia, meticulously searching through

the papers, announced that she could find only a few references to them, and nothing at all exotic. The most recent paper to have arrived, the *Neue Züricher Zeitung*, was the last to which she turned. Looking at its front page it suddenly seemed to her that she had lost her ability to read German. *"Grenzmord in Berlin,"* one of the captions said, but as she read the German made no sense to her. The meaning of the report she had grasped at a glance, as she would have done had it been in English, but when she attempted to read the item line by line syllables blurred and jumped.

"Is something wrong?" Ernest asked.

She turned to him in bewilderment, her mouth opening for a second without speech, a puzzled smile flitting over her face, as though to make apology for her stupidity. "My German seems suddenly to have gone to pieces. I can't understand this. It's so silly of me."

He was beside her at the table where they had all got into the habit in the last days of going through the papers, Mrs. Dartley's room having finally become inundated with print. "Which one?" he asked.

She pointed. His eyes swept over it. He turned to her with the slow, almost angry expression of a man who at last understood all.

"Please," she said very rapidly. "Please read it. Read it now. Go ahead. Translate it for me. Please. I'm fine."

When he still did not speak she said, *"Please.* I have to be sure."

Ernest Campion, reading from the German, put steadily into English: "Berlin, November 5. A man identified from his papers as a Canadian was shot to death on his way out of the Eastern sector at approximately five P.M. today. Witnesses in West Berlin said that at about thirty yards from the border he broke into a sudden sprint and was felled by bullets just as he reached the line. His assailants continued the pursuit, evidently with the intention of pulling their victim back into the Eastern sector, but fled when several West Berliners reached the body first. It is widely thought in official Berlin that the murdered man was a member of the United States Central Intelligence Agency, but no statement of confirmation or denial is yet available."

Fifty-four

George Bingham had once promised Sylvia that he would do his best to arrange a way for her to be told if anything should happen to him. It was a promise he had kept. In a surprisingly short time she received a letter from a high-ranking official at AMPERE, who regretfully informed her of the sad and sudden death—in London, of pneumonia—of his friend and colleague. The final rites had been by cremation, and the ashes conveyed to a distant and surviving relative in Vermont. He was a man who had "lived austerely and left little behind," the letter said—words which fell like iron rain upon her. But he had wanted the one object among his personal effects which had meant the most to him to pass to her in the event of his death. It would be sent to her just as soon as it was "feasible." Sylvia knew what it would be: his ring, the one that had belonged to the Greek great-grandfather, the one with the family crest. When the package came, she did not open it. To Ernest she had said only, "Yes, it was true. It was he. He's dead." She did not speak again of George Bingham. Ernest saw her as a grieving, mourning figure, someone not yet to be approached too closely, someone who was traveling the far distant reaches of suffering and would make her way back when it became possible for her to do so, someone it was worth waiting for.

Posy and Marshall returned, and were both scolded and praised. Mrs. Dartley now seemed relieved that the Phantom was gone, and gone it was. Marshall, acting on instructions from her, had sought a buyer for it in Vienna, and making a virtue of the commercial talents of his forefathers had driven a hard bargain with a Hollywood producer who had arrived in Vienna to rush before the cameras—hurriedly, hurriedly, before the world forgot—a film about the Hungarian revolution. Mrs. Dartley spoke frequently of how impossible keeping up such a car would have been in the life that lay before her. But Sylvia did not think this was the whole story. Something had happened to Mrs. Dartley. She could not quite say what it was. But it was as though she too had crossed some mysterious border. A terrible restlessness had seized upon her, and there were also passing moments when, for the first time, she seemed weak, almost helpless. Perhaps *uncertain* was the word that best described her. She made and changed plans constantly.

She had entirely given up the idea of ever returning to America. She spoke of moving to England, where she still had some money—she was now revealed as being almost hopelessly bankrupt, and this too, like the loss of the Rolls, she seemed oddly to welcome. She spoke of buying a small chalet she knew of high in the Engadine. She spoke of moving to the Balearics. And of other possibilities, but was unable to decide. Enough of the television program had gone out to have aroused a little interest in her; had she wished, she could, with the assistance of the publicity people and other agents who now offered their services, have contrived a brief popularity, and she could certainly, even after paying the agents, have made a fair amount of money. But all such offers, most of which involved television appearances, she turned down. "I am a *personage*," she told Campion. "And the exploitation of personality isn't a form of exploitation that has ever greatly attracted me," which, even if it was not entirely true, was not under the circumstances to be argued with. On another occasion she may more nearly have stated the deepest reason for her attitude toward these offers; she knew what it was like to have been famous and then forgotten, she said; it was not an experience she cared to repeat.

A number of good and reputable publishing firms had also approached her, urging her to write her memoirs, and her old house urged the reissuing of one of the novels, *A Sunken Journey*. When she gave vague replies they suggested a ghost-writer, though they used a more tactful phrase for it. She responded with contempt, they with appeasements and improved terms. But still she procrastinated. Campion did not think she would ever say yes or ever write her memoirs. One offer she did take, from the same American magazine for which she had written during and immediately after the war: a respectable sum for twelve articles on anything she wanted to write about in the next year. When the advance on this contract came she intended to give it as quittance to Giovanni and Celeste. Ernest, however, wondered how many even of these she would ever actually write. She talked suspiciously about some sort of machine she claimed to have heard of which you could "chat into" and then push a button and a perfectly ordered text and typed-up pages would appear; a "magic writing box" was her term for it. Perhaps she did not seriously believe in the existence of such a machine and only referred to it as a way of getting a reaction out of Sylvia—which it always did, even when Sylvia was

most extremely withdrawn. Each time, her tone always faintly put
out, Sylvia would assure, or warn, Mrs. Dartley that the sort of
machine she had in mind simply did not exist, and never would.

Benjamin Knox had left the day after the American elections, a
look of gathering bewilderment on his face. He had had his moment, but he would never quite understand what had happened to
him. Bledder he had of course got rid of. Knox was on his way to
Germany. Mrs. Dartley had told him about the Greifenberg papers
and had at last interceded for him with Andreas Greifenberg's
widow, who had agreed to meet and talk with Knox. Mrs. Dartley
did not think anything would or could really come of it, but you
never knew, and she felt it was the least she could do for Knox
considering the perplexities he had undergone at Kilchberg. Although she was not entirely sure that she had done him a favor.
"Anna Greifenberg's an unusual woman," she had said at one
point, and then a most curious slow smile had come across her
face. "But then Andreas only liked unusual women," she added
softly.

Marshall and Posy stayed at the villa for a week, packing their
belongings—the brass-rubbings were, as always, an enormous
problem—and waiting for certain arrangements to become definite. A great flow of letters now reached them from friends and
family in America. Posy's mother was quite frankly dining out
regularly on her daughter's brief appearance in the newspapers,
and she had thought it so "absolutely smashing" of Posy to have
helped out with all those poor Hungarians that she had even written her a letter about it. Marshall's parents revealed all too clearly,
though without knowing it themselves, that what had worried
them all along was what their friends would think of *them* for
having a son who so poorly fit the only pattern that was approved
of in their little world. Now they had a story to tell, or thought
they did, one that would make the flute-playing all right. Marshall
had proved himself to be a man and a red-blooded American, his
father actually wrote him. Other phrases in his letter indicated that
he took Marshall's "exploits" to mean that his son now shared his
own special neurosis, the one that manifested itself as a conventionally mindless but fervid hatred of "The Reds," a category
which for him rather tended to include nearly everyone. Marshall
was generous and did not disabuse him, grateful for the continent
and ocean that lay between them and that helped make his gener-

osity possible. He was charitable too, and accepted the check that
was included in a letter from his mother along with the statement
that she and his father had decided it would be all right for him to
keep the money from the money order (he had already written to
say he had cashed it and for what purpose).

Marshall's and Posy's plans were now quite complete. From
Kilchberg they were going to Austria, where they and other
young volunteers from all over western Europe would be building
the barracks now so desperately needed for the refugees—Hungarians still came, each day by the thousands, along the winter
roads and over a border the Russians had not yet chosen to close.
Then in January Marshall would take up residence at the Mozarteum, and Posy would settle in Munich, working as an apprentice to the couple that put back together again the sunbursts,
Cupids, and putti, the Daphnes, Apollos, and miraculous doves, all
the worshipful baroque divinities, profane and sacred, which had
once graced church, hall, garden, and theatre in south Catholic
Germany. In the early summer they would be married.

Both Mrs. Dartley and Ernest had heard from Elsie; the first, a
long letter written from London just after Lily's funeral, had been
to Mrs. Dartley but had been meant for all who had known Lily.
Ernest's even longer letter came later, from Texas, full of characteristically cynical phrases, but full of feeling too. She had not yet
made up her mind about marrying Beau; he continued to fascinate
her and she was certainly tired of being "arty-tarty and trampy-
vampy" but she wasn't sure she could adjust to all those wild
animals she sometimes met at the parties he took her to, all those
marvelous-*looking* people—they didn't even have circles under
their eyes—saying the most barbaric things. And most of them
college graduates too, which you'd think would make a difference.
It frightened her. ("For me it's terrible, it's like being back in
Hungary during the Nazi time when I hear some of the things
they say. I don't get it.") Beau would never leave Texas, she knew,
and she wouldn't want him to; he loved it, and it needed people
like Beau, people who could change. But she had the feeling she
was only making trouble for him. Now that he'd taken to reading
The New Republic and the *Times* he'd already had some fights at
the hospital. And what about her? Wouldn't they end up lynching
her? And what about children? Would they mind being *Misch-
linge?* Money helped, of course, and Beau had that, and all that

kindness. Well, she had sort of said yes, to tell the truth, but in the meantime she had a chance to join a new repertory theatre that had just opened in Seattle. Probably the rubes there would be just as rubish as anywhere else west of the Hudson, but it would give her a chance to be really sure about Beau. At the end of the letter, under her signature, she wrote, "She came back, didn't she? Good luck, darling. I hope to God she knows how lucky she is."

Only one thing brought out the old fire in Mrs. Dartley, the deep tones of outrage and sorrow, the energy, and mixed through it all—inexplicable, not yet to be grasped—an occasional clear cadence of hope, and that was the Hungarian revolution. This event, this "high deed," as she was now in the habit of phrasing it, she set herself to defending with ever-recurring vigor, and not blindly but with knowledge. "It will be the task of my old age," she told Sylvia. "It will be my last passion." She was in correspondence with Anna Kéthley, who had tried to get back to Budapest when she heard of the Russian attack but had been stopped at the border and who had then flown to New York and was waiting in vain to be allowed to address the United Nations. She talked by phone with many of the correspondents who had been in Hungary during the victorious days of the revolution and who had left after November 4th. She was collecting every scrap of information she could find, from every source. That nothing much would result from this did not seem to Sylvia to be the point. Mrs. Dartley saw a guilty world turning rapidly away, soothing its conscience by taking, sometimes, refugees, many of whom would no doubt prove disappointing to benefactors who would not easily be able to understand the daily discouragement of such an uprooting.

But the real lessons in what had happened Mrs. Dartley did not believe could be forgotten, not in the East, not in the West, whatever efforts to distort the truth might be made, were already being made. A small people, suppressed by force, physically tormented and intimidated, lied to and indoctrinated, kept in terror, had risen overnight to demand its freedom. Superior force had put them down, but not before they had shaken an empire, not before they had shown that perhaps after all totalitarianism was not to be borne forever. In Csepel workers affixed to the walls of empty factories this sign: "The 40,000 aristocrats and fascists of Csepel strike on." In Budapest on the ruins: "Attention! Ten million counter-revolutionaries are at large in the country!" Nothing could ever be quite the same again. Mrs. Dartley did not know what would come, what would happen, what changes there would be—but that there would be changes she was sure. It had been the purest revolution ever. There had never been a nobler attempt on the part of a people who had suffered most terrible cruelties to triumph over the blood lust that is in every breast. And if perhaps it was the last revolution of its kind, it might also turn out to have been the greatest.

Never had Sylvia admired Mrs. Dartley more than she did now, when she listened to her talk of this. For the first time too she felt really close to this woman who for all her strong passions was also a little unapproachable. Signs of weakness and old age had, if any-thing, given her a kind of greatness. She wanted to stay close to her; she felt that Mrs. Dartley's very existence made for a hope which at that moment was otherwise hard to find, especially as the days passed and the full horror of what was happening in Hungary became clear. Hungary was being sealed off completely now; it was a prison with the walls closing in, filled with hungry and defeated people who were nevertheless turning to passive resist-ance and protest; a torture chamber; a charnel house. And only Mrs. Dartley believed it had not all been in vain. Sylvia saw in Ernest the same reaction to her, although they did not speak of it. They did what they could to help her, listened chiefly, helped her to sort through that incredibly confused and endlessly growing mass of newspaper clippings, although it was obvious that they would never now be brought into any final order.

Sylvia welcomed the chance to be doing something; it helped her to bear her own private sorrow, sorrow of a magnitude she could never have anticipated. It helped her to overcome a little those personal worries and anxieties which in comparison to the Hungarian tragedy seemed so trivial and unimportant. Or ought to have seemed so, but didn't, for with each passing day they came ever more to take on that absolute importance of something which is happening to the self, even if in the shadow of much greater events. She was still putting off decisions, but she could not do so for much longer, and she now had very little hope. If her own life was not in ruins, then at the least it was turning in an unimaginable direction, one that would alter irrevocably the preparations and hopes of a lifetime.

When, toward the end of November, in the midst of another

moving-to-England phase, Mrs. Dartley suddenly decided that she must fly to London, Sylvia thought she detected some peculiar reluctance in her, as though she wished to undertake something she was not certain she had the strength for. In a moment of quick insight Sylvia asked if she would like her to go along. She would.

They were only to be in London for two days, and the ostensible purpose of the trip was to look for a flat. But when they got there Mrs. Dartley did not make the slightest gesture toward doing so. The first day they spent a painful hour with Margó. "How awful for Lily, how awful," Mrs. Dartley said several times afterwards, but that was all. On the second afternoon they went to visit Lily's grave, Mrs. Dartley having hired a car and made arrangements by phone with the sexton. They drove for nearly two hours and came at last to a small village whose prize was its Norman church. Lily was buried in the churchyard. There, it turned out, Bob Dartley was also buried, along with a great many other members of the Dartley family. The stone marker over his grave had a worn and permanent look to it and when Sylvia read its dates it struck her with force that he had been dead now for nearly forty years. She looked at Mrs. Dartley, walking about among the tombs with complete composure. There too, astonishingly, was the grave of Louisa Campion. For a moment it seemed very disturbing to Sylvia to be standing beside the grave of Ernest's mother, to think that all those once burning feelings and terrible conflicts which must once have driven her had so long been put to rest. Had Ernest stood there too? Undoubtedly he had. Would they one day come here together? It did not now seem so. Nearby was a small memorial stone, which, after great and violent conflict with the rector, Gwendolyn had had placed there: "To the memory of Andreas Greifenberg, born in Marienwerder 1892—died in Dachau 1944. Loved in death as in life by Robert Alexander James Dartley and Gwendolyn and by Louisa Phipps Campion." Sylvia thought it the most remarkable inscription she had ever read; it had neither beginning nor end; and as she stood before it she felt that she was very near to comprehending some profoundly complex yet simple truth . . . And just then a great cry of pain broke from Gwendolyn Dartley, a high sob, a lament; it shook the air. Hearing it, Sylvia turned and saw the blind suffering face, the groping hands, and hurried toward her. The tall body bent forward and the face was hidden now in the hands. Sylvia put her arms around her and felt how the whole frame was shaken. She did not speak. Slowly she led her to the car.

When they returned to Kilchberg one problem at least had been solved, the problem of Anton. It appeared that Rudi's modest estate, a small savings account and an insurance policy, was to pass to him. And the furnishings of Rudi's bed-sitting room in Küsnacht. Anton had recovered some time before from his cold. Slowly his spirits were improving too. He needed a scapegoat, and he had at last found one, the caretaker of the Wagner collection at the Wesendonck villa, an old man of his own age with whom he now spent long hours in happy argument.

A few days after the return from London Mrs. Dartley decided to go to Vienna and talk to refugees for herself. This time it was Ernest she wanted to go with her. It was Sylvia who made him feel that he should, who even made him feel that if she were alone for a time now she might better pull herself togehter. Yet he left reluctantly, and after only three days in Vienna abruptly flew back to Zürich. When he got to Kilchberg he found that Sylvia had gone, leaving behind not a note, not a trace.

Fifty-five

A few days before Christmas Ernest Campion entered the villa to find a letter for him propped up on the hall table. It was postmarked Munich, and though the envelope was typewritten and carried no return address, he knew it was from Sylvia. He knew too that Gwendolyn had seen it, and had also guessed. Standing there in the empty hallway he opened it with stiff fingers and read.

Dear Ernest—

I've no idea of whether you want to hear from me again or not. Something tells me that you do, but I may be wrong. If so, this is a small enough risk to take, considering everything. Certainly I don't "deserve" your interest, or your love. But I am at last free to write you, and I haven't been till now, and I'm going to. I'm not in Munich, incidentally, though that's probably where this will be posted from, and there's a firm there that forwards mail to me. I'll put that address at the end, just in case you want to write to me.

I left Kilchberg—and you—because I thought I was going to have a child, his child. I wonder if you guessed that this was my reason for running. Gwendolyn did, I imagine. I now find—to my great relief, I must admit—that I was mistaken. It was nature, my nature at any rate, stopping in its tracks for him, mourning. The medical version is different, I learned yesterday: nervous strain, shock, can do this for a time to a "sensitive" woman's body. We all have our different languages for describing agonies of the spirit. My body at least has unburdened itself.

Do I still mourn him? Yes. Often there's something almost impersonal about it now, above all the feeling that there *was* a loss—though perhaps it took place before his death. If I were a Catholic I should light candles for his soul. I've wished there were *some* rite I could perform for him, and it's bothered me that there hasn't been. Perhaps if, like Antigone, I could search out his bones and throw a little earth on them? But they're gone too, and that hurts—someone who loved him ought to have been there at the fiery moment. I ought to have been there. I can't really think of him, you know, in terms of Christian placations, and sometimes I'm haunted still by a dark figure, half shade, half flesh, creaking beneath the weight of heavy unbuckling armor—oh how heavily it must weigh on him, I often think—moving uneasily, perpetually, from shore to shore. And then when this happens I think too, almost at once, of the man I knew, see him at the keyboard trying to get the Bach to come out right, and a considerable amount of real, quite personal pain begins all over again.

Is it terrible to write all this to you? Probably. But it would be worse to make a beginning (I catch my breath at that—do you?) that isn't an honest one. You must know what real ghosts trail me about, so that you don't invent and struggle vainly with phantoms of no consequence. His is real, and of consequence. But it will cease to be, and he will fade. That is the saddest part.

During this time of grief and mourning (and not only for him) and shocked uncertainty about my own future—the last sort of future I could ever have imagined for myself, of course

—and almost unbearable loneliness, my work, strangely enough, has gone on. Do you see what you might be in for? What sort of unfeeling beast I am who, in the midst of so much personal anguish and so much general slaughter and suffering, goes about her tasks with almost heightened powers? Where, I have asked myself, do these forms come from? What is the source of this incredible, independent life of their own which they seem to have? And I have no answer. It is a mystery, and I am content to leave it at that. I only know that I have felt sometimes as though I were almost anonymous, as though my own life is, if not unimportant—at least not to me—then certainly irrelevant to the possibility, the privilege of art. And why do I tell you this too? Because these "tasks," while not phantoms, *are* obstacles, and they are much more formidable, I am sure, than his poor ghost. Do you understand what I am really saying, what a very very bad bargain you would be getting?

Oh Ernest, Ernest, has ever a woman said to a man less graciously—yes; even, if you *do* still care, yes I will marry you. For if you must have to wife someone who's defying gravity, a woman who is an artist, then I am she.

Oh Ernest, shall we be like those Egyptians, husband and wife, one sometimes sees in the old wall paintings, faces turned exactly to each other, holding each other, your arm about my waist, my hand upon your shoulder, standing thus in a world of abounding cruelty? I sometimes see us so.

I am often afraid now. Sometimes I awaken in the middle of the night and it all seems too much and nothing at all, everything that has happened and that will happen, a second's dream in the mindless spaces of a purely chance universe. And death seems ever near. And yet, I don't despair. There's a letter that Mozart wrote once, to his father I think, I'm not sure, but in it he called Death "man's trustiest and truest friend." He said something too about the daily knowledge of death teaching serenity, brotherly love, and even the will to live. Well, I am no Mozart and *his* serenity's as much beyond me as the smallest little phrase he ever composed, but, still, it is true what he said, and it helps knowing it, feeling it working as truth in one's self—even, sometimes, for just a second or two, at the worst moments, a sort of lightness, a something that is almost serenity even. Though that part, as I've said, is the most elusive, for there is also in me—surely you have seen this?—a wild fury, a terrible rage that possesses me from time to time, a rage at all the *horror*. And in some way my gift depends on this too. Could you bear this, bear it without hating me? Could you even forgive me? Just enough to make it possible to bear *me?*

And something else. In spite of what I've told you about my work, I'm far from being all spirit pure and brave in quite another sense. I've missed you terribly. I've found the idea that I may never be with you again almost unendurable. Not quite, but almost, and more perhaps than I could admit to myself.

What will it be like if we do cast forth together? Will we be free, equal, loving, harmonious? Probably not, for all the high hopes. Probably that won't come yet, not in our time. But we must try. Let us cling to each other, as men and women are meant to do, but please I beg you that we not let marriage turn us into provincials. It's this really that I've always feared most— not the conventional surrenders that both must make, but a narrowing of the *spirit*. I could not bear it, and I could not bear the sort of tyranny that would say that because I love you I must love no one else or love in no other ways. But you are no savage, no brute, and no child—and you have not bought me! Oh darling, forgive me, *laugh* at me and forgive me—old fears die hard, and old rages flare up. I shall have to take my chances with all the other daughters of time, and you with all the sons.

Do you remember the day we went to the gardener's cottage, just before we buried the fish? Do you remember all the hats and my searching around among them? To tell you the truth, I was looking for a pair of Florentine hats; you know, like the ones Rubens and his bride are wearing in that painting where they're sitting in the honeysuckle bower. I had some sort of memory, or thought I had, of Posy and Marshall on the lawn one day, seen from a distance; I was sure they were wearing such hats. I was a little disappointed at not finding any. And then later I thought, well of course not, how inappropriate if I had, not at our stage of knowledge of the world; Posy and Marshall yes, but not us. Besides, I was meant to go bare-headed into the world. And you too, I think. Let the young beget the young and the no longer quite so young (I shall be thirty-four in June) sing their praises, and also the praises of higher things, of all the cycles, those within nature and those without.

But don't come for me yet, darling. I'll write again in the spring and tell you where I am, and—if you still want me—I'll be ready for you then, and for life too. Meantime, don't ask to know too much. I've got to stick it here alone for a while yet. And there is, yes, my book. I must finish that.

Give Gwendolyn my love. I hope she's forgiven me. Any message to her would be superfluous.

And how dare I sign myself to you? For whatever you may think it's worth, with love, my dear, with longing even, with the great and undeserving hope that I shall see you again. Sweet Limmat, flow gently until then.

S.

P.S. Later. My courage failed me, and I put this away. But I *am* going to send it. I've just remembered something that Gwendolyn said a week or so before everything started breaking up. She and Anton were talking about art, and she remarked that today an artist has to be like one of those olive trees one sometimes sees in Attica, able to survive and flourish in the stoniest and driest of environments. And I said, "And a woman who wants to be an artist? What about her?" She looked at me—well, you know how she can look sometimes, those eyes, and said, "She must *be* the olive tree." Ernest, you don't want, you can't possibly be mad enough to want to involve yourself with a woman who's trying to become an olive tree, can you? But if you *are* that mad . . .

When Campion had finished reading the letter he went to Mrs. Dartley and told her briefly and very generally the import of what Sylvia had written. "And there are no obstacles?" she asked him.

"There are no obstacles," he replied.

Fifty-six

Ernest Campion had left his suitcase downstairs in the hallway. He stood now in front of Mrs. Dartley, who did not seem surprised to see him.

"You're leaving," she said.

He nodded.

"Going to Sylvia?"

"Yes."

"Now? At once? You're not going to wait until spring, as she has asked you to?"

"No, I'm not."

She smiled at last. "A wise decision. I've been sitting here for the last several hours wondering if you would see this."

"She's very alone," he said, almost to himself.

"Ah yes, and underneath that brave bearing of hers a little afraid, I suppose."

He did not answer.

"Like all of us," she added.

"Yes, but . . ."

"Yes but love makes it seem otherwise? You're quite right. That is what it's for. Chiefly. Besides, you have other reasons for going to her now, equally good ones." She leaned forward and as she did so her spectacles swung forward from their chain, catching what little light there was in the room, glinting like disembodied eyes.

"Yes, I don't want to risk losing her again," he said.

"I don't think you will lose her, but you are right not to take any chances."

"I won't stay long with her now. A few days, a week, whatever seems right. Then I'll go away—I'm going to be tied up in America for the next few months anyway, as it turns out—and go back for her in the spring. The Greifenberg papers are finished, as finished at least as I can make them. You're the one who'll have to decide what to do with them now. Everything's in order, all the original notebooks, the letters, and my struggling transcription from them. I'm leaving them all here."

"I had assumed you would." She hesitated. "And what are you going to do with your life?"

"I haven't quite made a final decision yet. But something."

"That seems certain now." Gwendolyn Dartley turned slightly to the window. "We survivors have special obligations."

Campion had an instant's hesitation then—he saw *her* aloneness, saw even the day when, enfeebled, she would totter towards a desk, eyes uncertain, hands trembling, spilling the cup of cognac-milk or fumbling helplessly with the top of an ink bottle, enveloped in the cloud of unknowing, old age. Could he leave her? Was it not a desertion, especially now when everyone else had gone, when there was so little money, when Kilchberg itself would have to be abandoned, and she herself had not even made up her mind about where she was going to settle? Yet precisely as he thought these things he could feel her sending him away—did she *want* to be rid of him?—and in the second that he felt this a last great wave of resistance to leaving her welled up in him. Then it was all over. She was looking at him with the old familiar expression, the one that said so blandly, so arrogantly, that she knew more about what was going on than anyone else. It never failed to annoy him, to give offense, not even now, and he waited for what was coming.

"And exactly where do you expect to find her, your bride? Do you even know where to look?"

So that was it. But he felt great relief. She knew where Sylvia was and would tell him. Good. That would save him time. Of course she would have to turn it into some kind of game.

He said, "It's not an impossible task. I'll find her. Some of her mail still goes to Munich, I know, and presumably it reaches her from there. That's where I've always planned to start the search. She has to stay in touch with someone." He had guessed it was Stefan Zimmermann.

Gwendolyn Dartley, smiling, alert, in that moment as sure of herself as she had ever been, opened the music box on her desk. A peal of Mozart came floating out—*Eine kleine Nachtmusik*, absurd, perfect. Lying in among the cigarettes in the box was a slip of paper with something written on it. Prolonging her moment to just the right degree, she let her hand hover near it, teasing, dominant; then she picked it up, flicked to the lid of the box, and put the paper into his hand, saying, "I haven't entirely lost my touch. I confess she angered me a little, running away from us that second time. Once was enough. And the first time was in a sense not wholly voluntary; it was a little an abduction. It was possible at any rate to see it as such. But the *second* time, no, that was too much. I'm sure she had good reasons, excellent ones—I rather imagine I know what they were. Nevertheless it was foolish, *extreme* . . . and therefore typical of her. Also ungenerous to her friends. Or so I thought. And if she needed help . . . which she might well have . . . so silly of her, that hiding out among strangers

. . . what an act of *pride* . . . as though she were saying to the world that if anything went wrong with *her* life, especially anything that might give the savages—to use that word she was so fond of—a hold over her, then it would be so earth-shaking that she would have to go off and stalk around in obscurity forever. Oh she has struggles ahead of her yet . . . and *you* . . . oh you, Ernest, you are somehow the man, oh just the man for this. But I dare say you know that, and I dare say there will be some very difficult times . . ."

She paused. A small gush of light, quick, almost girlish laughter came and went. "And some very marvelous ones. In any case, I forgave her when I found out *where* she'd gone. First, it isn't so very far away this time. She did not run very far. That even made me pity her, that reminded me of the little child in her, the child I love so dearly and who is her good genius as well as her bad. She ran because pride forced her to, but she did not want to. She wanted to stay and be comforted by us. Especially by you. That much was immediately clear to me, and her love for you. I should never have forgiven her if she had not loved you. This is unfair, I know, irrational, but it is also the truth. And other things were clear to me too; her sense of order, her incredibly fine sense of the symbolically appropriate, and then that funny little quirk she has of trying always to bring about reconciliations of a very high and mysterious order. All of these things restored her wholly in my eyes. Look at that slip of paper, Ernest. Look at it."

He had hardly heard her, and he had controlled himself only with the greatest effort. Now at last he was free to look. He opened his fist. And there it was: *Alterbrunnen*. Andreas' village. Oh my brilliant girl, he thought, oh my darling. It was the message of messages; it told him everything that the letter had not. A great stream of fire seemed to run in his blood, a great impatience too. At the same time a shudder of another sort went through him, a fear almost: her expectations for them both would not be small. He must hope this knowledge would fortify him, he must try never to forget it, or to forget to help her bear all the limitations, all the reminders in daily life of frailty and imperfection.

To Gwendolyn Dartley Campion looked now as she had always hoped to see him. She felt too his impatience. "Hurry, why don't you?" she said. "If you catch the early train from Zürich tomorrow you can be with her by noon. What are you standing there for? Go on. Before we begin to bore each other. One should not prolong fine high moments." She laughed. A car swung into the driveway. They caught the reflection of its lights in the semi-darkened room. "Besides," she added, "that, I imagine, is your taxi." She stood up.

"We'll come and visit you in the spring," he said.

"Will you? Where will that be?"

"Wherever you are."

"That will be lovely. If it works out, if it fits your plans. Wait and see. There's no point in planning so far ahead." She fingered the thin golden chain to which her spectacles were attached. It was held together at one point by a rather awkward-looking knot, he noticed. He tried to think whether or not it had been there before, but his mind went elsewhere. Then she said, "Give Sylvia my love. Tell her too that I await the day when I shall hold her new book in my hands." She frowned briefly, and downstairs, far away, on the other side of the door, a bell was pulled at sharply, once, twice, three times, its insistent ringing muffled to an almost gentle, almost pleasant sound by all the corridors it had traveled through to reach them. "Bring a child or two into the world, if it suits you," she said, "but if you do it at the expense of her books I shall never forgive you."

"Books last, children don't? Is that the idea?" He already seemed to her halfway out of the room, though he had not moved.

She let out a long, low, disturbing laugh; it carried him back to a hospital bed in New York and he was suddenly all attention. Then she said, "Oh no, no, no. Nothing *lasts*. I only meant that there are not many women who can bring forth children of the spirit. But it is certainly none of my business. On the contrary, it was an intrusion to have mentioned it at all." She seemed to dismiss the whole subject then with a small, austere movement of her right hand.

"We all owe you a great deal," Ernest Campion said.

"You owe me *nothing*." Her tone was cold, almost angry. There was a silence. "Come," she said then, "kiss me good-bye."

He stepped quickly forward, their lips brushed against each other, her arms were about him, then with a thump on his back she released him. Smiling, she said, "Have a good journey."

"You too," he replied, and left her, and did not wonder until he was halfway down the stairs why he had said that.

Gwendolyn Dartley sat by the window, watching. She felt as

though the moment of his departure, shattering though it was, was something she had waited for all her life, a necessary pain, a sending forth. She felt too that Ernest and Sylvia were making her some very great gift, for which she had no name, and needed none. A kind of exultation was flowing through her. No doubt by the next day it would not seem so important; she would be full of uncertainties again, irascible, perhaps even find fault with Ernest's leave-taking, criticize Sylvia for her artist's way of sweeping all before her, in order to be able to bear not having them with her. But tomorrow could not change what she was feeling now. Oh it was all worth it somehow, all. Now what did she mean by that, she asked herself; *what* was all worth it? Why, living, she supposed, loving, losing, having to die.

Outside, the lights of the taxi swung abruptly around and into the night. It startled her. Her heart hesitated, then made several elaborate misbeats, and her breath . . . She forced herself to rest one arm calmly on the window sill, to lean forward. Nothing but the darkness now and those two converging beams of light, searching through it for what? The taxi was pulling away, starting down toward the main road. She followed it with a slight, assentive, rocking motion of her head.

Inside the taxi Ernest Campion had forgotten for the moment everyone, everything, except the woman who existed beyond that darkness. My love, my love, he whispered from time to time.

Gwendolyn Dartley watched the light swiftly receding, now into a single beam, now into an occasional brightness that was flickering on and off in the expanding dark. No, not flickering on and off really; it was only the distance that made it seem that way. As steady a beacon as one could hope to find in a world of motion. Even when it had passed entirely beyond her vision that would still be so. But before she had quite lost sight of it she turned away from the window. She did not need to sit there staring out at a dark landscape. She knew how mightily it stretched around her.

ABOUT THE AUTHOR

Born in Indiana, JANICE WARNKE lived in most parts of America and attended over fifteen schools before entering the University of Washington. After graduating, she found it difficult to decide between her interests in acting and literature but finally chose to continue her studies and took her M.A. in English at Columbia. Most of her adult life has been spent in New York, where at various times she has taught at NYU and CCNY, and in Europe, particularly in Germany, Holland and Italy.

Mrs. Warnke's short stories have appeared in The Yale Review, The London Magazine, *and elsewhere, and her first novel,* The Narrow Lyre, *was published in this country in 1958. At present she and her husband, Frank, a critic and scholar, live in Seattle in a newly built house with two cats and a view of Lake Washington.*